Season of
Innocents

Carolyn Haines

Copyright © 1993 Carolyn Haines

The right of Carolyn Haines to be identified as the Author of
the Work has been asserted by her in accordance with the
Copyright, Designs and Patents Act 1988.

First published in Great Britain in 1994
by HEADLINE BOOK PUBLISHING

First published in paperback in Great Britain in 1994
by HEADLINE BOOK PUBLISHING

A HEADLINE REVIEW PAPERBACK

Published in the United States of America
by Dutton under the title SUMMER OF THE REDEEMERS

10 9 8 7 6 5 4 3 2

ISBN 0 7472 4593 2

Typeset by Letterpart Limited, Reigate, Surrey
Printed and bound in Great Britain by
Cox & Wyman Ltd, Reading Berks

HEADLINE BOOK PUBLISHING
A division of Hodder Headline PLC
338 Euston Road,
London NW1 3BH

This book is dedicated to my parents, Roy and Hilda Haines, to my grandmother, Hulda Nyman McEachern, to my brothers, David and Andy, and to Venus, the best dog a girl ever had.

ACKNOWLEDGEMENTS

Many things go into the writing of a book, and many thanks are necessary. First I'd like to thank my agent, Marian Young, who read my work with insight and a firm grasp of where I needed to go. The Deep South Writers Salon – Rebecca Barrett, Renee Paul, Stephanie Rogers, Susan Tanner and Jan Zimlich – gave me that solid, unshakable support that is so necessary. I'd like to thank Elaine Koster and Audrey LaFehr at Dutton and Anne Williams at Headline. They made the process of publishing this book a real joy. And a special thanks to the mischievous friends of my childhood, without them this book could never have been written. Diana, Marie, Becky, Debby and Janey – there was a time when we shared the most amazing and wonderful adventures through the freedom of imagination. A special acknowledgement goes to the late Rebekah Freeman. No one who knew her fails to miss her.

Chapter One

Maebelle VanCamp Waltman disappeared from Kali Oka Road one October day when the grape smell of kudzu rose thick over Chalk Gully. The afternoon hung suspended forever in the golden light that happens only during Mississippi's fall.

Halfway buried in a small cave I was excavating, I heard Agatha Waltman's shrill cry of discovery when she realized her baby was missing and not just misplaced. The shriek of fury and fear traveled the quarter mile from the Waltman house to the gully. Abandoning all of the clay I'd worked so hard to collect, I grabbed my bicycle and pedaled fast for home, the scream still echoing in that place beneath the tongue where fear can be tasted. Even then I knew what had happened. Without a single specific or detail, I understood what that long wail of despair had to mean.

And I knew I was to blame.

Word of the baby's disappearance rushed down that red clay stretch of road flanked by barren cornfields all the way to Cry Baby Creek, the end of the road. The place where that other little baby had been found more than ten years before. Though I rode as hard as I could from the back of our property, through the woods and pecan orchard to the house, I wasn't as fast as the gossip. Mama Betts was waiting at the screen door for me.

'Somebody's stolen the youngest Waltman,' she said.

'Maebelle?' I could picture the infant, only eight months old with brown eyes and a thatch of red curls. She was a frisky baby but hardly big enough to support her name.

'Effie's gone to town, but when she gets back, she's going to want you to go over to the Waltmans with her.'

My knuckles burned against the screen door. I'd meant to push it open, but my arms were jerky, unable to respond, and I'd rasped my fingers down the screen. 'No. I can't.'

'Alice will need you.'

Mama Betts' eyes bored into me, watching, calculating. I finally opened the door and walked past her to the other side of the screened porch. Her soft voice held me prisoner.

'It was ten years ago almost to the day that Evie Baxter was stolen. Everybody on Kali Oka remembers, but nobody wants to. They've forgotten that baby's name.'

Mama Betts remembered everything that had ever happened in Chickasaw County since the turn of the century.

'That's the baby in Cry Baby Creek, isn't it?' I knew parts of the story, what I'd overheard listening to adult conversations and in the whispered warnings from Mama Betts. My brother and I had spent many a night down at the creek listening for the ghost of the poor murdered baby. We'd heard it, too, one clear night when we'd almost given up hope. It had made my skin prickle, that pitiful crying of a helpless creature in distress.

'I knew when those church folks moved on Kali Oka it was going to be trouble,' Mama Betts said. 'I told folks about the past and how it charts the present, but no one wanted to listen.'

'That first baby, Mama Betts, how did they find her?' Barking came from the backyard, and I walked to a corner of the porch where I could look for my dog. I'd been so

2

busy hoofing it from the gully I hadn't thought to wonder if Picket was with me. But then Picket was always with me. There wasn't any tricking that dog.

'They found that other little baby in the tree roots along Cry Baby Creek. If it hadn't of been for those roots, that baby would have floated on down the creek to the Pascagoula River and right on out into the Gulf of Mexico.'

Mama Betts had blue eyes, like mine, and they were almost like a touch as she waited for my response. She waited for me to turn around, but I wouldn't. 'In the roots?' I saw it clearly. Those willows grow out of the bank and make a canopy across parts of the creek. It's a snake haven, and in low water the roots would make a perfect little nest for a dead baby.

'A piece of ricrac on the baby's little white gown hung up. The creek was low and the current couldn't tug her free. Hadn't of been for that ricrac, they'd never have known she was dead. They could have gone on pretending she'd just simply disappeared.'

The oak tree beside the house was ready to drop its leaves. Acorns littered the ground, a feast for the gray squirrels. In the distance the pecans clustered against the sky. Daddy had said it would be a big crop this year. We'd have to find workers to help pick them all up.

'I told you to stay away from those people at the end of the road, didn't I?' Mama Betts asked. 'Those fanatics.'

'Yes, ma'am.'

'And that crazy woman. Her too. Didn't I?'

'Nadine doesn't have anything to do with this.' I could hear my heart beating. My ears were drums. Nadine Andrews was different, a single woman with a barnful of prize show horses and some strange ways. But this business with Maebelle was something else. Something more sinister.

3

'That remains to be seen. But you remember, I told you.'

'Yes ma'am, Grandma, you did.' I could hardly speak. She had warned me to stay out of all the comings and goings that happened along Kali Oka Road in the summer of 1963. Bad influences had been stirred, she said, giving her head three little nods that meant business. Bad results were on the way.

Maebelle VanCamp Waltman was gone.

In a way no one else would understand, I knew I'd brought it on. If it wasn't for me, Maebelle would be sleeping snug in her pillows on the bed in the room Alice shared with four of her sisters.

The best way to explain any of it is to start back at the beginning of the summer. That was when the bad influences began on Kali Oka. Or maybe it was just the time for old deeds to rise up again. Mama Betts is always saying not to stir the past. She says it was never as great as we remember it, and if we have to meet it again, it won't be with smiles.

That summer two things happened. The Blood of the Redeemer churchers and Nadine Andrews. It wasn't hard to steer clear of the church folks. With their tall hair and gray dresses, they seemed gruesomely cheerless. No point in lying and saying they didn't prick my curiosity, they did, and I spent many a summer afternoon spying on them. But Nadine was another matter altogether. Not the threat of the Blood of the Redeemers' hellfire could have kept me from biking down to Nadine's whenever Mama Betts or Mama blinked an eye and I could shake free of them. The Redeemers were a curiosity; Nadine was a craving.

Mama Betts said right off the bat when Nadine moved in the old McInnis place that she was unnatural. No one in their right mind would move into that place alone, with all those cats, dogs and horses.

4

What she meant was no woman. No single woman without a man. No twenty-four-year-old single woman with bleached blond hair, tight pants and boots who rode horses like she thought she was Jacqueline Kennedy, yet lived in a house that Mama Betts said she could smell from the road.

Nadine was an amazement to me, too, but not for the reasons Mama Betts listed. It was the horses, plain and simple. They were the most wonderful creatures I'd ever seen. Shiny and tossing their heads.

Those horses had come straight from my dreams to land not a mile away from me on Kali Oka Road. Mama Betts knew about the past, but I recognized destiny when I saw it.

Nadine and the Redeemers hit Kali Oka at the same time. Actually, the Redeemers came first. Six old yellow schoolbus-loads of them, women and children staring without a twitch or a smile as they passed the house. It was a bad omen. There'd been talk up and down Kali Oka all spring that the church property at the end of the road, closed since Evie Baxter's untimely end, had been sold.

Property changing hands on Kali Oka was always good for rumors and speculation. Folks clung to their land like it was blood kin. Old feuds were a matter of pride and there wasn't room for newcomers.

Kali Oka was farmland, most of it from original home-steads when the southeastern portion of the state had been settled back in the late 1800s. Jexville, with a population of two thousand, was a stable town. No crime. No trouble.

Though Jexville was the heart of the county's business, in the summer of 1963 it was far removed from my world. Kali Oka was south of town, and that long stretch of red clay led directly from the present to the past. Our last taste of religious sects had resulted in scandal, murder and the pathetic cries of a dying baby that could still be heard along the creek on clear summer nights. The ghost of Evie Baxter still haunted that twisty little creek. Mama Betts said when poor little Evie was thrown into that cold artesian water, she fulfilled the prophecy of the creek. If anyone except her murderer had been around to hear her wails and cries, she might have lived. As it happened, though, she spent her last minutes crying to the black heart of her killer.

All of that happened when the Live for Christ Church owned the property at the end of the road. The Lifers, as they were known up and down Kali Oka, built the original church and parsonage down at the end of the road and set up what Mama called a commune. That was a word that upset Mama Betts, so whenever she said it, she'd make her eyes round and act like she was callin' up Satan.

At any rate, after the Evie Baxter murder, the Lifers were run off the road by public sentiment, and the church remained empty. No one was real excited to see the Redeemers move in, and I guess that Nadine arrived with her nine horses, fourteen cats, and five dogs without creating the stir she would have if the Redeemers hadn't stolen center stage.

That summer was one of the hottest folks could remember. The first week or two, Alice and I rode our bicycles, tended her baby sister Maebelle V., and tried not to sweat to death. It started as a typical Kali Oka summer. Daddy had gone to school in Missouri, but it was something we didn't talk about to anyone. Mama had grown up on Kali Oka, but Daddy was a different case. He was a Yankee. He was always winning trips to schools to study or teach. Since Arly and I couldn't talk about it, I never paid much attention to what he was really doing. We just said he was working away for the summer, and that satisfied most of our friends. Lots of daddies on Kali Oka were working offshore or over at the shipyard in Pascagoula.

Mama wrote books for children. We didn't talk about that either. It wasn't a secret, but Mama said it made other people ill at ease, so it was better not to talk about it. Maybe one reason Nadine held such appeal for me was because we were a family of secrets. Even our names had been changed. Mama Betts said she had been under the spell of fairies when she named Mama Erin Clare after the old country. Mama Betts said it affected Mama's brain and that she'd grown up fey and with a wandering mind and had earned the name Effie. That was why she could think up all those stories for children but couldn't remember when she'd put a pot of dumplings to cook on the stove. When Mama Betts would get mad, she'd say that Mama would get 'caught up in the raptures of a sentence and burn the house down.'

The other extreme could aggravate her just as much. She called Daddy the Detail Man 'cause he was always so precise about getting every little fact. I think that was how he came to be called The Judge, though his name was Walter Arlington Rich the third. Everyone just called him Judge, even though he didn't have a thing to do with the courthouse at Jexville or the law. He was a teacher at a university and a writer for those magazines that folks put out on the living room coffee table but never look at. He and Mama met at some writers' gathering, and his family was still upset that he'd moved off to Mississippi, where Mama Betts said they thought we still dug a hole in the woods to do our business. Details and Daddy's family could work Mama Betts into a righteous frenzy at times.

So that leaves Arly, whose name was Arlington and caused him to get into at least one fight every school year. And my name is Rebekah, from the Bible, and Brighton, from some of Daddy's kin, but everyone calls me Bekkah, the full name being too solemn for Mama's

taste in the 1960s. Oh, yes, and Mama Betts. Her name
was Beatrice O'Shawnessy McVay, but everyone calls her
Mama Betts, except for her oldest friends and they call
her Beatrice. She said she lets them do it because their
bones are too brittle, and if she hits them they might
break.

All of those secret names twisted up inside our big old
house must have counted toward my penchant for
secrets. Mama Betts said that there were times when I
didn't know the truth. She said if the truth and I walked
down Kali Oka Road together, neither would recognize
the other. Mama said I had a healthy imagination and to
leave me alone. Daddy wanted to know 'the specifics'
about my 'lies.' Mama Betts was the one I had to watch
out for whenever I started going down to Nadine's house
to see the horses. Mama Betts was the one who'd check
my blue jeans for horse hairs and the smell of leather and
sweat. She knew me best, I suppose. Knew how hard I
fought to get something I really wanted. If I hadn't been
so intent on getting my way, maybe Maebelle V.
wouldn't have disappeared.

Chapter Two

June 7, 1963

The attic fan was pulling in a good breeze from the kitchen window, and me and Mama Betts were skinning the tops off strawberries for a pie while Effie read aloud to us.

Mama Betts stood at the sink, her knife nicking back and forth so fast that I stopped to watch her. Her left hand was bent and gnarled from arthritis, but it didn't interfere with her work. The warm, sweet taste of a berry exploded in my mouth as I watched and listened and idled. Mama wasn't happy that I was using a sharp knife for anything, but Mama Betts had decreed that I was old enough. Effie read the last page.

'Well, what do you think?' Mama stacked the pages neatly. Her voice was catchy, excited and a little apprehensive.

'For a woman who writes so well about allowing children to grow up, it would seem you could practice it.' Mama Betts' knife clattered in the sink. She dried her hands on a dish towel and then went to the table where Effie sat, dark curls unbrushed and glasses perched on the end of her nose. 'It's a beautiful story, Ef. Each time you get better and better.' She kissed her daughter's head.

'Nothing like a prejudiced opinion.' Mama looked up at Mama Betts, and the tiniest pink touched her cheeks.

'If it was two-bit trash, you'd love it.'

'I'd *say* I loved it. Lucky me, I don't have to lie. Now that you've finished the masterpiece, how about rolling out some pie crust for me?'

'Yeah, yeah, a man can work from sun to sun, but Effie Rich's work is never done.' She put the pages in a neat stack on the table.

'What about it, Bekkah?'

'It was great.'

'It's written for a child younger than you, but you've always been my best audience.'

'I wish things could work out like they do in your books.' I snipped the last berry, washed it and popped it into my mouth. 'Everybody always understands each other in your books.' Only the night before, my request to go with a school friend and her family to the Gulf for the weekend had been denied. Mama didn't know the family well enough. They might not watch me. The undertow in the Gulf was deadly. A young girl had disappeared from the beach the summer before. It might rain and the roads would be slick and dangerous. She didn't know what kind of driver Mr. Nyman was. Castro or a Kennedy – they were both equally odious – might snatch me. The list went on and on. The end result was always the same. No.

The breeze from the kitchen window became hot, suffocating. 'I'm going outside.'

Mama Betts' hand rested on Mama's shoulder as I walked past the table and out the back door.

'You've got to ease up a little,' Mama Betts said softly. 'Bekkah's thirteen now. Won't be long before . . .'

The slam of the screen door drowned out the last of it, and I went out to the old live oak tree and sat down on one of the big roots. Arly and I had played there as little children, building dirt roads and making secret caves and towns in the root structure. Fancy in-town yards always had grass growing around all the trees. Our side yard, where the oak, magnolia and cedar trees were, was raked up neat and clean, brown dirt in contrast to the red ribbon of Kali Oka that ran only fifty yards in front of the house.

For the past thirteen years, Kali Oka had been my road, my territory, my place. I'd ridden the entire fifteen-mile length of it, from where it joined Highway 613 to where it dead-ended in the church cemetery just past Cry Baby Creek. I knew the ditches and the fields and the berry patches and plum trees all along its banks. The property lines were common knowledge. The fact that Marvin Shoals slapped his wife, Connie, around on weekends when he was drinking and that Carrie Sue Parker's third baby died from an RH factor were part of the road. I could read the signs of past and present just the same way I could tell which animals had journeyed down Kali Oka during the night by the evidence they left. I could even tail Arly to wherever he was hiding out by the bicycle tire tracks in the dirt.

Kali Oka was the world. It had always been plenty for me, until this summer.

Black army ants marched along the roots of the old oak. They didn't bite, so no one seemed inclined to bother them. Besides, Daddy said it was 'instructional' to watch them. All they did was work. One ambitious yeoman had a piece of grit or stale bread twice as big as he was, and he was truckin' it along the tree roots making for home. The moral Arly and I were supposed to pick up on was that work and discipline were good things.

I put a stick down across the ant's path, hoping to add a bit of adventure to his life. He never faltered, just climbed over. I was considering an aerial attack to take the ant's goody when I heard the sound of a car coming down the road. One thing about Kali Oka, there wasn't a prayer that a robber could come down the road and get away. Everyone on the road watched like hawks whenever a car or truck came along. We knew who owned what car, and when a strange one entered the road, all alerts were given.

This didn't sound like anybody's car I knew. It took a few seconds of listening to realize it was more than one vehicle, and it was something big. Like the school bus coming every morning to get me and Arly. Except this bus was coming fast.

The screen door banged, and Mama and Mama Betts walked out onto the porch. They looked like they needed some air and an end to whatever conversation they'd been having. Both were flushed, and there was that wary distance, only inches but so telling, that indicated there'd been words between them.

When the first bus came into view, we each stood in our places, watching. It was a rickety old bus, yellow but faded. The spot where the school's name should have been was painted over, and the words BLOOD OF THE REDEEMER had been hand-lettered on. It ended with a cross dripping blood. Up above the name were gray faces at dirty windows. Women and children, mostly. A few hollow-faced men. They stared at us. Sort of the way Arly and I would stare at cows in a field. Not with much thought about it at all. The idea entered my head that maybe they were some kind of prisoners. Like those people on trains in World War II who were being taken off to gas chambers. These folks looked about that happy. Before I even knew I was doing it, I was standing at the outside screen door, close to Mama and Mama Betts.

The second bus rolled by, then the third, the fourth, the fifth. The sixth bus came along in a great cloud of dust.

'Locusts,' Mama Betts said mostly under the breath.

We couldn't see the faces in the last bus windows, but we could make out that Blood of the Redeemer name.

12

Then the blood-dripping cross, leaning just a little bit to the right, as if someone hadn't set it up properly.

'Carrie Sue said her husband heard it in Jexville that someone had bought that church property.' Mama Betts wiped her hands on her apron.

'The summer was going along too peacefully.' Mama pushed her glasses up her nose.

'I'm going over to Alice's.' I wanted to know if she'd seen the buses and what she thought about it.

'Be back in an hour,' Mama said. 'And take Picket with you.'

Picket was a part collie, part shepherd mix who would take anybody's head off who came within ten feet of me. I didn't bother to point out that I never went anywhere without Picket. She was my closest friend, after Alice Waltman.

'Don't make me come over there after you,' Mama called as I walked around to the back for my bike. It was only a short ride through the pecan orchard and a brief stretch of woods. If I'd had to go the road, it would have taken longer, and been a lot hotter baking on the red clay.

We didn't farm our property like most of the others. We had the pecan orchard and some woods, and that was it. Daddy said he'd live on the land, but he wouldn't work it. Not that he didn't like the idea, but he was never home and he killed everything he planted. Besides, he said the wild things needed a place to hide out. Every time they tried to walk across an open stretch of ground, some jackass blew them to bits. At least they could hide in our woods and be safe. He said every living thing needed a sanctuary.

I loved the woods. If I hadn't been in such a hurry to talk with Alice, I'd have stopped to play at the spring where we made wishes and confessed our deepest secrets. But the six buses loaded with churchers was burning a hole in my mouth. I had to talk.

13

Our land bordered the Waltmans', which was little more than a scraggly acre, mostly dirt with a weedy garden. Alice was sitting in a swing made from a two-by-eight and chains. She was holding Maebelle in her arms, singing softly.

Since her back was turned to the woods, it was the perfect opportunity for a sneak attack, but I was afraid she'd scream and drop the baby. Maebelle VanCamp hadn't been unexpected, but she was something Alice and I couldn't help but resent. In the hierarchy of Waltmans, Alice was born fifth, and at the age of thirteen, she was considered old enough for permanent child care. Maebelle VanCamp was Alice's total responsibility. Mrs. Waltman was already pregnant again, and the children younger than Alice had been assigned to some of the older kids for care. At least Maebelle was an infant and couldn't listen in on our private conversations the way some of the other children did.

Kali Oka was only a rock's throw from the Waltmans' front door, so I knew Alice must have seen the buses.

'Let's ride down to the end of the road.' I grabbed the bottom of the swing and gave her and little Maebelle a push.

'What am I supposed to do with this?' Alice asked, indicating her sister.

'We could leave her in the woods.'

Alice laughed. 'Yeah, and she'd choke or some critter would drag her off. Then I'd be in trouble.'

'Might be no one would notice.'

We both laughed. It was a joke between us, the idea that there were so many Waltmans one missing wouldn't matter.

'You think those folks are gonna live down at the old Lifers' church?' Alice asked. She shook her head to thwart a pesky gnat that was determined to get near her eyes. Strawberry blond bangs bobbed on her freckled nose.

'Looks that way. Carrie Sue's husband heard in Jexville that they'd bought the property. Mama Betts said so today.'

Alice nodded. 'Folks ain't gonna like it. Not a bit. Not after those last church people who lived down there.'

'Think they'll have another commune?' I was proud of the word that made everybody so upset.

'What's that?'

'Where they all live together, like a tribe or something.'

The idea struck Alice as too stupid for words. 'None of them must have nine brothers and sisters, or they wouldn't want to be a tribe.'

'We could put the baby in my bicycle basket.'

Alice pushed the swing slightly with her toes. Maebelle VanCamp slept on, her rosebud face turned to Alice's flat chest.

'You know why Mama named her VanCamp?' Alice asked.

I had my theories. Brighton was my middle name, sort of a family tradition, as Mama Betts said, but she snorted when she said it so I couldn't tell if she was fibbing or not. 'She liked the name?'

'The whole time she was pregnant with Maebelle, she craved VanCamp's pork and beans. She couldn't think of anything else, so when they asked her for the baby's name, that was the first thing she came up with. Daddy made her put the Maebelle first.'

'It sounds like something out of a history book.'

'I hope she's not thinking about a loaf of bread when the next one comes. Can you imagine a kid sister named Sunbeam?'

'Or Clay!' I was laughing.

'Clay! That's a California name. What's Clay got to do with anything?'

Her laughter had disturbed the baby. Maebelle's solid brown eyes turned toward me, and she stared as if she, too, were waiting for an answer.

'Mama Betts said that some of the black women eat clay from Chalk Gully when they get pregnant. She said it was like some kind of awful craving, and that the doctors try to keep them from doing it because it sucks the blood out of the babies, or something like that.'

Alice's laughter was dead. 'That's terrible, Bekkah. Why do they eat it if it sucks the blood out of their babies?'

'They can't help themselves. They've just got to have it.'

'If this next one is a boy, I won't let Mama name it Clay. That's a promise.'

'Maebelle's awake. Get your bicycle and let's ride down the road.' I took a couple of steps towards the woods where Picket and my bike were waiting.

Alice cut a look over her shoulder. There was no sign of her mother's face at the window. 'You'll ride real slow and be careful.' She hefted the baby in her arms to calculate her weight and how much she'd bounce in the basket.

'Real slow and we'll come straight back. Mama said I had to be home in an hour. You can stay for supper at our house, and that way your mama won't think to wonder where we've been. Mama Betts is making one of her strawberry pies.'

'Okay.' She handed me the baby while she slipped around the corner of the house to get her bike. She was back in a minute, pushing the bike while I carried the baby into the woods. 'I shouldn't do this . . .'

'I've got to see what those Redeemer folks are doing down there. They might be getting ready to worship—' I stopped. Alice could get funny about religious things at times. I didn't want to scare her out of riding down to

Cry Baby Creek to check out the church folks.

'Worship what?'

'That's what we're going to find out.'

I got my bike and made a comfortable little nest for Maebelle in the front basket. It was a deep basket and there was no chance she'd fall out. The only concern was that the road got a little rough in places, but I could get off and push the bike and she'd be none the worse for it.

Picket was right beside us as we rode through the woods, cut behind my house and finally pulled out onto Kali Oka about half a mile from our driveway. Alice and I shared a look of excitement. We were both dying to see what the new residents on Kali Oka were going to do.

Chapter Three

The bridge over Cry Baby Creek is wooden. The creek itself is only about twelve feet wide with amber shallows and a few deep pools. There are places where logs have jammed and the water flows over the top with the sound of a mountain stream.

Old and dilapidated, the bridge is dangerous. Since it only leads to the church property and that's been vacant for the last ten years, no one worries much about it. Vines growing over the side of it made a good place to hide for me and Alice and Maebelle. The baby was sleeping soundly as we crouched down by the bank and peered through the honeysuckles.

The buses were all parked side by side to the left of the old parsonage. The church folks, seemingly mostly grown-ups, were milling about the grounds, staring up at the sky or into the trees, looking everywhere but at each other. No one seemed to be in charge.

Undisguised by the dirty bus windows they were even scarier than I first thought. Especially the children our age. They reminded me of winter trees, still and solemn and asleep, as if their faces and minds were dormant and waiting for spring. I could not imagine those children playing football or hide-and-seek. I hadn't caught a glimpse of the really young children yet.

'Creepy,' Alice whispered.

'Zombies.'

'I wonder what they're going to do down here at the end of this road.'

I couldn't imagine; but then I did, fevered images of singing and chanting and snakes. Embellished by my imagination, the churchers were frightening – and compelling. 'Wonder if those kids are going to school with us? Mama Betts said no one in Mississippi had to go to school. She said we were one of the only states without mandatory attendance.'

Alice jiggled the baby as she leaned on one elbow and held her with the other arm. 'Not likely. The old church set up their own school, or at least that's what Mama remembers. She'd never just come out and say it, but I heard her whispering with old Mrs. Shoals that the people from that Life church sold their babies for money.' Her voice dropped to a whisper. 'The girls who had the babies were almost slaves.'

'Selling babies?' It was an incredible idea. Who would buy one?

'Yeah, like puppies or horses. Girls in the church would have a baby, and then they'd sell it to someone who couldn't have one.' Alice tickled Maebelle and was rewarded with a few healthy kicks and a lopsided grin. 'I'd like to sell a few of ours.'

'Alice!' I wasn't really shocked 'cause I knew she was just talking. 'Look.' Several of the men had gotten together and were talking and pointing around the church grounds. It wasn't clear what they were saying, but words like nursery and housing and duties were part of it. They called one of the women over, and she nodded her head and then went into the old parsonage.

'They're acting like they don't know what to do.'

Several of the men walked over to the buses and began to unload suitcases from the back.

'They're going to stay here.' Alice inched up the bank

for a better view. 'They're going to all sleep in the church.'

She was right. The men were moving the suitcases into the sanctuary. There was only the church building and the parsonage. By my guess there must have been fifty or sixty families. As the men worked, the women began to form a line. The lack of laughter or conversation made it eerie.

'Let's get out of here before they see us.' Alice inched down the bank toward the creek. Maebelle shifted in her arms and let out a small cry.

The closest group of Redeemers turned our way. I was still at the edge of the creek, buried in honeysuckle, I hoped. I waved Alice back into the protection of the vines in case anyone came over to look.

Maebelle gave another gurgle. Sweat trickled down my cheek. A middle-aged woman and two girls were looking our way. The woman stepped forward, her eyes scanning. The first sign of life shifted across the faces of the girls. One had long brown hair that hung, uncurled, down her back. The mother wore hers up, sort of like some of the high school girls did, but the effect was completely different.

Her eyes locked on me and I stopped breathing. She turned, called something over her shoulder, and one of the men started walking toward her.

'Run!' I tore free of the honeysuckle and slipped down the bank of the creek. Alice came out from under the bridge, and together we waded the shallow water, not concerned for our shoes, only worried about our lives.

'Run, Alice!' I climbed the opposite bank in front of her so I could help with the baby. Maebelle let out a terrible cry as if we were snatching her bald-headed.

'Hey! You!' the man called.

'Run!' I cried. I had Maebelle in my arms and sprinted toward the edge of the woods where we'd left the bicycles. Alice was behind me, dragging in air.

A brown and white streak erupted out of the woods, headed straight for the bridge over the creek and the tall, thin man who was coming for us.

'Picket!' I thrust Maebelle into Alice's arms and turned back toward the church. The man had stopped on the bridge, his face contorted with fury as Picket squared off at him, her hackles raised and her teeth barred. If he made another move toward us, she'd latch onto his leg. Instead of staring at the dog, the man was looking at Alice and Maebelle.

'Picket! Come here!'

She ignored me, her focus never shifting from the man. She could sense his rage as easily as I could see it written on his features. There was no way she was going to relax her guard. Several other men had clumped together, and a teenage boy ran into the church and returned with a gun. He handed it to one of the men.

'Picket!' I could hear the fear in my own voice. They meant to shoot her.

'Bekkah!' Alice grabbed my arm as I brushed past her, running toward the bridge. 'Bekkah, don't!'

My fingers found the collar in Picket's thick fur, and I pulled her back with me. Toenails screeching in the wood of the bridge, Picket was rigid, and a fierce growl erupted from her teeth. At the edge of the bridge I looked up at the man. There was a terrible smile on his face.

'That's a dead dog,' he said softly. The man with the rifle cocked it and aimed.

Picket weighed nearly fifty pounds, but at that moment it didn't matter. I gathered her in my arms and fled.

'This here's private property,' the man called after us. 'Come here again, and you'll be sorry. We'll get the sheriff on you and that cur!'

Maebelle's descent into the basket was less than tender. Alice held my bike for me and then got hers. The man was sauntering across the bridge as we pedaled furiously away, Picket at our side.

'Whose baby is that anyway?' the man called. 'That ain't no way to treat a youngun'.'

My bicycle chain whirred, and Maebelle had begun a soft, steady cry. The motion of the bike seemed to soothe her a bit, and I wasn't slowing down for her anyway. At least not until we were well clear of the Redeemers.

Sweat was dripping down Alice's face, and mine, when we pulled over in the shade of a mulberry tree that had sprung up wild in P. C. Harless's fence row.

'Those folks are crazy mean,' Alice said as she took Maebelle out of the basket and rocked her in her arms. 'It's okay, baby,' she crooned softly. 'Hush, hush, baby.' She was about to cry herself.

Neither one of us wanted to talk about how close we'd come to serious trouble, but we couldn't pretend nothing had happened. 'It looks like they're all going to live there together, doesn't it? Mama's gonna die when she finds out they're going to have a commune.'

'Mama said if Daddy stayed home all the time, I'd have twenty brothers and sisters instead of just ten,' Alice said. She made a face at Maebelle. 'I couldn't stand it.'

'Me either. And they sure didn't look like happy people. They were mostly wandering around like lost souls.' There had been something definitely eerie about them. Not a single spark of laughter or enthusiasm. It was as if they'd been drained of all vital juices. Sucked dry. 'Until they got the gun.'

'You were right; they're zombies.' Alice hefted the baby to her shoulder. 'We'd better get back. Mama'll be lookin' for me to help with supper.'

I could see she'd abandoned the plan to eat with us. It had been too close a call. We needed some time to think about it. 'Maybe we can go for a swim tomorrow.'

Carolyn Haines

Alice shot me a quick look. 'Not at Cry Baby Creek.'
'Why not?'

'You just want to go and spy on those Redeemers. You don't care a fig about swimmin'.' Her freckles were startling across her white, white skin. 'After today you'd go back there? You don't have a lick of sense, Bekkah Rich.'

'Sure I want to go swimmin', and I want to look around the church a little more. If we hadn't had Maebelle—'

'And your dog! Chances are I'll have her tomorrow, and the next day, and the next, until school lets back in.'

Complaining that it wasn't fair didn't do a bit of good. Alice didn't like it any better than I did. Still, part of my dissatisfaction with Kali Oka Road had more to do with Alice being pressed into child labor than with anything else. I missed my friend and the time we once had together.

'Maybe Julie Ann will keep her.'

'Yeah.' Alice put her back in my basket and signaled to go. She didn't have to say that Julie Ann would never keep the baby. Julie was two years older than Alice, but she was the special child. Asthma had weakened her lungs, and she couldn't do any of the chores. If any new clothes were purchased, they were for Julie and handed down to the other children. Those above Julie in age got even more work and less attention. In the Waltman household, Julie was the watershed. She was the best embroiderer in the state, too. That's all she did, pull those pretty threads through that hoop of cloth until she'd made a picture.

At the cut through in the woods, Alice left her bike and took the baby. I rode on to the house, back in less than the hour Mama had given me.

'How were the church folks?' Mama Betts asked as I pushed open the screen. She was standing in the door-way, concealed in shadow.

24

'Spooky.' There was no point lying, exactly. 'They acted lost.'

'Stay away from those folks, Bekkah. Nothing good will come of them.'

'I'm only lookin' at 'em. There's no harm in doing that.'

'And when they go to talk to you, what are you going to do then? Act mute?'

'They won't talk to me. They don't want any of us around there.'

'Did they run you off?'

Mama Betts was too smart. She had a way of tricking all the details out of you just the way she squeezed a lemon for her pies until even the rind was dry. 'Not exactly.' If she found out about Picket and the gun, I'd be in really big trouble.

'But they weren't too happy to see you, were they?'

'Not really.'

She laughed. 'Effie called your dad and told him all about it. He said to keep you away from them, that you'd be joining up like it was the circus.'

'Will Daddy call back?' I hated it when Mama called him and I wasn't home. It made me feel like I'd been cheated out of a treat.

'Tonight. Just to talk with you.'

'And Arly?'

'And Arly.'

'Where is he anyway?' I hadn't seen him all day. 'Does he know about the Redeemers?'

'He knows. He was all for running down the road to look for you.'

'He couldn't have made it worse than Maebelle V., whining and crying.'

'You took that baby?'

Her tone of voice made me realize how critically I'd messed up. 'We only rode down there and back. The baby likes bicycle rides.'

'You're going to give that child brain damage. I know Mrs. Waltman has more than she can manage, and pregnant again, I hear, but it seems like she wouldn't allow—'

'Alice takes care of the baby. Mrs. Waltman has other things on her mind.'

Mama Betts raised her hands to her hips. She didn't like sass. 'I know it isn't fair, Bekkah, but a lot of children work harder than Alice. Maybe with Alice tied down with that baby you two won't get into trouble this summer. And don't deny it. I see it simmering in those devil blue eyes.'

Chapter Four

The bite of the creek was cold, even set against the June sun and the sweat we'd generated on our bicycles. Cry Baby is fed by artesian springs that flow out of the hard clay earth fresh and icy. In places the bottom of the creek is pure clay and slippery as a buttered hog. Alice and I, little Maebelle secure in a sling we'd constructed across Alice's chest so that she had full use of her hands, made our way past one of these slippery places to the slide. This was our favorite part of the creek, where the fast-running current had cut a gully in the stream bed about four feet wide and eight feet deep and ran for about fifty feet, ending in a quiet pool. It was a roller-coaster ride of intense joy and fear. Picket was at my side, intent on scouting squirrels along the bank.

'You go first and then you can hold Maebelle,' Alice suggested as she took a seat on a flat clay rock beside the cascading water.

Edging into the icy water, I held my breath, partly from the shock of the cold and also from fear. The water churned around me, pushing, tugging, clutching at my skin and the second skin of my suit. It wanted me, and it was exhilarating and terrifying.

'Go!' Alice urged. 'Go!' The sun, penetrating the trees on each side of the bank, dappled her skin with larger freckle shadows.

With a squeal I pulled my feet from the rocks and

shunted down the roaring channel of water. I tumbled up and down, over rocks and around curves until twenty seconds later I jetted into the calm of the open pool. The clay sides were hard to grasp, but I pulled myself out and into the shallows.

'You looked like a pink cork,' Alice said as she waved me back to the head of the slide.

My suit had taken a hard knock against a jag of clay, and the yellow dirt was embedded into the pink of the nylon. My hip would bear a bruise, but it had been worth it for the moment of complete and total surrender to the grasp of the water. Maebelle was transferred into my arms as Alice took her place in the water. With a cry she launched herself in a more daring head-first journey. I lost sight of her completely, and for an unendurable few seconds feared she might have struck her head on one of the rocks. When she surfaced, she was flushed with the joy-terror of the ride and from holding her breath.

'Why didn't Arly come with us?' she asked after she'd clambered into the shallows.

'I didn't invite him.' He'd tattle on us if we went near the Redeemers. Arly would hold onto information until he wanted something or he wanted to get even with me, then he'd blurt it out. 'Mama, did you know Bekkah was snoopin' down at that church?' I could hear him clear as thunder.

'We're not going near those church folks,' Alice said, reading my mind. 'I mean it. They scared me and next time no telling what they'd do.'

'You can stay here, then.' I'd already thought it out. I could wade down the creek and check them out from the eastern side. Cry Baby sort of crooked around the church and parsonage. The bridge was due south of the church, but upstream from there the creek angled northward in a sharp bend. That bend would be a perfect vantage point, and they'd have no way to suspect we were there.

'You're going to get in serious trouble, Rebekah Rich, and your mama and granny are gonna tan your hide.'

'They won't know unless you tell them.'

'Or unless Picket attacks one of those Redeemers again.'

'We can tie her by the bicycles.'

'And what if she sets up a howl?'

'She won't.'

'Like Maebelle V. won't cry?'

'Maybe she won't.'

'And if she does?'

'Then we'll leave. Besides, they might own the church property, but they don't own the creek. The bridge was built with public money, so the creek is public property.'

Alice snorted. 'Says who?'

'My daddy.' He'd never said any such thing, but it made for a sound argument. Alice had some sort of fixation on Daddy and never argued with a thing he said. I smiled as I watched her face.

'Okay.' She hefted the baby onto her shoulder. Maebelle V. was smiling and laughing, a regular little red-faced adventurer.

'See, Maebelle wants to go. She wants to know all about those wild folks who've taken up at the end of our road.'

'I'll just bet she does,' Alice said, kissing her sister's nose. 'She'd rather have a bottle and a nap, I'm sure.'

'Well, dig out the bottle.'

I called up Picket while Alice fed Maebelle. The dog was smart enough to know I wanted her for something. There were times I brought shampoo to the creek and gave her a bath. She hesitated on the high bank, looking down at me, her tail wagging. She heard me and understood what I wanted. She simply had no intention of obeying me. Daddy said she was smarter than all of us put together, and I believed him.

'Let's just go home,' Alice tried again. 'Really. We were down here yesterday. Let's give them some time to settle in. There won't be anything to see for a while. Maybe Sunday we could sneak back and listen to part of their service. They might scream and shout and play the drums.'

'Or handle snakes.'

'Uh-uh.'

Alice thought I was kidding. 'Some of those strange religious sects do.' I'd paid a lot of attention to Effie and Mama Betts discussing this the past night. Sect was a word I was glad to acquire.

'Why on earth?'

'To prove they have faith. They believe God will protect them and let them handle the evil snakes. It's a test of faith.'

'And if they're bitten?'

'Well, I guess they didn't believe strong enough.'

'And if they die? Does that mean they went to hell?'

Effie hadn't gone into such depths. 'Straight to hell-fire.'

'Let's go home. Maybe they keep their snakes down here around the creek.'

'Rattlesnakes don't particularly care for the water, and they always use rattlers. The noise makes it more dramatic, when they have all those rattlers and the tambourines going. Then they get out the tubs and start to washin' each other's feet.'

'I don't believe a word of it, Rebekah Rich, you're just pullin' my leg.'

I'd led Alice off on a dangerous bend, and now I had to get her back. 'Maybe, maybe not,' I said with a smile. 'While we're here, let's sneak a peek. Maebelle's out cold after that bottle, and we need a little time before we ride back. All that jostlin' around will make her upchuck her milk.'

'Just a peek, then I have to get home.'

By a streak of luck, Picket trotted down the bank, and I got her collar. I'd brought a piece of rope for the express purpose of tying her out of harm's way. I hated to do it. She looked as if I'd beaten her and then spat on her, but I left her secured to a big magnolia with lots of shade. She didn't howl. She was too mortally wounded by my betrayal to make a sound. Daddy had said that he'd never have a dog that had to be tied or chained. He said no creature should have to live on the end of a rope. Tying Picket was against everything I'd been taught, but I had to keep her safe. Alice wouldn't even watch when I did it.

'Guard the bikes,' I told the dog as I left. It made me feel better, as if I'd given her a job.

The creek grew too slippery to stay in the current, so Alice and I, baby Maebelle tucked in her sling, made our way up the far bank, actually on the church property. The path was on that side, and I saw no reason to push through vegetation and brambles so thick that it would take an extra half hour on the opposite bank.

It wasn't hard to imagine the creek back in the days when the Pascagoula Indians roamed freely. Most of the woods had been logged when the area was settled, but there were some stretches of virgin pine, especially in the Pascagoula River Swamp, which was about ten miles south.

The Pascagoulas had been a small tribe, living mostly along the banks of the Pascagoula River but moving inland to places like Cry Baby Creek to hunt and fish. There were burial mounds all over the place. Effie had found several. She'd unearthed pottery, arrowheads, beads and bones and finally called the state archives so that a team of archaeologists could come down and do a proper job of it. We hadn't heard yet if the remains were Choctaw, Pascagoula, Chickasaw or some other stray band that camped on the banks of the creek. Mama Betts said it was positively Chickasaw, and she insisted that Kali Oka was the Chickasaw word for 'the edge of the spring water.' She even broke it down, declaring that Oka meant spring and Kali-sita was the Chickasaw word for edge. She said no matter what the 'experts' determined, she knew the truth.

The woods were loaded with deer and squirrel and rabbit. There were wild boars, too, something that I'd learned to keep a sharp eye out for. Folks argued both ways whether the wild pigs were there before or after the Indians. It wasn't much of an important issue when one of those pigs with red eyes was thundering after you. The big ones weighed in at better than four hundred pounds, and they could hamstring a grown man with one slash of their tusks. They were big, mean, and quite willing to hurt anyone who trespassed on their turf. It made me nervous to leave Picket tied, defenseless.

I was deep in my Indian thoughts when a covey of Redeemers broke to my right. Alice and I both slithered down the bank of the creek at the same time.

There were five boys, bigger than me and Alice. They all wore white shirts and gray long pants, even in the June heat. They were walking like they had some place to go. They'd been quiet, but they were obviously in the middle of a conversation. A hot one.

'He put his hands on her breasts.'

Hidden below the bank, we couldn't see who was talking.

'He did not!' another boy answered.

'He did too. I saw him. He came up behind her and put his hands on her breasts. She was wearing that white dress she sings in.'

'I'm going to bash your brains out. My sister wouldn't let him touch her. She hates him!'

The argument was between only two boys. The other three were staying silent.

'She might hate him, but he put his hands on her breasts and sort of squeezed them.' There was a taunting note in the boy's voice.

'Maybe she was afraid to stop him.' This was a new voice, a softer boy's voice.

'That's right. Rev. Marcus does whatever he wants, and we all know that, don't we, Tommy?'

There was rough laughter, an undertone I didn't fully catch. It was as if the boys didn't like each other, but there was some type of mutual thing between them.

Alice's fingers pinched a blister on my underarm. I almost squealed with pain. 'What?' I hissed.

Maebelle was shifting in her arms, squinching up her face as if she was going to cry. Alice jostled her a bit, trying to ease her out of her bad mood.

The plump boy was talking again. 'I'm going to tell Mama about Rev. Marcus. You said it was Sunday?'

'Just after your sister sang that sweet song about being safe in the arms of the Lord.'

The mockery was clear in the first boy's voice. He was also angry. I couldn't stand it anymore and edged up to the lip of the creek bank. The boy who had just spoken was the tallest. His dark hair was poorly cut and hung ragged in the back. His pants were baggy over his thin body, and his arms dangled. But he was fierce. He stood with his elbows bent and his fists clenched. He wanted to fight, and he didn't care who. The boy who was defending his sister was better fed, better groomed, and very worried.

'Mag wouldn't let him touch her unless she didn't have a choice. She hates him as much as we do.'

'Ask her,' the first boy challenged. 'And just remember, you go tattlin' to your folks and who're they gonna believe? You or Marcus?'

33

The question hung between them. 'Let's go,' one of the other boys said. 'Let's take a swim.'

They hurried along the path, headed up the creek. Alice and I could move on down to the parsonage or try to double back and beat them to the swimming hole. With Picket tied, I didn't have a choice. We crossed the creek and started up the other side, hindered by the vegetation and by Maebelle in the sling. Where I could duck and twist around the brambles and undergrowth, Alice was slower with the baby.

We were about there when I heard the howl. There was no mistaking Picket's voice, and this wasn't a bark of anger. She was in pain.

'Run!' Alice pushed me ahead of her. 'We'll catch up! Run!'

Cursing myself for everything I was worth, I ran. I didn't feel the briars or the limbs. Picket's howl of pain came again, and I thought my heart would burst. She was defenseless. I had left her that way.

Chapter Five

The tall boy was backing away from Picket when I crashed through the undergrowth. His hand was bleeding, and every hair on Picket's body was standing on end. She wasn't making a sound.

'Get away from her.' I went to stand by Picket. Very carefully I began to run my hands over her fur, to check and see where they had hurt her. She gave a sharp whine of pain as my fingers pressed her lower spine, at her rump. Beside her were two heavy sticks.

The boys had shed their white shirts, and their skin was alabaster in the shade of the woods. Ribs protruded on all but the plump boy, making them look helpless, somehow shamed. Blood streaked the tall boy's hand. It ran down his middle finger and dripped to the ground very slowly.

'Let's get out of here,' he said, and the others followed him as he backed away.

'What did you do to my dog?' Picket was tense, ready to strike, but she wasn't barking. Deep in her throat she growled, a sensation I felt more than heard. No one answered my question, and I wanted to strike them, to pick up the heavy sticks and whale away at them until they would never hurt another dog again. Not a single one of them answered me. They stared until the tall boy turned away.

'I said let's go,' he commanded. The boys fell in with him in a ragged line.

'If you ever hurt my dog again, I'll get even. You'll burn in hell, Redeemer boys!'

The tall boy paused as if he was considering my words. Then he turned and faced me. He was smiling. 'You'd better be careful who you threaten, girl. Don't you know you shouldn't be out in the woods alone. No tellin' what might happen to you. No tellin' . . . '

'Bicycles!' The cry rang out over whatever else the tall boy had intended to say. The plump boy had found them, the one who earlier had been defending his sister.

They pulled the bikes from the foliage where Alice and I had hidden them. They were jubilant with the discovery, intent among themselves. One of them danced and hollered like an Indian around my Schwinn. Very carefully I loosened Picket's rope from around the magnolia tree. If I let Picket loose, she'd go after them. It would be worse than one small bite. But even as much as I wanted to let her go, I was afraid of the tall boy. He might really hurt her. Or me, and he might enjoy doing it. There was also Alice and Mae-belle V. to consider. I held Picket tight.

The boys picked the bicycles up and started running across the creek with them. They meant to keep them.

I spoke softly to Picket, pressing my fingers along her back once again. Except for that one sensitive spot she seemed to be okay.

'Bekkah!' Alice broke through the tangle of huckleberries behind me. She took in the disappearing boys and our bicycles. 'Oh, my God,' she whispered as she leaned against the magnolia. 'What are we going to do now?'

I didn't know. I still had Picket on the rope, and I got her to walk with me. She could move, and she didn't limp. My biggest worries began to disappear, replaced by a fire that was new. Something in the center of my chest burned. I wanted to hurt those boys. I picked up the bigger of the two sticks they'd thrown at Picket. It weighed as much as a small bag of sugar. It must have hurt when it hit her.

'Mama's gonna skin me when she finds out about the bicycle.' Alice's voice wavered. Maebelle V. echoed her sentiment with a lusty cry.

I held the rope to her. 'Hold Picket and I'll go get them.'

'No!' Alice's face registered shock and fear. 'No, Bekkah!'

'They stole our bikes. We can't let them take them. Take Picket and Maebelle and head back to the road.'

Alice pushed my hand with the rope away. 'I won't do it. No matter what you say, I won't.' Her blue eyes didn't flinch as she looked at me, and I knew she wouldn't budge.

'Those little bastards.' I wanted The Judge to be at home. But the whole summer might be gone before he came back, and I needed him now. Effie wouldn't do, and Mama Betts wouldn't be any help either. Tears prickled and burned. I could tell by the noises Alice was making that she was fixing to cry too. 'We'll get them back.'

'How?' Alice pointed across the creek. 'They're gone.'

'They can't take them to the church. How're they going to explain where they got them? And they can't ride them in the woods too easily. They'll have to get out on Kali Oka to ride. We'll get Arly and some of his friends to help.' Arly didn't warrant a lot of my faith, but in a crisis he could be useful. Especially a mess like this. Alice was justifiably concerned. It would be impossible to tell our folks that the church boys had stolen our bikes. We weren't supposed to be around the church.

Something white fluttered across the creek. 'Hold Picket.' I gave her the rope before she could decline again. In a flash I'd waded the creek and was climbing the other bank. Those stupid boys had gone off and forgotten their white shirts. I gathered the five shirts, all hanging together on a scrub oak branch. Clutching them like valuable treasure, I hurried back to our bank of the creek. Panting, I held them out. 'Now we have something to barter with.'

Alice smiled. Even Maebelle V. paused in her crying. 'They can't go home without their shirts, can they?'

'Not likely.'

'Then we'll wait.'

'Nope. We're going home. We can get around the bicycles for a few days. They can't. If they go back to that church without their shirts, everyone will know they've been in the woods with their clothes off. Maybe this is a lesson those boys need to learn.' I took Picket's rope from Alice. We all started walking home. It would take better than an hour, probably closer to two with the baby. There would be lots of time to plot revenge.

Before we broke out of the woods, I bundled the shirts up and hid them in a clump of dogwood trees. The boys weren't likely to find them, but I'd know where they were. Just to be on the safe side, I broke off two huckleberry limbs at the roadside to mark the spot. When I'd finished we started walking. As we were leaving squatty footprints in the sandy part of Kali Oka, I kept thinking about the tallest boy. He was about my age, or maybe Arly's. He was the leader. He was the one who'd thrown the sticks at Picket while she was tied.

We were coming up on the McInnis place when Alice finally spoke. Maebelle V. had been crying for the last half hour and there wasn't a thing we could do. We'd stopped and given her the rest of her bottle. She wanted some food, and so did we, but we still had another two miles to go at least.

'Do you still believe that place is haunted?' Alice asked, nodding at the old yellow house and the barn that had once been home for some of the finest blooded walking horses in the South. The roof sagged in several places. Alice and I had spent a lot of the past summer exploring around the barn. It had been vacant for about two years. Mama Betts said everyone who moved in there fell on hard times and couldn't stay.

'Mama Betts says it is.' A ghost story would help pass the last half hour. The driveway was lined with china-berry trees, and I squatted down in the shade of a big one for a few minutes. My feet were burning hot from the sand and clay of Kali Oka. It was June 8. Our twentieth day of summer vacation. Daddy had said the cities were even hotter, especially this summer when Negroes and whites were eyeing each other like hungry dogs.

'Hey, do you want to take a minute and go look in the barn? Remember last summer we left some soft drinks hidden in there.'

'They'll be hot.' I leaned against the tree trunk and closed my eyes. I didn't want to move, but I could hear Maebelle V. frettin' and gurglin'. She was bound to be half starved, and a little hot Coca-Cola would tide her over until we got home.

'I know you're not afraid of the Redeemers, but you might be afraid of old Sheriff Sidney Miller.' Alice nudged me with the toe of her shoe. She was already standing up, and I could hear Picket breathing at her side.

The McInnis barn did bother me. It was big, with a loft and twenty stalls, and doors that were locked but were said to lead down to underground living quarters. Mama Betts said it was all a crock of bull. At one time the McInnis place had been the premier plantation in Jexville. Rathson McInnis, the original, had arrived in Jexville in the early 1800s, along with his slaves and family, and started the farm tradition in the county. We'd studied about Rathson McInnis in Mississippi history. He was famous for his ideas in farming, and later for getting himself killed in the Civil War.

He carved out more than three thousand acres of the best land in the county and built a plantation house and the old barn. The plantation had been burned by the Yankees after the war. Mama Betts said that a cease-fire had been negotiated when a band of Yankee troops rode through and burned the house to cinders while Mrs. Rathson McInnis stood in the yard with a portrait of her husband, the only thing she'd been able to save before the fire was set.

After there was nothing left of the house, the Yankees ran their swords through the portrait as Mrs. McInnis held it. The story goes that one blade cut her palm, and as the blood dripped onto the ground, she cursed anyone other than a McInnis who would ever attempt to live on their land.

But it wasn't the Rathson McInnises, either the mister or the mistress, that made me feel ill at ease in the old barn. It was Sheriff Sidney Miller. I was eight years old when he lost his mind, shot his wife and two children and hung himself from a chinaberry tree. It was his ghost, the sheriff's badge glinting in the sun, that I'd seen in the barn. He'd been holding the end of his rope in his hand.

'Hey, come on.' Alice nudged me with her toe.

It was pointless to hang back any longer. My eyes were sun-blinded for a moment as I stood. Behind me a soft breeze ruffled the chinaberry leaves. An old sign, hung by rusty chains, creaked a warning.

'Let's just go on home,' I said.

'Maebelle needs the sugar. We left those Cokes behind that old tire, remember? It won't take but a minute. Last year you weren't too scaredy cat to even walk in the barn.'

Last summer Arly had dared me to go in the barn alone. Alice and I had been in every stall and even climbed into the loft where the old bales of hay smelled

40

like dirt and Mama Betts' herb plant, that curly purple-leafed one that she said smelled like an angel's armpit. 'Last year I hadn't seen old man Miller.'

Alice rocked back and forth on her toes. Maebelle V. was shaking her fists and crying now, a thin, tired wail that was beginning to worry me. She might starve or die of thirst or something even worse. We hadn't thought to bring diapers, and she was sorely in need of a change.

'Let's go get the Cokes.' I didn't want to. Alice was looking for a rush of goose bumps. She'd wanted to go into the barn ever since I'd told her about the ghost business last summer, but I'd never go back in there no matter how much Arly teased me. Now I was going.

The double doors creaked, and once again I wondered who would paint a barn white with pale blue trim. It was awful-looking. Barns were red with white trim. This just made the bigness and the oldness of the place seen even more peculiar.

The plantation had never been rebuilt, and even the stone chimney had been picked clean by fortune hunters over the past thirty years. Sometime during the 1920s someone had built a small cottage beside the barn, and that was the house Sidney Miller and his doomed family had occupied. He'd shot his wife on the back steps and his two children in their beds. Folks said he just lost his mind for no reason. Or as Mama Betts said, no one ever found the reason. He'd been right popular, for a sheriff.

The barn was dark. Slats of light fell through the bars of the stall windows, making narrow trapezoid patterns on the red earth floor. Alice pushed the door open wider, a hiccuping Maebelle V. making her shadow seem two-headed and sinister.

'Just behind the old tire near the last stall,' Alice said. She wasn't coming in with me. She was going to stand at the door, holding the baby and watching me. It was fair. If she had the baby, she wouldn't be able to run fast enough, just in case we saw something we didn't want to hang around and talk with.

Off to either side there was the scurry of small creatures, rats more than likely, unused to the tread of a human foot in their barn. Above, the loft creaked, as if the great weight of hay was being shifted ever so slightly. As if some sleeping entity had been roused by the smell of three small girls below. Shift. The groan of old, tired boards. Or bones. At the end of the barn a clump of moldy hay fell. It had to be rats. They could climb as good as any cat when they took a notion.

I was halfway down the long aisle of the barn when the bird swooped in front of me. Although I didn't scream, I ducked and threw up my arms. Alice laughed, until the bird struck the window at the end of the barn. The thud was so loud, so powerful, that we knew the bird had broken its neck. We'd panicked it and now it was dead.

Turning back, I looked at Alice. She wasn't laughing any longer.

'Get the Coke, and let's go back to the tree,' she said, her voice eerie in the barn.

Before my nerve completely disappeared, I turned toward to the last stall. Walking real slow, I pretended each stall had a beautiful horse in it. At the very end was the black, my own horse. It tossed its head and whickered a greeting. Ever since I'd been able to walk I'd wanted a horse. I even begged Mama to get pregnant again because I knew she'd have a foal for me. Mama Betts had told Effie not to indulge me in such foolishness, but for a long time Mama let me believe that it might happen. Until Daddy said that it was cruel to build up my hopes. He said I could have a horse, but Mama said no. She was afraid I'd be hurt. Horses were unpredictable, dangerous, big, capable of bizarre behavior. Mine wouldn't be, but Effie had no faith in that.

'Hurry up, Bekkah! Quit standing around daydreaming!'

Of course the last stall was empty, except for two old tires, some rotting blankets, an old halter and the three Coca-Colas we'd hidden behind the tires. I got them all, hoping never to make another trip into the barn. At the door, Alice's shadow extended almost to the middle of the barn. It was growing very late. Bikes or no bikes, we were going to be in trouble.

We made sure to close the barn door just as we'd found it. Although we didn't have a bottle opener, Alice was able to force the top off one bottle by using the edge of the step. We filled up Maebelle's bottle, and she took to it with a greedy sucking sound.

'If I had a horse, we'd be home in two minutes flat.'

'If you had a horse, the poor thing would probably be living in your bedroom. Don't let her have too much too fast.' She motioned for me to pull the bottle out of Maebelle's mouth. The result, not to my surprise, was a wail of protest. I gave the nipple back to her.

'She'll gas up and puke on you,' Alice warned, then shrugged. She was constantly amused by my lack of know-how when it came to babies.

'She's starving to death.'

'Let her digest what she's had.'

Alice knew her business when it came to babies, so I removed the bottle and contented myself with listening to Maebelle's angry frustration. We picked up our gear, leaving the two unopened Cokes behind the chinaberry tree, and started on our way home. Even though we were rested, our steps were slower. Effie would be fit to be tied, worried about me. Mrs. Waltman didn't seem to worry much, but she'd be mad at the state Maebelle V. was in. She was dirty, soiled, and now beginning to erp and drool. Upchuck was not far behind.

'I'm hungry,' Alice finally said. We'd gone all day

without anything to eat. It was close to three.

'Mama Betts will have something good made. Since we're in trouble, you might as well stop by and have a bite.'

'Maybe we could clean Maebelle up a little.'

'Sure.'

'Maybe we should tell the truth about the bikes.' Alice had no stomach for fibs, or the resulting trouble they always caused.

'If we don't say anything, we might get the bikes back.'

'If we don't say anything, that's not really a lie.'

'Right. And I get a feeling I'll hear something from that tall skinny boy real soon. Like tonight.'

We'd just come to a big curve in the road. At the sound of a loud motor, we both automatically moved into the sandy ditch and up the bank to high ground. At the curve some of the boys drove wild. If the road was rutted real bad, like it was today, the cars would sometimes begin to jump and quiver on the washboard ruts and the driver would lose control. Then the car would slam into the ditch. Kali Oka curve was good business for the body shops around Jexville.

'That ain't nobody we know,' Alice said, listening to the voice of the motor. 'It's straining, like it's big.'

Before I could hypothesize, an old truck pulling a long horse van rounded the curve. I knew what the van was because I'd read about them in my books. The English called them vans or boxes, and Americans called them trailers. When I pretended that I had a horse, I also pretended I was English, like Velvet Brown.

The sun was bearing down right in our eyes, and I couldn't see in the truck very well. Most of my attention was focused on the van anyway. I couldn't see anything through the tiny little windows, but when it passed, I might be able to see the horses' tails, if it was loaded.

'Look!' Alice squeezed my arm and pulled me around to look behind us.

A skinny little arm poked out to left-hand-turn, and the truck and trailer disappeared down the chinaberry driveway of the old McInnis place.

'Are they moving in?' I could hardly breathe.

Before Alice could answer, there was a loud scream from a horse. Not panic or fear, but a call, as if the horse was hoping for another horse to answer.

Picket's interest picked up immediately. Her ears stood up and quivered, and I knew I had to get her home. The thick chinaberry trees blocked our view, but we stood for a moment longer listening.

Several horses called in that wild, anxious manner. I knew just how their nostrils would flare and the forelock would hang wild in their eyes. Then there was the sound of a metal door banging open and a woman's voice shouting commands.

'Let's go,' Alice said. She grinned. 'I've been praying that something would happen to take your mind off those Redeemer folks. The Lord works in mysterious ways.'

Chapter Six

'Well, you girls look like you bathed in sweat and powdered with Kali Oka dust.' Mama Betts took the baby from Alice with a look that spoke her displeasure. 'What have you been doing with this child, using her for a kick ball? I've never seen the like. Thunderation, her little tummy is tight as a drum with gas, and she smells like she hasn't been bathed or changed in a week. There should be a law . . . '

She took Maebelle V. and walked into the house with her, headed straight for the bathroom and a soapy tub. As soon as she'd passed through the kitchen, Alice and I hit the refrigerator. There was part of a coconut custard pie and some cold milk. We ate out of the pie tin, not even bothering with saucers. Then we moved on to some bread and pimento cheese spread that Mama Betts had made up fresh that morning. She put olives in it, my favorite way. And though I liked it toasted in the oven, I didn't bother with the niceties. We were too hungry for such.

'Where were you girls at lunch?' Effie had walked quietly into the kitchen from her study. Her glasses were down her nose, and her hair was curls all standing on end. I could see where she'd been dragging her fingers through her hair as she wrote. Whenever I did that, she fussed at me and said I'd make myself bald. My hair wasn't as curly as hers, and I wore it in braids.

'We went for a swim,' I answered around the half of sandwich I'd stuffed in my mouth.

'I was beginning to think you'd drowned.'

'We had a little trouble with the bikes on the way home. Somebody moved in the old McInnis place. A woman with horses.'

'Horses?'

Alice looked from me to Effie and back. Before I could answer she jumped in. 'Yes, ma'am, she had a big old truck and a trailer filled with horses. They were all crying and screaming when she pulled up at that place.' Alice stopped when I kicked her under the table.

'They weren't really screaming. They were just talking.'

'Forget it, Bekkah.'

'Forget what?'

'The idea that you're going down to the old McInnis place.'

Effie knew how bad I wanted to ride. I could see how much it scared her to think about it. She'd been dragged once as a young girl and almost killed. She was deathly afraid of horses, and she just didn't want me around them at all. She didn't seem to want me to do anything that was new or fun. Even Mama Betts said so when they thought I was asleep.

'I'd better get the baby and go on home to help Mama with supper.' Alice stood up, picked up her napkin and threw it in the trash. She wasn't about to mix in the great horse war that was raging between me and Effie. She hurried from the room to the back of the house, where Mama Betts was playing with the baby.

'I'm telling you right up front: stay away from those horses.'

'Yes, ma'am.' I rolled my crumbs into a little ball and mashed it into the tablecloth.

'Emily Welford called and said she had some new

potatoes and okra if you or Arly would come pick it.'

'I'll go as soon as Alice leaves.'

'Take Emily a jar of the strawberry preserves Mama Betts put up.'

'Okay. Where's Arly?' I didn't mind digging the potatoes, but the okra made my hands itch and burn. I wanted either Arly or his gloves.

'He's running an errand for me in Jexville.'

'In town?' He would be sitting at the drugstore sipping on a fountain Coke and reading a comic book in the Kool air-conditioned store. 'How'd he get to town?'

'I took him right after lunch. We looked for you, but we couldn't find you.'

That was it, then. It was my fault that I was walking down Kali Oka in the hot sand with the sun scorching the part on my head while Arly was living it up in town.

'See you tomorrow.' Alice walked back into the kitchen with a much cleaner and happier baby in her arms. Mama Betts had also supplied her with a fresh bottle of evaporated milk, water and a little sugar. The baby was sucking and gurgling with contentment.

'Are we still on for swimming?' I made it sound like we'd talked it over.

Alice looked at me as if I'd turned into a toad. She knew we weren't going to walk all the way to the end of Kali Oka again. And we didn't have our bikes.

'Swimming?'

'At eleven. The picnic, remember?'

'Oh, yeah, the picnic.'

Effie watched us, but she didn't say anything for a moment. 'Maybe Mama Betts will pack a lunch for you.' She turned and left the room.

'She doesn't believe us,' Alice hissed. She clamped my shoulder with her hand. 'She knows we're lying.'

'She thinks it's the horses.' I knew she did. She thought I'd spent part of the day at the old McInnis place.

I knew the look of disappointment on her face at the idea I hadn't told her the truth.

'What are we going to do?'

'Give those boys a chance to redeem their shirts.' I could imagine how the scene would go. It would be sweet revenge to make those boys say uncle. We'd have our bicycles back in a flash, and then I'd tell them where to find their shirts.

'Be sure you leave Picket at home. They might try to hurt her.'

Of all the disturbing things I'd ever thought, it had never crossed my mind that someone would hurt Picket to get at me, until today. It had already happened. Alice was right.

'Meet me in the woods at ten. That should give us a chance to walk a ways down the road and find a good picnic spot.'

'And those boys will find us, right?'

'If they're smart they will.' And if they weren't, then I'd have to bring Arly into my confidence. Arly, sitting at the drugstore counter. Effie must have given him money to spend, too, 'cause he'd already gone through his allowance and tried to borrow some from me.

'See you at ten.' Alice let the screen door slam behind her as she took off for home, humming a little song to the baby in her arms.

After Alice left I went to Emily's for the potatoes and okra. There would probably be peas and corn too. She had a daughter my age, Jamey Louise, who hated picking vegetables. Emily always sent her out in the field to help me, but all she ever did was dig her bare toes into the hot dirt and complain.

Emily and Gustav, her husband, and their three daughters, Jamey Louise being the youngest, lived about a mile down from us on the right side of the road. Gustav, better known as Big Gus, worked as a carpenter at a factory, and he farmed forty acres on the side. Emily, who was nearly six feet tall and had the biggest chest in all of Chickasaw County, put up a lot of vegetables and was always real generous to share with us. We in turn gave her lots of fruit and preserves and pecans from our trees. Daddy didn't farm, but Mama Betts had a way with fruit and nut trees and berries. When nobody else in the county had pecans, we did. Big old Stuarts and those long papershells with hulls so thin anybody could crack them.

There was talk that Libby Ruth, the oldest girl, gave Emily a lot of trouble. Libby liked nice things. She liked boys and fast cars, and she liked to laugh. She was homecoming queen last year, and she looked more beautiful than any other girl in school even though she was taller than a lot of the boys. She was always real nice to me, even when a lot of the high school kids were around. She drove the tractor in the field in her two-piece swimsuit and had the best suntan of anyone near Jexville. I thought she should be on television, and I told her so, which made Jamey Louise squinch up her face and pinch me. She said I shouldn't encourage Libby in that kind of thinking because all she ever did was read magazines and listen to the radio as it was.

Walking over to Emily's, I hoped Libby would be at home. There were four Welfords in all, but Buck, the oldest, was long gone, working the oil fields in Texas and making a fortune. Mama Betts said he was the handsomest young man she'd ever seen, but I hardly remembered him at all. The middle girl, Cora, was pretty too, but she wasn't as much fun as Libby, or as tall. And Jamey was no fun at all and the runt of the litter. It was like the juices had all been spent on Libby. She had all the best of the looks and a happy way. The others just sort of dribbled along after her, even though Jamey Louise was thought by all the schoolboys to be a real dish and it looked like

51

she was going to take after her mother's chest. I didn't bother to go in the house when I got there. I got the shovel from the shed and found a pail and headed toward the long rows of potatoes.

I liked the way Gus's shovel felt. The handle was worn smooth, as finely worked as if someone had rubbed it down with sandpaper. Arly's gloves weren't in his top dresser drawer, so I was working bare-handed. Gus had taught me the art of "tater diggin" and said I had a natural feel for it. The tip of the shovel was placed about eight inches from the plant and then pushed down with a smooth thrust of the foot. When the dirt was turned, the potatoes were clumped up in it. The smell of the earth was rich, warm and somehow comforting. Even the feel of the sun on my shoulders and back was pleasant. Over toward the house I caught sight of Picket trying to ambush one of Emily's guineas. Good luck, Picket. Those mean old guineas would turn on her in a second and send her scooting for the safety of the potato patch. As I watched the hen spun around and launched herself at my dog, old leathery chicken claws extended. Picket was in it more for the sport than the kill, and she didn't have the heart to pursue the game. Tail tucked, she came back out to my side and laid down in the row where I'd just turned the earth up.

'Mama says to tell you there's fresh lemonade.'

Wiping the sweat from my eyes, I looked up to see Jamey Louise standing at the end of the row. She had on a dress and lipstick. A big straw bonnet protected her face.

'You'd better get you a hat or those freckles are going to get thicker and thicker until you look like a monkey, or one of those Waltman girls.'

'I like freckles.' I liked Alice's freckles, but I hated the ones that were across my nose and were slowly growing on my shoulders and arms.

'Freckles are ugly, and none of the magazines recommend them.'

'That's too bad, Jamey Louise.' I stepped down on the shovel and realized too late I was too close to the potato mound. I could feel the blade as it sliced several taters in half. 'Why don't you give me a hand with this, and we can dig some for Emily while we're at it?'

'I hate potatoes. They're nothing but dirt.'

'What's wrong with dirt?' I was goading her and we both knew it.

'One day I'm gonna live in a big house with white columns and a marble dance floor imported from Italy. We'll never serve potatoes, or butter beans, or peas at my house.'

Jamey Louise considered herself a tap dancer of great talent. The boys loved to watch her because it looked like some wild animal was loose in her sweater. 'What are you going to eat, hamburgers and ice cream?'

'French qui-sine.' She dared me to comment. 'Libby says that President Kennedy and the First Lady have a cook who prepares French qui-sine. Mrs. Kennedy also has a French designer who makes her special clothes. They come all the way from France.'

'Why would an American president's wife want clothes that came from France? Seems like she'd want to wear American clothes.' I had a mental picture of a very neat dark-haired woman with this dorky little round hat on top of her puffed-out hair.

'You have no couth, Rebekah Rich. You'll never get a boyfriend.' Jamey linked her hands behind her back. 'There are some cute boys down at that church, but Libby says they're a waste of time.'

Shovel tip in the ground, I stopped and looked at her. This was a new gambit from Jamey Louise. What was she driving at?

'Libby said the boys from the church don't have cars or

money. She said even if they are cute, they're a waste. Do you think they're a waste?'

'I suspect Libby knows more about boys than I do.' Jamey Louise had rocks in her head if she was interested in boys who would beat on a helpless dog and steal bicycles, but those weren't facts I felt free to divulge to her.

'There's this one boy, tall with dark hair. I saw him this afternoon riding by--'

'On a bicycle?' I dropped five potatoes in the bucket and determined that I had enough for me and the Welfords for supper. I could move on to the okra.

'Yeah. It was a girl's bike though.'

'A white Schwinn?' That bicycle was my pride. The idea that those boys might leave it out in the weather tormented me. I'd had it for a year and there wasn't even a dent on it.

'Yeah, a white bicycle.'

'With a deep front basket?'

'No,' Jamey Louis smiled. 'There wasn't a basket. If that bike had had a basket, it would have looked just like yours.'

'Are you sure?' My palms felt hot and sweaty, and a stinging sensation started on the top of my scalp. Either I was going to faint or I had been gripped by a fury so powerful that I'd never experienced it before. Had they dared to take my basket off?

'I'm sure. You think I don't know a basket on a bike?'

'What time?'

'About half an hour ago.'

So that explained the bonnet, the lipstick and the dress. Jamey Louise was sick, sick, dressing to catch the eye of one of those Redeemer boys. She obviously didn't think it was a waste of time no matter what Libby said. 'Did he say anything?'

'He asked me if I knew a girl with pigtails and another

one with blond hair and freckles. He said they had a
baby. Sounds an awful lot like you and Alice and her kid
sister.' Jamey's eyes were small and brown. Hidden
under the shade of her hat they had a distinctly pig-like
quality.

I wanted to tell her that he'd stolen my bike and hit my
dog with a stick, but the horrendousness of those acts
would wash over Jamey like a cloud across the sun.
Besides, she'd twist it up and gossip it all over the road.
Before I knew what hit me, it would be everywhere that I
was consorting with the Redeemers down in the woods.
Mama Betts would have my hide.

'He must have seen us when the buses went by. All
those folks looked spooky to me, like zombies all going
down the road in a bus to hell.'

'I'm telling on you for cussing.'

'Be my guest.' I looked up at her. 'Shithead.' That did
the trick. She tore out of the field as if I'd thrown roaches
on her feet. Emily wouldn't believe I'd called Jamey a
shithead. Emily thought I was the most courteous child
she'd ever met.

I put the shovel back in Gus's shed and found a
sharp garden knife he kept on hand for cutting vegetables. There was a store of paper sacks out there, too,
and I got a big one. I'd cut it full and then take the okra
and potatoes up to the house to divide with the
Welfords. Mama insisted that whenever I picked vegetables, I was always to pick enough for us and for
them too. The pleasure of the afternoon was lost,
though. I couldn't shake the image of my bicycle
stripped of the basket and God knew what else. I felt
more helpless than I'd ever felt in my life. Totally
hamstrung. It was at that moment that my decision to
go back to the McInnis place crystallized. If I hurried
with the okra I'd have time to get down there and back
before anyone missed me.

Chapter Seven

The green Chevy and rusted old trailer were parked at the end of the driveway, just inside the gate. It didn't look like much of a rig, but I could imagine that it had been all over the world. I'd read about the MacClay and Madison Square Gardens and the Grand Prix. Never in a million years had I dreamed that a little piece of that world might drive down Kali Oka Road. Not until today. All I had to do was walk into the barn to see those horses and the woman who rode them.

Picket and I stood in the driveway in the shade of the biggest chinaberry tree. The big barn doors were open wide. In the dim light near the front of the barn, a small shape flitted through the shadows. Beside me, Picket tensed. I grabbed a firm hold on her collar and spoke softly to her. Not all chickens were as savvy as the Welfords'. Whatever was in the barn, I didn't want Picket chasing it. I didn't want to have to go in that barn after her. We surely hadn't been invited.

For a long time we didn't move. Deep within the barn something repeatedly stirred, but it wasn't a sound I was familiar with. As much as it shamed me, that barn still scared me. By all reasons of logic, there were supposed to be horses in there. What if it was something else? I didn't have to go in there. I could always walk home, picking up the sack of potatoes and okra I'd left by the Welford fence.

Walk home in defeat, a coward twice in one day!

I had a mental picture of my bicycle, stripped of its basket and neglected in the sun and rain. I started walking toward the barn. The Redeemer boy had sent me a challenge, and I'd failed to answer him. I would not lose the entire day.

There was a big iron gate that allowed the truck and trailer to pass into the barnyard, and there was a smaller gate for people. It was latched with a rusty hook on part of an old dog leash. Only that morning there hadn't been a hook on the gate. I opened it and walked through, still holding tight to Picket's collar. A yellow streak zipped by the barn door. Cat. Picket tugged against my hold. She liked to chase cats. She'd never hurt anything. Like with the hens, she liked the sport. But I suspected that the cats and chickens didn't much care for it, even though Addy Adams' big tabby cat Mr. Tom seemed to take delight in taunting Picket whenever we went over there. Addy said her cat was smarter than most people and that Picket didn't stand a chance. That cat was something. He'd lead Picket a chase all over the yard and then end up in my arms, purring away, just to get Picket's goat. He was a special cat, almost like a child to Addy.

Picket wanted to go after the yellow cat at the barn, but she knew I had a hold of her, so we let the gate bang shut behind us and walked across the red clay barnyard to the open door. It was late afternoon. Later than it should have been. The sun was hovering above the tallest oak tree along the fence row, and it was about four-thirty by my best calculations. I didn't have time to dally if I wanted to see the horse woman and get home before Mama was really irritated.

There was the sound of something big shifting around in the darkness of the barn. Picket lost interest in the cat and turned her attention to the interior of the barn. Her ears perked forward. Something cool touched the backs of my arms and made my teeth clench. That barn was so scary. It was almost as if it breathed, waiting for me to walk inside. Waiting for a chance . . .

I forced myself to walk to the open door where a shaft of light stretched deep into the gloom. As my eyes adjusted I could see four horse heads sticking out of the first stalls. They were all looking at me. With their bodies hidden behind the doors, it was a creepy picture. It was like their heads were disembodied, hanging over the stall doors.

Then I saw her. She was sitting on a cement block at the end of the barn, up against the right wall. Light from the west side of the barn poured in through the barred windows and fell in these slatted trapezoid patterns across her face. She was wearing dark clothes and her blond hair was spun gold in the intense June light. Her shirt was sleeveless, and her slender arms showed muscles. She was staring straight at me and didn't make an effort to move.

Deep in her throat, Picket growled. 'Easy,' I whispered. I couldn't tell if it was the horses or the woman that made Picket anxious. We were all frozen in place, horses and woman staring at me and me and Picket staring back.

'I'm Rebekah Rich from up the road.' My voice echoed in the barn. It almost made me step backward into the full protection of the sun. My eyes had adjusted to the dimness of the barn, and the woman shifted, putting more of her face in the light. She had brown eyes that seemed to catch the light and send it up the barn to me.

'Welcome, Rebekah,' she said. The features of her oval face never changed expression. Her skin was unmarred by freckles or any other marks. 'I'll bet you've wanted a horse all your life.'

Her voice was slower than mine, tinged with some strange accent that I couldn't place. She wasn't Jexville, that was for sure.

'When I was a young girl like you, all I could think about was horses. But my mother didn't want me to ride. She was afraid I'd be hurt.'

She stood up and walked toward me, stopping in the next pattern of light. Her blond hair was shoulder-length and tangled-looking, as if it had been whipped by the wind while she was on the back of a galloping stallion. She took another five paces and stopped in the next pool of light.

'I don't know why mamas always think they can keep their babies safe by never letting them experience life. Do you?'

I thought my throat had rusted closed, but my voice was strong. 'No.' I gathered my courage. It was necessary to tell her. 'My mother would skin me if she knew I was here.'

The woman's laughter was soft and rich and easy, like water over rocks. It made me smile too.

'She must love you very much,' she said. 'Isn't it odd how something as wonderful as love can be so smothering?'

She didn't really expect an answer, I could tell by the way she asked the question. Besides, to answer honestly would have made me feel as if I'd injured Effie, and Mama Betts, and even Daddy. This woman understood, and I didn't have to say anything.

'Would you like to ride?'

My fingers almost lost their hold on Picket's collar.

'Go ahead, let the dog loose. I've got fourteen cats out here, but they've all gone up in the loft.' She motioned for me to lift my hand from Picket. 'She's a fine-looking dog too. Very smart. I've got five dogs, but they're in the house. I had to give them something to make them sleep on the trip down here. They probably won't wake up for a while.'

'Picket may chase the cats.'

'Let her. They need the exercise.'

Her laughter seemed to dance in the sunlight. My fingers slipped from Picket's collar, and she was trotting down the middle of the barn, stopping at the first horse to sniff and explore. She seemed perfectly at home.

'Well, do you want to ride?'

I could tell by the sunlight that it was getting late. Very late. Mama Betts would be waiting on the potatoes. They were more than likely destined for potato salad, and I should be getting home with them. They had to be washed and peeled and boiled and then chilled.

'Can I just sit on one?'

'I have five more horses that I'll get at the end of the week. These four are my best. Which one appeals to you?'

The entire time I'd been talking, I'd been noticing this one horse, middle stall on the left. A white blaze started between her eyes and moved down her nose to end in a curl over the left nostril.

'So it's Chameleon, is it?' There was approval in her voice. 'A good choice. I see you have an eye for horse flesh. Cammie is perfect for you.'

'You named her after a lizard?' She was such a beautiful animal to be named for a lizard.

'She can change her looks.'

'How?'

'Well, in the show ring she's all fire and flash, but when we're working, she's very reliable.'

'Where did you come from?' The question was rude, but it popped out before I could stop it. 'I mean, I live just up the road. I've always lived there, my entire life.'

'I'm from Cleveland. Not the city in Ohio. I'm from the Mississippi Delta. You know anything about the Delta?'

I knew there were cotton plantations and rich folks, and poor Negroes. Since this woman was white, it followed that she was rich. That and the fact that she had nine horses. What was she doing on Kali Oka Road?

'My parents died in a car accident. I didn't want to stay in Cleveland, so I decided to move around. It's not so easy with nine horses, fourteen cats and five dogs. Before you ask, my name is Nadine. Nadine Andrews. You can call me Nadine.'

'Where's your husband?' She was older than I'd first thought. There were tiny lines around her eyes and mouth. She'd walked up a little closer, and I could see that her hair had a funny cast to it too. And it was considerably darker close to her head.

'I don't need a husband. Where's yours?'

'I'm too young to have one.' She was smiling, and I could see she was teasing me.

'Well, I've had three, and none of them suited me. My advice to you is do without as long as you can.'

I almost asked her if all three of her husbands had died, like her parents, but I knew that would be rude too. Besides, she'd turned away and had picked up a halter from beside Cammie's stall. With practiced moves she slipped it over the horse's head, unlatched the door and led Cammie out into the center of the barn. In a few seconds she had the horse tied on both sides to ropes hanging in the barn. She was an enormous horse, bigger than any I'd ever seen before in my life. I couldn't see over her back – withers was the correct term I'd learned from all of my reading – and I was tall for my age.

From inside what I'd supposed was the tack room she returned with a basket full of brushes and supplies. She explained the different combs and brushes and showed me how to use them, and then how to saddle the horse. The little saddle was light enough for me to carry, even though I had to stand on a cement block to put it on Cammie's back. As much as I was learning and enjoying myself, I couldn't forget that I was due home.

'Maybe I'd better wait until later to ride, Mrs. . . .

Nadine.' We had Cammie saddled and bridled, but it was five o'clock at least.

'Mama gonna fuss?'

'I'm supposed to be getting some potatoes for supper. She'll be waiting for them.'

'Jump up on Cammie for a few minutes, and I'll drive you home.'

'No!'

She laughed, easy and deep.

'I mean, I couldn't put you to that trouble, Mrs. Andrews.' I'd really stepped in it, but I knew from looking at her that Effie and Mama Betts would take an instant dislike. She wasn't like them, or anyone else on Kali Oka. Nadine Andrews was not going to fit in.

'It's Nadine, and I'll drop you off before we get to your house. That way your folks won't see you consorting with me.'

My face burned. She knew exactly why I couldn't let her take me home.

'Listen, Rebekah, I gave up a long time ago worrying about whether folks approved of me or not. The truth is, I've got enough money to do whatever I damn well please.' She cupped her hands beside the horse, and I put my foot in them. Two seconds later, I was in the saddle.

It was better than I'd ever dreamed. Cammie shifted beneath me, and I felt it. My body went right along with her. My fingers tangled in her mane until Nadine handed me the reins and showed me how to hold my fingers so that they worked as springs against the horse's mouth. Then she walked me out in the yard and turned me loose.

Picket danced beside me, as eager as I was. In a matter of minutes I'd mastered walking and turning. Cammie was a dream. In the sun her coat was a deep brown. Nadine called her a mahogany bay, with two white stockings on her back legs. She was better than anything I'd ever imagined. We trotted, and even though I bounced for a while, I finally got the idea of posting.

'You have a real talent, Rebekah. You and Cammie seem to have a special bond.'

I felt it. It was everything I'd ever wanted. *Black Stallion*, *King of the Wind*, *Silver Birch*. The potatoes and Mama Betts and Effie disappeared. There was only the sensation of moving with Cammie, of riding high in the sun and the afternoon, of Picket trotting beside us and of Nadine's smile of approval.

'You'd better call it a day and get home.'

Nadine's words brought me back to hard reality. It was at least five-thirty. Before Nadine could help, I slid from Cammie's back, just as I'd read in my books.

'Perfect dismount. This time I'll untack her, because we're in a hurry. But from now on it's your responsibility.'

'I can come back?' Although my dread of going home was multiplying with each second, the thought of riding again gave me a jolt of pure bliss.

'I hope you'll come and take some lessons from me. I'd love to teach you.'

'Maybe.' I knew Mama would never give me money for riding lessons. She'd been trying to coerce me into piano for years, and I'd held out. Horses were out of the question.

'You could work for your lessons.'

Nadine showed me the door to magic and then gave me the key. Somehow I'd manage to have them. My hand lingered on Cammie's warm shoulder as Nadine removed saddle and bridle and returned her to her stall. In a few moments we had unhitched her truck and were bumping over her driveway to the road.

At the Welfords' fence I stopped her and got out to get the potatoes and okra. She drove to the edge of our property, where I directed her to stop. Chances were that Mama had already called the Welfords, and that Emily had told her I'd left better than an hour before. I was in big trouble.

'Whatever punishment they give you, remember Cammie,' Nadine said, brushing my bangs from my forehead. 'You didn't do anything wrong, Rebekah. You wanted something bad enough to take a risk. That isn't bad. What's wrong is that no one understands or appreciates your dream. I do, because it's the same one I have.'

Clutching the bag of potatoes and okra, I got out and closed the truck door. Tears threatened and I called a thanks and hurried away before she saw them. Nadine Andrews wouldn't cry in public. Cutting through part of the yard, I hurried to the screen door. The porch was ominously quiet. I almost tripped over the pile of metal that had been assembled near the door.

It took a full ten seconds for me to recognize the two wheels, the curves of fenders and the once white seat that had been my bicycle.

The entire thing had been taken apart piece by piece. Even the basket was mixed in the wreckage. That Redeemer boy had destroyed my bicycle and then brought the parts of it to my very yard.

The sack of potatoes slipped from my hand and bounced lightly on the ground. I knelt beside the pile of metal, fighting back the tears. In a second I was glad to feel the surge of anger that saved me from crying like a baby. I'd kill that bastard. He'd torn up my beautiful bicycle and left it destroyed at my own front porch.

Chapter Eight

I didn't know how much time passed, at least fifteen minutes. I was so caught up in the rage and loss that I lost track. Voices coming through the kitchen window brought me around. A shaft of inviting yellow light beckoned me inside, but I hovered outside, listening. My fingertips traced the back fender of my bike.

'Effie, you want me to run over to Alice's house and ask her?'

Arly's voice floated out the open window, eager. He could sense the depth of the pit I'd fallen into, and he smelled blood. If anyone outside the family tried to hurt me, Arly would tear them apart. But inside the family we were competitors. Mama Betts said until I was born, Arly had been the sun. Every time he burped or fizzled they thought it was a sign of genius. Then two years later I came along. Mama Betts said I'd never understand because I'd always lived with Arly, but he had that distant memory of being the only child, the best-loved baby.

Now Arly had entered the ranks of male teenager, and he was girl crazy, though he hid it pretty well from Effie and Mama Betts. Daddy suspected, but since he was away this summer I couldn't be sure how much he knew. Anyway, if Arly could keep the spotlight of Effie's fear focused on me, then he'd have more freedom to do as he pleased. I understood his strategy, and I wanted to choke him. I held myself still while Mama talked.

'If she isn't home in ten minutes, I'm going to call Joe.'

'Now, Effie. You're getting hysterical.'

'Her bicycle is in pieces! What sane person would do that? I should have called Joe when Arly found the bike! What if someone's taken my baby?'

Mama's voice had gone past anger, climbing higher and higher into the zone of panic. Joe Wickham was the county sheriff. I'd really stepped in it now.

I stood up. There was no point delaying, but my legs didn't want to work. Man oh man. I forced myself over the bicycle and onto the porch. Since I was a coward, I let the screen door slam. That gave them a little warning that I was home. The scraping of chairs in the kitchen was distinct, a harsh noise that foretold of things to come.

Dusk had begun to settle over Kali Oka Road, and when the door opened, the light spilled out and over me. I stood transfixed, like a 'possum staring directly into headlights. I had to fight to keep my hands from going up as if I expected to be struck.

'Rebekah!' Effie and Mama Betts spoke together.

'Man, you're in some shit now,' Arly offered and failed to even earn a reprimand for his language. He stood behind them, peering over their shoulders.

'Where have you been?' Mama and Mama Betts both lifted their arms to their hips. 'Well, answer me.'

It was as if they'd rehearsed together.

'You'd better hope you were kidnapped by communists, because if not, you haven't got an alibi and you're going to suffer big time.'

'Shut up, Arly.' I was trying to think what to tell them. They knew about the bicycle, but they didn't know who had done it. 'Someone stole my bicycle.'

'Rebekah Brighton Rich.'

Effie's voice simmered. She was over the fear and had notched up to a pure fury that was the by-product of intense relief. She'd be over the worst of it in a matter of minutes, if I lived that long.

'Your father is sitting in an office halfway across the country, worried sick about you. I've been about to tear my hair out, and Mama Betts has been terrified thinking of all the things that could have happened to you.'

'I'm sorry.' Indeed I was, but I knew apologies would go unheard at this point.

'She didn't ask for a character reference.' Arly had stepped back from the door. Mama Betts' hand clamped down on his shoulder with a suddenness that made him jump.

'Someone stole my bike, and I was trying to get it back.'

'Who took it?' Effie held the screen door open for me to enter.

The crisis was over. At least the worst of it. She was asking questions and maybe willing to listen to my side. 'I don't know.' I was still carrying the potatoes and okra, and Mama Betts took the bag from my arms.

'Arly, go wash some of these potatoes.' She handed the bag to him, and I felt a surge of satisfaction.

'You'd better explain yourself right now.' Effie pointed a chair at the kitchen table.

I told them about going to the creek swimming and how we'd left the bikes along the bank and how they were gone when we went back for them. It was not a lie, only the timing was a little off. 'That's what took us so long to get home. We had to walk. Alice begged me not to tell because hers is the family bicycle and now it's ruined.' I was about to cry, thinking about the trouble Alice would be in if her bike was sitting in a heap in her front yard. Mrs. Waltman was known to slap first and never listen. With eleven kids she wanted results, not excuses, as she said.

'Arly said he thought he could put it back together.'

'Really?' My beautiful bike, whole and wonderful again. 'Alice's too?'

'If all the parts are there.' Arly spoke over his shoulder, his hands in the sink. 'It's going to cost you,' he mouthed at me so that no one else could hear.

'I'll bet the child is starved,' Mama Betts said. She reached into the oven and brought out a plate of food.

I was famished. My ribs ached I was so hungry. Fried chicken, rice and gravy and crowder peas. Without okra. I was the fault of that, but I picked up the fork Mama Betts gave me and dug in.

'Look at her scarf her food,' Arly said. 'Maybe there's a contest we can enter her in.'

'Chew your food, Bekkah,' Effie said automatically. 'And swallow that mouthful and tell us where you've been.'

I chewed for a long time. 'I was hoping whoever took the bikes would leave them along the road. Like a prank and all. So I was down the road, sort of along the fence rows.' Even though it wasn't a complete lie, my eyes wouldn't lift from my plate.

'Did it ever occur to you that I would have taken you in the car?'

'I wanted to find it myself.'

'Little Miss Independence.' Mama Betts put a slice of hot cornbread on my plate. Her knuckles brushed across my arm. 'You were always that way, Bekkah. Headstrong and determined to have your way. It's going to cost you one of these days. Gonna cost all of us.'

Guilt mixed in with my fond desire to save my hide. Mama Betts had been worried sick. She never threatened unless she'd been badly scared. 'I'm sorry, Grandma.'

'You can't help your nature, child. That's something you're going to have to learn. And that stubborn streak is gonna cost you plenty in the future.' She kissed the crown of my head. 'Yes ma'am, like I said, that streak is gonna cost you, and yet it may be the thing that holds you up in the worst of times. That's what you learn when you get old. There's a blessing and a curse in everything. Just like loving you children. It brings me my greatest pleasure and worst pain.'

Not even Arly had anything wise to say after that. I felt about as big as a sun-baked cow pie. Even the fried chicken had lost its taste. I chewed on, determined to finish or Arly would comment.

'When you finish, we'll call your father.' Effie took a seat beside me at the table.

I pushed my plate back. It was silly to pretend I wasn't upset. I could see that Effie had been crying. Mama Betts had been worried sick, and Daddy was probably pacing the office of his strange house in Missouri. All of this misery brought on because . . . because I'd ridden a horse. The thought of Cammie touched me like a gentle hand.

We dialed the university where Daddy was living in some faculty housing for visiting teachers. It didn't even ring one good time before he snatched up the phone.

'Daddy, it's Bekkah.'

'Then you're safe. When Effie told me about the bicycle, I was afraid . . . '

What could possibly have made him so afraid on Kali Oka Road? Parents had a way of worrying all out of proportion to what was going on.

After we talked a few minutes and he finally believed I wasn't hurt at all, his mind started working again.

'Who took the bicycle, Bekkah?'

Somehow, a thousand miles away, he knew that I knew more than I was telling.

'I'm not certain.' I didn't know their names.

'Listen to me, girl. Whatever mischief you're up to, don't you ever worry your mother that way again.'

'I was right on Kali Oka. I didn't go anywhere—'

71

'Rebekah, you're old enough to begin to understand. You have a responsibility to me and Effie and Mama Betts and Arly. You have to use good sense and make certain that nothing bad happens to you.' He paused. 'You can't risk yourself, Bekkah.'

'Yes, sir.' They'd all gone off the deep end. I was just an hour or so late. You'd think I'd been playing with dynamite. Effie had stepped back in the kitchen, away from the telephone in the hall. 'Daddy?'

'Yes?'

'If I had a chance at something I wanted more than anything else, something that wouldn't hurt anyone, would it be wrong me for to try to get it?'

'Hypothetical questions are impossible at this distance. Would you care to be a little more specific?'

The Detail Man. He couldn't be happy with a simple question. 'There's a woman at the old McInnis place. Her name is Nadine Andrews, and she's offered to give me horseback riding lessons if I'll work at her barn.'

'What does Effie say?'

'I haven't told her.'

'So, that's the story of where you were and how you lost your bicycle.'

'For the most part.' It would be stupid to drag the Redeemer boys into an already complicated story.

'You couldn't have picked up the telephone and called your mother?'

'Nadine just moved in. I don't think her phone is hooked up yet.'

'Bekkah, I know how bad you want this, and I don't personally see any harm in it, but I can't say yes if Effie's dead set against it.'

My only hope faded. 'Don't tell her, Daddy. Let me work on it.'

There was a long pause. 'Promise me you won't run off and worry your mother again. Work it out between the two of you, but don't leave her wondering if she's going to find your body in the ditch somewhere.'

'I promise. How are things in Missouri?'

'Far removed from the things that are worrying me about Mississippi.'

Daddy suddenly sounded tired. He was always worried about things that couldn't be helped. He talked about perceptions and how people got tied down in one way of thinking and couldn't see the truth. He said that the South was in for a hard time because some northern folks had time schedules in their heads and were determined to keep them. Not a lot of what he said made sense to me, but it troubled him. And Effie too. I had the idea that it had something to do with communists, but somehow Negroes were involved in it too. We didn't have any Negroes living on Kali Oka Road, so it didn't seem as if it could really have too much effect on us. Besides, the ones I knew in Jexville didn't seem upset about anything.

'Daddy, we're all fine down here. Don't worry about us.'

'Put your mother on the phone, Bekkah. I love you.'

Daddy wouldn't tell on me about the horses. We had a deal. I called Effie to the phone and listened for a few minutes as she talked about Jexville and some argument at a juke joint up near the forks of the river at Merrill. A Negro man had been selling shine, and a white man had killed him. The Negro's brother had then taken a shotgun and blasted the white man in half. I'd heard Effie and Mama Betts talking about it in whispers. It sounded like it was all over to me. The white man had started it, and he'd been killed. There was obviously something more to the whole story because whenever Effie started to talk about it, she whispered and tried to talk in code so that Arly and I wouldn't catch on. Arly and I, for the most part, weren't interested.

'They've got him in jail.'

There was a pause while Daddy talked.

'No, none of the lawyers will represent him. I'm afraid they're going to send someone from out of town.'

There was another pause.

'No, Joe says the jail is secure. He wants him moved, but there's no place to take him.' Pause. 'No, Greene County would be worse. They'd hang him in his cell. Hattiesburg, maybe.'

There was a lot longer pause, and Effie cast me an accusatory look. 'I'm not afraid to let her grow up. That's not fair. You're not even here.'

Before I could be pinned by Effie's evil look again, I went to my room. I got out my old yellow notebook that had been bought for math notes, which I hated, and started to draw pictures of Cammie. Somehow I'd get back to Nadine's. Mama Betts said that opportunity only knocks once, and I knew that this was it for me. I took my notebook into the bathroom and ran some hot water. When I took off my jeans, I could smell Cammie on them. How had they not noticed? Somehow I was going to have to leave a pair of jeans at the barn, so I could ride and then change to go home. I'd work it out. As I slipped beneath the hot water in the old claw-foot tub, I let my body float and tried to recapture the feeling of complete freedom I'd felt on Cammie's back.

Chapter Nine

Alice's bicycle was returned – intact. She found it the next morning parked under the tree with the swing. The Redeemer boy had singled me out as a particular target. It was personal between us now.

I was caught between a rock and a hard place with Arly. He put my Schwinn back together, as good as new. Every bolt and nut that had come out of the bicycle had been returned. But I needed Arly's help to get even with the church boy, especially since Alice was reluctant to go on any more adventures down at Cry Baby Creek. She counted herself lucky, she said, to have escaped without getting in hot water over the bike. Mrs. Waltman was cranky and mean in her fifth month of pregnancy, and Alice was walking a thin line with her already. If I got Arly to help me, I'd have to spend a lot of time with him, and I couldn't stop thinking about Cammie and Nadine. Arly could not be trusted with that secret.

Two of the longest days of my life passed while I stayed around the house and tried to make it up to Effie and Mama Betts for all the worry I'd caused them. I washed venetian blinds in the bathtub and ironed curtains and scraped dead wax out of corners until my knees were red and sore. I thought it was a suitable penance. There weren't any Catholics on Kali Oka Road, probably not even any in the county. But I'd read somewhere that Catholic women had been known to walk to certain sacred places on their knees. It was their way of showing they were worthy of a miracle, and I needed one where horses were concerned. At the same time, I couldn't help but wonder what the Redeemers considered a suitable penance. Remembering their gray clothes and faces, I shied away from that thought. It would no doubt be harsher than knee-walking.

The third day of my rehabilitation, Mama Betts and I went plum picking down Kali Oka. She suggested the trip, a sign that I was making it back to a state of grace. Walking with an easy step, pails swinging in our hands, we passed the old McInnis place, and Mama Betts gave it a thorough sizing-up.

'Needs a good cleaning. I can't imagine how someone could live in that house without doing some hard scrubbing. Now, how old did you say this woman is?'

'I don't know.' I sought Cammie in the pasture beside the barn, but there wasn't a single horse out. The barn doors were closed, and the old truck and trailer were gone. Nadine had probably gone to get the rest of her horses. I wondered when she would be back, and who was feeding and taking care of her animals for her. There was no sign of the dogs out either, and five dogs, even if they were those little frou-frou house dogs, should have made a racket. Picket, for her part, was eagerly eyeing the area for any cats to chase.

'I thought you said the woman had horses.' Mama Betts walked on, pail swinging and an old straw hat pulled down over her eyes. She had pretty white skin and hair, and she said she'd never been in the sun without a bonnet or a hat.

'She does.'

'Why aren't they out in the sun? Livestock needs sunshine. Can't keep 'em cooped up all day. It's inhumane.'

I shrugged, feigning a lot less interest than I had. 'You

think Mrs. Mason's trees will have any of those big juicy plums?'

'We'll stop and ask. Brenda won't mind giving us enough for one batch of jelly.'

'Jelly my foot, I want some to eat.' We were past the old McInnis place, and my spirits sank. This would be another day when I didn't get to see Cammie.

'You haven't had much to say about your bicycle.'

Mama Betts' statement made me misstep in the loose sand of the road. 'What's there to say? Arly fixed it.'

'The Bekkah Rich I know would be fuming all over the place wanting to get even with whoever did such a thing . . . unless she knew who'd done it and was feeling guilty.'

'When I figure it all out, I'll get even.' I picked up a big white rock and threw it down the road.

'Things are changing, Bekkah. You know it as well as I.'

Beneath the floppy hat Mama Betts' face was shadowed, but there was no denying the sadness along her mouth.

'Not really. Every summer we pick plums and make jelly. It's the same as it's been every year.'

'Child, child.' There was amusement in her voice. 'I can remember days when cars hadn't been thought of. When your grandfather and I first moved here to Kali Oka, I was seventeen. We hauled water from the little spring in the woods until we could get a well put down. I've seen a lot of what folks call progress, and when I was younger, I thought that some of it was good.'

'You'd rather haul water in buckets than turn a faucet on?'

'Not on your life. The point is, things change. There's no helping it, and even if we could all go backward, nobody would vote to do it. But now things are moving too fast.'

Nothing in my life had moved an inch. The past three days had been a slow, twisting eternity. 'You're just being silly, Mama Betts. What do you mean?'

'Have you ever noticed how chickens will hear a noise and go to squawking and running all over the yard? They don't even know what the noise is, but they go to pieces, feathers flying everywhere, and sometimes they even trample their own chicks.'

We didn't keep chickens, but I'd seen it happen at the Welfords. 'Chickens aren't real smart.'

'Neither are people. Chickens and people have a lot in common sometimes. People hear a rumor and go to running and squawking, and before they know what's happened, they've hurt someone. Maybe even someone of their own.' She took a breath. 'Television and radio give people too much news. Folks don't have time to digest it slowly. They just hear it and react.'

'But you like television.' Arly and I didn't watch much TV, but we loved some of the shows. Even Mama Betts was hooked on *The Edge of Night*. Every afternoon at three-thirty, just when the bus pulled up at the house during school days, I'd hear the *Edge of Night* music. The big star was Mike Carr, a lawyer. He always did the right thing.

'At times. Bekkah, there are two things I have to tell you. One won't make much difference, not to you and not today. Later on you'll understand how much this summer changed your life.'

A knot of apprehension twisted up in my gut. Was it something about the horses or the Redeemers?

'There's a Negro in prison in Jexville. There's trouble brewing about him.'

'Yeah, he shot a white man.' I wasn't deaf as a post. I'd heard Effie and The Judge batting it back and forth on the phone. They were very troubled, but I didn't know why. 'We don't know anybody involved in it. Why is Effie so worried?'

'Well, baby girl, your mama and daddy believe that Negro should get a fair trial. There are those who think he should be sent to the gas chamber.'

'What would it hurt to give him a trial? He was only killing the man who killed his brother.'

'Sounds simple to you, doesn't it? Well, it isn't. Just listen to me when I tell you that times are changing. Folks are on the telephone gossiping back and forth. News gets twisted and changed. Folks get to flapping and squawking like chickens, and someone's bound to get hurt.'

The sun was hot and I wanted to get to the shade of the plum trees, but Mama Betts was dawdling in the road talking about things I didn't understand or even care about. 'Whatever happens in Jexville won't change my life. Not Kali Oka Road. It will never change.'

Mama Betts' arm slipped around my shoulders, and she pulled me to her. She smelled of vanilla and a lemony bath powder she used. No matter how hot the day, her skin was always dry and cool. She said it was because she was so old she didn't sweat anymore. She was old. Close to seventy-five. But she didn't act old, so it didn't matter.

'Baby girl, Kali Oka Road is changing now.'

This time I laughed. Heat devils danced in the road ahead of us. The pecan trees along the ditches were in full green, and there was the distant call of a mockingbird. The road hadn't really changed since I could remember. The Welfords had lost a big oak tree in a storm two years before. It was hit by lightning, and for several months it seemed as if part of the road had gone bald, but that was the biggest change I could remember.

'It's the same, Mama Betts. Look at it. Nobody's even put up a new fence in the last five years.'

'It's not the physical nature of the road, though that will change too.'

She was so sad that I took her free hand and held it. 'What is it?'

I could taste it now, the terrible sadness that I'd failed to notice for the past day. She'd taken me plum picking deliberately, to get me away from the house to tell me something. 'What is it? Tell me.'

'Someone killed Addy's cat.'

'Mr. Tom?' Addy didn't have but one cat, but it couldn't be Mr. Tom.

'Yes.'

'They ran over him?'

'No, Bekkah. They killed him in a terrible way. It was deliberate and cruel.'

Mama Betts was staring straight ahead. Her lips were white and I knew something horrible had happened to Mr. Tom. 'But why?'

'It isn't much of an answer, but just for meanness, I suppose. Some folks are stupid and don't know better. And some know better and are mean.'

Since I couldn't swallow, I couldn't talk. We walked along in silence. I fought hard not to cry, and when I finally did, I didn't make a sound. The road danced and curved ahead of me in the heat. I walked, trying not to think. 'Why Mr. Tom? He liked everybody.'

'There's a new element on Kali Oka Road. It could have been someone driving by, but that doesn't seem likely. It was probably someone on the road, somebody who lives here . . . now.'

'Arly and I'll find 'em, and we'll make them pay.' It was easy to say, but who on the road would do such a thing? I couldn't imagine.

'If I could find the person, I'd be inclined to hurt them myself,' Mama Betts said slowly, but it was clear from the way she said it that she couldn't. 'Addy is heartbroken. That cat was her company, her friend. We can't figure it out why anyone would do something like that to hurt her. She stays home and minds her own business.'

'How did they kill him?' I didn't want to know, but I had to.

'Addy found him in her front yard. There was a rock with blood all over it. His head . . . They had tied him up first.'

Tied him to deliberately kill him. A helpless animal. Oh, how I wanted to make that person pay. But who?

'There were two footprints in the dirt by the cat. Not a grown man but a boy's shoe. And bicycle tracks. Effie and I think whoever took your bicycle might have killed the cat. There's never been any mischief like this on Kali Oka before. Did some of those church people steal your bicycle, Rebekah?'

In the hot sun of the road, she stopped and faced me. Beneath the brim of her hat, her blue eyes searched my face.

'Yes, ma'am.'

'You know which ones?'

'Not by name.'

'And would they have a reason to want to hurt you back?'

'Maybe.'

'And what is that reason?'

'I took their shirts when they took the bicycles.'

'Where are the shirts?'

'I hid them in the woods.'

Mama Betts stared at me. I couldn't tell what she was thinking, but it made her very sad.

'I was going to give their shirts back to get the bicycles back.' Deep breath. 'They hurt Picket.'

'I see.' She shook her head. 'Go get the shirts.'

'Why?'

'We're going to launder them, iron them and take them back to those boys.'

'Mama Betts!' I couldn't do such a thing. Even Mama

Betts had made it clear she thought those boys might have killed Mr. Tom. I'd never give the shirts back. I'd tear them into rags and leave them scattered on the public road in front of the church property. I'd get Arly, and we'd ambush those Redeemer boys and beat them to a bloody pulp.

'Do it. Now.' She turned away from me. 'I'm going on to get the plums.' She started walking. 'And don't be talking this to anyone. We don't need any chicken stampedes on Kali Oka today.'

'No, Mama Betts. I won't do it. Those boys are mean and I won't do it!'

'Yes, ma'am, you will. You had no right to steal.'

'They took the bicycles and they hit Picket with a stick.'

She stopped walking, but she didn't turn around. 'And how did they catch your dog to hurt her? Picket's smarter than that.'

I swallowed.

'You had her tied up so she wouldn't follow you around that church property, didn't you?'

'Yes.'

'Then part of the fact that she was injured lies on your head, Rebekah. You don't leave an animal defenseless.'

'And Mr. Tom, did he deserve to die because he wasn't afraid?' The words tore at my throat and made it raw.

'When we take those shirts back, we'll have a little talk with the minister. What happened to Mr. Tom will be told, as well as what happened to Picket. Those boys have to be taught some decency and compassion. But that doesn't excuse your part in this. Go get the shirts.'

'They're almost all the way to the creek.'

'Better start walking, then. Effie won't like it if she has to hold lunch for you.'

Chapter Ten

Revolt boiled in my heart. Mama Betts had betrayed me for a principle that had nothing to do with what had happened between the Redeemer boys and me. Instead of getting the shirts, I walked on down to the creek for a swim. Hot, angry and frustrated, I needed the cooling water of Cry Baby Creek. It would also give me a chance to spy on the Redeemers again.

Shucking my shoes and socks, I stepped into the cool sand that bordered my side of the creek. Overhead, the branches of the trees were thickly laced and the sun filtered down in a gentle pattern. Some of the anger slipped away as I eased into the icy water. I'd give the damn shirts back, but it wasn't over yet. The water flowed over my knees and thighs, catching the hem of my shorts. I hadn't bothered to undress because I'd be more than dry by the time I got home. Alice and I skinny-dipped in the creek plenty of times, but it was different now. The Redeemer boys had tainted the place. It wasn't mine anymore. I hated them.

Shoes and socks in hand, I made my way up the bed of the creek, careful not to slip and fall in. I'd get as close as I could before climbing the other bank for a look-see at the church people. It was strange wading the creek alone, without Alice or Picket. Mama Betts had taken my dog with her. She didn't want to risk any more trouble with the Redeemers. It was another small but infuriating point that Picket had been denied a trip to the creek because of those boys.

Sound carries a long distance over water, and I heard the axes and exclamations long before I could see the boys. Edging up the bank, I found them about fifty yards from the creek. They were chopping down saplings with a lot of vigor but not much skill. One, two, three, four. They were all there except the tall, skinny one, the leader. I got comfortable on the edge of the bank with some scrub oak and dogwood seedlings for cover.

The plump boy was wielding the ax, and his blows glanced off the tree, sliding down toward his leg. With any luck at all, I wouldn't have to extract any revenge from him. He was about to chop his own stupid foot off.

'Give me the ax, Georgie.' The blondish boy took it. So the fat one was Georgie. It was a gold nugget of fact.

'Greg said for us to have ten trees chopped by the time he got back.' The blond boy spoke again. Greg was obviously the leader.

Greg. Greg. 'Greg.' I whispered his name. I had a little piece of him. 'Greg.' My fingers clenched in the dirt.

'Yeah, well, fuck him. Why isn't he here working?' This from the fourth boy. He was the skinniest. I thought he was the one who'd brought the gun the first day. 'You're as bad as Greg, Jim. You think when he's not around you can give orders.'

The blond boy, Jim, shrugged. 'Suit yourself, jerk-off. When Greg gets back he'll kick you out of the club if you haven't done your work.'

Jim picked up the ax and lit into the tree. His strokes were cleaner, more directed. The tree shook as if it were having a fit of the ague. There was only the sound of the ax biting into the tree until there was the whoosh of the leaves and the small crash of the trunk finally falling.

'Come on.' Georgie signaled the others, and they dragged the tree into a small clearing where Jim could trim the branches. They were building a fort. I watched for a few minutes. The boys were dangerous with the ax. Arly could have felled the trees and had the supports for the fort in place by the time they chopped another tree down. My guess was that they were getting everything ready for Greg to return and supervise the actual construction. He'd have to have more sense than his cohorts if they hoped to make the fort stand.

Watching their clumsiness, I couldn't help but wonder where the boys had grown up. They'd never built a fort before. What had they done? How had they escaped from the dour-faced church people? And if Greg wasn't with them, where was he? A sense of dread prickled the hair on the back of my neck. Without meaning to, I turned around to check behind me. There was the feeling that maybe he was standing behind me, watching.

Some squirrels were busy frisking in the trees across the creek. A few birds rustled in the brush. But there was no sign of a human presence. I backed down the bank and returned to the water; I'd seen enough for the day. It was harder to wade against the current. Where was Greg? It was a question that had taken on tremendous importance. I knew instinctively that he should be with the other boys. He was absent because he was up to something. It was time to leave.

The shirts were exactly where I'd left them. They seemed none the worse for wear. It was going to be a long walk home, and a sense of urgency drove me forward at a brisk pace. I needed to talk with Alice and tell her of the latest development. Even with the inconvenience of Maebelle V., I wished my friend were with me.

Kali Oka stretched before me, hot and red and as familiar as members of my own family. I'd make it home before lunch. Mama Betts would have the plums and she'd be waiting for me. Our annual plum picking was over, ruined by the Redeemer boys and an act of cruelty. Thoughts of Mr. Tom kept coming at me, and I dodged as many as I could. Was it partly my fault that he was dead? If Greg had killed him, maybe it was. The thoughts I was thinking made me walk faster, even though the sun was broiling my neck and shoulders. Mama Betts had a point about her hats.

As I left Cry Baby Creek behind, something else made my steps faster. I was getting closer and closer to the McInnis place. What harm would it do to stop and look in the barn at Cammie? Maybe just to check and see if she had some water. It wouldn't slow me down too much. I'd still get home with the shirts.

Even though it was hot enough to fry eggs, I jogged. That would give me a little more time to spend with Cammie. By the time I rounded the bend before the McInnis place, I was soaking with sweat. Even my eyes were stinging. The cool shade of the chinaberries was an oasis. The old sign creaked on rusty chains, and I flipped the latch on the gate. Two yellow blurs sped around the corner of the barn, but there was no sign of Nadine's dogs. Not even a bark. Inside the barn there was a soft whinny. Cammie was calling me.

At the barn door I stopped. Nadine's truck and trailer were still gone. My fingers clutched the handle of the door, and yet I paused again. The barn terrified me, even knowing Cammie was inside. Why were the doors closed? Had Nadine closed them? Or had someone else?

Cammie's soft call made my decision. I slid the doors open wide enough to enter. The sound of soft scurrying was all over the barn. Cats, rats and . . . nothing but the horses shifting in their stalls. Nothing more. There was a light switch by the door, but it didn't work.

After a few seconds my eyes adjusted to the darkness. The horses were all hanging over their stalls watching me. I wondered if I should let them go outside in the sunshine like Mama Betts had said. Nadine must have left very early or she would have put them out.

Cammie's call of recognition drew me on into the barn. I rubbed her velvet muzzle and whispered her name. The barn was dim, especially in the stalls. My fingers found her halter on the hook beside her stall, and I slipped it over her head. Surely I could groom her the way Nadine had taught me. Cammie eagerly followed me out and I hooked her to the ties in the center of the barn the way Nadine had showed me. When I finally turned to look at her, I stopped dead. She was covered in a heavy canvas blanket with fur lining. I ran my hand under the edge of it and felt her sweating body. It was at least ninety-five degrees outside, and though the barn was shady, it was still hot inside. Even in the dead of night Cammie wouldn't need such a blanket. Without further thought I found the hooks that crisscrossed under her belly and the front buckles. Dragging the blanket off her I realized it was soaked with sweat. I draped it over an empty stall door to dry out. Poor Cammie actually trembled in relief.

Curiosity prompted me to look at the other horses. It didn't seem possible, but they were blanketed too. What had Nadine been thinking? Even though I was a little afraid of the other horses, I went in to the stalls and took their blankets off. Only one, the tall bay male horse that Nadine said was the most expensive one, tried to bite me. He was restless and ill-tempered, flattening his ears and showing his teeth. I was tempted to leave his blanket on him, but I was afraid he might get sick. It was a chance to prove to Nadine that I could be trusted, that I could take care of her horses even when I was afraid.

The horse's name was Caesar. When I entered his stall he shifted to a corner and swung his tail at me. I'd read plenty about horses, but reading and doing seemed to be two very different things. The books all said to use a riding crop or bat on the horse's hindquarters if he swung them toward the rider. I doubted beneath the thicknesses of his blanket if Caesar could feel such a disciplinary move even if I had nerve enough to make it. Instead I pushed him in the side, and he obligingly shifted over against the wall. Even though he danced as I worked the buckles, he made no efforts to swing on top of me, and I'd learned the art of the horse blanket and had him stripped down in a short time. Clutching the blanket, I stumbled out of his stall, heart pounding with success and fear. One of the blanket straps had dropped to the ground, and I stepped on it. Somehow my foot tangled and with the heavy, sweat-soaked blanket in my arms, I stumbled forward. The momentum was about to throw me into the aisle and directly under Cammie's feet. A firm grip on my arm pulled me upright.

'Hey, thanks.' My face was buried in the smelly blanket. When I looked up, I froze. The Redeemer boy was standing right beside me, his hand still on my arm. Up close, he was older than I thought. His shirt was off and he was sweating too. He was thin, but it was a wiry thinness. He was stronger than I'd thought. 'What are you doing here?'

'I could ask you the same thing.' He grinned in a gesture that held no friendliness, only success. 'Did you have permission to take those blankets off?'

'I work here.'

His face was pale white, and in the poor lighting his eyes were shiny black wells, pulling me in.

'So do I.'

'That's a lie!'

'Ask Nadine. She needed some heavy work done. I was up in the loft when you came creeping in here. I thought I'd wait around and see what you were up to.'

The blanket was heavy and stank unbearably. I turned away from him to put it on another stall door to dry.

When I was finished, I faced him. 'If you work here, why didn't you take the blankets off the horses? They were about to sweat to death.'

To further my advantage I went into Cammie's empty stall. Her water bucket was bone dry. 'And they don't have any water. Horses can die without water. Especially if they're standing around sweating like . . . ' He was grinning at me.

'Nadine put those blankets on those horses, and she didn't tell me to water. She told me to clean the old hay out of the loft and to kill the rats up there.'

For the first time I saw the heavy stick he was holding in his other hand. It had fragments of blood and skin on it.

'Jesus Christ,' I whispered, falling back from him. He was clubbing the rats to death.

'What? You think anyone would let me use a gun?'

I had to get out of the barn. I had to get away from him. He was worse than anything I'd ever imagined about Sidney Miller's ghost.

'You're scared of me, aren't you . . . Miss Rebekah Rich?' He tapped the club against his leg and stepped toward me.

'Come one step closer and I'll spit in your face.' I thought of Picket. Never in my life had I gone anywhere without her. Until today. 'Who told you my name?' I couldn't let him know I was afraid.

'Cute little girl who lives down the road. She was all too willing to tell me all about you.'

Jamey Louise Welford, that little twit.

'She even helped me take your bicycle apart. She thought it was a big, magnificent joke on you. You know, I don't think she likes you very much. You or your best friend, Alice Waltman.'

'She's too stupid to live, Mr. Greg Redeemer Boy.' I threw my tiny crumb of knowledge at him. Jamey

Louise had told him everything. Even about Alice. 'Jamey Louise doesn't know half what she thinks she does.' My hand brushed across Cammie's chest. It was still damp but drying, and the hair was clumped and matted. I had to show him I wasn't afraid. I walked down the entire length of the barn to the tack room and got the grooming kit. His eyes followed me, but I refused to turn around. When I came back, kit in hand, I stared at him the whole way. He stepped to the side into one of those little rectangles of light from the windows. The sweat on his chest and the gore on the stick were highlighted.

It was foolhardy to stay in the barn with him, but there was nothing else I could do. Cammie had to be returned to her stall, and the horses had to have water. I picked up the curry comb and began to work over Cammie's body the way Nadine had shown me. He didn't say a word for the ten minutes it took to work around her. Then I took the hard brush and smoothed out the hair I'd roughed up.

'She seems to like that,' he said.

He'd moved to one side and was leaning against an empty stall.

'Nadine says it stimulates the blood supply to their coat, the same as brushing a person's hair.' As awful as it was to talk to him, the silent watching was killing me. I wanted to pound him with my knowledge, with my bond with Nadine. There wasn't a place for him there, and he had to know it. I hated the way he lounged against the stall, but he was alert. He didn't miss a move.

'I like your pigtails, Bekkah.'

The only sound was the snap of the cross ties as I released Cammie and returned her to her stall. I removed the halter and hung it back on its hook, then latched the door.

'Is there a hose?'

'I haven't looked for one. I found two Coca-Colas under the chinaberry tree. I've been drinking them.'

Damn him! He'd found our Cokes. Behind him I caught a glimpse of coiled green, the hose. 'It's there.' I pointed. He turned to look, and the trapezoid of light fell across his back. Long, deep cuts had scabbed over. There were at least a dozen, and they crossed and crisscrossed each other. He'd been beaten severely.

The sharp intake of my breath made him whirl back to face me. 'Did you get your eyes full?' He was angry, coldly angry. 'Don't stare at me.' He stepped forward.

'Who beat you?' I knew suddenly. It was because of the shirt. He'd lost his shirt and he'd been beaten with some hellacious switch or whip. 'Were the other boys beaten?'

'Only Jim. But his father doesn't enjoy it so much as mine.'

'The shirts are out by the chinaberry tree. My grandmother was going to wash and iron them and take them back. Maybe that isn't such a good idea.'

'Maybe it isn't.' He backed into the shadows. 'I'd better get home. Nadine didn't say how long I was to work, and I got some things to tend to before dark.'

The fort. I knew but I didn't say. 'The shirts are—'

'Don't worry, Rebekah Rich, I'll get the shirts. I always get what's mine.'

'Greg, stay away from my house and my dog. I mean it.'

'You gonna stay away from us, Rebekah Rich? Aren't you the one who started all this anyway?' He walked down the barn and picked up another white shirt that was hanging from a nail. He put it on, fastening the buttons as he walked back toward me in those fleeting but intense patches of light. His hands worked down the shirt, moving from button to button like animated images in a cartoon. When he was beside me again, he stopped. 'I'll see you later. Since we both work for Nadine.'

He walked out the crack I'd left in the door, and then suddenly slammed it completely shut behind him. The angle of light from the door disappeared. I was alone in the dark old barn.

Chapter Eleven

The scene I'd anticipated with Mama Betts over the shirts never happened. When I got home, Effie was crying in her room. The noises she made were soft, like a fall rain, but they also had the sound of winter in them, as if they'd never stop. It was not the tears of anger or frustration that came with trouble with her books. Those tears were hot and stormy. Electric tears that burst into angry exclamations and arguments on the telephone. These were the worst tears, the ones that meant Effie was badly injured and grieving. She and Daddy had been fighting again, and this time over the telephone.

'There's a bag with some sandwiches. Take them over to Alice's and have a picnic,' Mama Betts said as soon as I entered the kitchen. She was making a pot of coffee, and her hands trembled.

'Is Daddy coming home now?' I needed him, and I knew that he wasn't.

'Rebekah Brighton Rich, take those sandwiches and get out of this kitchen.'

Though her back was turned to me, I knew she was crying. Mama Betts hardly ever cried. She said she'd expended all her tears raising her children and she had none left except for extreme emergencies.

'Is Daddy sick?' A long-suppressed fear rose up and turned my gut to liquid. Three years before there had been whispering, telephone calls, trips to the doctor, and finally the hospital where Daddy was forced to stay for weeks while they made test after test. He'd been very sick, and no one would tell me or Arly what was wrong.

There was a morning, with the sun streaming in the blinds of the hospital room in Hattiesburg, when he'd lain in bed, eyes closed, his breathing hard and slow. Effie had gone for some coffee, and I was watching him sleep. I hadn't been allowed to see him for two weeks, and I wouldn't leave. If I could stay with him, I could make him better. There was a drip in his arm, and his hand was cool on the sheet. I woke him. I knew that if I didn't wake him up and take him home, he might never come home again.

He said he was just tired and needed to rest, for me not to worry. He went back to sleep, and Effie came back into the room and took me home. In a few weeks he did come home, and the rest of that fall he stayed home and wrote, like Effie. He wasn't completely well, but he was getting better. In the winter he went back to work and nothing more was said about his sickness. But the mantel in their bedroom was filled with tiny pill bottles that we were told never to touch. He took medicine in the morning and when he came home from work, and he took it to work with him so he could take it at lunch.

Mama Betts put her hand on my shoulder and pulled me into a hug. 'Your daddy's fine, Bekkah. He's just fine.'

'Is he coming home?' He had to be. Something was terribly wrong and I knew it. 'When is he coming home?' I spoke into the fabric of her dress. She smelled of sugar cookies and lemon.

'Not for a while.'

My heart twisted so painfully I thought I might cry out. He wasn't coming home any time soon. Something was wrong. They'd been arguing, Daddy and Effie, and it had gotten bad.

'How would you like to go up and visit your father?'

'To Missouri?' That question put a gentle brake on my fears. I wanted to see him more than anything.

'It isn't that far. You could take a bus. Or maybe even fly there.' She was thinking out loud, weighing the possibilities of travel.

'Could I?' And in that same instant: 'Effie won't let me. She won't even let me go to the beach.'

'This time she might not have as much say as she'd like.'

Mama Betts was finished crying. She had a plan, a goal. She patted my back. 'Take those sandwiches and go play with Alice for a few hours. Let me talk with Effie. I'm beginning to see where a little trip for you might be good for the whole family.'

'And Arly?' He'd burn with jealousy if I got to go see Daddy. Especially if I got to fly.

'I'm not so sure about Arly. It might be better if you and The Judge had some time together alone. You're very much like him, Bekkah. Perhaps the two of you can work out . . . the details.' She smiled and lifted a weight off my heart.

Perhaps it wasn't as bad as I thought. Daddy and Effie fought. They had since I could remember. There were arguments at the supper table about events so far removed from Kali Oka that Arly and I never even noticed who said what. Many times they agreed in what they called principle, but they had different ideas about how to go about changing things. Some of this talk was about Negroes. Some about poverty. Some about Europe or Mexico or other faraway places that were only names on a map. These arguments were part of the rhythm of Kali Oka Road. They were part of the smell of cornbread baking in the oven and the pop and sizzle of chicken frying. 'Pass the mashed potatoes' would be spoken in the middle of a long speech on the

brutality of immigration laws. It was the fights that
went on behind the bedroom door that were the bad
ones.

Sometimes at night, no matter how much I didn't want
to hear, there would be words that crept over the transom
and into my room, dancing and pointing at me. One
word they threw back and forth at each other was
opportunity. Another was control. Dependency. Agreement. Promises. And my name. Bekkah. They argued
about me. And Mama Betts.

Arly, stuffed full of supper and dreams of the girls he
was going to kiss, would sleep like a log in his room. Or
at least he never admitted that he heard any of the fights.
Maybe he didn't because I never heard his name batted
back and forth like a shuttlecock.

'Now take these sandwiches, and you and Alice have
some fun. Just keep an eye on that baby. I wonder why
Mrs. Waltman allows the two of you to go off with that
infant.'

Mama Betts was pressing me out the door. The sack
she'd handed me was filled with sandwiches and cookies
and wedges of cheese and small bags of potato chips.

'She doesn't even think about it. Alice says that since
she's got another cake in the oven, she doesn't have time
to worry about the one that's already baked.'

'Rebekah!' Mama Betts' arms went automatically to her
hips, the stance of shock and disapproval.

'Well, Alice said it, not me.'

'And don't think that I've forgotten about those shirts,
young lady. We'll attend to them later.'

'I ran into Greg, and he wanted them right then, so I
gave them all to him. I told him we were going to wash
and iron them and bring them back,' I hurried on,
because I knew she'd be angry that I'd gone against her
plans, 'but he wanted them right away. He said he
wouldn't go home without them.'

Behind her glasses, Mama Betts blinked twice. 'Well, maybe it's for the best. The incident is over. You and Alice have the bikes back, and the boys have their shirts. And if you're up in Missouri, I won't have to worry about what the two of you are getting into with the church people.'

'Since they were their shirts, I didn't know what else to do.'

'Where did you run into that boy?'

'I didn't go on the church property, if that's what you're asking.' The bitter evidence of the lashes across the boy's back almost made me flinch. I saw him again, chest glistening with sweat and then the sight of his back. I wanted to tell Mama Betts, but I couldn't. It wasn't right that I'd seen the boy without his shirt in the barn. There had been something wrong about it, something I couldn't even begin to put my finger on. I just knew that I couldn't talk about it.

'Rebekah, I'm an old woman. I grew up in the days before cars and televisions.'

She was staring at me, and I had no idea where she was going. I shifted my weight from foot to foot. Mama Betts was up to something, circling all around me with words to set the trap firm.

'From the time when I was a little girl, there's a smell I remember. When I hugged you up close, that old familiar smell came back to me.'

The horse blankets soaked in sweat!

'I'm not telling you your business, but if it were me, I'd get some fresh shorts and a blouse, and I'd take a bar of soap and go for a dunk down at the spring on the way to Alice's house.'

'Thanks, Mama Betts.' I started back to my room.

'What were you doing in the McInnis barn?'

'I took the blankets off the horses. They were sweating and Na – Mrs. Andrews was gone.'

'Blankets on horses in June?'

I shrugged. It didn't make sense to me either. 'She'd gone to get the rest of her horses, I think. Maybe she forgot to take them off.'

'I know a little about horses. Blankets in June is asking for pneumonia. Why, the nights are hot already. Too hot for a sheet, even for an old body like mine with no hair and thin blood. That woman must not have good sense, or she must be a Yankee.' I nodded. The horses had been slick with sweat, but surely Nadine knew what she was doing. After all, she had nine horses and knew how to ride them.

'Maybe it's because they're special show horses.'

'Harrumph,' Mama Betts snorted. 'Even fancy horses sweat and get sick when they're not cared for properly. I've been around stock, fancy and plain. And another thing, Rebekah, I don't approve of you sneaking around behind your mother's back with those horses. Don't go back there until you have her permission.'

'I didn't ride them. I only took the blankets off.'

'No matter. Effie has to say yes before you go back.' She paused. 'Do I have your word?'

'Mama Betts . . . '

'No dancing around, Bekkah. I want your word.'

It wasn't fair. 'She's offered to let me work there for lessons. Daddy said that I—'

'Your father isn't here. Effie is, and she's the one who worries about you.'

'She doesn't worry about Arly the same way!' Arly was always going and doing just as he pleased. He played sports and ran around town and got to go camping with his friends and on trips to Jackson and Mobile . . . and to the beach.

'Your word, Rebekah.'

Mama Betts' patience was wearing thin. 'Okay.' I whispered it because I knew it was a lie. Probably the first intentional lie I'd ever told. But I was going to see Cammie and the other horses. No matter what the cost. No matter how big the lie.

'When you get back from Missouri, we'll talk about those horses. It might be a good idea for you to take lessons. Maybe it wouldn't worry Effie so much if she thought you'd learn how to ride safely.'

'It isn't just the horses and you know it. It's everything. Mama won't let me do anything! She's always afraid I'll get hurt, but the truth is she doesn't want me to do anything at all except stay right here!' The tears were burning my eyes and throat.

'Your mother loves you too much, child.'

'Yeah, well, that sounds good, but it feels awful.' I took the sack and hurried out the door before I started to cry. It was a matter of pride. I didn't cry in front of anyone, except maybe Alice and Picket.

By the time I got to the Waltmans', I'd calmed down. Alice and I enjoyed the lunch. We tempted fate and gave Maebelle V. a taste of pimento cheese. She seemed to like it as much as we did, but Alice was cautious. She only let the baby have a taste. Picket liked it, too, as well as the chicken salad and the peanut butter cookies that Mama Betts had baked the night before. While we lazed in the shade near the spring, I brought Alice up to date with the Redeemer boys and Nadine, and my forthcoming trip to Missouri. I tried not to sound too excited, 'cause Alice had never been farther away than Jexville.

During the summers when Daddy wasn't working away, we had always taken vacations to places like the Grand Canyon and the Rocky Mountains or Rock City in Tennessee. Daddy liked to travel, and he thought it was good for me and Arly to see the country. He said we could better appreciate the diversity of the people and their beliefs if we saw it firsthand.

Whenever we went away, it always took about a week

for me and Alice to get back to the place where we'd left off. She acted as if she expected me to change while we were on vacation. I tried not to brag too much about what we'd seen and done. Once Effie asked Mrs. Waltman if Alice could go with us to Florida for a vacation at the beach. Mrs. Waltman said Alice had too many chores at home to be gallivanting all over the country, so Alice didn't get to go. A lot of the fun of that vacation was gone because the whole time I missed Alice so much.

When I told her about Missouri, she got kind of quiet. I told her something was wrong with Mama and Daddy, that they'd been fighting on the telephone.

'How come your Daddy stays gone so much?' Alice was changing Maebelle V.

'His work. Lots of people's daddies are gone to work all the time.'

'Not like yours. They go and come back every two weeks if they work offshore. Yours is gone for months and months.'

'It's because he works at universities and for magazines. Sometimes he has to go for long jobs.' She was hitting at something that had only begun to bother me.

'Then why don't you and your mama and Arly go with him? Your mama could write her books anywhere, couldn't she?'

That was the crux of it, and part of the fragmented arguments I heard through my bedroom transom. Daddy wanted us with him, but Effie wouldn't go. It didn't make sense to me, except that I wasn't all that keen on leaving Kali Oka Road to go someplace where I wouldn't have Alice or any of the other people I knew. Still, we could have been with Daddy, and that would have made a difference.

'Mama doesn't want to go, I guess. She has deadlines and things, and she says she can't concentrate anywhere but in her study. She says she doesn't have to worry about me and Arly when we're on Kali Oka. She says the road is the safest place in the world.'

Alice put in the last pin and righted Maebelle V. up on her shoulder. 'I see,' she said, and I knew that she did. Effie didn't want to go.

'What about those Redeemer boys while you're gone to Missouri?'

I'd thought about this on the way over to Alice's house. 'I'd stay clear of them.' I also had a favor to ask. 'Would you keep an eye on Picket? I mean go and get her and take her for a walk back here in the woods, away from the road?'

'You think that Greg boy might hurt her, don't you?'

I nodded. 'Someone killed Mr. Tom with a rock. Mama Betts thinks it was the Redeemer boys because of the shirts. And that stupid Jamey Louise told Greg all about me and you.'

'I'd like to fill her mouth with chicken shit.' Alice was holding Maebelle V. in a standing position. The baby was making struggling movements, as if she really wanted to try to walk. She was getting stronger and stronger by the day.

'Fill it full and then tape it shut,' I added. Jamey Louise had been a big-mouth from the first day in school. 'Want to go pay her a visit?' Mama Betts had told me to stay away from the house for at least three hours. I had time to kill, and I didn't want to go in Alice's. That house was in constant motion with a pitch of noise that would drive anyone crazy. There weren't enough chairs to sit on, and the house was in steady decline. The floors tilted in all directions, and there were places where they'd rotted through because of leaky pipes or something. It didn't seem to bother Mrs. Waltman. Alice had said one time that pregnancy produced some type of chemical or hormone, as she

101

called it, that made women oblivious to what happened around them. She said her mother was a drug addict for that hormone, and that once she had a cake in the oven, she forgot there were holes in the floor.

'Naw, I don't want to see Jamey Louise. If we get in a fight with her, she'll end up telling on us and I'll get in trouble.'

Alice was right. Jamey Louise was a big-mouth and a tattle tale. She didn't have a single redeeming quality.

'If your daddy asked you to stay with him, would you?'

Alice's question was a lance in my heart. 'That would mean he wasn't ever coming home. That he and Mama wouldn't be married anymore.'

'People get divorced.'

Other people, but not my parents. Effie was hottempered, everyone knew that and gave her plenty of room. But Daddy wouldn't just stop coming home altogether. It wasn't possible.

'Hey!' Alice punched my arm lightly. 'I didn't mean it. It was a stupid question. I was just wondering if you had the chance, would you live somewhere different?'

'I could never leave Kali Oka Road. I expect I'll die here, just like Mama Betts is going to do.' There were plenty of places to visit and see, but I wouldn't want to live anywhere but where I was.

'I'd move to Paris.'

Alice was looking at Maebelle, but she wasn't seeing her. She was seeing a picture of a slender blond woman in a chic red dress and hat walking a poodle on a leash and going down a street with little cafés with umbrellas. The men at the cafés were watching the woman walk her dog. I knew this because the picture was hanging in our house, and Alice looked at it all the time. The Eiffel Tower was in the background. Alice loved that picture and she wanted to be the woman in it.

'What would you do in Paris?' I'd never thought to ask

her. Where was the woman going with the dog?

'I'd be a model for painters or for fashion photographers.'

Would they have a model with freckles? I knew better than to ask the question, but I thought about it. Alice had beautiful blue eyes and pretty hair. She was skinny enough too. But I'd never seen a model with freckles.

'You'd make a lot of money. Maybe when you got tired of standing still in front of the cameras or the artist, you'd become a movie star.'

'Maybe.' She closed her eyes and smiled.

More than anything, in that second I wanted to give her Paris. Now. While she really wanted it, before she got older and quit wanting it.

'And what about you, Bekkah? What would you do?'

'If I could do anything right this minute, I'd go down to the McInnis barn and learn to ride. Then I'd take Cammie, and we'd go around the world jumping and winning every show.'

'You think a horse would enjoy traveling around the world?'

'Cammie would. If she was with me.'

Alice smiled, and I knew she thought my dream was as silly as I thought hers was. We both lay back in the mossy ferns that grew beside the spring. I'd taken a quick bath before we picnicked, and my hair was spread out around me drying in the dapples of sun.

'Bekkah?'

'Yeah?'

'That Redeemer boy, Greg. Did his daddy beat him because we took his shirt?'

'I don't know. He didn't say.'

'What do you think?'

'Maybe.' I was almost positive, but there wasn't any point in making Alice feel bad when it had really been my doing.

'Maybe we should have been nicer to those boys.'

'Fat chance. They hit Picket.' I refused to take on any guilt. The Redeemer boys had started it. I'd simply taken up for myself with the only opportunity I had.

Alice was silent for a moment. 'I didn't think they'd get a beating.'

'The other boys seemed fine. It was only Greg, I think.'

'Bekkah, you've never had anybody hurt you like that.' Her voice softened until it disappeared. 'I mean it would be scary. Nobody around to help . . .'

'Alice, they started it. They hit Picket and stole our bicycles, if you remember. They left mine in a heap at my house. I could have been beaten, you know, if Effie had a mind for it.'

'Your folks wouldn't do that. They never hit you or Arly.'

'Well, we don't do anything to deserve gettin' beat. At least we don't get caught.'

'And you think that Redeemer boy deserved to be beaten that way because he lost his shirt?'

There wasn't an answer to that one. The sun was soft and reassuring as it filtered down on my face and hair. I kept my eyes closed, fighting hard against the image of Greg's back cut open by whatever he'd been hit with. Alice was right. At no time in my life had I ever had to worry that someone would hurt me. She made me feel small and mean.

'Tomorrow's Sunday.' My mind was on the Redeemers. Maybe Greg's plight deserved a little more sympathy. 'Remember what they were saying about that minister and the chubby boy's sister.'

'Yeah, so what?' Alice's voice was guarded.

'Maybe we should check out what's going on at that church. Maybe the police should be called.'

'Maybe you should call the police and let them take care of it.'

'They won't come unless they have some evidence.'

'Just make it up, Bekkah. You have a real knack for that.'

'Be serious, Alice. Maybe we could find out something that would get the police down there to check it all out.'

'You just want to go nosing around, and you're trying to talk me into it.'

I leaned up on an elbow. Alice still had her eyes closed and was lying back on the ground. Her mouth was pressed shut real firm. It was going to take a lot of persuasion to make her see things my way, but I had the entire afternoon to work on her.

Chapter Twelve

For the first time since Maebelle V. erupted into the world, Alice and I were going to be without her. Alice had been reluctant to lie to her mother, but heavy persuasion had finally won out. We told Mrs. Waltman and Effie that we were going to church at the new King James Baptist Tabernacle in Buzzard's Roost with a school friend, Sandra Rogers. I'd been brought up in the Sweet Water Methodist Church, but no one in the family except Mama Betts took much pleasure in spending Sunday in church, and Effie and The Judge figured it wasn't fair to make me and Arly do something they wouldn't do. At any rate, it was a pleasant surprise for Mama Betts when I said I was going to church – even if it was a Baptist one.

Effie, still upset over my impending trip to Missouri, didn't ask many questions. It was as if I was already halfway to Missouri and she couldn't see or hear me real clearly. She was mad, and it was her way of punishing me because I wanted to go to Missouri. In her mind it was a betrayal of some kind. I didn't fully understand it, but I knew what she was doing and why. She was hurt and angry, so she acted as if I wasn't a real person anymore. If my mind hadn't been so bent on getting down to the Redeemers, I would have been hurt and worried myself. As it was, I had on my starched petticoats and my best robin's egg blue dress. Of my entire wardrobe I hated this dress the most. Effie loved it, and the sight of me duded up in it didn't even move her cold heart an inch.

I left the house torn by excitement and sorrow. I was also a little worried Alice might not show up. Agatha Waltman was irritated that Alice had finally figured out an excuse to escape Maebelle V. that she couldn't deny – church. According to Agatha, we could drag that poor little baby up and down Kali Oka Road in the blazing sun in a metal bicycle basket. We could haul her around the creek like a rubber ducky. We could take her to Chalk Gully to dig out clay for the potters who claimed Kali Oka clay was the best in the world for throwing pots. We could lug her around everywhere we went. Except church. Agatha Waltman thought that babies could squall and scream anywhere in the world but church. I wasn't about to let Alice tell her mother that there were nurseries for babies at church now. Not on your life! We'd finally found a way to get rid of that baby, and we were going to take advantage of it.

Cloaked in the guise of holy children and our best Sunday dresses, we made an escape from our homes and met in the woods where we'd hidden the bicycles the day before. I'd even had the foresight to shut Picket on the screened porch, though it nearly broke my heart to hear her whine as I walked away.

When we were deep in the woods, we stripped off our dresses to reveal swimsuits. I'd had all of that frothy blue dress I could take, and Alice's patent leather shoes pinched her feet. Stepping out of those shoes put the first grin on her face all morning. When we had shed all the trappings of going to church, we pedaled furiously toward Cry Baby Creek.

My plan was simple. We'd enter the creek at a point far above the slide where we liked to play. We'd make our way down the creek until we could hear the carrying-on in the church. Once the Redeemers got in full throttle, we'd sneak up to the windows and peek in. I'd left Alice with the impression we were staying in the creek bed and listening, but if the Redeemers were going to be handling any snakes or washing any feet, I wanted to see it. I'd also heard some things about pew jumping and speaking in tongues. I couldn't have stood it if we'd gone at night, but in the daylight I didn't think I'd be too afraid. As awful as it sounded to 'speak in tongues,' I just had to see it for myself if it really happened. This might be my only chance before I went to Missouri. If there was something unnatural going on at the end of Kali Oka Road, I wanted to be able to give Daddy all the details. The Judge would ask for every little nitpicking thing. I'd have to know all the specifics.

We left the bicycles far enough up Kali Oka that we felt certain the church boys would never find them. Alice was quiet as we walked to the creek, and I knew her heart wasn't in the adventure. I couldn't understand why she didn't want to know about the church folks as much as I did. She had her answer ready when I asked.

'Maybe it's none of our business. Maybe they just want to be left alone down here at the end of the road.'

'Maybe they're doing something illegal.' Alice was working on making me feel guilty. I'd been taught that everyone deserved a chance to lead their own lives as long as it didn't hurt anyone else. The Judge was a big believer in the First Amendment, and he talked about it a lot at supper. I didn't plan on telling him about this little adventure unless I found some serious trouble.

'I wore my watch, Bekkah. I'll stay twenty minutes, and that's all. Then I'm going home. Mama's already going to be fried because I left. If I'm not back exactly when she thinks church is over, she'll make me pay.'

'Twenty minutes. That's fine.' We eased down into the water, and for a moment my mission was forgotten in the icy caress of Cry Baby Creek. The sand slipped between my toes as I led the way down the creek bed.

'What if we hear something awful?' Alice touched my shoulder.

'Naw. It's a church. It's not like they practice voodoo.' I hadn't told her about the speaking in tongues. 'They'll probably be singing hymns, just like at our church. We'll probably listen for a minute and get bored and be ready to go home.'

In that moment the clear contralto of a young girl cut over the creek. I felt that voice along the base of my spine. It was so sad, so filled with longing. I didn't recognize any of the words, but I didn't have to. The message came from the melody and the young girl's heart.

'Sweet Jesus, she can sing!' Alice pinched my arm. 'You think that's the little fat boy's sister they were talkin' about?'

I hushed her so we could listen. Until the end of the song we stood frozen, then we hurried on down the creek. Even Alice seemed more enthusiastic.

We were within easy earshot of the church now, and since it was summer all the windows were open wide. When I climbed up the bank, I could see the flick of fans moving back and forth as women held them. I didn't know about the Redeemers, but at our church those fans came from the funeral homes. They were put out in the churches as a form of courtesy and mostly advertisement. There were two competing funeral homes in Jexville, not counting the colored one, and Effie often said they didn't let a body get good and cold before they were vying for it.

'Get back down here!' Alice tugged on the leg of my swimsuit. She let the elastic go with a loud and irritating snap.

'I'm only listening.' I eased down from the bank. There

was a hubbub in the church, but it sounded like the collection plate was going around. I wondered how the Redeemers made any money to put in the collection plate. As far I knew, none of them except for Greg had left the church grounds since they'd arrived. Mama Betts had been talking about it the night before, saying the men at least would have to have some kind of work.

Alice was getting ready to cut and run when there was a loud round of applause from the church. Drums and guitars and banjos and tambourines surged together in a lively tune. It sounded like a regular hoe-down.

'Listen!' I urged, but Alice was already listening to the voice of authority. The preacherman was talking over an irregular patter of 'Amen,' 'He's blessed,' and 'He's sure 'nuff touched by the Lord.'

'And now we'd like to welcome the little man with a big voice.' The preacherman sounded like he thought he was Ed Sullivan.

'God saw fit to skimp a little on arms, legs and a trunk, but he gave Brother Rueben the biggest voice in the kingdom.'

Hallelujahs broke out and ran around the church. I edged up the bank so I could hear better, and at least get a glimpse of the church.

The front door was closed. If I ran straight from the creek to the side of the building, I'd be in the open no more than ten seconds. If I ran hard. Alice's hand grabbed my calf.

'What are you thinking, Rebekah Rich?'

'I want to see this little man.' Somewhere in the church a woman cried out, 'I feel the Lord a "workin" in this room.' I had to go look. I couldn't stand it a minute longer.

Alice's fingers tightened painfully.

'You promised! You said we'd stay in the creek and listen. You said we weren't on church property this way and that we couldn't get in any trouble.'

'If we get caught here, no matter whose property we're on, we're in trouble. This ain't the Tabernacle Baptist Church, Alice.' While those words sank in, I shook loose of her grip.

'You deserve to get in trouble.'

I turned back and saw the tears of anger in her eyes. 'Alice, I've got to see what they're doing. It's eatin' me up. I'm goin' off to Missouri tomorrow, and I want to be able to tell Daddy what's going on here. What if—'

'Go on.' Alice turned away. 'Just go on and get it over with. You won't be happy till you get up to that window.'

I climbed back to the lip of the creek bed and stopped. Alice was back in the creek. She was seining pebbles from the sandy bottom. Her blond hair was pulled back in a ponytail, but her bangs hid her face from me.

'Come with me, Alice. See for yourself. That way there will be two of us.'

'You want to see this, Bekkah. I don't. You think you're going to see something gruesome or fantastic. You're just going to see a bunch of folks dressed up and sweatin' on church pews. Just 'cause you imagine that it's going to be special, you think you can make it that way.'

Alice didn't look up the whole time she talked. Behind me, the frenzy in the church was building. How could I make Alice understand that I had to see it? 'If I knew what I'd see, Alice, I wouldn't have to look.'

'Sometimes lookin' is stupid. Sometimes it pays not to look.'

'Daddy says to name your devils.'

'Some devils don't come till you call them by name.'

Alice could be as stubborn as a rock. 'If there's anything going on, I'll signal for you to come. Watch for me.'

Alice looked up and her eyes weren't angry. 'If they

catch you, Bekkah, I'm going home, and I'm going to pretend I wasn't here.'

Before the consequences of that remark sank in, I made a dash for the church. The building was white clapboard, and in the few days since I'd gone down there someone had slapped a fresh coat of paint on it. I pressed up hard against the clean white paint and let my heart stop hammering. I hadn't realized I was afraid until I stopped running. The window was just about chin level, so it wasn't going to be a problem to see in, and I could hear a man singing in a deep voice. As I crept toward the window, the backs of people's heads came into view. They were nodding and clapping and singing a phrase here and there with the man. A few shoulders were rocking side to side in 'the sway.' Every now and then two arms would shoot straight up in the air followed by a 'Praise the Lord.' There was a powerful emotion sweeping back and forth across the room. Several women had sweated through their Sunday dresses, and up two pews I could see plump Georgie wiping his brow. He was squeezed between two grown-ups who appeared to be his parents.

The Redeemers were caught in the rapture of the moment, but I hadn't seen a sign of any snakes. It wasn't until I was right at the window that I caught a glimpse of the singer. That's when the full impact of the preacherman's words came back to me. The 'little man' was a dwarf. He was dressed in a perfect little suit with a perfect pompadour of blondish hair, and he was holding a hymnal in one hand, giving it a good shake now and then and singing to beat the band. It was incredible that such a deep, full voice could come from someone no taller than my chest. I was struck with the impossibility, and if there had been a fat old blowfly around, it could have gone straight in my mouth.

I'd been taught that physical deformity wasn't any-thing to gawk at, so I tried to look away, but I couldn't. Brother Rueben was making a show of his size. He was strutting up and down the little stage that served as a platform for the preacher, shaking his hymnal and his slightly long hair. His hands seemed to be normal size, which only made the rest of him look more ungainly. I knew I shouldn't look, but I couldn't help myself. Every-thing he did was exaggerated, grand, to draw attention to himself. I thought of the carnival that came to Jexville every fall and the shows that were for adults only. Arly had sneaked into one by paying three times the amount, and he'd said there was a fat woman with hair on her face and chest and one who, for an extra five dollars, could smoke a cigarette with her private parts. Right behind her had been a row of jars, and one had con-tained a real pickled baby. There had also been a dwarf man and woman, and Arly wouldn't tell me what they did to make money.

All of those stories Arly told me churned through my mind like a runaway train. Try as I might, I couldn't stop the images, and I couldn't stop staring. The little singer was ablaze, and the Redeemers were feeding the flame. Someone in the congregation handed him a towel, and he mopped the sweat from his brow without missing a note. The action caused a woman in the front row to stand up and throw up her hands, shouting gibberish I couldn't understand. Her fingers stretched wide as she threw her head back and let loose a hoarse, guttural cry. In a second she was falling to the floor. The two people sitting beside her pulled her up on a pew and fanned her face with one of the cardboard fans. Shouts of 'Amen' crisscrossed the church, coming from men, women, and children. It was as if someone had turned up the heat in the church. The little man sang, and the congregation began to boil.

114

I didn't know the song. It had nothing in common with the more solemn hymns I remembered from the Methodist service. I listened to the words and was shocked by the gory depiction of Jesus suffering on the cross. Since the words made me feel bad, I put more effort into watching the congregation. They were rocking and swaying with a vengeance. Up in the left-hand corner there was a woman playing the heart out of a piano and a young boy with a guitar. Standing slightly behind him was a girl in a white dress with a tambourine. She was about my age, and she looked like she was going to cry. She followed every strut and gesture of the little singing man, Brother Rueben. Whenever he came her way, she looked out at the congregation.

If this was Mag, plump Georgie's sister, it was obvious that Georgie ate his share and hers too. This girl was skinny as a stick, like Alice. Or else she worried the weight off. She was turning and twisting and watching Brother Rueben, and she never missed a lick with that tambourine. From behind the piano another boy stepped forward with a saxophone and joined in the chorus. The entire church was alive. Pews rocked with folks jumpin' up and shouting and falling back against them. Several women started talking that gibberish and fell out in a faint.

When it seemed that the congregation would surely jump up and bust out the doors, the little singer called a halt to it and turned the show back over to the preacherman. The boys had called him Brother Marcus, and I was eager to see what he looked like. The man who walked up to the edge of the stage was tall and lean, younger than I'd expected. His chestnut hair was pomaded back and it glistened in waves under the hanging light bulbs. The crease in his pants was razor sharp, and his jacket hugged him tight and had big padded shoulders. The attention he gave his clothes was very different from the

115

way the congregation was dressed.

For the first time I noticed the plain walls of the church and the lack of any softness. The floor was unpolished wood and the pews were unrelieved by any cushions. There weren't any plants or flowers on the little table up front, and even in their Sunday best the women were as drab as female mockingbirds. The men weren't any better in their dark suits and white shirt collars. I could only see their backs, but I knew the shirts were buttoned tight with subdued ties.

In the very front of the church there was a hand-carved crucifix. At first I didn't pay much attention to it because it was all dark wood. Something in the shape caught my eye. On closer examination, I saw that the figure of Jesus was expertly cut. I could almost feel his anguish and the blood coming from his hands and feet. The more I looked, the more I realized the crucifix was one of the most gruesome things I'd ever seen. The nails in Christ's palms were so real, the thorns digging into his head. But there was something beautiful in the man's body. It was the way the wood curved and twisted, shaping the torment of the man. Brother Rueben and the crucifix were certainly the most awe-inspiring things in the church.

The preacherman called for testimonials. This was something new in my experience. I knew what court testimony was, when people swore under oath at a trial. I'd never heard of it in a church, though. To my surprise, the girl with the tambourine took a few steps forward and then stopped. She stared into the audience. It looked as if her whole body quivered, poised on the edge of some tremendous decision.

Before she could do anything, a man in the middle of the church stood up. Beside him a slender woman grabbed his arm and cried out.

'Please, Lucas, please don't!' She clung to his arm, and

as he struggled to move in the aisle, he pulled her along with him. She was holding his arm and crawling on her knees after him, begging.

'Well, Brother Simms, do you have a confession?' the preacherman asked. He acted as if the woman did not exist.

Brother Simms was a tall man, his body filled out with muscle. His gray suit was neatly pressed, and except for the woman clinging and begging, he looked to be a regular man. I could only see the back of his head, though, so I was unprepared when he turned to angrily look at the woman who clung to him. His face was twisted with hatred.

'This woman suffers from the sin of vanity, Brother Marcus.' He spat the words in the woman's face. In the hush that followed, he shook free of her and she fell to the floor. 'My wife is vain. She's consumed with her looks and her mirror.'

Amens skittered around the room, but all the hand waving and speaking in tongues had slowed up.

'She thinks she's better than us,' a woman near the front stood up and said. 'She won't answer to her church name. Her husband names her right. She's bitten by the demon of vanity.'

'Save her, Jesus,' another woman cried. 'Save her soul from damnation.'

The woman struggled to her feet in a half crouch. She ignored the congregation and reached up for her husband's arm. 'Lucas, please don't do this. It wasn't a crime, what I did. Please!'

From his pants pocket the man she called Lucas pulled out a flattened piece of cardboard. He took it to the minister, covering the church in six long strides.

'Hair color,' he said as he turned back to face the congregation. 'It's the box the hair color came in. My wife bought herself some Lady Clairol. She didn't want to look old. She wants to stay young. She thinks going gray is unattractive. She thinks she knows better than the Lord what color her hair should be.'

Still crouching, the woman buried her head in her arms and cried. She was wearing a pale pink dress, something that would have looked more in place on a young girl.

The man walked back to her and roughly pulled the pins from her hair. It came down in a tumble, just below her shoulders. It was a dark brown color, a pretty shade.

'She looks like a whore!' her husband cried. With a savage jerk he pulled her to her feet. Grabbing hold of both shoulders, he turned her around in a circle. 'See her hair. Ain't it beautiful? She looks like a young woman, doesn't she?'

My fingers bit into the windowsill. The poor woman was crying, the tears running off her face, but she didn't make a sound. At first she tried to hide, and then she got a little backbone and finally held her head up.

'Brother Simms, bring your wife to the front of the church. I think the sin of vanity is one that we can all learn from.'

The woman didn't make any effort to resist as her husband half pushed her ahead of him to the small stage. The preacherman walked up to her and lifted a strand of her hair and held it aloft. 'A painted woman will never enter the gates of God's kingdom,' he said in a loud whisper. 'We must save your soul, Sister Florence.' Brother Marcus motioned to the piano player, who jumped up from her seat and rushed out a back door.

'My name is Susana,' she said in a soft voice. 'Susana Hebert. There is no such person as Sister Florence. I've done nothing wrong. You may think what you want to, but I know I've done nothing wrong.'

'Hair dye is a tool of Satan,' Brother Marcus thundered at her.

'My husband has a fondness for the young girls,' she whispered, but it carried clearly throughout the still church. 'I was only trying to look young for him.'

Lucas Simms slapped her hard across the face. 'Watch your mouth, wife,' he said in an ugly tone. 'You're getting old, and you can't face up to it.'

The piano player returned and approached the stage with caution. Brother Marcus waved her forward, and in the flicker of an eye he took something she handed him.

'We're going to redeem your soul, Sister Florence.' Before the woman had a chance to react, he grabbed a handful of her hair. He opened the scissors the piano player had given him. With a quick motion he cut the hair a half inch from the woman's scalp.

The dark brown tresses fell over her pink dress and to the floor. In the hushed silence she didn't move or cry out.

'Save her, Brother Marcus,' someone called from the audience. 'Save her.'

The dwarf motioned to the piano player, and the rousing chords of a new hymn echoed in the church. The dwarf sang while the preacher sheared. The congregation was louder and more excited than ever before. It wasn't any snake handling or foot washing, but it was the most dramatic thing I'd ever seen in a church.

'Now take her home and teach her that her value comes from being a good and obedient wife,' Brother Marcus directed Lucas Simms as he snipped the last of her hair. He gave the woman a little shove down toward the congregation as he picked up his Bible and began pacing the stage.

When there was a pause in the singing, he signaled for quiet. 'Now who else has a sin to confess? Any gamblers?' He looked about the room. 'No gamblers here, praise the Lord.'

The congregation responded with applause.

'How about dope fiends? Any dope friends in this house of the Lord?' He paused dramatically for a moment. 'Well, I didn't think we had any dope fiends among us. Satan doesn't work that angle here on Kali Oka Road.'

It was shocking to hear him say my road as if he belonged there. It reminded me that I was an eavesdropper, and that if I was caught, the penalty would be severe.

'What kind of sinners do we have?' the preacher asked. He rocked back and forth on his heels and thrust his Bible forward so that the light from the windows caught the gilt edges of the pages.

The young girl with the tambourine stepped toward him. She said something no one else could hear. The preacher stepped back from her, his face going colorless. He tried to reach out and touch her shoulder, but she jerked back from him. She faced the congregation.

'I got to say this.' She looked wildly about as if searching for someone she couldn't find. 'I don't have a choice. I got to say this to save my soul from hellfire.'

From the middle of the congregation plump Georgie stood up. He stared at his sister, and some signal passed between them. 'Don't, Mag, don't do it. Nobody will believe you.'

He didn't speak loudly, but I heard him. I felt what he said, the fear and pain. Then he cried out loudly, 'Don't do it. Mag! Don't! It won't do any good.'

The girl wavered and looked as if she might cut and run, but she didn't. Behind her the preacher stepped forward. Whatever indecision had held him in its grip, he'd come to terms with it. He reached out to put his hands on the girl's shoulders, but she sidestepped him. She spoke again. 'There's someone in this church possessed by evil.'

Her words flamed around the room, quieting all talk

120

and movement. In the back row two men stood up and started forward. The girl saw them, and she pointed at them.

'They're coming up here to quiet me so there won't be trouble, but I got to say my say. Rev. Marcus has called for testimonials to the Lord. He's called on sinners to unload the burden of their grief at the altar of God. I saw the forgiveness this congregation showed Mrs. Simms.' She smiled bitterly. 'Well, I'm here anyway, and I don't expect no kindness. I only want to confess.' She took a breath. 'I've been fornicating.'

'Listen to this poor wayward lamb of God.' The minster shook his Bible behind her. 'Poor little child, she doesn't know what she's saying.'

Georgie lurched forward and was jerked back into his seat. He struggled to stand again, and beside him a tall, heavy-set blond man held the boy in place. The man stood up slowly and stared straight at the girl. 'Magdeline Scott, get down from there and come over here to your family!'

The words were dark thunder. They rocked the girl until she dropped to her knees. Behind her the preacher stood transfixed, his eyes staring into the back of her head with a look that would have drilled through to her brain if he'd had the power.

'I've sinned against the Lord and my family.' The girl buried her face in her hands and started to weep. 'I have to confess to save my soul and the soul of—'

The preacher's hand on her hair was nothing short of a jerk. It was almost as if he lifted her to her feet by the hair.

'This poor lamb has gone hysterical on us. The power of Brother Rueben's singing has churned up her spirit and confused her mind. We all know Magdeline.' He turned her so that her face was pressed into the lapel of his jacket. He held her with his right hand hard against

121

him. 'Magdeline Scott is no whore of Babylon.'

'My name is Maggie!' the girl cried out. 'Maggie! Not Magdeline, just Maggie!'

The first whispers began to stir in the congregation. It was as if everyone had held their breath and finally let the air out.

The preacher still had a grip on her hair. 'Magdeline is a lamb of God, a sweet child with a voice touched by the Father's hand. She's confused. In her desire to seek his grace, she's imagined herself as a sinner. Isn't that so, Magdeline?'

His fingers were buried deep in her hair. The girl turned slowly to face the congregation. Her expression was contorted. 'Yes, Brother Marcus, whatever you say.'

'Poor Magdeline wants some attention from us church folks. She craves the limelight, and not even her beautiful singing is enough.'

'She needs some attention at home.' A heavy woman from the back of the room spoke up. 'If she's not whoring, she shouldn't claim to be. If she's lying, she deserves to be punished for that.'

'Well, it appears that Magdeline has something to atone for, the sin of lying. And lying to achieve prominence and self-importance. I think that's a sin we can work on together, Magdeline.' The preacher lifted his hand from her hair and stroked her head gently. 'Now run along and think about this. I'll see you in my office after lunch, and we'll talk about this need you have to draw attention to yourself.'

Magdeline Scott fled the little stage. She ran behind the piano and disappeared into the darkened corridors of the church. There was only the sound of her hard-soled shoes on the linoleum and the slamming of a door.

I felt as if a giant fist had unclenched on my ribs. Magdeline Scott. And Georgie. I peeped at him through the window. His face was turned down, and something that looked suspiciously like a tear was hanging off the end of his nose. The two adults beside him, the heavy-set man who had stood up and called Magdeline, and the thinner woman had lost all semblance of life. They were stone. They both looked straight ahead, without expression. Somehow the rest of the congregation had shrunk away from these three. They were isolated and alone in the center of a crowded pew.

From the middle of the church a young man stepped forward. He smiled to the left and right as he went up to the stage.

'Timothy!' The preacher's greeting was warm.

'That poor little girl standing up here makin' up stories to tell just broke my heart. Especially when I was so full of sin myself, before the Lord touched my soul. Poor little thing can only imagine what sin is. But I'm here to tell you I know sin. I've walked hand in hand with Satan, and I've felt the worldly pleasures he tempts all men with.'

He stepped up on the stage and turned to face the congregation. 'I came to the Blood of the Redeemer's Church last month, as most of you know. From Texas. Some of you know about my dealings out there, and some don't. But it was Brother Marcus, when he was out there on his May ministry, that took a moment out of his life and changed mine completely.'

Timothy was glib. No one in the congregation seemed to notice when Brother Marcus backed into the shadows and disappeared. Everyone was enthralled with Timothy's story of sex and drugs in Texas.

I saw Marcus leave. He went out the same door Magdeline had left through. Georgie and his parents sat like rocks in the pew. I felt a sudden need for action, to hurry around the church and see about the girl. There didn't seem to be anyone who would make sure she was okay except Georgie, and he wasn't about to move off his pew.

I'd come to the church to see something, and what I'd seen was more than I'd expected. I knew what fornicating meant. Effie had talked about it. Married people did it, but they didn't call it fornicating. They called it making love or making babies. Teenagers and boys called it fucking. The only time I'd tried to call it anything I'd gotten in big trouble. I couldn't imagine standing up in church and laying claim to fucking. Not a girl no older than me. I wasn't certain what it all meant.

Timothy was still talking, and Brother Rueben had joined him on the stage and was leafing through the hymnal for his next selection. I was suddenly aware that someone was looking at me. Greg was seated in a pew all the way across the church, but he was staring directly at me. The tiniest smile touched his lips when he saw that I saw him. I knew what he was thinking – I couldn't leave them alone. I was inviting him to do something. I drew back and pressed hard against the white wall, even knowing that it was too late. Greg had seen me.

Chapter Thirteen

Pressed hard against the wood, I waited for Greg to sound the alert. My life flashed before my eyes, or at least parts of it that I didn't want to remember. The past summer, against Mama Betts' iron will, I'd convinced The Judge to take me to see *Invasion of the Body Snatchers* at the Jexville Theatre. It had taken the movie five years to make its way to Jexville, and I'd been waiting for half my life to see it. Mama Betts said the movie had permanently scarred me because I was always talking about pod people and invasions.

Sweating against the white wood of that church, I knew real terror. The Redeemers were worse than aliens. If Greg screamed that I was at the window watching, they'd pour out of that church with the single-mindedness of ants. They'd catch me and drag me inside and pretty soon I'd become one of them. I was terrified. Paralyzed. I had the sudden urge to pee.

I thought I was going to wet myself right there on the spot when a rock thudded about an inch from my head. Alice was half crouched at the creek, waving me toward her. She was ready to cut loose with another rock if I didn't respond. My fear broke and I took off running.

I was about twenty yards from the creek when I heard the scream. It was followed by a plea. 'Stop! Please don't!' and then the sound of crying.

'What the hell's going on?' Alice asked.

I almost tumbled headfirst into the creek. 'Come on.' I urged her. 'Let's get out of here before they all come out.'

'Bekkah! What happened?'

The sound of screams rose again on the air. 'Jesus Christ! I hope he doesn't hurt her bad.'

'Bekkah Rich, who's screaming and crying like that? I'm not going another inch until you tell me!'

'Fine time for bravery, Alice. It's Magdeline Scott. She confessed to fornicating, and the preacher is probably beating her.'

'Holy shit.'

We ran to the bicycles and pedaled toward home. We'd gone about half a mile when Alice suddenly braked. 'We can't just run off and let them beat her.'

I stopped, too, sweat running down the leg that I braced in the hot sand. 'What can we do?'

'You were so all-fired ready to get evidence to call the police. Let's stop at Connie's and call them.'

For the first time since we'd left the church, I stopped to think. The Judge had taught me to 'weigh the evidence.' He was always talking about news reporters and how they had to be observant and how they had to weigh the evidence of what they saw and what they were told.

'I didn't see anything real.' I traced the sweat that ran down my dirty leg. I was ashamed of myself. I'd cut and run when I should have stood my ground and watched. So what that Greg had seen me? The Redeemers weren't really aliens. They wouldn't have hurt me. They might have gotten mad and called Effie, but they wouldn't have hurt me. But they had hurt the girl called Magdeline Scott.

'If they beat her, that'll be evidence enough.' Alice wiped the sweat from beneath her blond bangs.

'She said she'd been fornicating.'

'With who?'

'She didn't say. She just got up in front of the church and confessed to fornicating. Just like she said she'd been eating Fig Newtons.' I was still amazed.

'Libby Welford fornicates.'

I cut a sharp glance at Alice. 'How do you know?'

'I've got an older brother, remember?'

'Are you saying that Jimbo and Libby fucked each other?'

'No!' Alice frowned. 'He didn't fuck her. Harley Adams, the mayor's son, did. But Harley told everyone he'd done it with her. He told Jimbo she was real good too. That she knew how to make him feel like a man.'

It made more sense that Libby would do it with Harley than Jimbo. Libby didn't hang around with boys who weren't worth her time. Jimbo didn't have any money and he didn't have a car. Harley had both. It was something to think about.

'What are you going to do?'

Alice's question hung in the air. What was I going to do? What could I do? If Magdeline Scott was going to be hurt, she already was. I hadn't seen anything, not really. 'Let's get back to the woods. We'd better rinse off and put our dresses back on.'

'We're going to pretend we went to church, aren't we? We're not going to do anything about the Redeemers.'

It was almost an accusation, but not quite. Maybe it was just that I felt so damn bad about it all. 'When I get back from Missouri. I'll think of something by then. I'll talk to Daddy.'

'When are you coming back?'

'Sunday. I'll be gone a week.'

'I'll miss you. Of course, that girl could be dead by then.'

I gripped my handlebars. 'I wish you could come with me, Alice. I'm not so sure I'm going to like flying.' That was a lie. I knew I'd love it, but I didn't want to rub it in that I was going.

'Maebelle V. and I'll be back here, waiting.' She sighed and we both started pedaling home. 'We'll be right here on Kali Oka Road, where nothing ever happens when you aren't around.'

Missouri was a different country. Hills rumbled to the horizon, and the university was like a town for grown-ups only. I felt like a munchkin, and The Judge was too quiet. On Tuesday we ate breakfast and then I went with him to his office at the liberal arts building. That morning I stayed in the classroom and listened to him lecture. It wasn't a bit like school. The students were grown and they sat quietly and asked questions like they were really interested. It reminded me some of the dinner table talk we had at our house, except no one in the room would disagree with Daddy the way Effie did. It didn't seem to be much point to talk if all they did was spew back what he said. There was one girl with long blond hair who practically hung on every word he said. After the class, she waited to talk with him. She kept looking at me like she knew who I was.

'Bekkah, this is Cathi Cummings. She's a graduate student from Hushpuckena, Mississippi.'

The way Daddy said it, I knew the word tickled him. He liked the odd Indian names for some of the little towns around the state. When I got up close to the girl, she wasn't really a girl, she was a woman. Her long blond hair made her look younger from a distance. I knew graduate students were older than regular college students. She dressed older. Instead of the denims that most of the other students wore, she had on a real short skirt and a matching jacket. She looked like she had a job instead of going to school.

'Cathi graduated from Ole Miss with the highest

honors in her journalism class. She worked up in Washington, D.C., at the *Post* for a few years before she decided to get her master's.'

Daddy was looking at Cathi as he talked. It was hard to figure out what he was thinking, but it was easy to see that what he said pleased her. Something about it didn't sit right with me. It felt almost as if she was trying to crowd into my life.

'What kind of place is Hushpuckena?' I didn't want to talk to her, but I had to say something or Daddy would be disappointed with me.

'Not much bigger than Jexville,' Cathi answered. She had a drawl, but it wasn't like mine. It was somehow familiar, but I couldn't place it. Maybe it was just after all of those flat mid-western voices I was glad to hear something I knew.

'I've told Cathi a little about Jexville and the Ollie Stanford trial.'

Ollie Stanford was the Negro they were holding in the Jexville jail for murder. I hadn't come all the way to Missouri to talk about the same thing I heard at home all the time. 'Are you married?' I asked Cathi Cummings.

'In fact I am,' she answered with a short laugh. 'My husband is not very happy that I'm in school, though.'

She surprised me. There was a sharpness in her voice that let me know she wasn't kidding around. She was angry with her husband for being angry at her.

'Is he a student too?'

'Not on your life.' She looked at Daddy. 'My husband is an editor at the *Post* in Washington. His career is safely tucked in his pants.'

Daddy laughed and I didn't understand exactly what she meant, but it sounded funny so I laughed too.

'When your father talks about you, Bekkah, it reminds me of my own childhood. I had an older brother who deviled me to pieces, and I found plenty of adventures to get into. Your father says you like horses. Maybe we can go to a stables this week and ride.'

Cathi had really nice eyes. They were green and they crinkled whenever she smiled. Most of The Judges's students didn't even bother to say hi to me. She was working hard to win my approval, but I couldn't think why.

'I don't know,' I answered softly. I had a sudden feeling that Effie would feel doubly betrayed by my riding, especially with this woman.

Cathi touched my shoulder. 'Well, think about it. I promised your father that I would entertain you while he worked. He's promised to give me an A.' She looked at The Judge and laughed, and he laughed along with her. They were friends, and she did sound like a lot of fun. The temptation to ride was hard to resist.

'There's a new woman on Kali Oka Road and she has horses. She wants to give me riding lessons and teach me to jump.' I cut a look at The Judge.

'Bekkah's mother is afraid of horses. She thinks Rebekah will get killed. This is a ploy by my daughter to put me in the middle.'

'Horses are safe, if she learns to ride properly,' Cathi said. 'Lessons would be excellent for her, if this woman really knows what she's doing. Why don't I take her for a ride or two and see how she does?'

'Nadine has nine horses,' I added quickly. I was liking Cathi despite myself. 'And five dogs and fourteen cats.'

'Sounds like a humane shelter to me,' Daddy said. 'How about some lunch? Cathi, will you join us?'

I wasn't certain that I wanted Cathi along, but it was too late to protest. 'Is there a McDonald's here?'

The golden arches were the biggest craze. Jexville didn't have one, and probably never would. Mobile had just built one, and in the first few months they'd sold over a million hamburgers. Or at least that's what the sign by the golden arches said. We didn't get a chance to go to Mobile often. Effie hated the traffic and Mama Betts said she hadn't lost anything there. But Arly and I loved it. There were department stores and drive-in burger places and movies and motorcycle shops.

'There's a local joint that specializes in malts and burgers,' Cathi said. 'It isn't McDonald's—'

'Thank God,' Daddy said under his breath.

'—but I think you'll approve. They have the best chocolate malts in the world.'

'And fries?'

'The crispiest.' Cathi laughed. 'Your father is an old man. He doesn't remember how important a good burger can be in a girl's life.'

We ate the burgers and talked. Cathi told me my father was a genius, and that the university wanted to hire him full time. Daddy didn't say much. He was watching me. I didn't say anything. I couldn't help but wonder how Effie would react to this. Cathi and I arranged to go riding the next afternoon when Daddy had a faculty meeting. Cathi had a lot of free time on her hands because she wasn't working while going to school. Even though her husband didn't want her there, he'd decided to pay for it.

Those days in Missouri passed in a blur. Cathi and I rode three times. She was a very good rider, and she taught me a lot. We were becoming friends, but we both held back a little. I wasn't certain why, and I didn't give it a tremendous amount of thought. We rode the horses and didn't push each other.

Cathi had dinner with us several nights, and we played card games and laughed. She tried very hard to make my stay fun and exciting, but it wound up making me feel like I was a guest. And no matter how much Daddy laughed and joked with us, he was sad. I would catch him staring at me, and it was like he'd said goodbye and was going on a long trip. As soon as he realized I saw him, he smiled and tried to act normal. That only served to frighten me more.

At the university he seemed happiest. The students there all smiled when they spoke to him. A couple told me he was a wonderful man. They said he was hard and sometimes difficult, but fair. It seemed important for them to tell me.

I liked the students. They weren't like any of the high school kids in Chickasaw County. These boys and girls acted like friends. They weren't sneaking off to hug and kiss and giggle with each other. When they did that stuff Cathi assured me that they hid it pretty well. She said the students were idealistic, but that underneath all of the idealism were the bodies of young people, and they enjoyed hugging and kissing and giggling. She said that one day I'd enjoy it too. When she said it I thought of Jamey Louise and gave a silent prayer that I'd never act so dumb for a boy.

The last night before I was ready to go, I told Daddy that I had to talk with him. The Redeemers had been heavy on my mind, especially the girl who had fornicated. I'd as much as promised Alice I'd have a solution when I came back, and I hadn't thought up a thing on my own. Daddy had to be consulted.

After a supper without Cathi, I went to his study and waited for him. The faculty housing was small but cozy. He had a two-bedroom house with a study and a fireplace. He'd already told me he could get a larger house for very reasonable rent if we should all end up in Missouri. There was a picture of Effie and me and Arly on his desk, and I looked at it while I waited for him. It was Halloween and we were all dressed up. Effie was a really scary-looking witch, and I was a goblin and Arly was Satan. Daddy had said we were the perfect family when he took the photo. He didn't dress up.

I was putting the picture back when he walked in the room. 'Whatever you're thinking, don't worry about the family. You know I love all of you more than anything. I'll do whatever it takes to keep us all together.'

That scared me more than anything he could have said. I knew he and Effie fought, but I hadn't realized they'd actually talked about not being together.

'After this week with you, Bekkah, I couldn't leave my children. Or my wife.' He smiled. 'Your grandmother was very wise to send you.'

'Arly wanted to come too.'

'Arly might have made me decide the other way.'

'Daddy!' I ran into his arms and he held me tight.

'I love you, baby girl. More than you'll ever know.'

I could have stayed in his arms, safe, forever. It didn't matter that Mama Betts had used me as a tool of blackmail. What mattered was that whatever had gone wrong between Daddy and Mama had been set right.

'When will you come home?'

'At the end of summer term. In August.'

'Summer will be over then.'

'Maybe we'll take a trip in the fall. I've been thinking about the Grand Canyon. How would you like to see that?'

'I'd rather take riding lessons this summer.'

To my surprise, he laughed. 'Your grandmother says that you get that stubbornness from me. I think it comes from your mother's side of the family. Or maybe it's just the female nature.'

'Daddy, Nadine is a wonderful rider. I want to learn, and she'll teach me for the work I can do. If I don't do it this summer, school will start and I won't have time.'

'I'll talk with your mother, Rebekah. That's all I can promise.'

That was enough, for right now. The Redeemers still had to be dealt with. 'Daddy, you know how you told me that when someone is doing something wrong, it's up to me to address that wrong?'

'What have you done, Bekkah?'

'I went down to that church and spied. I went down there last Sunday, and I heard a girl about my age confess to fornicating, and I think they beat her.'

'Did you see them strike her?'

'I got scared and ran away, but I heard her scream. And beg. Alice heard her too.'

'You went to all the trouble to spy and then didn't see anything?' Daddy could make me feel shame like no one else. Effie and Mama Betts were better at remorse. With Daddy it was total shame.

'You don't know how those people are. They beat Greg, the Redeemer boy.'

'In church? You know this for a fact?'

'No.' I shook my head. 'His parents, I think. It was over his shirt.'

'The shirt that you took?'

I looked up at him. He'd been talking to Mama Betts. 'That shirt.'

'What is it you think should be done?'

'Daddy, those boys said it was the preacher who was touching that girl. They said—' I stopped.

A terrible look crossed his face. 'You've been talking about this with those boys?'

'Good grief, no! I eavesdropped on them.' He must have thought I'd lost my mind talking about fornicating and touching with boys.

'Bekkah, I'll talk to your mother about the horses, but I'm telling you, stay away from that church and those people. When I get home, I'll make it a point to see about them if they haven't already moved on. They have a right to their beliefs and their privacy, as long as they aren't hurting anyone.'

'What about that girl? She might be getting hurt.'

'I'll have someone look into it. I promise you. Just stay away.'

The Judge was mad, but I couldn't tell if it was at me or at the church people. All I knew was that the subject was closed. He had walked away from me and was staring out the window into the early night.

'The stars aren't as bright in Missouri,' he said.

'There's more lights around than on Kali Oka Road. You said that lights take away from the splendor of the night sky.'

'You were only about six when I told you that. You have a very good memory.' He turned back to me and he was smiling.

'I'm precocious, remember?'

He laughed out loud. 'You're arrogant.'

'Mama says I'm just like you.'

'Your mother is vicious. If she'd put that in print it would be grounds for libel.'

'She says that you'd never win in that case because truth would be her defense.' We were both laughing. Daddy came to me and hugged me hard.

'I don't want you to go home, Bekkah. Why don't you stay the rest of the summer with me?'

'Oh, Daddy. I have to get back to Kali Oka Road.'

His laugh was sad again. 'What is it about that road that the women in my life can't seem to leave it behind?'

Chapter Fourteen

Mrs. Welford and Jamey Louise met me at the Mobile airport. It was an unpleasant shock to my system to see Jamey Louise waving at me like I was some kin to her. I tried to ignore her, but she squealed and ran out across the tarmac to meet me when I started down the steps of the plane. She reeked of Evening in Paris cologne, and she had on silvery pink lipstick that made her look like she wasn't getting enough blood to her face. On Jamey Louise's insistence, I had to ride in the backseat with her so she could whisper to me all of the things I'd missed in my week away from Kali Oka Road.

Jamey Louise was delighted to report that Alice had been slapped by her mother Thursday afternoon in the Waltman front yard as the Welfords were driving by. Arly had also been in trouble, something I found not unusual. Jamey Louise didn't have all the details, but she'd heard he kissed a girl in one of the booths at the Jexville Drugstore. Old Mr. Hartz, the pharmacist, had seen him do it and called Effie. Such public displays weren't in good taste.

Someone had given Addy a new kitten, and she was keeping it in her house for fear someone would hurt it. Instead of a gray tabby, it was a marmalade. Carrie's plums had gone ripe, and everyone on the road had picked at least a bucket for jelly. The Spooners got a new car, a '62 Chevy, red with white interior.

I listened, waiting for a chance to ask where Effie and Mama Betts had gone. I'd looked forward to seeing them at the airport. Truth told, I was sort of homesick to see them. I'd never been away from Effie before. She'd been angry with me when I left. Even though it upset her, she had taken me to the airport and watched with her lips tight as I went through the door that led outside to the plane. In so many words she said I'd betrayed her by going off to Missouri. She made it seem as if I'd chosen travel and seeing Daddy over staying on Kali Oka with her. But even mad, she would have been at the airport to get me. A knot of worry was growing in my stomach. Something bad had happened.

'Why didn't Mama and Mama Betts come for me?' I finally got a chance to ask Emily Welford.

She tried to avoid the question, but Jamey Louise was sitting on ready. 'It's that nigger they've got in jail. Someone tried to break in the jail and hang him last night. Your mama's down there standing vigil.'

By the way she said it, I could tell that no one in the Welford family appreciated what Effie was doing. Jamey Louise was just spouting off what she'd heard at her dinner table.

'Why'd they try to hang him? He hasn't had a trial yet.'

'No need for a trial,' Jamey Louise said, her chin lifting a bit. 'He's guilty. He didn't deny it. He said he killed Mr. Fallon.'

'But Mr. Fallon killed his brother.'

'Yeah, but he was just a nigger. That don't count.'

Maybe it was the way she said it. I knew suddenly that Effie was at the jail to protect a Negro man she didn't even know. Folks around Jexville were thinking like Jamey Louise. That Ollie Stanford had killed a white man without good cause. In their minds there was no reason for a nigger to fight back. They could fight among

138

themselves, but they couldn't fight a white man. It was the law, unwritten but very real.

'Take me to the jail.'

'Your granny said to bring you straight on home,' Emily Welford said, already sounding nervous.

'I want to go to my mother.' I was scared, and it made my voice sharp.

'Don't go getting on your high horse with my mama,' Jamey Louise said. 'You can't order us around like you do Alice and the others.'

'Mrs. Welford, I've got a terrible feeling that Effie may need my help. Is she down there alone?'

'I don't know,' Emily admitted. 'Not many folks feel the same way she does. Not white ones, at least. And the Negroes are too scared to go down there.' She cast a nervous glance in the rearview mirror and our eyes met. Emily Welford would never admit in public that she agreed with Effie, not about a black man. But she felt something, and a reflection of it was in her eyes. She frightened me.

'What is it?'

'I heard there was a crowd gathering at the jail. Joe Wickham called her and said the men folks had been drinking and were getting rowdy. Your mama called some lawyers in Hattiesburg, but they couldn't get to Jexville in time. That's why she went down there. She was afraid something violent would happen. She went to stop it.'

'By herself?'

Emily nodded.

Mama was alone. In all of my life, I'd never been afraid of the people living in and around Jexville. There was always talk about fights and brawls, but none of it touched Kali Oka Road. These were folks I'd grown up with, or at least heard about. Now I was afraid for Effie. She'd stepped over the line by going to the courthouse.

'Take me to be with her. If there's trouble, we'll both ride home with you.'

'Now, Bekkah, your granny said—'

'If Mama gets hurt, Emily, it's going to be your fault.'

Cold and flat, the words made Jamey Louise gasp. 'Well, I never heard such a thing in my life. It won't be anybody's fault but hers. No one made her go there. No one—'

'Jamey Louise, you'd better shut up.' I was rigid with fear. The Welfords' old Plymouth rattled toward Chickasaw County,

'We'll ride by the jail,' Emily said slowly. 'We can see if your mother's okay. Then we'll decide. If it looks dangerous, I'm not going to stop. Your mother is an adult. Besides, the sheriff is there with her. Nothing bad will happen.'

'It already has,' I whispered. I could feel it. There wasn't a name for it, not exactly. In a week's time, though, something very important had changed. 'Please hurry, Mrs. Welford.'

It was only another twenty minutes to town, but it seemed as if my eyeballs had gone completely dry. I couldn't blink. The white lines disappeared beneath the front of the car and the tires whirred. Pine trees whipped by, followed by red dirt roads cutting into the woods. More pines. A few fields. A house here and there. The outskirts of Jexville. There wasn't any air in the car. My fingers gripped the back of the front seat until the little plastic bubbles on the seat covers were permanently indented. There was the Soloman wrecker business that marked the east side of town, junked cars parked all around a nice house. Then the little house on the right beneath the hill, where one or another of Effie's school friends had been beaten by her husband with a dog chain. I never knew the whole story but I'd heard Mama Betts and Effie whispering about it.

140

The old stores of downtown crested the top of a hill. There had once been enormous oak trees that canopied the main street, but the power company had cut them all down. What was left was a flat, ugly, half-mile strip of shops that needed a lot of paint and a lot of money. I knew every business on the street. Arly or I could walk in any of them and charge anything we wanted by saying our parents' names. Most days I enjoyed shopping in Jexville, but I didn't see the display of summer shorts in the window of the Dale Shop. The dark recesses of the Jexville Drug held no secret promises of ice cream and comic books. I wanted my mama. I wanted Effie, to feel her hand on my shoulder or tugging my braid.

Emily turned left at the second red light and drove the two blocks to the county jail. Old and square and red brick, it was surrounded by a twelve-foot chain-link fence with rolled barbed wire along the top. I knew it was bad when I saw the men standing in the jail yard with rifles held across their chests.

On the east side of the jail a large crowd had gathered. They were milling and talking. Mostly men, there were a few women scattered in it, and a handful of children. There wasn't a sign of a Negro anywhere.

They didn't seem to be doing anything, just staring at the old jail. Two stories with crumbling masonry, the jail operated on a mutual agreement basis. Convicted felons agreed to do time in the jail so they wouldn't be sent to the state pen in Parchman. The jail wasn't exactly secure, and often the prisoners were allowed out to pick up litter or to walk down to the Coffee Cup to get their lunches handed out of the kitchen door to them. About five times a year one of them would tie his bed sheets together and escape from the second floor of the jail. Since the crimes committed were seldom worse than burglary or public drunkenness, nobody got terribly upset. Joe Wickham would generally wait for the prisoner to get his business done and return to jail voluntarily.

What struck me, though, was that if the jail couldn't keep prisoners in, it certainly couldn't keep that crowd of people out. From the distance of the courthouse yard, it didn't look too bad. But there was something about the crowd, like a pot just getting ready to boil over. When it happened, it would be sudden and dangerous.

Emily Welford slowed down when several of the men walked across the street in front of her car. They acted like they had more right to the road than she did, and she obliged them by almost stopping. It was my chance, and I opened the back door and made a dash for the court-house. I knew where Joe Wickham's office was, and I was hoping Effie was in there. I hadn't seen her anywhere else, and I knew she wasn't mingling with the crowd.

For all the hubbub outside, the courthouse was quiet. The heavy wooden door to the sheriff's office was hard to push, but I slipped in. I'd been in there several times with Daddy and Mama, and it was normally a place where the men leaned back in their chairs and talked on the phone or joked among themselves. There was only one sheriff and one deputy, but there were always a handful of men who volunteered to be constables. They liked the law enforcement work. Daddy said they were bullies by nature and deadbeats by fact. I didn't fully understand what he meant, I just knew he was careful around them. He didn't like any of the officers except Mr. Wickham, yet he was always harping how they needed more pay. There were lots of things about Daddy I didn't understand, but as I walked up to the high wooden counter, I would have given anything I owned to have him with me.

'Where's Effie Rich?' I asked. I was tall enough to see over the counter, so I saw the glance the men exchanged. There were two volunteers and the deputy sitting around a scarred old desk. They were all smoking and drinking coffee from thick white mugs.

Not a one of them answered me.

'Where's the sheriff?'

'He's busy.' The deputy smiled at his friends and then walked over toward me. He was holding his cigarette between two fingers stained yellow. 'He ain't got time for little girls.' His name tag said WAYLON SMITH.

'I'm Rebekah Rich, and I'm looking for my mother.' He frightened me. He was playing with me like a cat plays with a mouse, and I didn't know why.

'Tell me something, Rebekah Rich. Do you like niggers as much as your mama?'

One of the men at the desk laughed. The other one put his coffee cup down and slowly stood up. 'Maybe that ain't such a good idea,' he said to the deputy.

'I simply asked Miss Rich a question. She looks like an educated young girl. She can answer a simple question, can't you, Miss Rich?'

My lips were very dry and my tongue was sticking to my teeth. I knew they were being mean, but I didn't understand why. I had the sudden thought that the plane had brought me back to a place I didn't know. I'd come home to the wrong Jexville.

'Maybe Miss Rich only talks with niggers.' The deputy leaned on the counter. 'Is that the problem? Am I too white to answer?'

The man at the desk laughed again. With a grumble of disgust, the other man left the office. He banged the door hard behind him.

'I want to see my mother,' I said, trying not to let my voice shake but doing a bad job of it. I grabbed the edge of the counter and held until my knuckles turned white. 'Where is she?'

'She wanted to be with her nigger friend, so we put her in there with him.'

The deputy's little brown eyes were rimmed in red. As

he leaned over the counter, his breath smelled of winter-green. He'd been eating Life Savers. The roll was still in his shirt pocket.

Mr. Wickham had given me a tour of the jail the past year when The Judge had taken me to the courthouse while he bought a car tag. The only way to get to the jail was through the sheriff's office and out a back door that opened up in the jail yard. I'd have to run across the open space of yard to the jail building. That was a big metal door that required a special kind of key. I remembered Mr. Wickham showing me the key and how he hung it by the back door. With that mean deputy watching, I knew I couldn't get the key and get inside, but I could call out for Effie and make sure she was okay.

The deputy and his friend were chuckling at some-thing else he said. Part of the counter swung up and revealed a door. I knew how it worked because Mr. Wickham had shown me. While the deputy was half watching me, I lifted up on the countertop with all of my strength. The wood, though heavy, swung up easily on well-oiled hinges. When I had it about halfway up, I felt a sudden resistance followed by a yelp of pain. I gave it an extra heave and it broke free of whatever was holding it. I didn't realize I'd hit the deputy until I'd swung it wide open and was rushing through. When I looked back, I saw the deputy grabbing his nose. Blood gushed out from between his fingers. I ran as hard as I could. The door out of the office was unlocked, and I pushed through it and ran to the outside door. In a few seconds I was sprinting across the jail yard.

'Mama!'

My cry caught the attention of the milling crowd outside the fence.

'Hey! Hey, you!' Several men in the crowd challenged me. 'You, girl! Get out of there.'

'Effie! Mama! Mama!' I had to find her before the

men with the rifles came to stop me.

'Bekkah?'

The voice that answered me was incredulous. 'Rebekah?'

'I'm down here, Mama. I came to help you.'

There was the slightest pause. Behind me the crowd was pushing toward the fence. Fingers laced into the chain link and the crowd surged. For a moment it looked as if the fence would give.

'Rebekah Brighton Rich, what are you doing here in this jail?'

'I came to be with you, Mama. Mrs. Welford brought me.'

'Emily Welford hasn't got the sense of a runover dog.'

Mama's voice was coming from one of the barred windows, but I couldn't tell which one. The crowd outside the fence was growing louder. It buzzed, sort of like an insect. Occasionally someone's voice would rise above the hum and say something about nigger lovers. It was only men talking. None of the women said anything.

'Must be nigger-loving runs in the family,' someone yelled.

I turned to look at the crowd. Shock must have registered on my face because there was a sudden tiny silence. I couldn't believe I saw Mr. Sargeant, the butcher-shop owner with a rifle. He still had on his apron smeared with blood. And there was Theo Fontaine who ran the Western Auto where Arly and I got new bicycles for Christmas every four or five years. They were looking at me like I was something terrible. I turned back to the old red brick wall. 'Mama, why are you in jail?'

'According to Joe, for my own protection.'

Effie was pissed off in a big-time kind of way. I couldn't believe Sheriff Wickham had put her in jail, but he had. And when she got out, he was going to pay.

'Mama, let's go home.' There were four windows on

the bottom and four on top. I was having to talk loud for her to hear me, and I thought her voice was coming from the upper right-hand window, just above me. Sure enough, she stuck her hand out through the bars.

'Bekkah, get out of this yard and back inside the courthouse. Just wait in the sheriff's office for me. I can't leave here until some of the people from Hattiesburg get here.'

'I'm not leaving here without you.' I'd expected the men with rifles to run me out of the jail yard, but they were too intent on watching the crowd. The insect noise had increased. The air hummed all around me.

'Rebekah!'

Mama's hand pointed down at me.

I didn't see the glass until it struck the dirt at my feet. It was heavy and green, a vicious jag from a 7-Up bottle. Part of it had a dark stain on it. When I bent down to look at it, another spatter of red fell on my hand. I looked up and saw the blood on Effie's arm.

'That's for you, you nigger-loving bitch!'

The voice that came out of the crowd was young. It was taut with fury, a boy's voice breaking with emotion. I searched the crowd and no one would look back. The hum had stilled. There was only silence. When I looked back up at the window, Effie's arm was gone. There was a streak of blood on the bricks at the windowsill.

Chapter Fifteen

The twenty-seven stitches in Effie's arm brought Daddy home. The university paid for his flight. Mama Betts said they were courting him hard. She said that like an anxious groom they were willing to buy anything to win his favor. That wasn't true. Daddy had already told them he wasn't going to stay there and work for them. I tried to tell her that, but she wasn't inclined to listen. She was too upset over Effie, her own one-time baby. The shock of someone hurting Effie was almost too much for Mama Betts to take in. She was also upset that she'd been home on Kali Oka when it all happened. In Effie's hour of need, Mama Betts felt like she'd let her down. Of course that wasn't true. Had Mama Betts been there, nothing would have gone differently.

The ruckus at the jail died down shortly after Effie was carried out by ambulance. She lost a lot of blood real fast. No one in the crowd really wanted to hang around once they realized she'd been cut bad. A few people, including the deputy, grumbled that she'd gotten what she deserved. Mostly they just sort of drifted away, one or two at a time, until there wasn't anyone left standing outside the fence. When the ambulance got there, it drove right to the jail. They carried Effie out on a stretcher, and I rode in the ambulance with her to the hospital. There wasn't a sign of Emily and Jamey Louise. For that I was thankful.

147

Daddy's flight came in that night, and Arly and I rode with Effie to get him. Even though it was against the law, Effie let Arly drive. Her arm hurt, and she was sick to her stomach. The doctor had wanted to keep her at the hospital, but she was so mean he finally let her go.

Once Daddy got off the plane and slid behind the wheel, my whole world started feeling better. Arly was in the back seat with me, where he belonged, and Mama and Daddy were together.

'You did a brave thing,' Daddy said to Effie as we headed down the dark road to Jexville. The traffic was sparse, and there were long passages of time when there was only the glow of the dash to illuminate the car.

'I only intended to go there until the defense lawyers from Hattiesburg could arrive.'

'You made the effort, though, Effie. You stood up for what you believe.'

'And it shouldn't have been a big deal. Every man deserves a trial. Why is that so hard for those people to understand?'

''Cause he's a nigger,' Arly piped in. I could tell by his voice that he wasn't being smart-alecky. He was trying to explain it to Effie. I also knew he was in for it now.

'I didn't realize that was a word my son used,' Mama said softly.

'Well, that's what folks are saying.' Arly's voice was edgy. He knew he'd stepped in it. 'I don't normally say that word, but that's what folks are saying and that's why they don't think he deserves a trial.'

'And what does my son think?' Effie asked.

'Let it go tonight, Effie,' Daddy said softly. 'We're all tired. The children have been scared to death. No one's thinking right.'

'I've got twenty-seven stitches in my arm because someone disagreed with my views. And my child is in the backseat of our car aping the words and attitudes of the type of person who cut me.'

The more she talked, the higher her voice went. She'd held back in the hospital. It was all about to boil out and burn us.

'Arly didn't mean anything,' I said. 'It's what people are saying. Jamey Louise said the same thing to me today.'

'Jamey Louise is a moron. I expect better from my children.'

'We know better, Mama. Arly just slipped up.' I wasn't in the habit of defending him, but I wanted everything to be good. Daddy was home. I didn't want any fighting. What got started between Mama and Arly could carry over to Mama and Daddy. It had happened before. In the back of my head I remembered the past week in Missouri. Me and Daddy and Cathi hadn't argued for a minute. That scared me. I kicked Arly as hard as I could in the shin. His fingers dug into my arm, and it was all I could do not to cry out.

'Apologize, you idiot,' I whispered.

'For what?'

'For saying nigger in front of Effie.'

Arly's grip loosened. 'Mama, I didn't mean to say that word. It slipped out because I've heard it so much today.'

Mama's sob was so sudden and unexpected that nobody said anything. It sounded like it tore her throat.

'Mama, I'm really sorry.' Arly was worried. 'I won't say it again. Ever.'

Daddy's arm drew Mama across the seat until she was nestled against his side. He spoke softly to her in words I didn't quite hear, but it seemed to help. Arly and I sat back. The rest of the ride was in silence. By the time we got to Kali Oka, Effie was sound asleep and no one wanted to wake her.

Alice was waiting for me the next morning. I didn't tell

149

that I knew her mother had slapped her. It would only have made Alice feel worse. She had Maebelle V. strapped in the papoose-like carrier on her back. She'd ridden her bicycle the short distance through the woods and was parked, ready to ride, at the edge of our yard.

'Let's go to the Redeemers,' she said before I could even say hi. I looked at her like she was crazy.

'Why?'

'Old Doc McMillan had to go down there the Monday after you left. We saw his car. He's gone back every day. Somebody's bad sick.'

It was nearly me. I had the horrible idea that maybe they'd beaten Magdeline to near death. Looking at Alice, I could see she was feeling the same thing.

'It ain't her,' I said. 'There's a hundred people living down there, and most of the boys look wormy. It could be any one of them.'

'I want to make sure. If it's the girl, then we're to blame.'

'Stop it, Alice! We're not to blame. We didn't make her stand up and confess to fornicating. And we didn't make them hit her, if they did. They do what they want to do. We just happened to see it.'

The trouble with my argument was that I knew Alice was right. We were to blame. Or more rightly, I was to blame. Alice would have gone to the police and admitted eavesdropping and spying. I was the one who wouldn't do it.

'Let's ride down there and look.'

'I don't know.' I wanted to go down there, but I was worried about Effie. Her arm was swollen, and Daddy was putting compresses on it. He'd called a doctor in Mobile, and they were going over there for a consultation. 'Mama's pretty sick.'

Alice looked at the ground. 'I'm sorry she got cut. Why'd she have to go to that jail anyway?'

I shrugged. 'She said it was the right thing to do.'

'It might have been right, but she could have gotten killed. It's strange, but grown-ups do that kind of thing all the time. Then when we try to do it, we get in trouble.'

She was dead right. 'I'll get my bicycle. We'll just ride on down there and see what we can see. Maybe we'll see the girl playing and we can come home in peace.'

'That would be wonderful,' Alice said. Her smile was thin. 'I've been worried crazy. I could hardly wait for you to come home. I almost went over to your house and got Mama Betts to dial you, but I was afraid she'd listen in and get us both in trouble.'

'I missed you, Alice. And we're not going to move away. Not ever.'

The sun broiled down hotter than ever on Kali Oka Road. The green hills of Missouri were a fading memory as I gave myself to the heat and red dirt of my home. After a week of not knowing where anything was, of being dependent on someone else to take me everywhere, I was home. I could get anywhere I needed to be on my bicycle or on foot. I had Picket at my side, and Alice as my best friend. Even Maebelle V. wasn't much of a bother.

Kali Oka seemed shorter than it ever had before. We were at Cry Baby Creek before I got good and winded. Alice was blowing hard, though, and Maebelle V., in the basket of my bike, seemed a little rattled by the fast ride. I got her out and was surprised to see that she'd grown much heavier. She was also straining her head up and grabbing hold of things with her hands. Pretty soon she'd be trying to crawl, and she was already making a lot of different noises. Too many and too much.

During my stay in Missouri I had Cathi take me to a pet store, and I bought a leash. Alice and I left the bicycles a long way from the creek, and I put Picket on the leash and took her with me. Maebelle V. was in her papoose, cooing and drooling all over Alice's back.

The closer we got to the church, the harder it was for me to breathe. I hadn't told Alice about the 7-Up bottle. I'd sort of buried that thought from myself.

'What are we going to do?' Alice asked.

We'd gotten off in such a hurry, I didn't even have a plan. It was Monday, so there likely wouldn't be a church service. We could wade down the creek until we stumbled across someone or something. That seemed like a waste of time, though. I kicked at a stick floating by in the creek. 'I don't know how to get to the girl and check on her. We could just walk up, I suppose.'

'Yeah, sure.' Alice eased the papoose around to her front and took the baby out. Maebelle V. chirped with delight at the feel of the cool water on her legs as Alice dangled her in it.

The truth of the matter was that I didn't know what to do. Since it wasn't a Sunday, those Redeemers could be anywhere in the area. They wouldn't be all gathered up in church for our convenience to spy on. I'd been listening close, and there wasn't a sound of the boys, even though we weren't all that far from the place where they'd begun their fort. With no better plan, the fort seemed the best place to start.

We waded along in the creek. I couldn't help but remember the summer before – before the Redeemers and before Maebelle V. – Alice and I had dreamed together back then. Now it had changed, and I couldn't put my finger on exactly how. Everything had changed. Part of it was Missouri, and even part was a green 7-Up bottle flying through the air and blood dripping in the dirt. Part of it was a singing girl and too many secrets.

When the boys' fort was across the creek from us, we stopped. There wasn't a sound in the woods except for the small animals and birds hustling about their business.

'She's dead, isn't she?' Alice asked out loud.

'Good lord, no.' I asked Picket to sit beside me as I sank into the creek. She was straining at the leash. Squirrels danced on the rim of the bank, tempting her almost beyond endurance and the strength of my arm to hold her. At least she didn't bark.

'You think she's hurt, don't you?' Alice sank into the cold rush of water beside me.

I did, but I didn't want to say it out loud. I didn't want to think about it. 'We didn't even go to the water slide. Last summer we wouldn't have missed a day. Now June is half over.'

'Bekkah, what are we going to do?'

'What do you want us to do, march in there and demand to see a girl named Magdeline?' Instead of angry, I was tired.

'Let's find that chubby boy, Georgie. He could tell us where his sister is.'

'Like he would if they've killed her. The Redeemers are a sect, Alice. They do everything together. They'd never go against their leader. Mama Betts said they're almost as bad as a cult. None of them even have jobs, that we know of.'

Sand was slipping under the elastic of my underwear. My sneakers had already filled with it. The current was so shallow and fast that it moved over my lower body with a relentless power that suddenly made me even tireder. I didn't want to take on the Redeemers. Effie getting her arm cut had done something to me. Those folks outside the jail, they'd changed me. If the Redeemers had done something terrible to Magdeline, what could I do about it? The answer was nothing.

'I'm going to take a look,' Alice said. She thrust Maebelle V. at me and churned off down the creek. I held the baby, dangling her feet in the water and then pulling them out, until Alice disappeared from sight. Maebelle

V. and I sat for another five minutes before I got up and started after Alice. It wasn't fair to make her go by herself. She was always going with me.

It didn't take me long to catch up, and I know she heard me splashing behind her even though she didn't turn around.

'I'm not afraid,' I said as I touched her shoulder.

'I didn't say you were.'

'You think I am, though.'

'I think you're different.' She shook her head and made her ponytail jiggle. 'We both are, I suppose.'

She took the baby in her arms and led the way toward the church. We had both changed. Alice had gained guts and I had lost them.

We hadn't gone too much farther when we heard the voices. The boys again. It was crucial that we kept Maebelle V. quiet, and Picket too. She was straining at the leash again and growling low in her throat. She hated those boys, and if anyone doesn't believe a dog is a good judge of character, they just haven't known any smart dogs.

Alice slung Maebelle V. back in her papoose and I kept one hand on Picket's back. It seemed to keep her calm to feel my touch. Like some soldiers in the war movies, we crept up the bank and fell on our elbows to spy on the boys.

They were in the old church cemetery. Alice and I exchanged looks, and if I had the same wild-eyed stare she had, we were a fearsome-looking duo. The boys had a shovel, and they were going to town on a hole.

Jim, the blond boy, was digging while Greg supervised. At first I didn't see Georgie, but I heard him. There was this soft choking sound coming from behind one of the old tombstones, and it took me a minute to locate Georgie sitting there, crying. The worst sensation ran down my spine.

'They're burying her,' Alice said, awe and terror in her voice. 'They killed her and they sent the boys to bury her.'

'That's impossible.' But I knew it wasn't. One thing I'd learned this summer was that anything was possible. People could be as nice or as mean as they could think up to be. They didn't need a reason to be either one.

'Bekkah, they're digging a grave.'

'Maybe it's treasure.' I wanted it to be treasure. I hoped they found a million dollars each. I didn't care how rich they became, I just didn't want them to be digging a grave.

'In a cemetery?' Alice scoffed. 'Not much chance of that.'

'Alice, if they've killed her . . . ' We would have to call the police. 'Let's just watch for a minute.' The time before, I'd run off without my evidence. This time I wanted to see for sure.

Jim dug the hole diligently. He was knee-deep and working it into a square about three by four. But we couldn't be sure of the size of the hole, because our view was on the same level.

Alice's fingers were digging into the dirt of the bank, and to my complete relief Maebelle V. had dozed off in her papoose. Even Picket was lying right beside me, her eyes alert and watching but her mouth closed.

From the woods near the boys there was the sound of terrible weeping. Alice gripped my shoulder and nearly broke the bone she squeezed so hard.

I wanted to break free of her, but I was afraid to move. A white shape flitted through the woods. My heart notched up to a faster rhythm, and I had to force myself to hold my ground and watch. The white shape came closer and closer.

The boys didn't seem to notice it. Jim kept digging. Greg supervised right on, and Georgie sat behind his tombstone with the other two boys. He was still crying, and they were talking to him.

None of them acted as if they heard whoever was coming through the woods crying like they'd lost their only friend. It was a terrible sound, that crying. I'd never heard anything like it. It was so sad that it tore at me. I looked at Alice and there were tears in the corner of her eye.

'We're a fine pair, crying over God knows what,' Alice whispered. 'Who is that and what's wrong with her?'

All we could tell was that it was a female. She was draped in white and she wore a veil that obscured her face. She went to the edge of the grave where the boys were working. She stood for a moment, looking down into the hole and crying.

Jim got out of the hole, and the boys over by Georgie pulled him to his feet. When he turned toward us, he was holding a blood-soaked towel in his arms. There was blood on his face where he'd rubbed his hands at his eyes. Beside me, Alice made a dry, retching sound. I gave her a hard elbow in the ribs and stopped her before she could start vomiting.

'What is it?' she asked weakly.

'Shusssh!'

The boys and girl gathered around the grave. Georgie, crying loudly this time, still held the bloody parcel. I could see by now that it was something wrapped in the towel.

Out of the clear blue, the girl's voice rose in a hymn. The words of 'Softly and Tenderly' floated from the graveside in a tone so pure that it made my skin jump. She sang one verse and the boys took the bloody towel and put it in the hole in the ground. Without another word Greg took the shovel and started covering it up.

Georgie and the girl we both recognized now as Magdeline broke into fresh tears.

'They didn't kill her,' I told Alice, though she could plainly see it for herself.

'No, they didn't kill her.'

Her voice let me know she was thinking of something almost worse than killing her. 'What are you thinking?'

'Maybe she *had* been fornicating, and she was pregnant. Maybe they beat her until they killed the baby.'

'You think they were burying a dead baby?' That idea was more horrible than anything I could ever have thought of.

'Not a complete baby.' Alice slipped back into the creek where we could talk easier.

'What are you getting at?' I wasn't following. It was either a baby or it wasn't. Unless someone had cut it up!

'Well, babies grow. If they don't get a chance to grow enough, they come out, and they aren't real babies. They're just part of a baby. If she was pregnant and not too far along, she could have lost her baby when they hurt her.'

'This is crazy, Alice. Where did you learn all of this?'

She dropped her head and turned away from me.

'What?' I was getting upset. Where had Alice heard these things and why hadn't she told me before? We'd never had secrets. 'Where did you hear all of this stuff?'

'Jamey Louise.'

I couldn't believe it. 'Jamey Louise Welford?' I was completely betrayed.

Alice nodded. 'Jamey and her sister, Libby.'

'While I was gone to Missouri?'

'Yes. Jamey came over and asked me to go bicycle riding with her. She wanted to come down here to the creek, but her mama wouldn't let her come by herself.'

'So she asked you to be her nanny?'

Alice frowned. 'She was lonely. She's not as bad as you think, Bekkah. That Libby is something else. She knows

157

everything there is to know about sex and boys and that kind of stuff.'

'Libby said they could beat Magdeline and kill her baby if she was pregnant, right?'

'That's what she said. That's why I've been so worried.'

'What if she wasn't pregnant?'

'Then what were they burying?'

'I don't know, Alice. Why don't you ask Jamey Louise? She seems to be quite an authority on these things.' Before she could respond, Picket and I started back up the creek to the point where we'd entered.

Chapter Sixteen

Behind me, Alice called my name once, then fell into her own angry silence. I could hear her splashing after me, but I only pushed harder to leave her behind. Picket was an asset, straining forward and pulling me. Alice had the baby to drag along. By the time I left the creek bed, she was far behind.

I got on my bicycle and pedaled fast toward home. My heart was burning with a strange emotion. It wasn't fair to get mad at Alice for being friendly to Jamey Louise, especially not when I had been off in Missouri. But it was so hard. And they'd been talking about the Redeemer girl. Alice had told our secrets. The pain in my heart barely left enough room for my lungs.

When I got to Nadine's driveway, I didn't even hesitate. I rode straight in. The barn doors were open wide, and I dropped my bicycle in the shade by the chinaberry and ran toward the barn. I was panting when I stopped in the dim coolness, a bit startled by the sudden quiet.

Cammie's head was hanging over her stall. There were more horses, but I ignored the new arrivals and ran toward Cammie. I wrapped my arms around her neck and buried my face. She was damp, and I drew back to take a look at her.

There was a light blue sheet over her. I slipped the latch and went into her stall. I felt her all over. She was wet, but a cool wet. Not the sweat of being heavily blanketed.

'I gave her a bath.'

Nadine's voice shocked me, but I didn't let it show. I walked back to the stall door and looked down the hall. She was sitting on the cement block, just as she had the first time I met her. Her legs stuck out of a pair of short, short cutoffs, and she wore a tiny top, like part of a bikini. Her skin was very white and her dark eyes watched me closely.

'How often do you bathe them?' I asked. Every week or two we gave Picket a bath, which was quite a chore. I couldn't imagine that Cammie would like it any better.

'Once a week, at least. It depends on show season. The fall circuit will be coming up soon.'

I counted nine heads of horses, and I latched Cammie's door and walked toward Nadine, taking in the little I could see of the new horses.

'I went to Missouri and rode,' I told her. 'I learned how to post properly.'

'I thought maybe you'd moved away.' Nadine stood up. 'Since you didn't show up to work for lessons, I hired someone else.'

A giant rock plunged through me, knocking my already injured heart around. All of my summer dreams disintegrated. I'd gone to Missouri for one week, and Alice had a new friend, and Nadine had found someone else to work. Greg, the Redeemer boy, hadn't lied.

'Is Greg a good worker?' My voice trembled, but I was trying hard to be polite. I was also looking for any cracks there might be in this new arrangement.

'Greg? Why do you ask?'

'Didn't you hire him?'

'For labor. I hired Jamey Louise Welford to help with the horses. Her daddy farms and they own stock.'

I could have swallowed my tongue. 'Jamey Louise is a

160

moron,' I said sharply. 'She hates animals. She doesn't care two figs for the horses.'

'Maybe not. But she doesn't come in my barn and take the blankets off without permission.'

Nadine's voice had a snap to it, but she was still smiling. At least it looked like a smile.

'They were sweating. I thought I was doing the right thing.'

'You could have given them pneumonia, Bekkah. They got too cool too quickly. They could have gotten very sick.'

'They were sweating! Cammie was trembling!'

'If you knew the first thing about horses, I might be interested in hearing your opinions. I think, though, that if you're going to come on my property, you need to realize that I know what's best for my animals.'

Of all the things I'd expected to find at Nadine's, a reprimand wasn't one of them. I'd only been trying to help. I thought I'd done something she'd thank me for.

'I didn't mean any harm.' I forced the words out. It was all so unfair! Alice and Jamey Louise, and now this! No matter what I did, it was wrong.

'I know that, Bekkah. It's just that in acting without knowledge, you could have killed Cammie or one of the other horses.'

Her hand on my shoulder was small, but the fingers gripped hard.

'It's okay. I'm not angry and no harm was done. Maybe if I explained about the blankets you'd understand.'

I nodded. I needed a few minutes to compose myself, so I walked back to Cammie's stall. Her forelock needed straightening, and I reached up to comb the tangle of hair with my fingers.

'Show horses can't have winter coats. They have to be very thin-skinned. They can't get out in the sun and get bleached out either. They have to look perfect.

Sometimes, in a ring, there'll be two horses tied for first place. When the judge hasn't got any other criteria, he'll use appearances. That gleaming coat may be the only thing that gives me a blue ribbon.'

'And the blankets keep the hair thin?'

'Right.' I started to tell her what Mama Betts said, but I knew my grandma didn't know anything about show horses. Nadine's horses were special animals with special needs. Mama Betts only knew about ordinary stock.

'Where have you been today?' Nadine asked. She slipped Cammie's halter over her head and led her to the cross ties. 'Tell me while you groom Cammie for a ride. I think it's time for your lesson.'

'I can't take lessons . . . I was going to work them off, remember?'

'There's plenty of work for you and Jamey. In fact, she should be arriving just about the time you finish riding. You two can clean the stalls together.'

I'd rather have danced with the devil, but I wanted to ride so bad I couldn't complain. After I thought I'd lost my chance, I wasn't going to say anything else about Jamey Louise. Nadine could find out on her own.

Cammie was drying out, and as I ran the stiff brush over her body I told Nadine about going down to the creek with Alice and Maebelle V.

'It's a wonder you two don't kill that little baby,' she said. 'I saw y'all bumping down the road with her.'

'Maebelle's tough. She can take it.'

'Tell me about the Redeemers.'

'Greg should be the one to tell you.' I didn't know what to say. There was a lot I wanted to tell Nadine, but since Greg was working at the barn, it didn't seem right.

'Greg won't talk about the church people at all.' Nadine laughed. 'His lips are tighter than the cheeks on an elephant's behind. You'd think they were all a bunch of cannibals, the way he acts.'

162

'I don't know about cannibals, but they're some mighty strange folks.' The image of those kids standing around the grave with that blood-soaked towel came back to me. Right along with the thought of Mr. Tom, his brains bashed out. 'Alice and I went down there to check on a girl we thought might be mistreated.'

Nadine's voice was conspiratorial when she spoke again. 'I saw Greg's back. I didn't comment on it, but somebody beat the bejesus out of him.'

I swallowed. Like everything else that had gone wrong this summer, that could come roosting at my door too. 'Yeah, I saw his back.'

'Tell me about the girl. What did you see?'

While I put the saddle and bridle on Cammie, I told her about the singing dwarf and the hair shearing and Magdeline's confession, and then about the screams. I finished off with the burial scene we'd just witnessed that morning.

'Was it a baby, do you suppose?'

'Alice said it might be, or at least part of a baby. Like before it's a real baby.'

'A fetus,' Nadine supplied. 'If they beat her hard enough, she could abort. With a horse, sometimes a storm or some severe excitement can result in miscarriage. People aren't any different.'

It was a gruesome thought, and Nadine's willingness to believe such a thing had happened made it seem more probable.

'Should I go to the police?' I asked. 'Alice wanted to.'

'You don't have any evidence. Maybe you could sneak to the cemetery and dig up whatever they buried.'

'It's right by the church! They'd catch us in a minute. Why don't you ask Greg?'

'That boy wouldn't tell the truth, not about that.' Cammie was perfectly tacked up, and we walked outside into the hot afternoon sun. 'More than likely it was some dead animal they found. Maybe a pet.'

I hadn't thought about it until Nadine spoke. 'They don't have pets. I haven't seen a cat or dog around that place.'

'Well, I'll gladly give them a few,' she said. 'Those dogs are driving me crazy.'

I hadn't seen a trace of them around the barn. I wondered if they were house dogs.

'The cats have all gone wild.' She shook her head with a bemused look on her face. 'I'm having more success taming the rats in the barn than I am my own dogs and cats.'

I laughed. The idea of tame rats was funny.

'You think I'm kidding, don't you? I've tamed two of the rats in the barn. I'll show you after we finish your lesson.'

'Yeah, you can tame rats, but the real question is can you make Jamey Louise work?' I thought I scored a good one with that remark.

'Oh, Jamey will work,' Nadine smiled a Cheshire cat smile. 'I have something she wants very badly. Very badly indeed. And Jamey will work when she's motivated.'

'What do you have?' I knew it wasn't horses, cats or dogs. I couldn't imagine what Nadine would have that would interest Jamey Louise. I mean Nadine did dye her hair and all, but she didn't wear gobs of makeup or dress all frilly.

'I have Greg,' Nadine said softly. 'Greg the Redeemer.'

Now, that was something Jamey Louise would relish. Time alone in the barn with the Redeemer boy. I was awed by Nadine's brilliance. She has read Jamey through and through. Poor Greg, though. If he didn't know any bad habits, Jamey Louise would sure enough teach him a few.

Before I had a chance to answer, Nadine gave me a leg

up and told me to put Cammie into a working trot. Since my three rides in Missouri, I had a lot to show her.

At the end of the hour-long lesson, my legs were trembling but my heart soared. I'd ridden a canter, and Cammie had taken a two-foot jump, all with Nadine's plentiful praise. Alice and the burial and even Jamey Louise's imminent arrival were forgotten – at least for the moment of glory.

It didn't last long, though. I had just untacked Cammie and was brushing her down when I heard Jamey Louise's sugary voice.

'Well, well, Bekkah Rich, how did you ever talk Miss Effie into letting you around these horses? Or does she know?'

'It was a family decision,' I answered. 'When I was in Missouri, I went to a stables and started my lessons. Now I'm taking them from Nadine.' Bravado was my only weapon. If Jamey Louise thought she had me squeezed up, she'd either try to blackmail me or simply go to Effie for the sheer pleasure of making my life a living hell.

'I'd like to hear Effie's side of this.'

I looked up at Jamey for the first time. My mouth fell open. She was wearing a sun dress, a straw hat with a pale blue ribbon and white sandals. Her chest had been growing.

'I hope you brought work clothes,' Nadine commented as she walked by leading Caesar. 'You'll get worms working in the stalls in those sandals. You need some good solid shoes like Bekkah's. And by the way, Jamey Louise, not a word of what goes on here leaves the place. If you go running up and down the road gossiping, I'll have to fire you.' She snapped the two cross ties. 'And I suppose Bekkah would have to entertain Greg then.'

I wanted dance. I wanted to sing. I would have kissed Nadine. She'd put a wooden stake in Jamey's black little heart, and she'd driven it in with a sledge-hammer. I turned back to grooming Cammie so Jamey couldn't see my smirk.

'I thought I'd help Greg in the loft today,' Jamey said sweetly.

'You can play in the loft with Greg after you've cleaned the stalls. Bekkah will take the right side and you the left. The first one finished gets a free lesson.'

Jamey had one less horse than I did, but I knew I'd beat her. The idea of shoveling horse manure would slow her down considerably, especially in open-toe sandals.

'Greg!' Nadine called. 'Greg!'

I'd left him back in the church cemetery. During our lesson I hadn't seen him arrive either.

'What is it, Nadine?' His head came over the side of the loft, just above Jamey Louise. A little landslide of hay fell onto Jamey. She brushed at her chest and giggled.

'Hate to interrupt your work, but it would appear Miss Welford went to a lot of trouble to look nice for you. I thought you might want to see her before she cleans the stalls. I don't imagine she'll look the same afterward.' Nadine's drawl was longer than necessary.

'Too bad to see such a pretty girl get all dirty,' Greg said slowly. 'Such a pretty dress too.'

He was looking straight down Jamey's bosom. She sort of squeezed her arms to her sides so that her breasts looked larger. I wanted to groan out loud.

'Well, Jamey has to learn to dress to work in a barn.'

'She could take that pretty dress off,' Greg suggested. 'In this hot weather it's easier to work without a shirt.'

I remembered his whipcord-thin body and the sweat – and the lashes across his back. Jamey Louise giggled.

'You young folks better behave. Y'all start taking your clothes off in my barn, and I'll get a bad reputation. Greg, those church people of yours will be comin' down here and accusing me of all sorts of evil things.'

Whatever Nadine believed, she wasn't worried one whit about the church people. Nadine didn't gave one flying damn what anybody thought about her. She'd told me that herself.

'You can be our baby-sitter, Miss Nadine,' Greg said. He laughed and he sounded more grown-up than when he talked. 'The one you got to be worried about is Miss Bekkah Rich. She'll run home and tattle to her mama if she thinks there's a whiff of fun going on around here.'

'I don't tattle,' I said stiffly. I didn't know why he had to turn the conversation around on me, except maybe to impress Jamey Louise. And it was working.

'Miss Effie hardly trusts Bekkah to take a bath alone. She's afraid she'll drown in the bath water.' Jamey laughed. 'Bekkah's a titty-baby.'

'Is that so?' Greg hung out a little farther from the loft. 'Her mouth ain't deformed. Least not yet.'

Even Nadine laughed. Jamey Louise would pay dearly for her comments. She thought she was such a little charmer. I put Cammie away and got the pitchfork and wheelbarrow from the end of the hall. Nadine had Napoleon tacked up, and she left us to our own devices in the barn. I set to work shoveling, ignoring Jamey and Greg. They were talking at the far end of the barn, where Greg had come partway down the ladder. Jamey Louise had her hand on a wooden rung, and her arms squeezed tight to her sides again.

'Don't get a hernia, Bekkah,' she called. 'I don't want any riding lesson, so you can have it.'

'You'd better get to work.' I kept the rhythm of my shoveling. The stalls weren't that dirty. There were fresh shavings in them and clean hay.

'Shovel horse poo? You've got to be kidding. Greg's going to help me, aren't you, Greg?'

She spoke with such persuasion in her voice it made me almost retch.

'And what are you going to give Greg in return, Jamey Louise? What do you have that someone else hasn't already sampled?' I knew the words were vicious, but they weren't any worse than what she'd said, at least not in my opinion.

I was rewarded with a loud burst of laughter from Greg and the sharp sound of a palm meeting naked skin. Whether she'd slapped him on the chest or the face, I didn't know or care. I only hoped it had been enough to keep him from doing her chores. I moved down to the next stall, where Caesar stayed. He was a big bay gelding with two white stockings. Really magnificent and the most expensive of all the horses. There was something wrong with one of his feet, but Nadine had said it wasn't serious.

When I took a pause from the constant lifting of the pitchfork, Jamey was standing at the stall door. 'Greg said you and Alice were down at the creek today.'

'I've been taking a riding lesson, and I'm about to get another one because you aren't doing your work.'

'He saw you. Both of you.'

'Good for Greg. Why doesn't he file a police report.'

'You'd better stay away from down there, Bekkah. They don't like you, and they don't want you there. Everybody on Kali Oka Road knows you and your family are trouble.'

'Like everybody knows you and your sisters are whores?' I hated to drag Libby and Cora in on the brawl, but Jamey was aiming at my whole family. Fair was fair. Her face went white with fury.

'Just remember, before you pop a gut, you started this, Jamey. I'm just going to finish it.' I heaved another forkful of manure at the barrel. My aim was off a bit, and a small turd hit Jamey in the arm.

'Sorry.' I couldn't hide my smile. 'Maybe you'd better stand back. I'm trying to work.'

Jamey looked at the stain on her arm. She whirled around and marched down the barn aisle toward the water hose. I was tempted to lob another forkful of manure at her, but I didn't want to mess up the aisle.

'Nice shot,' Greg said. He was up in the loft just above my stall.

'Thanks.' I was burning to ask him what they'd buried that morning.

'Your friend is cute. Why does she always have that baby?'

'It's her sister. Alice has to take care of her. Mrs. Waltman's expecting again and she can't take care of Maebelle.'

'Well, she's a cute girl. I like blondes.'

'I'll tell her. I'm sure it'll make her day.'

Greg chuckled softly. 'You don't like us, Bekkah, but you can't leave us alone. You'd better be careful what you come down to the end of the road to see. You might see something you don't want to.'

'How's the girl who sings?' I couldn't help it. 'She has a pretty voice.'

'Yeah, she does. Magdeline has a lot of pretty parts about her. And—'

'They didn't hurt her, did they?'

He stopped talking.

'I'm not going to tell anybody. I just wanted to make sure she wasn't really hurt.'

'What you know and what you think you know are two different things. Stay away from the church. That's for your sake and Maggie's. If they had any idea she was talking to you—'

'She hasn't. She hasn't talked to me or anyone else.'

'Stay away, and keep your friend and that baby away from there.'

He went back to his work in the loft, the sound of the pitchfork turning the hay again and again with a brute frenzy. I finished HiJinx's stall and moved down the line to Heathcliff. I had some thinking to do. For the first time Greg had sounded concerned, as if he was worried something would happen to me and Alice if we went back down there. All of my deepest suspicions were roused again. Maybe Alice and I would have to go to the cemetery and try to dig up that fetus they had buried. That would be enough proof to get the sheriff and the FBI down there to save Magdeline. And maybe even Greg.

Chapter Seventeen

Two weeks passed and I didn't see Alice for the first time. None of the Waltmans attended the Sweet Water Methodist Church Fourth of July Dinner on the Ground, even though Alice and I were supposed to sing a duet together. It was an omen that fretted me. Alice's older sister, Sukey, played the piano for the church, and she never missed an event at the old white clapboard. Sukey was planning on being a missionary to Peru, and she was going 'to take the word of God through music to the savages of the rain forest.'

I wasn't real certain the rain-forest savages were going to like the way Sukey intended to introduce them to Christian music. She pounded down on hymns like 'He Lives' and 'Onward Christian Soldiers.' Taken from the viewpoint of a savage, those songs might be sort of scary, especially with Sukey, her curly red hair wired in every direction, striking the piano like she meant to bust it apart.

Since Sukey wasn't there, Miss Ethel Scarborough played, but she lacked the fervor of the young Miss Waltman. That cut me out too. Without Alice, who could really sing, I wasn't willing to do it by myself. No one pressed me very hard either. The truth was, the dinner wasn't much to enjoy without Alice to talk to. Jamey Louise was noticeably absent also. I knew where she was, lurking around the barn and Greg. Not even the sumptuous foods at the dinner could tempt her away from Greg, and I avoided her mama and daddy for all I was worth. I didn't want to be answering any questions about how I liked working with Jamey Louise. Nadine's edict about gossip was still in effect, and I didn't want to be banished for having a loose tongue. Besides, Jamey Louise was keeping her mouth shut tight about my jumping Cammie. As long as she kept quiet, I would too. Mama Betts would say it was a pact made with the devil, and I'd probably have to agree with her.

Effie and Mama Betts and I ate watermelon and home-made peach ice cream and pound cake and potato salad and Mrs. Spooner's pickled okra and fried chicken and enough other things until we were stretched out on the ground under a big oak tree. The late afternoon sun beat down hard on the church grounds until even the little children were tired enough to sit and listen to different ones of the congregation sing and talk. Several of our neighbors dropped by and visited with Mama Betts and Effie. I caught a glimpse or two of Arly's friends on the fringes of the crowd. He was spoonin' with one of the Carpenter girls. I think it was Rosie, but I couldn't be certain. Talk around school last year was that Rosie was the best kisser in Chickasaw County. Leave it to Arly to follow the scent.

The day wound down to an end, and when the boys lit the fireworks and set the dusky sky on fire I realized with a bump that summer was half over. School would start the last week of August. I'd be in the seventh grade.

Riding back home in the velvety night with the car windows down, Mama warned me that when school started up I was going to have to wear a brassiere, whether I needed one or not. She said we'd go to the Dale Shop the next Saturday and get fitted. That took what little magic there had been out of the night.

I rode my bicycle down to Cry Baby Creek several

times during those two weeks, and I even hid an old shovel down there so I could dig up whatever had been buried in the cemetery. Picket and I hunkered down in the creek bed and spied on the Redeemers, but there was never a time when no one was about long enough for me to rush across the creek and dig. Nothing was happening that I could tell. Women walked along by themselves or with other women. The men were invisible. They stayed indoors, it seemed. And the five Redeemer boys came and went, but they always looked as if they were doing something important. At the barn, Greg refused to talk about the Redeemers at all, not even when Nadine teased him about worshiping Satan and other strange rituals.

Daddy did talk with Effie, and it was agreed that I could work at Nadine's barn for riding lessons. It was all settled with a lot less commotion than I'd ever thought possible. Daddy had to finish out his contract in Missouri, but he was home every two weeks for three or four days. Effie was trying really hard to make life easy for Daddy. I know he never told her how close he came to staying in Missouri. He didn't have to tell her. Both she and Mama Betts seemed to know. In the kitchen when they were cooking, Mama Betts would say something about Daddy's favorite dessert being apple pie, and that would be exactly what Effie had planned to make. That glance would pass between them, and the rolling pin would be put in the refrigerator to chill.

I got a card from Cathi Cummings, and I didn't show it to Effie. Or to anyone else since I wasn't talking with Alice. It was a cartoon card about dog days in summer and how she wished I'd come back to Missouri. She said she missed her horseback riding partner, and that made me feel good. She said that she was looking out for Daddy for me while he was still in Missouri and that she was going to miss him a lot when he came home to us.

That was the part that made me hide the note from

Effie. I'd given it a lot of serious thought, and I didn't believe Daddy and Cathi were fornicating. I think she wanted to, and maybe him too. But I don't believe it ever happened. If it had, they would have said they were in love, or something like that. But instead of being all cow-eyed at each other, Cathi always had that look of sadness whenever she looked at Daddy, like he was something she wanted but couldn't have. And The Judge just wasn't the kind of man who did the sort of thing that required sneaking around and lying.

It was hard not to think about fornicating when Jamey Louise was in heat every day. Working at the barn each morning, I was getting a real education about teasing boys. She kept Greg on a slow sizzle. Nadine was right about one thing: Jamey Louise knew how to work when the payoff was time alone with Greg. Since she wasn't interested in riding, she flew through her chores and was sitting like a cat at a milk saucer when Greg finished his. Then they'd disappear up in the loft and spend the next hour or so giggling until Greg had to go back to the church. He had a job there, too, but he wouldn't tell us what it was. Jamey didn't bother to talk to me at all, unless she wanted to trade some chore for another so she could be around Greg more.

Cammie and I were becoming a real team. I'd fallen off twice, but it had only been a few scrapes and bruises, and I'd taken great care to hide them from Effie. If she saw any marks on my body, she'd have a fit and demand that I stop riding. One time the stirrup leather broke over a jump, and I fell into the jump standard, and another, Cammie spooked when one of the cats leapt off the roof and startled us both.

We were getting good, though. We were going over two-nine jumps, and Nadine said I'd be ready to show over three-foot fences by September if Effie would buy me the boots and jacket. I hadn't asked her yet, because I was afraid if she knew I was jumping at all, she'd make me stop going to the barn. It was a hard situation because more than anything I wanted to tell her. I wanted her to come and see me and be proud. But she'd just be frightened.

Nadine said she wasn't going away for the fall circuit this year. She was tired and wanted to stay put on Kali Oka, so if Effie would spring for the riding gear, she'd take me and Cammie to the local shows in Mobile. It was more than I'd ever dreamed of, and I began plotting ways to get the boots and jacket. There were times I did Jamey Louise's chores and she gave me what little bit of pay Nadine gave her.

A routine of sorts began to build around my days, but there was a big hole in it named Alice. The barn kept me busy until lunch, and then Mama Betts always had a few chores for me to do. But by three o'clock I was always finished. From then until bedtime I hardly went five minutes without thinking of Alice. Mama Betts asked where she was, and I said she was too busy to play with me.

'She's too busy, and you're too stubborn to apologize,' she said.

'What have I done to apologize for?' I asked her back.

'I don't know, but it must be something. I know you, Bekkah Rich, and you've hurt Alice's feelings or she'd be over here.'

I stormed out of the kitchen, but it didn't take away the sting of the truth. It took me two weeks to decide to offer an apology, and by that time I wasn't certain she'd accept.

Jamey Louise hadn't spent any time with her, and though I couldn't prove it, I suspected Jamey had snubbed her good. Jamey had Greg. She'd never wanted to be Alice's friend, she'd just wanted someone to help her catch Greg's eye.

Picket and I took the path through the woods. We stopped for a while at the spring. I'd kind of hoped Alice might be there, where we could meet on neutral ground. But even though I dawdled for a good fifteen minutes, there wasn't a sign of her. We walked on toward her house, stopping at the edge of the woods. She was sitting in the swing with Maebelle V. in her lap. The baby had grown two inches and a good five pounds. Maybe all that jostling around in the bicycle basket had been stunting her growth.

Picket bounded forward and barked a greeting at Alice. I'd hoped to be a little more dignified, but my plan was lost when she turned around and saw me.

'I'm sorry I left you at the creek with the baby.' I wanted to go closer, but I was afraid she'd tell me to leave. To make it worse, I thought I might cry.

'We made it home okay,' Alice said. 'It didn't matter.'

'I felt like you'd taken up with Jamey Louise. It made me feel left out that you were telling her all of our secrets.'

Alice slipped out of the swing. Holding Maebelle V. on her shoulder, she walked toward me. 'I didn't tell her anything, Bekkah. You never gave me a chance to explain.'

'I—'

'I didn't know if you'd come back from Missouri. I wasn't certain you wanted to come back here. Maybe me and Kali Oka Road weren't enough anymore. You're going to go away one day. Maybe it was going to be this summer.'

The truth of what she said stopped me from saying anything at all. I hadn't wanted to come back, not completely. A part of me wanted to go, to see things I'd never seen before. One day I would leave. I'd be going to a university like those people in Missouri. I'd be sitting in a room with people from all over the place. The Judge expected it of me.

And Alice would not.

'I hate this summer,' I said. 'Why does everything have to hurt?'

'What's it like working with Greg and Jamey?' Alice's smile was tentative. There wasn't any apology to make right what had gone wrong. The only thing we could do was keep going, either as friends or not. I wanted to be her friend more than anything, except maybe riding Cammie.

'They smooch all the time, but you can't tell anyone.' Alice hefted Maebelle V. a little higher in her arms, and I whistled for Picket as we walked back to the spring. I had a lot of gossip to tell Alice, and it wouldn't be breaking Nadine's rules, because Alice wouldn't tell a soul.

Chapter Eighteen

The plan to dig up the Redeemers' cemetery took shape without any real effort on my part or Alice's. Mostly it was happenstance. Greg asked for three days off on the first of August, a request that ignited Nadine's curiosity. After weeks of routine, Greg was doing something different. Nadine demanded to know what it was.

Greg said only that the Redeemers were having some sort of congregational gathering in Hattiesburg and that the entire push of them were going to board up on the buses and drive there for the first two nights in August. Under Nadine's inquisition, with Jamey Louise helping out, Greg said it had to do with policies, but he wouldn't give any details. I personally thought maybe he didn't know any more about it, but for a couple of days, until she tired of it, Nadine tried to worm more information out of him. He told nothing except that a lot of the Kali Oka Road Redeemers were upset and that everyone had to be in Hattiesburg for the vote.

I was so caught up in riding Cammie that I didn't even realize the implications of what this information meant. Not until I was reading Mama Betts' almanac to find out about planting pansies did it dawn on me that August first was a full moon.

The perfect night for a sneak raid on the Redeemer cemetery.

Things were still a little raw between Alice and me,

and she agreed too easily to my plan. We were both trying hard to recapture the bond we'd shared so effort-lessly in the past. A grave-digging adventure seemed just the ticket, especially since the Redeemer girl Magdeline Scott was the subject. Magdeline and her plight had crossed us up, and now she'd get us back together.

I was so keyed up that morning that I had a lot of difficulty calming Cammie down enough to ride her. Nadine was impatient in her funny way, calling out orders and cursing when I didn't obey. I didn't mind Cammie's sidestepping and crow-hopping. She was just feeling good because she didn't get out of her stall except when I rode her, and she wanted to stretch out and shake out the kinks. I asked Mama Betts about this in an offhanded kind of way, and she explained that horses were grazing animals and that it was harmful to keep them pinned up in a little stall. Nadine was afraid Cammie'd scar her hide or twist a leg in the hardscrabble pasture.

Jamey Louise leaned against her pitchfork in the door of the barn. Knowing that Greg wouldn't be at work, she'd worn faded blue jeans and a red checked shirt, which was the most appropriate thing she'd worn to work yet. I could tell by the way she watched that she hoped I'd bust my butt right in front of her.

When the six Redeemer buses flew down the road, a trail of dust choking after them, I must have smiled.

'What's going on?' Nadine asked as she grabbed Cammie's bridle and brought her to a dancing stop. She motioned for me to climb down.

'Nothing. It's just the Redeemers leaving for the gath-ering in Hattiesburg.'

'Yeah, yeah' – she waved impatiently in the air – 'I know that. What's going on with you? You look like you won a prize.'

'Nothing.' I wanted to tell Nadine about the adventure

Alice and I had planned, but I couldn't. Jamey Louise was always hanging around and listening in on every private conversation. If she knew Alice and I were going to Cry Baby Creek, she'd insist on going with us. She'd be worse than useless too.

I guess I must have looked down the road, because Nadine smiled real big. 'What are you up to, Rebekah Rich? What's happening down at the end of the road?'

'When I was a little girl, my grandma used to tell me about the baby that drowned in Cry Baby Creek,' I answered. I was hoping maybe the legend would distract her. 'Late at night, have you ever walked down the road and listened? When it gets real still, you can hear that little baby a'crying so pitiful. They say she floated for a long time before she finally drowned.'

I walked Cammie into the barn, and Nadine followed. Jamey was still standing at the door, listening to every word that passed between us.

'So why did the baby's mother put it in the creek?' Nadine asked.

'It's a long story, and it goes back to the church people who originally lived down at the end of the road.'

'I got time, and Jamey can clean your stalls while you tell me,' Nadine said. 'Right, Jamey, since you're standing around doing nothing?'

'I know the story,' Jamey said. 'I'll tell it and Bekkah can clean her stalls.'

'Not this time,' Nadine said. 'Let Bekkah tell it.' She signaled me to continue. I'd put Cammie's saddle and bridle away, and she needed a few minutes to cool before I started grooming her. Nadine had jumped up to sit on Ceasar's door, and I leaned against the wall on the opposite side of the barn, rocking back on my heels so I could crouch and rest against the wood.

'Well, the young woman's name was Miss Selena Baxter. I remember because Selena was such an odd name. And her baby's name was Evie.' I was trying to remember exactly everything Mama Betts had told me, but I knew I was going to have to fill in with a lot of my own details. It was only this summer that I'd come to realize several important things about little dead Evie Baxter, and how that baby had come to be that way.

'Selena was a beautiful young woman with long dark hair and green eyes.' I was making all of this up, but it didn't really matter. Now, in my mind, when I pictured Selena Baxter, I saw Magdeline. 'And she had the most beautiful voice. She was thought to be truly blessed by God with the way she could sing. She didn't need a piano or anything else, just the words and a tune, and she made everyone believe that God was among them.'

'You're making this up, Bekkah,' Jamey accused. 'I know this story, and there wasn't ever anything about that girl being able to sing.'

'Shut up and shovel,' Nadine directed. 'I want to hear this.'

'Selena didn't have any real family. Her parents had died in an epidemic of some fever or something, and she was left all alone. Since she was too old to be really adopted and too young to live by herself, she ended up with the church people on the end of the road. It was the Church of the Risen Christ back then.' I couldn't remember for certain, but that sounded good enough, and I knew Jamey Louise wouldn't know any better.

'How'd she find out about them?' Jamey asked. She was still holding up the end of the barn.

'Must have been that one of her people knew about it,' I said. 'I'm not a historian, Jamey, I'm just trying to tell the story.'

'Go on,' Nadine urged.

'Well, Selena didn't always feel that she fit in with the church people. She'd been used to going to school and doing regular things, and now she was isolated down at the end of a red dirt road without any real friends. The only one who made her feel at all welcome was the preacherman who was in charge of the church. He was always telling her she was a beautiful child of God and that her voice was a special gift, a sign of God's pleasure with her.'

'I can see where this is going,' Jamey said darkly. 'He's going to rape her.'

'Not rape. It wasn't like that at all. Selena believed that he loved her and that it was God's wish that they join together.' I was proud of that phrase. I'd been wondering how I was going to skirt around the fornication issue. When Mama Betts told me the story, she'd avoided all mention of that. She'd only said that Selena Baxter had had a baby. Although Mama Betts had never come right out and said it was the preacherman's, I'd finally figured that part out.

'I'll bet it was the preacher who told her it was God's will,' Nadine said dryly. 'He probably told her that she was serving the Lord.'

'And he told her that he loved her,' I said. 'The preacherman was very handsome, and he was the leader of all the people. It made Selena proud to be chosen by him. And he said he would marry her and make her his wife. It didn't matter that she was lonely and treated like an outcast by the congregation. As soon as they were married, she would be accepted and loved, just like he was. But it didn't happen that way.'

'She got pregnant,' Jamey said. 'Somebody should have told her the facts.' She laughed and Nadine threw a clump of dirt at her.

'She did indeed. And when she told the preacherman, he said it wasn't his baby and that she'd been sinning with someone in the congregation. Selena was so upset that she fled the church and ran into the woods to think.

'Too afraid to tell anyone what had happened, Selena

spent more and more time alone in the woods. She walked beside the creek and tried to think of a solution to her problems. She had no one to turn to, and the members of the congregation, as her stomach started to grow, treated her very ugly. It was obvious she was pregnant, but she refused to name the father of her child.'

'Rebekah Rich, you're making every word of this up.' Jamey threw her pitchfork into the aisle. 'It isn't fair, me having to do all your work while you lounge around telling lies that anybody with half a brain could tell is a bunch of hogwash.'

'Are you implying that I don't have half a brain?' Nadine asked.

'No, but you're sittin' there listening like you believe what Bekkah says is gospel.'

'It's a good tale well told,' Nadine said. 'Maybe if you practiced your verbal skills instead of moaning and primping, you'd be able to tell a good story.'

'Moaning and primping will get me everything I want in life,' Jamey said with a grin of victory. 'All telling lies is ever gonna do for Bekkah is get her butt tanned and get her in a heap of trouble.'

'Go on,' Nadine said, laughing and shaking her head at Jamey. 'Tell the story, Bekkah. Jamey may not claim to like it, but she's listening, isn't she?'

I took a deep breath and gritted down for some more imagining. 'Well, as the time drew nearer for Selena to have the baby, she knew she was in a bad situation. The folks at the church shunned her. Nobody would talk to her, and she wasn't even certain they'd help her with the delivery when it came time. The preacherman wouldn't have anything to do with her and told her, in front of the congregation, not to come back to the church with her burden of sin. She could stay on the church grounds, because she had no place else to go, he said. But she was

184

unholy. He told her it was God's will that she give the child up for adoption to some loving family who would raise it in a Christian way.'

Nadine shifted her position on the door. 'You two girls may think this is a wild tale, but things like this happen all the time. Some of those religious groups even take the babies of young girls and sell them. They sort of use young girls, just about your age, like breeding cattle. They just order the men to fertilize them, and when the baby is born, they sell it like a crop.' She smiled her fox smile at the horror on our faces.

'It's true,' she said. 'I'll bet that's what got all the Blood of the Redeemer church people so upset. There was something on the news a week ago about selling babies out of a Hattiesburg home for unwed mothers.'

'A Redeemer home?' Jamey asked. 'The Redeemers sell babies?'

Nadine and I exchanged glances when we saw Jamey's hand go to her flat stomach.

'They wouldn't take a baby unless the girl wanted to give it away, would they?' Jamey asked. She came out of the stall and stood in the center of the aisle.

'Sure they would. Think about it. Most of those girls are underage. The ones in the unwed mothers' home, their parents have probably turned them out or sent them to the home because they're ashamed of them.'

'What about the doctors?' I asked. 'They wouldn't let that happen.'

'Who said there were doctors? Women have babies without doctors all the time.'

I was sorry I'd started this whole story. Nadine stood in a clear pool of midday sun, her amber eyes dazzled by the light. Jamey, only three feet away, was covered in a fine sheen of sweat. They were both upset, and all because of an old legend and a story on the news.

Nadine walked out of the light and back into the

dimness of the barn, and the intensity of the moment flattened out. 'Forget I interrupted. Go on with the story. So what happened to the baby and Selena? Did somebody steal her baby?'

Jamey snorted. 'Stole would have been a heap better than what happened. She murdered it.'

In all the times I'd thought of the legend of Cry Baby Creek, I'd never exactly pictured the mother murdering her child. It had been so much more tragic than that. The baby had been tossed in the creek and had floated, as if it might find a safe harbor. Jamey Louise made it sound as if the woman waded out in the middle of the creek and held that baby under.

'It wasn't exactly murder.' I knew it was going to be hard to upstage Jamey's version.

'What would you call it?' Jamey asked.

'Selena put the baby in the creek, but she didn't really know what she was doing. She had it in the woods alone, and she didn't know what to do with it.'

'Why did she have it in the woods?' Nadine asked. 'Could it be that she was afraid someone would take it from her, maybe sell it?'

I shook my head. 'I don't know. It's only a story anyway.'

'Not really. You can hear that pitiful baby late at night,' Jamey insisted. 'Libby said she was down at the creek just last summer, and the sound of that suffering baby made the hair on her neck stand on end.'

More than likely Libby said that because she was parking down at the end of the road and didn't want any interruptions from her little sister. But there wasn't any point in saying that; besides, I'd brought up the legend. Jamey's assistance only gave my story more punch.

'That's true,' I said. 'It was a tragedy. No one denies that the little baby, a newborn girl, drowned. Mama Betts said that Selena had washed the baby off and dressed her in an old christening gown.'

'There was blood all over Selena herself,' Jamey supplied. She'd inched closer to both of us and was crouching down against the wall near me. 'She was a gruesome sight. Mama said she must have lost her mind, like some women do when they have a baby. She chucked that poor little girl right in the creek in her white christening gown.'

'The baby floated with the folds of the gown billowing out all around her.' I had to jump back in the story or Jamey would try to steal it away. 'She had dark hair, like her mother's, and as soon as she hit that cold, cold water she started crying.'

'Babies can swim,' Nadine said softly. 'I mean they can swim naturally, I've been told.'

'Well, she floated for a ways because they said Selena ran along the bank with her hands over her ears screaming to try to block out the sound of the baby's cries. And then finally she went under.' I paused, looking from Nadine to Jamey. They both had big eyes and shut mouths, and I decided to go for the dramatic. 'And there was silence on Cry Baby Creek.

'Five days later, they finally found the body. Some of the lace on the christening gown had snagged on the root of a dogwood tree that was leaning down the bank.'

'The water must have been very cold, or the body would have decomposed,' Nadine said matter-of-factly.

'The baby didn't have a name,' I continued. 'But when the people of Chickasaw County got ready to bury her, they named her Evie, so she'd have a name on her tombstone.'

'Why Evie?' Nadine asked.

'I don't know. Mama Betts just said she was so perfect. It really upset everybody on the road. See, when Selena went back to the congregation with blood all over her and no baby, everyone started looking for the infant. The church people tried to keep it hushed up among themselves, but it didn't work. Soon the news traveled down the road and everybody got involved.'

'Maybe it wasn't Selena who killed the baby but the preacherman,' Nadine said. She rose to her feet, walked four or five steps away from us and then suddenly turned to confront us. 'Maybe he came up on Selena having the baby, and when she delivered, he took the child, dressed it, christened it and then drowned it.'

Nadine's brown eyes were alive in the dim barn. I could feel the skin beginning to crawl along my arms. Jamey Louise even shifted a little closer to me.

'Maybe that preacherman who killed Selena's baby is the very same one that lives down at the end of Kali Oka Road now. Maybe he's come back! They always come back to the scene of the crime.'

I took in a deep breath. It might be true. Who else would know about that church down at the end of an old dirt road? Based on the way he'd treated Magdeline Scott, he was mean enough to do anything.

Nadine looked from me to Jamey Louise, and I thought for a fraction of a second she might smile. Then she said, 'That poor little baby you hear late at night is crying out for justice.'

Chapter Nineteen

Nadine's interpretation of the story of Evie Baxter and Cry Baby Creek put a curl in my toenails on a hot August day, but it wasn't enough to derail my plans for that night. I wanted to tell Alice how Nadine had ended the story – how her version redeemed Selena Baxter and put the guilt on the preacherman. But Alice was on the touchy side about the horses and the barn. She didn't approve of Nadine. Nadine had a way about her that set Alice's teeth on edge and made her angry. Alice didn't care to talk about it much – didn't care to say Nadine's name, actually. She just stayed away from the barn. When I pressed her for reasons, she said Nadine reminded her of some of her relatives who were mean.

Living with all of those brothers and sisters had given Alice a different appreciation of other people's feelings. She was careful; she looked away when someone was exposed. She had a tender heart and it hurt her to see other people suffer. I guess with so many relatives poking and prying into her business, she valued keeping her private feelings private.

At the barn, feelings were examined, pulled apart. No one was spared. I don't think Nadine realized how the tricks and things she played on me and Jamey and Greg might upset someone like Alice. The truth was, though, Nadine didn't care. She was like that. It was what made her such a great rider.

Fear was Nadine's specialty. She was always saying to confront fear and beat it back. When I was afraid of a jump, she'd raise the standard three more inches. Her logic was that if I was afraid of a three-three jump, then to jump three-six would show me three-three was nothing to fear.

Fear was an ally, she said. Fear kept a rider alert and safe. All good riders felt fear. They just didn't give in to it. So she'd call Jamey Louise and Greg to watch as I jumped the brick wall with a rail set at three-six. They would witness whether I conquered fear or it conquered me. And Cammie and I would jump! And when we landed, I would feel the rush of victory over fear. Nadine would smile and in her eyes would be the look of a victor.

That was exactly the kind of scene that Alice hated. For her, fear and every other emotion were private. When she cried, she wanted no one to see. When she was afraid, she hated the idea of an audience, of a contest won – or lost – in public. She didn't realize that Nadine's way of confronting things was the way she'd learned on the national show circuit. There everything was public. Win or lose. Victory or defeat. She was a competitor.

I tried to smooth things over by inviting Alice to visit Nadine. I was surprised when she reluctantly accepted and agreed on a cloudless Wednesday. More than anything else, I wanted Alice to see how special Cammie was. I planned and planned. Mama Betts made a picnic lunch for us, and Nadine even promised to give Alice a lesson. I was going to pay for it with my work. Even Jamey Louise and Greg were excited by Alice's pending arrival.

As it turned out, Alice didn't have much chance to get to see the horses. Nadine had prepared her own special treat for Alice. She'd spent the entire summer training two barn rats to perform tricks. She'd taught one to eat out of her own mouth.

The first time I saw it, it made me feel a little queasy, but I caught on that Nadine did it just to see if she could unsettle someone. It was a test. And it was something Nadine liked to do in front of Greg.

There were two rats. One of the rats had been domesticated at one time, or so Nadine supposed because he was brown and white. She named him Charlie. The other rat was a grayish brown, and a little bigger than Charlie. He was Ernest. It was Charlie that Nadine had trained to walk up her chest while she reclined in the hay in the loft. First, Nadine would chew up some suitable food and then catch Charlie up and set him just about at her belly button. While she obligingly opened her mouth, the rat crawled up her chest until he put his feet on her chin and eased his head into her open mouth to eat off her tongue.

No matter how many times she did it, I watched in fascination. It was so grotesque that I couldn't stop myself from looking. And even when I didn't want to see it again, I looked.

On the day that Alice visited the barn, Nadine performed. I was hoping she wouldn't, but I could see it in her foxy eyes the minute she saw Alice and Maebelle V. First she asked to hold the baby, and Alice hesitated longer than I'd ever seen her hesitate before giving Maebelle over. Nadine was small but strong, and she lifted Maebelle high in the air and made her laugh.

'Cute baby,' Nadine said, handing her back. 'Let me show you mine.' And she led the way up into the loft.

I tried to catch Alice's eye and warn her, but she was intent on getting up the ladder safely with Maebelle V. in her little papoose. When we were in the loft, Greg came to stand by me, effectively blocking my chance of saying anything private to Alice.

'It's the rats,' Greg whispered. I thought there was a

hint of eagerness in his voice, but when I looked at him he was looking at Alice with concern. 'Nadine, maybe Alice won't like the rats.'

Nadine halted her search in the hay and looked at Greg. 'How is it that you know so much about what Alice likes and dislikes, Greg? Would you like to tell us?'

When he didn't answer, Nadine continued searching in the hay for several minutes before finding Charlie's hiding place. It was odd, but the rat seemed to try to resist. He squirmed and struggled to get free of Nadine's fingers, and then he quit. It was as if he fell under some spell. Once she placed him on her chest, he moved slowly up her ribs and between her breasts, one reluctant paw after the next, until he had both front feet on her chin and his hind feet on the pulse of her throat. Then his mostly white head would dart deep into her mouth and he would eat.

Alice gagged. Before I could say anything to help her, she climbed down the ladder and walked out into the sunshine. 'Why does she do that?' she asked, rubbing her right eyebrow with the back of her hand. 'She's completely crazy, Bekkah. Rats carry all kinds of diseases.'

'It's a test,' I whispered.

'What kind of test?' Hot color jumped beneath her freckled cheeks. 'To see how much someone will put up with before they pick up their things and go home?' She was doing just that as she talked. 'I know you love the horses, Bekkah, and I'm glad you get to ride, but that woman is sick in the head. I won't be coming back here. I don't like this place and I don't like her.'

She walked out of the gate with Maebelle V. bobbing and waving on her back. She latched the gate carefully, picked up her bicycle by the chinaberry tree where I'd parked mine, and she rode home without ever looking back once. She'd never come back and visit, not even to watch me jump. I knew it would be pointless to try to explain it all to Alice. She didn't understand that horse people were different.

So telling her about Nadine's version of Cry Baby Creek would be foolish. Because Nadine had said it, Alice wouldn't appreciate it. Besides, it was better to stay away from the legend if we were going to be sneaking around the old church in the dead of night. Of all the summer nights I'd gone down to the creek deliberately to hear the baby cry, I didn't want this to be one when it happened.

I took great care to make sure everyone in the house thought I was asleep. Getting around Picket was a lot harder than the humans, and Alice and I had decided to take the dog with us as a safety measure. Since all of the Redeemers were in Hattiesburg, there'd be no danger to her. Besides, Picket was a very comforting presence in the dark, and even though Alice and I were old hands at sneaking out of the house on summer nights, going down to the creek to dig up a baby's body was a little different.

When I could hear Mama Betts snoring over the sound of the attic fan, I slipped from the bed and hurried through the kitchen and out the door. I'd worn my shorts and T-shirt to bed, and my sneakers were on the screened porch. It was nearly eleven o'clock. Nobody else on Kali Oka would be awake. Alice and I could slip through the night like enchanted spirits.

Alice was waiting in the woods, her body unusually slender in the moonlight because she wasn't encumbered with Maebelle V. We got our bicycles and kept to the woods for as long as we could before we were forced out into the road.

The night silvered the old fence posts and trees. There was a magical quality about the most familiar mailbox. Even the air seemed sweeter, more filled with scents and noises. I looked at Alice and she grinned as we pedaled our way to adventure. The joy of escape filled us with a wildness that made any risk worth taking. We were free in the night, without the rules of daytime, without the need to be the people we normally were.

I wondered about the creatures that claimed the darkness as their turf. The owl and cat. Daddy had told me that their golden eyes enabled them to see more than other animals. They were nocturnal. And by escaping the bounds of our houses, Alice and I had become like them. Nocturnal creatures filled with the night.

Nothing looked familiar in the strange light of the moon, yet I felt more normal with Alice on Kali Oka Road than I had since the beginning of summer. We passed under the branches of Mrs. Spooner's most prized persimmon tree. In the moonlight the glossy leaves were black and silver, beautiful. Alice and I shared a glance, and a grin.

'We should sneak out every night,' Alice said.

'Maybe we will.' We pumped in unison and moved down the road. Picket seemed caught up in the specialness of the night. She stayed right beside my bicycle, never straying to inspect a yard or to bounce among the briars in search of a rabbit.

We parked our bicycles and found the old shovel I'd hidden. Alice gripped it while I slipped Picket's leash on her. I intended to let her run free just as soon as we made it to the cemetery.

'What if they left someone to guard the church?' Alice asked. We had both come to a stop standing in the road. Neither of us wanted to be the first to step into the cemetery.

I felt my resolve weakening, and I knew I had to do something or we'd both turn around for home. 'They didn't leave any guards. Greg said everyone had to go. There was some kind of vote to be taken.'

'They wouldn't let the children vote.' Alice looked

from the woods to the creek to the church to the cemetery. In the moonlight even her freckles were beautiful.

'They wouldn't leave children here alone.' I grinned in the silvery moonlight. 'We might corrupt them if they were left on their own.'

'I hadn't thought of that.' Alice grinned too. 'If not us, surely Jamey Louise.'

'Greg's a lost cause. Jamey's snatched his soul, and it's going to take more than a little redeeming to save him from the jaws of hell.'

We giggled and together took the first step toward the creek. We simply could not think that we were going to dig up a dead baby. Not even a part of one. Our footsteps were steady as we topped the bridge over Cry Baby Creek. The water, slow because the summer rains of mid-August hadn't arrived yet, gurgled below us. Even in the coolness of the night the water issued a tempting invitation. Maybe after we had our evidence we'd have time for a dip.

Alice must have been thinking the same thing because her steps slowed on the wooden bridge. We both looked over the side. In the moonlight the water was quicksilver.

'I'd forgotten how the creek sings,' Alice said.

The silence of the woods seemed to edge up closer on us. Only the creek made a sound. The hair on my arms trembled, and I tried to think of something to say to keep Alice from noticing how quiet it was.

'Maybe we should have invited Jamey Louise to come with us,' Alice said.

'Jamey? Why should we have?'

'Well, if something gets after us, we can both run faster than her, and we could leave her behind.' Alice giggled again.

She was teasing, but the idea of Jamey Louise as a human sacrifice wasn't half bad. 'Let's go,' I urged, forcing myself to move forward. Together, with a shovel and my dog, we stepped onto the promised land of the Redeemers.

I had no problem remembering which grave. Although weeks had passed, the earth was still raw. We stood looking at the grave. At this distance the creek couldn't be heard. There was only that complete, unnatural silence that made my body hair jerk and quiver.

'Want me to go first?' I asked Alice. We had to get going so we could get home.

She shook her head. 'You go last. I don't want to be the one who actually digs it up.'

I'd brought a knapsack and some old newspaper from the house to wrap it in when we finally got it. I didn't think that was exactly the right thing, but it was the best I could manage without getting Mama Betts to asking all sorts of questions. I hadn't told Alice about the newspapers, which were hidden in the knapsack that was stuffed in my bicycle basket. It was better if she didn't think that far ahead. I didn't want to spook her before we even got started, and the idea of carrying anything dead home in a knapsack would certainly upset her.

Alice put the shovel at the edge of the grave and rested a foot on it as she stared at me. 'Ready?' Her glance darted to the woods, which seemed to have inched even closer to us.

'Go on.' I folded my arms across my chest. Picket sat at my side as if we were part of some religious service.

'You're sure the Redeemers are gone?'

'Come on, Alice. I'm positive. Just get on with it.' My own nerves were jangling and it made me snappy.

Alice jumped on the shovel, and it went in the ground about three inches. The dirt only looked loose and easy to dig. Kali Oka was red clay and sand. Digging anywhere on it wasn't easy, and especially since it hadn't rained for at least two weeks. Alice set to work with all of her wiry strength while I walked around and brushed my fingers over the inscriptions of some of the older tombstones.

Picket heard the noise first. She didn't get up, she just shifted her weight so that she could turn her ears toward the creek. Since she didn't bark or ruffle her fur, I didn't think much about it. Probably a squirrel or something shuffling around in the underbrush attracting her attention.

Alice kept digging, hard-packed inch by inch. She had a little mound of red dirt beside a shallow hole. I knew I could dig faster because I was heavier, but she needed to dig. Her work preoccupied her and she hadn't heard a thing.

She stopped suddenly, shovel half lifted, and looked toward the woods. 'Did you hear something?' she asked.

'Just the normal stuff. What do you suppose Maebelle V. is doing right now?' I had to keep talking. 'I wish I had a flashlight so I could read these tombstones. Arly and I read them once, but he was in a hurry and wouldn't let me really dwell on them. Some of them are so old that the writing is almost worn away.'

'Shussh!' Alice lowered the shovel and waved her hand at me. 'Listen!'

But I didn't want to. We were trespassing, surrounded by dead folks and robbing a grave. It wasn't likely that we were going to hear anything we much wanted to hear, especially not from someone hiding in the woods.

'Alice,' I whispered, but all of her attention was focused just beyond the clearing of the cemetery in the woods.

'Some of these graves have verses, like poetry or Bible sayings. They're really morbid, but some are beautiful. Mama Betts said the graves are much, much older than the church.'

Without taking her eyes off the woods, Alice lowered the shovel. Her right arm came up in a point. Not wanting to but unable to stop myself, I looked down her arm to the tip of her finger and into the woods. There was total blackness.

'I saw something move back in there,' she whispered.

'Don't be silly.' I tried to be stern, but I ended on a giggle. 'You think it's a ghost?'

Alice giggled too. 'I'd rather run up on a ghost than one of those Redeemers,' she said.

That struck me as pretty funny. 'Yeah, those Redeemers are a lot scarier than any ghost.'

'They're truly scary,' Alice said, laughing. 'Remember when you called them zombies?'

I remembered. I glanced around the graves nearest us just to make sure nothing was peeking out to watch us. Alice picked up the shovel again.

'The ground's a lot harder than I thought it would be,' I said. Alice answered with a grunt. It didn't seem possible, but there was a root in her way. She was using the shovel to try to lever it up so we could chop it in half.

Picket had flopped down on her belly in some of the cool red dirt Alice had thrown out. Without any warning she rose slowly to her paws and growled deep in her throat. She was staring directly into the woods, and her hackles rose.

'What is it?' Alice asked. The shovel was under the root, and she was trying to pry it up.

'I don't see anything.' I didn't, but Picket's behavior made my skin crawl with dread. I looked around the cemetery again, checking to be sure no bony fingers were scrabbling to get out of a grave.

'Maybe we should go home,' Alice said. 'We can't dig this up.'

I took the shovel and turned the conversation to the only thing I knew never failed to get Alice's attention. 'Do you think Maebelle thinks you're her mother?'

Alice eyed the woods before she answered. 'I might as well be.'

'Will you get married and have ten children?' The future had become almost a forbidden topic between us, but I broached it as I put the point of the shovel on the root and jumped on it with all of my weight. For a moment the root held, and then the blade sliced cleanly through it.

'Well, I doubt I'll be going to Paris,' she answered. 'I can promise you, though, that I won't have ten children. It isn't fair. Nobody gets enough of anything. There's never any time. It's not like with you, Bekkah. You're special at your house, and what you want matters.' Alice took a seat on a big tombstone.

That painting of Paris with the woman in her red dress walking her poodle replaced the midnight splendor of the old cemetery for a moment. I could tell by the way Alice talked that she'd given up the idea of Paris. For one brief second I hated Kali Oka Road. I hated Paris. I dug with a vengeance.

I was about to jump on the shovel with my full weight when I heard the sound again. It came from the creek, and it was almost a laugh but maybe a sob.

'What was that?' Alice's blue eyes were enormous in the moonlight. Her freckles had disappeared in the whiteness of her face.

'Something at the creek. Some raccoon or something.' It was nothing more than that. The entire time we'd been in the cemetery I'd felt as if someone had put salt under my skin. Alice and I both were making every sound into something terrifying.

I hit the shovel hard, and it slipped through the heavy earth. I turned a big shovelful of red dirt out beside the grave.

'Be careful,' Alice cautioned. 'They didn't put it in a coffin or anything. We don't want to cut it in half.'

I moved out a little farther, making the grave wider.

A low wail came from the creek. It started out soft and mournful, then reached up higher on the register of horror to qualify as something that made the hair on the back of my neck stand up.

Alice abandoned her seat and edged toward me, close enough that I could feel the heat of her body in the sudden chill. Picket rose to a sitting position, ears alert and pricked toward Cry Baby Creek. That was when we heard the infant. At first it was a wail of anger, the shock of cold water on a little warm body. The baby's protest came just after the sound of something small striking the water.

'Holy shit,' I whispered.

'Bekkah! It's the baby! It's Evie!'

Alice's hand gripped my arm and her fingers dug deep. I didn't care. At least Alice's punishing fingers were real. What I saw at the edge of the woods was not. It couldn't be. Picket saw it, though. She stood up, and the hair on her back ruffled as a low growl rumbled in her throat.

'My God,' Alice whispered.

Dark hair streaming about her face and shoulders, a woman stepped out of the woods to stand on the edge of the clearing. She held out her hands in supplication to us. 'My baby,' she cried. 'Please don't hurt my baby.'

Alice's body jerked twice, and I grabbed her wrist with my hand. It felt like she was going to either run away or explode. 'Be still!' I whispered.

'Oh, my God,' Alice moaned. She jerked against my grip. 'I want to go home.' But the woman blocked our way to the bridge. My heart was pounding in my ears so loudly I could barely hear.

'Please,' the woman moaned. 'Help me save my little baby.' She started forward. She wore a white dress that was soaked in what looked to be blood.

Alice screamed, a loud, terrified wail that sliced clean through me. I felt as if I'd been electrified. Picket lunged forward, her teeth bared and a savage snarl coming from deep inside her.

The woman faded back among the trees. 'Help me,' she moaned as she disappeared into the trees. 'Oh, God, someone please help me.'

She was gone.

The sound of a baby crying came from the creek. It was pitiful, the sound of doom.

'The baby!' Alice wailed. She started toward the creek automatically and then stopped. 'What are we going to do?'

I held her arm. 'No! Don't look! It's a trick. There's no baby. It's a ghost. That baby's been dead for ten years.' I was staring at the place in the woods where the woman had disappeared. I had never been so afraid in my entire life. The one thing I knew for certain was that I wasn't going near that creek. I didn't want to see what might be waiting down there for us. What might look back.

We stood for several minutes, too afraid to move at all. My grip on Alice was clammy with sweat. I didn't want to take my eyes off the woods, yet I had to check around the cemetery. I had to be certain all of the graves were still secure.

'What are we going to do?' Alice said, tears in her voice.

'We should go home,' I said.

The baby's cries came from under the bridge.

'No!' Alice backed away from me. She looked from the bridge to the woods. 'I'm not setting foot on the bridge.'

'Maybe we can cross the creek down a little ways from here.' I didn't care which way we went, I only wanted to get home.

'No!' Alice's rejection of that plan was sharp.

'We have to go home!' I insisted as sharply.

A loud and horrible scream came from the woods. 'No! Oh, please, God, save me and my little baby.'

In the ringing silence that followed, Alice stepped back from me. 'I'm not going near that creek.' She gave up her search of the woods long enough to look directly at me. The baby cried, this time weaker and more pitiful. 'No matter what you say, Bekkah, I'm not going near that creek. I'll die here first.'

She meant it. I'd left her once at Cry Baby Creek. I wouldn't do it again. Not even a ghost could make me. 'Okay,' I said. There was no way I was going to spend the rest of the night in a cemetery waiting for something to crawl out of a grave. 'We can stay in the church. Just until daybreak.'

Alice nodded slowly. Arms brushing, we backed our way across the clearing to the front door and pushed it open. Stale air rushed out at us, the smell of the grammar school on the first day. We walked in together, Picket at our side.

Chapter Twenty

I spent the next five hours staring out the same window I'd peeped into the day I watched the singing dwarf. I must have slept, but I don't remember. I was very thirsty. I knew there was a drinking fountain in the corridor behind the sanctuary, but I didn't want to go there. As bad as Selena's ghost had been begging in the woods, I didn't want to see the ghost of the preacherman. Selena was sad. And the preacherman? Sometime during the night I had adopted Nadine's version of the legend of Cry Baby Creek. The preacherman was evil. So I stared out the window and watched, ignoring my dry mouth and the discomfort of the hard pew.

At times I thought I heard the faint crying of a baby, but I couldn't see the creek from my window. I could only be certain that Selena did not come out of the woods again. To my knowledge, Alice, Picket and I were the only presences at the end of Kali Oka Road.

Alice dozed beside me, her hand in Picket's fur. Only her greater fear of Selena and Evie could ever had driven her into the Blood of the Redeemers' sanctuary. Only fear could have drained her to the point that she could sleep on those hard pews. I was too afraid of what might be standing over me when I woke up to trust myself to the helplessness of sleep.

When the pink light of dawn touched the sanctuary

with the first hint of softness, I eased away from Alice's sleeping form. I had the creepy feeling that Jesus crucified on the cross was watching me. Hanging on the wall, he had nothing to do but suffer and watch me. His anguish was so plain, I felt it too. I needed to get outside where I could think.

Picket fell into step beside me as I walked out of the church toward the creek. In the gray wash of dawn there was no sign of Selena in the woods. Even as I looked, the possibility of her made the hair on my arms stand on end. Since I'd had most of the night to think about what had happened, I'd come to a few conclusions. It only made sense that one day we'd see her. If we could hear the crying of little Evie, then it was natural that Selena was not far behind. Whether murderess or helpless victim, she would have been near Cry Baby Creek when Evie died.

Maybe just a few feet inside the woods. Maybe she waited for someone to change history, for someone to save her baby and herself. Maybe she was waiting, and watching, now. My eyes caught a flicker of movement just beyond the trees. I had been staring so hard at them that I had to blink. In that split second I lost whatever had moved. Had it been a white dress gliding through the secret dark of the woods? My muscles clamped down with an unpleasant grip, and I had to force myself to take a step forward into the cemetery.

Our shovel was still lying on the ground near the small grave we'd excavated. In the growing light of dawn, I saw clumps of red clay and several fresh piles of earth scattered around the cemetery. The grave Alice and I had chosen was not the only fresh hole that had been dug. It looked as if several body snatchers had been busy, digging away for corpses. My body shuddered and I tried to push that thought out of my mind. I'd seen too many old movies and read too many scary books. Body snatchers weren't part of Kali Oka Road. They weren't even a part of Jexville.

Even though I'd seen it a hundred times, I found Evie Baxter's grave. The sod there was untouched, a flat surface of grass. My finger traced the contours of a baby angel that had been carved into the face of the granite stone. The inscription read: *And He called the innocents unto Him. Evie Baxter October 18, 1953–October 24, 1953.*

The residents of Kali Oka Road had paid for the tombstone. Mama Betts said everyone on the road had given something toward the cost. The church people moved on after that, but little Evie was left behind on Kali Oka Road. I guess maybe she belonged to the road as much as she'd ever belonged to the church people, or even Selena. Maybe the tombstone was right. Maybe she'd never belonged to anyone except God.

Stepping carefully around the fresh mounds of earth that pocked the cemetery – five newly turned mounds in all – I tried not to look into the woods. I had the creepiest sensation that someone, or something, was watching me closely. If I looked up and saw something, I'd panic. I didn't have time for that now. Alice and I were going to have to get home, and soon. To occupy my mind, I tried to think what had become of Selena. No one had ever told me that part of the story. Selena might still be locked away in Parchman State Prison, where murderers worked in cotton fields that stretched from horizon to horizon.

I'd never personally seen the state prison farm at Parchman that covered twenty-two thousand acres, but Nadine had. She'd described it one day, talking about the long sacks the inmates pulled behind them and filled with cotton as they sweated under the broiling sun. She said the top soil in the Mississippi Delta was eight feet deep and could grow anything, but that cotton was king, even in the 1960s, especially at the prison.

Nadine had volunteered to go there to do some research for a high school paper in her civics class. She'd gone there just to look, because she wanted to see for herself if prison was as bad as everyone thought. She said it was worse. The guards carried bullwhips and sometimes set dogs on prisoners.

The Judge and Effie talked about Parchman too. They said it needed to be reformed. Just recently they had said that Ollie Stanford was headed for Parchman, and he wouldn't be there a week before he'd commit suicide by jumping out of his top bunk with his belt wrapped around his neck and hooked to the bunk bed. The Judge said that type of suicide was a favorite of the Parchman guards. The way he said it, everyone at the dinner table knew Ollie wouldn't hang voluntarily. It would be a 'legal lynching.'

No matter how I turned my thoughts, they always seemed to lurch back toward something gruesome or violent or both. I guess I knew what was waiting for me. Before I woke Alice, I had to look down in Cry Baby Creek. No matter what was there, I had to look.

My mind conjured up terrifying images, and I fought against them with logic. There wouldn't be anything there. Ghosts didn't leave evidence, at least none that could be picked up or touched. Now that daylight was practically a fact, all traces of what we'd seen and heard the night before would be gone. All I had to do was look, and then it could all be over. I'd wake Alice and we'd go home.

My footsteps echoed hollowly on the wooden bridge, and just above the creek I stopped. When I looked down, I wasn't surprised to see the white lace of the christening gown floating in the creek. It was snagged on the root of a tree not three feet from the bridge. I didn't even take off my shoes when I slid down the bank and waded out into the shallow water to retrieve it. My legs were rubbery, and I fell once, sending cold water up to my crotch. I barely felt it, my mind was so set on getting that tatter of lace. When I reached out for it, I expected to look up and see Selena on the bank, or the little baby floating downstream from me, blue with cold and eyes rolled back in its head. But there wasn't anything. I touched the lace to make sure that it was real, and then I took it from the snag. It was very old, fragile in my hands. It felt like cobwebs.

On the bank there wasn't a sign of another human life – and no footprints except for my own. When I got out of the creek I went to the grave Alice and I had tried to dig. Working quickly, I smoothed it over and replaced the sod as best I could. I wanted everything done before I woke Alice. We had to get home. The sun was a third up on the horizon, and if we weren't in bed before everyone got up, we'd be in serious trouble. To sneak out was one thing. To stay out all night was a crime that deserved punishment – as Arly had found out only a few weeks ago.

I didn't think that spending the night in fear at the Blood of the Redeemer's Church would deserve the same punishment as spending the night in the backseat of a car with a snoring Rosie Carpenter, but I didn't want to press the issue. Maybe what I'd done was worse.

I showed Alice the lace clinging to a bit of torn gown when I woke her. She burst into tears.

'We could have saved that baby,' she said.

'There wasn't anything we could do.' But the christening gown belied my denial. I wasn't certain what to think about it. Sure, different folks, mostly teenagers, said they heard the baby crying in the creek. That was the legend. But what about the gown? No one had ever come back with evidence of the dead baby's ghost. And no one had ever reported seeing the mother, all bloody and anguished, pleading for help to save her child. Maybe if we had gone into the night we might have saved that little baby. But that was stupid. Evie Baxter was dead and buried in the churchyard cemetery.

'Hey,' Alice nudged my arm. 'You okay?'

I nodded. The gown was so thin that it was already drying in my hands. It wouldn't have given much protection to a newborn in October, not even on dry land. 'Let's get home.'

Alice ran across the bridge, the shovel in her hand. She was mounted on her bike and pointed toward home before I could even pick mine up out of the dirt.

'What about the grave?' she asked.

'There wasn't anything there. Even if there was, we were digging in the wrong spot.'

'How do you know?'

'There were five other graves. Or at least the ground had been turned. The place we were digging, the sod had just been lifted up. It looked like the right place, but it wasn't.'

Alice looked back over her shoulder at the cemetery. She stared like she was hoping an answer would appear. 'Are you sure?'

'If someone had dug there before us, the root would have been chopped already.' It was true. The question was why had someone made all of those pretend graves. And when?

She nodded. 'I thought about that.' She lifted her weight up on the right pedal and started home. We rode so fast there was no time to talk. When we got to the woods behind my house, breathless and sweating, the sun had inched into the sky.

'Come over this afternoon,' I whispered.

'Okay,' Alice answered as she disappeared down the trail to her house. I ran toward home, praying I could make it inside and duck under the sheets before Mama Betts got up to make breakfast.

I left my wet sneakers on the front porch and tiptoed barefoot back to my room. I'd just closed the door when I heard Mama Betts come out of her bedroom and shut the bathroom door. There was the sound of the toilet flushing and the tap running.

Without bothering with pajamas I tossed my clothes in a corner and slipped beneath the cool sheet. My own bed had never felt better. I looked around my room, taking in the shelves of books and the glass figures of horses that I'd collected for as long as I could remember.

The large gray Percheron The Judge had bought for me on a trip to his relatives in upstate New York was the last thing I remembered seeing.

'Bekkah Rich.'

I heard my name from a long distance. There was a lot of warm, soft cotton between me and my name, and I wrapped myself tighter away from the noise.

'Bekkah! It's nine o'clock. That Mrs. Andrews is sitting out in the yard in that old rusty truck with the motor running. She says you're late for work.'

Reality and panic hit about the same time. I sat bolt upright in bed to find Mama Betts standing beside me, arms akimbo. I could read a lot of things in her expression, but it all boiled down to disapproval. The list of my sins was long – I'd slept way into the morning; Nadine was in the yard; she hadn't gotten out of the truck but had probably blown the horn; she was waiting for me.

I started to throw back the covers, then remembered that I was naked as a jay bird. 'Okay, I'm awake,' I said. 'Please tell Nadine that I'll be there in a few minutes.'

'At least you know how to say please,' Mama Betts said as she left the room. At the doorway she turned around to face me. 'This afternoon I want to talk with you about your shoes.'

'My shoes?'

'Indeed. How did they manage to get sopping wet

209

sitting on the porch all night?'

'Damn!' I whispered as soon as she closed the door. Before I could get into any more trouble, I picked up my dirty clothes and bundled them into a knot. I stuffed them under the mattress as I made my bed, found some clean shorts and a blouse and grabbed another pair of sneakers. If I'd had a bit of sense I would have hidden those shoes. Mama Betts swept the porch every morning. I'd been so tired that I hadn't even stopped to consider that she would find them – and think it strange that they were wet.

I was about to race through the kitchen and out the door when Mama Betts stopped me. 'Here.' She handed me a brown paper sack. 'Take something to eat. You haven't even had any breakfast.'

'Thanks.' I kissed her cheek, breathing in the smell of lemon and vanilla. The sunlight through the kitchen window made her white hair silvery. Even when she was mad at me she couldn't stand the thought that I might be hungry.

'I put enough in there for you to share. You know it's rude to eat in front of others.'

'Thanks, Mama Betts.' I kissed her again, meaning it even more. Mama Betts didn't like Nadine a bit, but she would send her food so I could have some. 'I'll be home soon.'

'Emily Welford called this morning and asked that you stop by to see her on your way home.'

I balked. It was as if my feet refused to step forward, and I almost crashed into the kitchen table. 'Why?'

'She didn't say. But you used to like to stop by and visit Emily and Gus.'

Out the kitchen window I could see Nadine sitting in the truck with the engine idling. Ugly black smoke chugged out of the muffler. 'That was before the jail.' That day in Jexville had soured me on the Welfords.

They'd said things about Effie that couldn't be taken back. I knew Emily Welford had been afraid. Afraid for Effie, and afraid of what she was doing. Like most of the other mamas on Kali Oka and around Chickasaw County, Emily left those kinds of issues to the men folks. And especially Mama going down to a jail cell with a Negro man. It was a shocking thing to Emily. But Effie had been in trouble.

'Emily wrote your mother a letter. She was afraid for you, Bekkah. She knows how headstrong you can be, and how much trouble you can get into. She did her best.'

'Maybe you think so. If it had been left up to Mrs. Welford, Effie could have been hurt and bleeding to death. None of those people would do a damn thing to help.'

'Rebekah Rich! I won't have a child cursing in my home.'

I bolted out the door, letting the screen shut behind me. I was angry with Emily Welford, that was true. But I was also leery of talking with her. She was going to ask me questions about Jamey, and I didn't want to answer them. Most of all, I didn't want to lie.

'You look like you've been rode hard and put away wet,' Nadine said as I climbed into the cab.

'The day just got off on the wrong foot.'

'Looks like you didn't get much sleep.'

'Not much.' I stared out the truck window as Nadine drove.

'Looks like maybe you've discovered the pleasures of the flesh,' Nadine said. She was grinning to herself as she drove the old pickup with no attempt to avoid the washboard ruts.

I knew she was talking about fornicating, because she was always teasing Greg about sampling the pleasures of the flesh in regard to Jamey Louise. The idea of spending the night doing that was so far removed from what I'd been doing that I wanted to blast her with a scorching reply. 'I'm not so simple-minded I have to fuck some boy to entertain myself,' I snapped. 'I'm not Jamey Louise.'

'Boy-ee!' Nadine slammed the steering wheel with the butt of her hand. 'Only guilt will give a girl a reaction like that. Was he good, Bekkah? Did he make your bottom wink?'

The lack of sleep and the horror of the whole night made me suddenly too tired to argue. 'Have it your way, Nadine. I screwed my brains out.' I'd heard that one from Arly talking on the phone to one of his buddies. They lied all the time about what they did, and I knew for a fact Arly didn't have any brains, so he couldn't have ever screwed them out.

'Looks like you won't be fit to work or ride today,' Nadine said, her foxy eyes bright with amusement. 'Nope, I guess you rode a new stallion last night.'

'Right,' I answered. The day was already hot. Too hot. Black specks floated on the edge of my vision. I let out a startled cry as Nadine drove past the driveway to the old McInnis place. 'Hey! Where are we going?'

'You got me so interested in that Cry Baby Creek, I thought we'd drive down there and take a look. You aren't worth a hoot in hell for working. Maybe we'll just have ourselves a little adventure. Go ghost hunting.'

My stomach clutched. I was glad I hadn't eaten any of the breakfast Mama Betts had made.

'You haven't seen any of those Redeemers coming home yet, have you?' Nadine asked.

I shook my head no. I remembered the scrap of lace in the pocket of my shorts. I could only pray Mama Betts wouldn't decide to change the linens on my bed and find my dirty clothes. I was in enough hot water already. And I didn't want to go back to Cry Baby Creek.

'Something wrong?' Nadine asked, slowing the truck slightly.

'Couldn't we just go to the barn? I have a lot of work to do today, and Mama Betts has some chores for me this afternoon when I get home. She told me not to be late.'

'Jamey Louise volunteered to do all your chores for you.' Nadine hit the gas pedal again. 'Wasn't that sweet?'

'Hah! Jamey wouldn't give me the time of day.'

'Let's just say that I convinced her she wanted to clean your stalls.'

'I'm surprised she showed up for work at all since Greg's out of town.' The truck rattled down the road. It hadn't rained in over two weeks, and the red dust blew out behind us in a thick cloud. 'Her mama wants me to come talk to her this afternoon.'

'What are you going to tell Mrs. Welford?' Nadine cast a quick look at me.

I couldn't read her expression, but she knew that Emily Welford was going to ask me about what went on at Nadine's barn. Jamey didn't earn enough money to warrant working so hard. Over the course of the summer her arms had developed muscle and her legs were stronger. For the first time in her life she was working, and she was there every day.

What was I going to say? 'She knows that Jamey doesn't care enough about horses to work just to be around them.'

'It took her all summer to figure that out?'

'Maybe she's not the smartest critter upright and walking.'

Nadine laughed. 'Is it your mama or grandmama who says such things about people?'

'Both.' It was true. When the tongues started wagging around the dinner table, sometimes the comments got sharp. Nobody in our family, not even The Judge, had much tolerance for stupidity. Or mediocrity. Effie was always telling me that there were two things any person could accomplish – mediocrity and marriage. She said

213

even badness took a little more imagination. I started to tell all of this to Nadine, but then I remembered she had three marriages under her belt. She might think I was drawing some kind of comparison.

'So, what are you going to tell her?'

'That . . . we work real hard and don't have a lot of time to talk.'

Nadine grinned. 'Will that satisfy her?'

'I'm hoping. At least until I get off the property.'

Nadine pulled the truck over in the deep sand by the side of the road. One more curve and the bridge over Cry Baby Creek would be in sight.

'Why don't we ride the horses down here tomorrow?' she asked.

'Can we?' The idea was the best I'd ever heard. Sometimes I dreamed about riding down the road or through the woods. I could feel the flickering pattern of sunlight and shade on my skin during the dream. I could smell the pines and the cleanness of the suncharged air. But I'd never dared to hope that Nadine would actually let me ride Cammie down the road. She didn't like trail riding, as she called it. She said it ruined a horse's concentration for ring work.

'Tomorrow, if it doesn't rain.'

I automatically looked up at a sky that heat had almost burned the blue out of. Not much chance of rain. Relief was a physical sensation. 'Then let's get back to the barn. I really have a lot to do.' Just being that close to Cry Baby Creek made me antsy.

'We'll ride here tomorrow.' Nadine slipped the keys from the ignition. 'Today we're going to look for that ghost you're always talking about. That little baby that was murdered by the preacherman. We won't have another chance, Bekkah. The Redeemers are bound to be back in a day or two.'

'I don't know . . . ' I did know, and what I knew was

that I didn't want to set foot on the property again. I wanted to go home, to be with Mama and Mama Betts.

'You're not afraid, are you?' Nadine asked. 'You look a little pale, Bekkah.' She laughed and focused her bright eyes on me, taking in every detail. 'You look like you've seen a ghost.'

'I really want to go home.'

'Jamey Louise said you'd back out at the last minute.' Nadine jumped the keys in her hand a few times. 'She said you had always been a baby, afraid of the dark. She said you were yellow through and through. I guess we can just drive back to the barn and tell her she was right.'

'Let's go,' I said, not looking in Nadine's eyes for fear she'd see that I was afraid.

We got out of the truck and started toward the creek. 'What do you think you're going to see?' I asked. Nadine had never shown enough interest to drive down to the creek before.

'Well, since the Redeemers are gone, I thought maybe we'd explore.'

'You mean go inside the church?'

'Haven't you ever done it before?'

'When it was abandoned, Arly and I used to come down here. And Alice too. But nobody was living here then.' Reluctance tinged my voice. It didn't seem right to go on someone else's property when they weren't home. The night before, Alice and I hadn't had a choice. But we'd stayed just in the sanctuary, and we hadn't touched a thing. We weren't poking around in the Redeemers' private things. Nadine worried me. She hadn't been raised exactly the same way Alice and I had.

'Jamey Louise said you'd be too afraid to go inside. She said you were scared of my barn.'

'I am not.'

'Good. Let's go.'

Nadine didn't give me a chance to say no. She started

toward the creek and marched right over the bridge. She didn't even stop to look or listen before she pushed open the door of the sanctuary and went in. The door closed behind her while I stood on the bridge and watched. I had a powerful urge to walk home. Whatever Nadine was doing in that church, I didn't want to know. She had an edge to her, something just a little bit wild. I'd sensed it before, but never to the point where it bothered me like this. Sometimes when I was riding Cammie I felt that she was putting the jumps high because I might not be able to make it. The risk excited her. It excited me, too, but it also was a little frightening. I felt the same way now, but it was worse. I wasn't sure what Nadine was capable of doing.

Standing on the bridge wasn't going to solve anything. I went after her. Maybe when she saw there wasn't anything interesting in the church she'd leave.

When I pushed open the door, the stillness of the sanctuary rushed at me. The night before it had been different. At first I didn't see Nadine. She was standing at the foot of the crucified Jesus, staring up at it.

'These people are really sick. Who would want to worship something like this?'

She didn't really expect an answer from me, so I walked up behind her and stood without saying a word. Up close and in the bright light, I could see the cords in Jesus's neck as the drops of blood slipped down his face from the crown of thorns. His palms were split by heavy wooden spikes.

Sitting in the Sweet Water Methodist Church during Easter services, I'd always wondered why Jesus' hands didn't pull loose from the spikes when they nailed him on the cross. The weight of his body should have dragged him free.

The Blood of the Redeemers had taken care of that. Their Jesus was nailed *and* tied, his upper arms secured to the crossbar. Both feet were held with a single spike, and there was a bright red splotch of blood on the rag wrapped around his waist where the soldier had pierced him with a spear. All that was missing was the sponge filled with vinegar – a final cruelty for a dying man who had begged for water.

'How could anyone find anything of comfort or peace in this?' Nadine pointed at the crucifix. 'This is barbaric. These people love blood and suffering. Redemption has nothing to do with what they crave. The real show is suffering and sacrifice.'

Nadine took a step closer, and I held my breath. I felt like an intruder, someone who'd stumbled into the middle of something extremely personal. In a way it was like watching Nadine with the rats. I knew what I was seeing was not right, yet I couldn't look away. I was fascinated by her upturned face, the way she stared at the crucifix with what might be hatred, or maybe love.

'Nadine,' I whispered, 'let's go.' She was entranced by the crucifix. I thought she might reach up to touch it. Maybe even kiss it. Or else tear it apart.

'Nadine.' I started to touch her arm but stopped. 'Let's go home.'

'It's odd, isn't it? Have you ever seen a fat Jesus?' She turned around and looked at me, her foxy eyes filled with amusement. There wasn't a glimmer of the other emotion she'd just shown. 'A fat Jesus,' she repeated. 'Why is it that Jesus always has a perfect body? You know, the golden blond hair, even though he was a Jew, blue eyes, perfect body.'

'Because he's Jesus.' It was the only answer I had.

'Don't you think niggers think Jesus is black?'

'Negroes? Do they?' I'd never stopped to consider such a thing. Somehow it made me nervous, and I looked around to see if anyone had slipped up to the windows to stare at us.

'Well, it seems to me they'd think he looked like them.'

'Let's go to the barn,' I urged her. The sanctuary was charged with a feeling of impending doom. Any minute the Redeemers would return. They'd find Nadine and me inside their church and they'd . . . the least they'd do would be to tell Effie and Mama Betts.

'We haven't even looked to see where they live yet. Don't you want to know where Greg sleeps? I mean, maybe they all just get in one big room and screw as the mood strikes.'

Nadine was filling my head with wild images. 'We should leave. We don't have a right to look at their private things.'

'You stay here, then,' Nadine said. 'I've got every right.'

She went behind the piano and pushed open the door that led back to the Sunday school rooms and the hallway to the parsonage. I knew it from the days when Arly and Alice and I had spent time playing in the old church. I heard two footsteps on the linoleum, then she paused. 'Keep an eye on those windows, Bekkah. The ones facing the woods. I thought I caught a glimpse of someone standing at the edge of the woods. A woman, I think.' Her footsteps echoed away.

I ran after her. The least I could do was to keep an eye on her. She was standing in the doorway of what used to be an old Sunday school room. I remembered it when it was filled with long wooden tables and little chairs. Modeling clay and toys had once been available. Now there were mattresses all over the floor. Blue ticking peeked out from under gray sheets, and the smell of piss permeated the room. Clothes were hanging from two-penny nails that had been driven all around the room. Men's, women's, children's. At least twenty people slept on the floor, and some of them obviously wet the bed.

'It's a commune,' Nadine said. 'I'll be damned.'

I remembered the word, and I knew that it meant that all of them lived as one big family. But it was Nadine who'd supplied the true meaning of that word. 'Can you believe it? They all live here, screwing and pissing at their pleasure. All together in this one room.'

I turned away. 'Nadine, please, let's go. I don't like it here.' There was something about Nadine that bothered me too. She was always talking dirty in the barn, teasing and needling Greg and Jamey. This was different, though. She made the words sound dirtier here. Maybe it was just because we were in a church.

'Just be thankful you don't have to live in this shit. Can you imagine? No wonder Greg wants to stay at the barn. At least he doesn't have to witness . . . ' She cast her arm about the room. 'This!'

I touched her shoulder. 'Please, let's go. We shouldn't be here. We could get into serious trouble. Nadine, if this preacherman is the old one, the one who was here before, he could hurt us. He killed Evie.'

She turned to me. 'Did he, now?'

I nodded. 'I think you're right. I think he killed little Evie. Selena wouldn't have done that.' I leaned closer, my voice dropping to an urgent whisper. 'Please, let's get out of here. This place gives me the creeps.'

'Maybe we can get that old preacherman to come out,' Nadine said. She looked up and down the hall. 'Mr. Preacherman! Mr. Preacherman! Come out here.'

'Nadine!' I grabbed her arm hard. 'Don't do that!'

'Mr. Preacherman, there's a young girl right here with me wants to ask you some questions. Maybe you could . . . convert her.'

Her foxy eyes were glowing with amusement. Even as she looked at me, she shifted her gaze over my head, as if she saw something down at the end of the hall.

Involuntarily I stepped closer to her and grabbed her arm hard. 'We shouldn't be here.' I tried to hide my fear.

'Nobody'll ever know, unless you tell them.'

'Nadine, please take me home. Now.'

'Bekkah Rich, you're acting like a baby.'

'I don't care. We shouldn't be here. The Redeemers aren't the only things we have to worry about.'

If Nadine heard me, it didn't register. 'Let's look around the rest of the place.' She walked out of my grasp and went on down the hall.

There were five more old Sunday school rooms converted to mass bedrooms. A couple of showers had been rigged up in the bathrooms, and the smell of stale urine was even stronger here. It must have been awful trying to get up in the morning and get into the bathroom. At our house, with only five of us, there was usually a fight between Arly and me. I made a promise that when I got home, I wouldn't complain so much about the minor inconveniences. *If* I got home, I'd do a lot of things differently. Effie and Mama Betts were going to see a change.

We went on down the hall, Nadine leading and me lagging behind, until we opened the door to the preacherman's living area.

'Well, well,' Nadine said softly. 'Looks like being the leader of the pack has certain advantages. In this congregation being the shepherd is certainly preferable to being part of the flock.'

We walked in through the kitchen, which had an oven and a coffeepot. There were little straw trivets hanging, bright green, pink and yellow, around on the wall, evidence that someone had decorated for him.

The dining-room table was covered in papers, which Nadine riffled through without any hesitation. I held my breath and watched as she picked them up at random.

'Looks like a lot of church business,' she said. 'There're receipts for building supplies, charts for working.' She tossed them back and picked up another bundle.

'Nadine, that's private business.' The rule at our house was inviolable. No one touched Effie's manuscripts or The Judge's private papers. No one read anybody else's mail. Arly and I didn't get much mail, but I kept a diary on and off. Those things were personal. We could leave them in our room and know that no one would ever pry into them. Now Nadine was opening envelopes and reading away, as if she had every right. And the expression on her face notched my own worries up higher and higher.

'Fucking bastard,' she said clearly as she tossed a letter on the table. 'Mother fucker.' Her brown eyes pierced me and went straight through.

She swept the table clean with one long arm. Then she stood up and walked to the door. She didn't tarry long in the den area, which didn't have a television or a radio. She went back to the bedroom. There was a real bed in a bed frame, a chest of drawers and a closet filled with dark suits and two spare pair of shoes. I stood in the doorway and kept an eye on her. I couldn't stop her, and I couldn't leave.

'Well, well, the preacherman gets to have a few luxuries. I wonder if that's compensation for preaching or playing the stud.'

I looked around. I didn't understand. And I didn't say anything. Nadine was white-hot fury. I could see it in the way she walked, hips thrust forward and arms deceptively dangly at her side.

She went to the chest of drawers and pulled out the top drawer. 'Silk,' she commented as she held up a white shirt. 'Reverend Marcus has classy taste.' She shut that drawer and opened the next, going through each one. There were silk shirts, expensive underclothes and socks, all made by manufacturers Nadine knew. She said they were exclusive. In the bottom drawer she found several cheap sexy nightgowns. She held them up for me to see.

'Wonder what preacherman's doing with sexy sleepwear in his room? Think maybe he's fucking a few of the cows in his congregation?' She arched her brows at me. 'More likely it would be a few of the heifers, don't you think?'

I could only think of Magdeline, and I wanted to vomit. I kept hearing footsteps coming down the hall toward us. It didn't matter much to me if it was a ghost or the congregation coming back. The Redeemers wouldn't ever let us go. We knew too many of the preacherman's secrets.

With an expert flip Nadine tossed the mattress off the bed. Her arm swept across the top of the chest of drawers, knocking a bottle of men's cologne against the wall with a crash.

'Hey!' I called out, but it was too late. She bent over the box springs and came up with a small notebook in her hand. Her eyes were all sly. 'I found it,' she said softly, and sat down on the box springs to examine the papers. 'I knew he wouldn't leave it out on the table.'

I wanted to run and escape, but instead I walked to the bed and sat down beside her. The notebook was written in black ink. There were names and dates and addresses, and to the side an amount of money. 'What is it?'

'Just a record of babies who've been sold. The Redeemers are what you might call a breeding colony. I knew it all along!' There was victory in her voice.

I stood up and backed away from the bed. 'Put it back, Nadine. Let's fix the bed and get out of here.'

Now I knew we were deep in it. Nadine had the look of a person with a high fever. Her face was flushed and her eyes slightly glazed. I didn't know if she'd be able to drive the truck home or not. I could drive an automatic but not a shift. I wasn't even certain I could get her to the truck. All I knew was that I didn't want to stay in Reverend Marcus's place another minute.

Nadine tucked the lists in her pocket.

'Put those back!' I had to make her think about what she was doing. 'Nadine, if he comes back here and finds those lists gone, he'll know we were here.'

Her eyes focused on me and they seemed to clear. 'You're right. I'll have to copy this information.'

'We don't have time!' I went to her and grabbed her arm. I pulled with all my strength, bringing her to her feet. 'Help me with that mattress.'

Together we managed to put the bed back together. I smoothed the spread until it looked the way it had when we first entered the room. Then I made sure all of the drawers were closed properly. The preacherman was neat. He wouldn't leave any edges poking out of his drawers. I picked up the cologne and put it back on the chest of drawers. Some had spilled, but the bottle hadn't broken.

Nadine had taken a seat in a straight-back chair beside the bed, and she was copying the lists onto a spare piece of paper.

'I'm going to check and make sure everything else is just the way we found it,' I said. 'When I finish, we're leaving here.'

'Okay.'

She didn't look up, just copied away.

I tried to arrange the papers on the kitchen table just the way they'd been. That was the only other thing we'd touched. Walking down the hall, I paused at a door we hadn't opened. We'd gone so far, why not the rest of the way? I asked myself. I swung the door open and stood, rooted to the spot.

There was a narrow table covered in a starched white sheet. Beside the bed were two enormous tin bowls filled with towels. The room was antiseptic white, like Dr. McMillan's office in Jexville. There was a glass cabinet filled with medicines and a counter with some gruesome-looking tools and scissors. I recognized the scissors as the kind the doctor used to cut off bandages and things like that. Beside the scissors were several syringes.

My gaze swung back to the examining table. At the end, facing me, were two metal holders. Stirrups. Jamey's sister, Libby, had been to Mobile to some special kind of female doctor. He'd put her feet in stirrups, just like women who had babies. My stomach flipped and a chill raced up my spine until the hair on the nape of my neck stood straight on end.

It registered on me that there were no windows in this room. There had been one, but it was bricked up so that not even a trace of outside light filtered in. That was more horrible than anything else.

I closed the door before I started screaming. Five steps down the hall was another room we hadn't explored. I pushed it open to reveal a cot and a throw rug beside it. The only other furniture was a nightstand with a Bible on it. The room looked like one of the prison cells I'd seen on television. I told myself that what I was seeing wasn't real. It was like a movie that somehow I'd gotten started in my head and couldn't stop. That helped for a minute, until I imagined Magdeline in that antiseptic room. Once I thought of her, I knew I had to get out. The walls were closing in on me, very slowly and without a sound, but it was happening.

'Nadine, let's go,' I called down the hall to her. I couldn't believe I'd spoken. I hadn't intended to, and it didn't sound like me.

To my surprise, she came out of the preacherman's room and closed the door. 'Five babies, Bekkah. Just this summer. Five. And before they came here, there were others.'

'Did you put the list back?' I had to think clearly. We couldn't leave a trace that we'd been here. What we had found was frightening. I didn't completely believe it.

Nadine was good at making things up. She had a list, but that was all. And the rooms? Maybe they were just for sick people. With so many people living at the church, there was bound to be a lot of sickness.

Nadine waved the copy of the list at me. 'Put it just under the mattress, the way it was. Let's go.'

Nadine led the way through the house, back into the hallway and back to the sanctuary. I didn't notice she carried something else in her right hand until we were walking under the Jesus on the cross.

'Wait for me in the truck,' she said, and she sounded normal, like the old Nadine.

For a second I hesitated. She was staring at the crucifix again. I had no responsibility to protect the Redeemers from anything Nadine chose to do. The starched white sheet on the high, narrow table had relieved me of any charge of responsibility.

The sun was hot on my cool skin, and I realized I was sweating a lot. It had run down my back and soaked into my shorts, but my skin was still very cold.

Almost dazed, I stumbled toward the cemetery. The rawness of a fresh grave made me catch my breath. There was a pile of red dirt almost a foot high, with an old shovel sticking out of it.

'No,' I said, denying it even though I could clearly see it. Someone had been out in the cemetery digging while Nadine and I had been in the preacherman's home. Had they seen us? I dropped behind a tombstone and looked all around. There wasn't a sign of anyone.

I didn't want to, but I couldn't help myself. I crept toward the grave.

'Oh, no.' The words escaped with my last lungful of air. The open grave belonged to Evie Baxter. Somebody had dug up the dead baby's grave.

I think my intention was to put the dirt back. I grabbed the shovel and lifted a heap. When I looked down in the open grave, there was a little white christening gown lying in the hole. I dropped the shovel and the dirt and knelt down to pull the gown out. It was still damp, as if it had just come from the creek.

I struggled to my feet and stumbled out of the cemetery, the gown clutched in my hand. At the truck I leaned my head on my arms against the burning hood. I stayed there until my arms felt like they were going to catch fire. When I finally looked up, Nadine was coming around the curve. She was jogging and grinning.

'Let's go,' she said as she hopped into the driver's seat. She spun the truck around in the loose sand, not a bit concerned that she might get stuck. When we were headed toward the barn, she looked at me, not even noticing the white rag I held in my hand. 'Don't tell a soul we were there, okay? You can't ever tell, Bekkah, or we could both go to prison.'

Chapter Twenty-one

For the first time all summer, I contemplated voluntarily giving up my riding lesson. Jamey Louise was cleaning my last stall, so I told her I didn't feel well and I was going home.

'You look like dog poo that someone set on fire and stomped,' she said, leaning on her manure rake. Her head was tied in a bandanna, and there wasn't a scrap of makeup on her face. During the summer she'd lost the little bit of baby fat she'd started with, and her body was lean and better-looking than it had ever been. Maybe that was why Jamey Louise worked more willingly than she ever had before. She also said that her cup size had increased from a B to a C. And she'd turned thirteen.

Nadine had disappeared into her house and didn't come back out. I gave Jamey the breakfast Mama Betts had packed, and she settled down in the shade of the barn to eat the bacon biscuits with homemade scuppernong jelly. Even Jamey was smart enough to realize Mama Betts made the best biscuits in the world.

I went to the back door and knocked real hard, but there wasn't a sound inside. Nadine's dogs never barked. I couldn't imagine how she kept them so quiet. Picket would have torn the screen down trying to get at someone at our back door.

I knocked again and stepped back away from the house. It stank. Mama Betts was right that Nadine didn't keep a clean house. The trash piles had grown and grown over the summer. Kali Oka Road didn't have garbage pickup like Jexville had, but Nadine owned a truck and she could have taken her garbage to the dump. But she didn't.

It smelled like something had died in the kitchen, and I backed up a few more steps. I sure hoped she didn't ask me and Jamey to clean up the garbage mess. Shoveling horse manure wasn't bad. The smell coming from Nadine's house was enough to gag a maggot, as Arly was always saying.

On the third try, when Nadine never came to the door, I gave up and started walking home. It seemed like it took forever to make the short walk, especially when I got close to the Welford place.

Mrs. Emily Welford was the last person I wanted to see, so I just kept walking toward the house until I passed under the grancy graybeard tree and slipped into the old swing The Judge had made for me in one of the oak trees. Arly and I hadn't played parachuter a single time this summer. It was a game where we'd swing as high as we could and then jump out when the swing was at its highest point. We'd mark where we landed. The farthest parachuter won the game.

I smelled the delicious lemony scent of Mama Betts before I heard her.

'Bekkah, are you sick?'

'Maybe a little.' I was. My head ached and my stomach jumped and twisted. 'Maybe I'm just tired.'

'Where were you last night?'

'Alice and I went down to Cry Baby Creek.' The urge to confess was almost more than I could bear, but I couldn't. 'We were looking for the baby.'

'Come in the house and I'll make you some soup. You look positively gray, child. You don't have a bit of color.'

228

I followed Mama Betts like a puppy. 'Where's Effie?'

'Your father's coming home. She went to the airport to get him.'

'Daddy's coming home? For good?' It was too much to hope for. But even The Judge couldn't fix what Nadine and I had discovered.

'For the weekend.' Mama Betts gave me a look that took in a lot of territory.

'And Arly? Where's he?'

'He's working over at Arnett's Nursery this afternoon.'

No one would be home but me and Mama Betts. 'Can I have my soup on the sofa and watch *The Edge of Night* with you?'

She stopped walking and turned around to look at me. 'Of course. You must be feeling mighty bad.'

I nodded. 'I am.'

'Are you sick or guilty?' she asked, her blue eyes watching.

'Both.'

'Then you have some soup and a nap first, and then we'll talk.'

At last the tears came. They filled my eyes and spilled down my cheeks, but I never made a sound.

'Whatever you've done, Bekkah, it couldn't be that bad.'

No matter what I'd done, Mama Betts would never think the worst of me. 'I think I'm going to be sick,' I whispered.

'Sick in body or sick in spirit?'

'I can't tell.' I got a grip on my tears and fought them back. What would I tell my grandmother, if I could? That I'd been digging in graves in a church cemetery? That I'd broken into a church and torn up a preacher's bedroom with Nadine? That I thought maybe the Redeemers were selling babies because Nadine said so? And I wasn't even sure of that because she'd told

229

me not to tell anyone or we could go to prison. Surely Nadine would have to call the police if it were true. Mama Betts' hand on my forehead brushed back my hot hair. She lifted my chin and stared down at me through her thick glasses.

'No matter what it is, I'll still love you, and Effie and Walt too. Now stop crying in this heat or you'll make yourself throw up.'

I wiped the tears off my face with the back of my hand. I felt her arm around me, pulling me up against her stomach and bosom. The lemony smell was stronger than usual.

'I made your daddy a lemon pie,' she said. 'Just the way he likes them with meringue four inches high. That'll put him in a good mood.' She hugged me to her side as we walked across the lawn. 'I think Effie and Walt have been neglecting you lately. You've been so busy at that barn we haven't gone swimming or made ice cream. Maybe we should do that.'

I was afraid if I tried to talk I'd start crying again, so I nodded.

'Let's do that tomorrow. We'll all go to the Escatawpa River where it's really deep enough to swim. We'll take a picnic and that old hand-crank ice-cream machine, and we'll have us a time. Does that sound good?'

In the back of my mind I remembered Nadine's promise to take Cammie for a ride down the road. It didn't matter. I wanted to be with Mama Betts and Effie. I wanted The Judge to show me how to do the different strokes in the medley races. I even wanted to see Arly.

'That sounds great.' My voice was shaky, but it held.

'Can you get off work?'

'Yes.'

'Then it's settled. I'm declaring tomorrow a holiday. Nobody works, not even you or Arly. It's going to be a

230

family day like we haven't had in too long. Maybe after *The Edge of Night* you can help me peel some potatoes for a salad. And I'll fry up some chicken. I'll even make another batch of biscuits and some baked beans.'

'Can Alice come?'

'The child's practically family. Of course she can.'

Chapter Twenty-two

I stayed away from Nadine's for the next three days. Mama Betts and I had our picnic, with Effie, The Judge, Arly, Alice, and Maebelle V. Effie and Mama Betts took care of the baby so Alice and I could swim. Arly did his best to pester us to death, but we were having such a good time, we wouldn't let him ruin it. I kept looking for a chance to talk with The Judge, but there was never a moment when we could slip away privately without making it obvious. He and Effie were thick as thieves.

I was afraid, too, of what I'd done and what I hadn't done. Daddy was only home for a few days, and then he would be gone. I knew the bitter disappointment he would feel, and I didn't want to tell him when he was going away. Truth was, I didn't know how to tell him. So for that short trip to the river, I let myself pretend that nothing had changed on Kali Oka Road.

The Escatawpa is one of the prettiest rivers in our part of the state. Alabama and Mississippi argue about who owns it – until it's time to improve the bridge. Then nobody wants it and the narrow, deadly bridge on Bloody Highway 98 never gets repaired. But we were upriver from the bridge, and we weren't concerned about political problems. We had cold water, hot sun and good food.

Neither Mama Betts nor Effie questioned me about not going to Nadine's. And Nadine didn't come up to the house, truck motor burping black smoke, saying I was late for work.

I helped Mama Betts in the kitchen and with her plants. When it got too hot to be outside, I lay on the sofa with my head in Effie's lap and read. It was like I'd gone back to being a really young child. Nobody seemed to care that I'd abandoned growing up, least of all me. If I wasn't old enough to understand what I'd seen at the end of Kali Oka Road, then I didn't have to tell about it. I could try to forget.

The Judge went back to Missouri, relieving me of opportunity to tell, and Alice and I played until night put an end to our visibility. We swung in the swing and hunted doodle bugs and even played Movie Star Hopscotch and jump rope. Maebelle V. would crawl around, eating grass and bugs. None of it seemed to hurt her, and she laughed about it all. We played at badminton until the baby crawled into the middle of our imaginary court. Then we'd stop and tickle her until she slobbered all over herself. Mama Betts would come out in the yard and rescue her when she thought we'd gotten too rough.

I hadn't told Alice yet about my trip to the church with Nadine. It was so ugly and frightening, I didn't want her to have to know about it. If I could have wiped it from my brain, I would have. And I tried. But my efforts to close my mind to what I'd experienced weren't working. I couldn't get the picture of that room with the table and doctor's tools out of my head. It got all mixed up with the crucified Jesus in my dreams. If I told Alice, it would only make her feel bad too. As it was, she didn't say anything about Cry Baby Creek, the Redeemers or the ghost we'd seen. We were both trying not to remember certain things.

The Redeemers had been gone for four nights, and there was no sign that they were coming back. Maybe they'd moved on. Maybe they wouldn't be back to Kali

Oka Road. I kept my fingers crossed and prayed that such was the case.

It was Wednesday when the old buses came rumbling by in dust even thicker than when they'd first arrived. Alice and I were sucking on lemons that we'd sprinkled with grape Kool-aid and sugar. Mama Betts said the lemons would eat the enamel off our teeth, but she let us have them anyway.

'I wonder if they know they live in a haunted church?' Alice asked. She picked Maebelle V. out of a clump of wild onions and instinctively pulled her to her chest. Happily unaware that she now stank to high heaven, Maebelle grinned, showing off the nub of her first tooth.

'I don't think they care.' The buses churned down the road. My stomach churned a bit itself. I'd really begun to hope they were gone. I'd prayed harder than I'd ever prayed before.

'Well, they can come back as long as they stay down at the end of the road.' Alice rocked the baby on her hip. 'We don't have to associate with them. Let Jamey Louise have all of them she wants.'

I didn't say anything, but I knew I'd be going back to the barn the next morning. Greg would be at work. I had to see how Nadine treated him.

'Want to go to the spring and take a bath?' Alice held up Maebelle V. to display the purple Kool-aid drool that had covered her little chest. We'd taken her shirt off to avoid ruining it.

'Sure. I'll bet Picket would like that too.' I whistled up my dog, and we all set off for the woods and a bath in the spring.

The next morning I got up early and got ready to go to work at the barn. Mama Betts didn't say anything, she just handed me my breakfast and then started making sandwiches for a lunch.

'Soon your daddy will be home for good, except for the days he has to go to Hattiesburg to teach. That'll be a good thing, won't it?'

'I'll be glad,' I said, wondering what she was getting at.

'When Walt gets home, maybe the two of you can have some time to talk.'

'Maybe.' I jiggled the brown paper sack with my lunch. 'I'd better go.'

'Bekkah, we never did talk about those wet shoes of yours. I sort of drew a parallel between those shoes and your sudden desire to hang around the house. Maybe you'll tell Walt what you saw down at Cry Baby Creek in the dead of night.'

'Maybe,' I answered, but this one had a definite hesitation in it.

'Think on it,' she said. 'Since you can't tell me or Effie, maybe you can tell your daddy.'

'Maybe there's nothing to tell.'

'Maybe cows can fly.' She turned her blue gaze away from the stove long enough to look at me.

I swallowed twice. I couldn't think of a single thing to say.

'Be careful,' Mama Betts said as she kissed the top of my head. 'Your mama and I are going to Mobile today to do some school shopping. Is there anything you want?'

'Notebooks. Pencils.' Damn! I wanted to go too. 'Is Arly going?'

'He needs some shoes and shirts and a couple of pairs of new jeans. He said he wanted to go. He doesn't want those jeans that bag in the butt.' She was laughing at him.

'I need socks and . . . ' I'd escaped the trip to the Dale Shop for a bra only because Effie had gotten busy with another book. This shopping trip would surely remind her. And Alice said she was going to start wearing stockings to school. She said she was grown up enough, and she had her older sister's garter belt and some old hose. I'd looked at the contraption, and it didn't seem worth the effort. Just to be on the safe side, we'd both agreed to take a razor from our houses and to meet at the spring and shave our legs the day before school started. Alice said nobody went to seventh grade with hairy legs, and I'd noticed Jamey Louise was already shaving hers.

'Socks and what else?' Mama Betts waited expectantly.

'Can we wear shorts in seventh grade?'

'No.'

'Jeans?'

'Not girls.'

'We have to wear dresses?' This was worse than I expected.

'That's my understanding. Mrs. Welford said she'd bought Jamey Louise several on sale. I think they should let you girls wear shorts. It's still hot as blue blazes at the end of August. If we see any little summer shifts, we'll get a couple for you. Something cottony and cool.'

'Okay. Thanks.' I hated stupid dresses. I could just imagine Jamey Louise brimming over with excitement. She loved dresses. She said they made her feel feminine. Dresses, talcum powder and Evening in Paris. And Greg kissing her lips and trying to feel her up.

It took me longer than usual to walk to Nadine's, but I was starting out nearly an hour early. When I got there I was surprised to see Greg off down in the back of the field digging. The red clay earth and the shovel sent a chill over me, but I walked down that way to talk a minute before Jamey Louise arrived. Jamey acted like she owned Greg. Whenever he tried to talk to me, she'd order him to get back to work and to stay busy. I'd started teasing him behind her back about being henpecked and not even married. To my surprise, he seemed to like being tormented in that way.

'How was Hattiesburg?' I asked as I was walking up.

Greg kicked dirt over something beside the hole. It was a blue towel with holes in it. There was something brown underneath it.

'Fine. Nadine said Cammie's stall had ants in it. She wants it taken down to the dirt so I can put in some lime. Good thing you came early. You'd better get busy.'

I looked at the towel. 'What are you doing?'

'Something Nadine asked me to do. You'd better get to the barn.' Something smelled terrible. As I was watching a big blowfly landed on the towel. Iridescent green, it shimmered in the sun. Then I noticed the brown paw half covered with dirt.

'What happened to the dog?'

Greg shrugged. 'Nadine said it died. She asked me to bury it.'

Greg's chest and back were covered with sweat. He worked without a shirt and his body was baked brown. The scars from his beating had slowly faded beneath his tan, but I could still imagine them.

'What did it die from?' Those dogs stayed in the house. It wasn't like it'd gotten run over or anything.

'She didn't say, Bekkah. She just asked me to bury it. That's what I'm doing. Now you'd better get to work. She wanted me to do this before you got here or she and Jamey got back. When the other two died, she said it would upset you if you found out.'

'The other two? Two more of her dogs have died?' My voice rose. 'When?'

'I guess it was about three weeks ago.'

'Is somebody putting out poison?' I couldn't believe it, but I looked around for Picket. If someone was putting out arsenic to kill strays, I didn't want my dog getting any of it.

'They died in the house.' Greg looked at me with a sharp, hungry stare. 'They hadn't been outside at all.

238

And they'd been dead a while before she asked me to bury them.'

I started to tell him what a liar he was, but I didn't. Something in the way he watched me made me hold back. 'Dead for how long?' Not even Nadine with her total lack of cleanliness could live in a house with a dead animal.

'Maybe a week.'

'In this heat, they'd a had maggots all over them.'

Greg wiped his lip on the back of his hand. 'They did. Right in her living room behind the sofa. Looked like they bled some from the mouth.'

I had the craziest notion he wasn't lying, but he had to be. His blue eyes watched me without flinching. He could lie as good as Nadine. Then I caught it. They had gotten together and made up a story to horrify me. They knew how much I loved Picket, so they'd concocted this gruesome story just to make me sick.

'Well, you'd better bury that one before the maggots hatch and carry you off,' I said, turning to walk back to the barn. I wouldn't give them the satisfaction of letting them see that it bothered me to realize Nadine's dog was dead. No matter how or when it died.

'You're pretty tough, aren't you, Bekkah?' Greg called softly. 'I wonder what it would take to make you cry.'

'That's one thing you'll never find out.' I threw the words over my shoulder, then thought better of them. I didn't really want to challenge Greg. His life was worse than anything I could make up. I turned back around, and he was still leaning on his shovel, watching me.

'People being cruel to other people, or animals. That would make me cry,' I said. 'I'm not as tough as you think.'

He wiped his forehead with the back of his hand. 'You like to do the unexpected, don't you? But one thing about you, Bekkah Rich, you don't lie.' He dug a shovelful of dirt, then leaned on the handle. 'You can't even imagine what real cruelty can be like.' He stepped down on the shovel and started digging.

After ten or so strokes with the shovel, it became obvious he wasn't going to talk to me anymore. 'I'd better take care of Cammie's stall. I don't want Nadine to be mad at me.'

'She said you hadn't been coming to work. She thought maybe it was you that really liked me more than Jamey.' He grinned again, a confident, boy grin.

'I had some other things to do. School's starting soon. Will you be going to Jexville Junior High?'

Some emotion I couldn't register passed across his face. 'No. I won't be going to school. We have our own.' He laughed, but it wasn't a pleasant sound. 'We learn what we need to get by. Books aren't important to Redeemers.'

He didn't try hard to cover the bitterness in his voice, and I suddenly knew that Greg loved books. It had never occurred to me. In all of the church I didn't remember seeing a book. Not even a hymnal.

'My father has a lot of different kinds of books. If you'd like, I could bring some for you.'

'If they found them, they'd burn them.'

'Leave them in the loft. Read them here.' I felt a tiny ripple of excitement. 'My mother writes books.'

'What kind?'

'Children's. They're really good, though. I like reading them, even though I'm too old now.' I wanted to tell him that I helped Effie by reading her books before she sent them away, but that would sound too much like bragging.

'Bring me one of hers. Bring me your favourite. Once I had a book by a writer named Poe. They were scary stories. I'd like to read some more of his stuff.'

'Okay.' I stood for another minute, but there was

nothing else to say. Greg and I had stumbled into some kind of uneasy friendship. 'I'll bring them tomorrow.'

'I won't let anything happen to them. I promise that.'

My father's study was lined with books. They were double stacked and piled on the floor. Effie went to the library in Jexville twice a week, and there were times she loaded up the car and took books there to give away. Books came in the mail, sent by friends, publishers and other writers. Effie bought them at yard sales and in stores. We had so many books that I never thought someone else might not have any. Even I had a full bookcase in my room that I'd read, but I didn't think Greg would be interested in Nancy Drew, the Bobbsey Twins, the Black Stallion. Robin Hood was a possibility. Arly had some Hardy boys. I liked them almost better than Nancy Drew, even though Arly said they were boys' books.

'Bekkah?' He called me back to the present.

'Yeah?'

'I didn't kill that old woman's cat. No matter what you think, I didn't do that.'

'I'll bring the books tomorrow,' I repeated, and then left him.

When I got to Cammie's stall, I couldn't find the ants, but I took the stall down to the hard-packed red earth. By the time I finished, Greg was through burying the dog, and he sprinkled lime around the floor of the stall, and I refilled it with clean shavings. Cammie stood in the cross ties, digging with her right front foot.

'She wants to run in the pasture,' Greg said from up above me. He was forever rearranging the hay, moving the old forward and putting the new up in back.

'I'd like to see her run.' I looked up and down the hall. Nadine didn't even like the suggestion of turning the horses out. 'Where is Nadine, anyway? And Jamey?'

'They were stewing up something together early this

morning. They went off about eight.'

'On foot?' The green truck was there.

'I guess.' Greg went back to his job, and I finished cleaning my stalls and Jamey's. She'd done it for me the past few days, I supposed. I was feeling left out. Where had they gone? The morning was almost over and it was time for my lesson.

I hayed and watered, just to kill time. Greg came down out of the loft and ate his lunch sitting on the cement block that was usually Nadine's perch. I couldn't tell what was between the two pieces of white bread in his sandwich, so I ate the peanut butter and jelly sandwich Mama Betts had made for me. She wouldn't make anything with mayonnaise because she was afraid it would go bad in the heat. I was getting pretty tired of peanut butter or cheese, though. I wondered if Greg's mother was so concerned about the lack of refrigeration.

I didn't have a chance to investigate. Greg finished his sandwich in two bites. He wiped his mouth on the brown paper sack and looked at me.

'What kind of jelly?'

'Plum. My grandmother made it.' I wiped my mouth with the back of my hand. There had to be jelly there or he wouldn't have known.

'Some of the wo – mothers made some dewberry jam before we moved here. It didn't last long.' He looked at my lunch sack.

Mama Betts always made more than I could eat. Usually I gave half of it to Nadine after we had my lesson. I passed the sack to him. With a deft motion he had the second sandwich out and half eaten.

'Great jelly,' he said.

I almost asked if he'd had time to taste it, but didn't. Maybe he was really hungry.

'Jamey usually gives me her lunch. I was worried when she didn't come back.'

'Yeah, well, you can have half of mine and I won't even order you around.'

Greg laughed. 'Taking a few orders is worth some of the food she brings. Her mama can bake a pound cake.'

Emily Welford was the undisputed pound-cake baker in Chickasaw County. To deny it would be a lie.

'Mama Betts makes the best pies. And biscuits. And mashed potatoes. And—'

Greg laughed again. He tossed my empty lunch sack back at me. 'And peanut butter and jelly sandwiches. They're my favorite.'

'Peanut butter?' I thought he'd lost his mind. I liked chicken salad with celery and crisp red apples. Or ham and cheese. Or fried oyster po-boys.

'Well, thanks for the sandwich, Bekkah. I guess I'd better head back for the church.'

'How was the meeting in Hattiesburg?'

His body seemed to pause, just for a second, like when the television rolled only once and then stopped. 'There were a lot of meetings. Me and the guys snuck off and went to a movie theater. We saw *Breakfast at Tiffany's*. Ever heard of it?'

I had, but I hadn't seen it. 'Was it good?'

Once again he gave me that look that said he was seeing something different in me. 'You'd like it. It had a happy ending, and the woman in it was very beautiful. Maybe one day you'll live like that.'

Since I didn't know the movie, I didn't understand what he was saying. 'What about the Redeemers? Is everything okay?'

'I suppose.' He shrugged and stood up, reaching for his shirt. 'There was a lot of arguing and carrying on, but that's grown-ups for you. They'd rather jawbone and fuss than just do something.'

If anyone had noticed anything amiss at the church, I couldn't tell by watching Greg. And Nadine obviously

243

hadn't said anything to him.

'Tell Nadine I left at twelve sharp,' he said. 'She likes to keep up with my time. She's afraid she'll pay me for five minutes I didn't work.'

'I'll tell her.'

Greg walked down the barn, moving in and out of the light that came through the windows. When he got to the door he turned and faced me.

'I forgot the rake up in the loft. If you're going to hang around here, would you bring it down for me? I'm late.'

'Sure.' Greg sometimes helped me finish my chores if I was way behind and Nadine was waiting to give me a lesson. I never went in the loft, though, unless Nadine was with me. The loft was Greg's domain, and to enter it without an invitation or without Nadine would be a violation.

He closed the door as he left, and I was alone in the coolness of the old barn.

There was still no sign of Nadine and Jamey, so I climbed the ladder to the loft. It was an eerie place with bales of hay stacked from the straw-covered floor to the eaves. Nadine had a thing about running out of hay. Since the horses didn't get any pasture, she said the hay was vital. If the horses missed their hay, they might get colic and die. One of Greg's jobs was to keep the oldest hay pushed to the edge of the loft so it could be dropped straight down into the hay racks in the horses' stalls. It was a very efficient system.

I moved around the bales to the end where Greg's rake was leaning against a support beam. Nadine didn't want any tools left in the loft. She was afraid one might fall and injure one of the horses. She said she'd boarded at a stables where that very thing had happened – a pitchfork had fallen and stabbed a horse. She said it was a horrible way for an animal to die.

I made sure I had a good grip on the rake. It was a

garden rake with heavy metal tines that Greg was using to clean up the loose hay. He was about three-fourths of the way through with the loft. In the section where he hadn't cleaned yet, I stopped to look at the hay. Nadine was always fussing about mold, but I'd never been able to find any. She complained about dust and briars, too, but it was mold that could kill a horse.

The tiny edge of white caught my eye. It looked like a handkerchief someone had lost. I could imagine that Greg would get another beating if he went around loosing items of his wardrobe. I pulled it out of the straw, intending to leave it tied to the ladder for him. But it wasn't a handkerchief. It was a dress. Soaked in blood.

I almost lost my balance. Only the support of the rake kept me from falling ten feet to the dirt aisle below me. The dress and the blood were so vivid; I couldn't think. Something horrible had happened, but I didn't know what.

The dress was familiar. Was it Jamey's? Had something happened in the three days I hadn't come to work? Surely Emily Welford would have called Effie and told her if Jamey had met with an accident. I knew the dress wasn't Nadine's, but the white dress had the look of Jamey about it – soft and lacy. I sank down in the hay and stared at the dress. The blood was a dark brown stain. Hay was sticking in it in places.

I smoothed out the skirt to get a better look. I knew then that it was Selena's. I'd seen it before – at Cry Baby Creek.

I suddenly remembered that I was alone in the old McInnis barn. Greg had gone home. Nadine wasn't around, and neither was Jamey. I was alone in a barn haunted by a crazed sheriff who'd killed his wife and children and then himself. I was alone in a hayloft holding a white dress marred and ruined by blood.

Chapter Twenty-three

'Bekkah?'

Effie came up behind me, slipping her hands on my shoulders and then letting them fall to scratch my back. The gentle pressure caused the swing to move ever so slightly.

'Is something wrong?' She found the place just at each shoulder blade where she used to tease me and tell me I'd been born with angel's wings. She said the doctor convinced her to let him remove the wings so I could be accepted by other children. I'd always believed it was a bad trade-off. 'Is there something you want to talk about?'

She and Mama Betts and Arly had come back from Mobile late, talking about the wild bus-load of people they'd seen in the McDonald's. Mama Betts said it was a disgrace that mostly grown Americans were traveling by bus-loads around the country making fools of themselves. They'd taken over the McDonald's, forming long lines, smiling and crying out 'Up, up, America!' while hugging each other.

Arly said one of them tried to hug Mama Betts, and she stomped his foot. He said he was mortified by her behavior.

Effie said they were some kind of chorus or singing family that all wore white dresses or white slacks and white shoes. She said the bus had red, white and blue stripes down the side.

Mama Betts said they looked like orderlies who'd escaped from hospital duty for an eating spree. She said they had enough strong white teeth among them to cannibalize half of Mobile.

Arly said they were all young, without any adults to boss them around, and they were having a good time. He added that if he could get on a bus and travel around the country eating McDonald's, he'd do it in a heartbeat.

They'd brought me a burger and some cold fries, which I ate without appetite while they rattled on about their trip. All I could think of was the white dress that I'd buried down by the spring. Selena's dress. I'd taken great pains to cover the area with old leaves and vines so Alice wouldn't see it. No one could see it. No one.

As soon as I could escape from the kitchen without causing too many questions, I'd slipped outside to the swing. I wanted to be alone, to try to sort through what I wanted to do and what I ought to do. If I could have brought The Judge home on a wish, he would have been standing there and I would have told him everything.

'Bekkah, if there's something you want to talk about, you can with me. Anything. You know I'll listen.' Effie continued her gentle scratching. It was the most soothing thing she could do.

I wanted to tell her. Somehow, though, it was as if I'd brought it all on. If I'd stayed home, if I'd never gone down to the end of Kali Oka Road, I wouldn't have a blood-soaked dress buried in the woods behind my house. Effie would know that.

'Bekkah, so many things are happening. It makes me feel old sometimes to watch the way you've grown over this summer. You aren't my little girl anymore, and it breaks my heart to think you're growing up.' She paused. 'Growing away from me.'

'I wish I could be five again.' When I was five, before I started school, Effie and I had spent the entire summer playing in the backyard and woods. We hunted elves and waited at the spring for a unicorn to visit. We picked berries and plums and made pies. We swam in the spring and took trips to the river. We made magic.

'I wish you could be five again too.' She picked up my hair and combed through it with her fingers. In a minute she was braiding. The gentle tug on my scalp reminded me of all the safe and wonderful mornings when she'd braided my hair for me, before I learned to do it myself. 'Bekkah, sometimes I love you too much. When I feel you growing up, growing away, I want to hold on too tight.'

'I hate feeling like this,' I said.

'Tell me how you feel, Bekkah. Maybe I can help.'

'The summer is almost gone and I feel like things have changed. Sometimes I think I've changed so much I don't know who I am. But then nothing has changed.' I wanted to tell her everything, but I couldn't. I'd fought so hard to get those riding lessons that now I couldn't tell her there was anything at all wrong at the barn. Things were so complicated between us now. With The Judge it was simpler. With Effie I felt that some process had started that couldn't be stopped, and it was pulling us apart. The truth of what I knew would only widen the gap.

She pulled me back into her arms, and I relaxed against her. 'I wish you could stay my little girl, Bekkah. It tears my heart out to see you growing up so fast. There are so many things out there that can hurt you. Kali Oka is our haven, our place to be safe. One day, when you leave, I won't be able to protect you.'

'Oh, Mama!' I fought back the tears. She couldn't protect me. Not even on Kali Oka Road. I'd fixed it so no one could ever protect me again. I already knew too much.

'You know what I'd really like?'

'What?' My heart was pounding. She was going to ask me to stop riding, to stay home with her for the last few days of summer. I would do it too. I needed it. I wanted to turn and hide my face against her and wipe out the memory of a blood-soaked dress and a room where babies were born. Just a few days weren't too much for me to ask.

'I'd like to come down to the barn and watch you ride tomorrow. I've been thinking about it. I must say your father has pointed this out to me too. He's made a great point of the idea that I should see you ride. I've been so afraid you'd get hurt that I didn't want to think about it. Can you understand that?'

'Yes, ma'am.' Confusion made me sound dull, sullen. That she wanted to come watch me ride was more than I'd ever dared to expect. A week before, it would have made me ecstatic. Now I didn't know if I wanted her at the barn.

'Can I come?'

'That would be great.' I tried to sound enthusiastic. She was making a big gesture, a serious move to make things completely right between us. 'I'd love for you to do that. And I think you'll like Nadine if you give her a chance.'

'Well, it's about time, isn't it?'

'That's okay. I'm just getting where my riding is good enough to watch.'

'I bought some things for you. They're in your room.' She hesitated. 'There's a bra. You're going to have to wear one, and if this one doesn't fit we'll take it back one day next week and get the rest of your school things then.'

'Okay, thanks.'

'What? No big argument about how bras are devices of torture?' There was laughter in her voice.

'They look like some kind of harness that you'd use to

250

walk a dog, but I guess I can get used to one.'

Mama rumpled my bangs off my forehead and kissed the top of my head. 'It's hard to watch my little girl grow up, but Walt has made me promise that I'll ease up on you. I was thinking when school gets started maybe you'd like to have a party here. Maybe some girls to spend the night or just a get-together after school. You're going to be a seventh grader now. You'll be going to a junior high where the children from all over the county go. There'll be lots of new faces. A party might be a good way to make friends.'

I spun around in the swing and looked at Effie. No wonder her voice sounded weird. She was crying.

'What's wrong?'

'I can't help but think that in a few more years you'll be gone from me. Walt is already talking about where you'll go to college. He says Arly can go to one of the junior colleges nearby because his grades are so poor. He says you'll get a scholarship, Bekkah. You can go away to school.'

A large tear hung on the edge of her jaw, a jaw that was square and determined, just like Mama Betts'. Just like mine. I brushed it away with the tips of my fingers.

'I don't think I'll want to go away, Effie. Couldn't I just stay here and go to junior college too?'

Effie sniffed. 'Walt said it would be a waste.'

I couldn't believe they were going to make me go away. It was like being cast out, driven from my home. My own eyes filled with tears. 'What if I don't want to?'

'Your father only wants what's best for you. He says you can be anything you want, Bekkah. He said there are no limits to what you can achieve.'

'What if I want to stay home with you?'

She rubbed the tears from her eyes with the back of her hand. 'I shouldn't have started this now. It's just that I talked to Walt this morning before I went to Mobile. He was raving about some new program that would be in place in Missouri by the time you get ready for college. I hate that state. Missouri. He . . . ' She sighed. 'He'll be home for good Friday. The quarter is over and he just has to pack up his things and have them shipped.'

'More books?' I tried to sound funny.

'More books. And papers. But it'll be good to have your father home with us, won't it?'

It would be good. The knowledge that The Judge would be there by the end of the week seemed to lift a heavy burden from my heart. I could wait until then to tell him about the bloody dress and all. I could wait two more days.

'Where's Alice?' Effie was deliberately shifting the subject.

'Mrs. Waltman and Sukey are over at the church. Sukey's playing the piano for a double wedding, and Alice got stuck with Maebelle V., Lucinda and Arlene to watch. She said it was too hard to try to bring them over here.' She'd asked me to go to her house, but I'd declined. The white dress was all I could think about.

'Well, come on in the house and try on your new clothes for me.'

I didn't want clothes. I didn't want to go to school, and I surely didn't want to go to college and leave Effie and Mama Betts on Kali Oka Road. I followed Effie back into the comforting smells of the kitchen and into my bedroom, where the clothes were neatly stacked.

The bra was as bad as I thought, but I put it on and then the dresses. Effie nodded. They would do. By mid-year I'd have grown out of them, she said. I was already too tall, with arms and legs that Arly said were apelike because of their length. The idea of additional growth was about as appealing as the other 'womanly changes' I'd been told to expect. It was going to be a great year.

I was unbuttoning the last dress when I heard something outside the house. It was that pleasant time of twilight in the heat of August when the first breath of coolness can be felt. It was almost as if the house sighed, and a breeze touched the sheer curtains in the windows of my room. I heard Picket barking in the yard before the lights of a car swung through my window.

'Who can that be?' Effie asked. 'Arly didn't say he was expecting any friends.'

'I guess not,' I added, unable to stop myself. 'Arly's friends are too stupid to pass a driving test.'

'I wish that were true,' Effie said under her breath as she went to the screened porch to see who'd come visiting.

There was the murmur of two female voices. I recognized Effie's but not the other. My curiosity got the better of me, and I put on my shorts and went to the kitchen. I almost swallowed my tongue when I saw Cathi Cummings sitting at the kitchen table.

Blond hair spilled down her back, and her skirt was tight and short. She looked at me in the doorway and smiled. 'Hello, Bekkah. I was driving through to Pensacola, and I promised your father I'd stop and see you.'

'Hi, Cathi.' I shot a glance at Effie. It was the complete calmness of her face that told me how upset she was. When Effie was angry to the core of her being, her face lost all expression. She looked at me with her mannequin face and her eyes glittered. 'What are you doing in Jexville?' I asked Cathi.

'Since I earned my master's, I decided to reward myself with a little vacation on the beach.'

She was smiling, but she was tense too. What in the hell was she doing in Effie's kitchen? 'Where's your husband?' I asked into the silence of the room.

'Phil couldn't turn loose of the desk long enough for a

break. He told me to come on my own and he'd try to join me on the weekend.'

'Cathi's husband is an editor at the *Washington Post*.' I wanted Effie to know she was married.

'He's a much better editor than he is a husband,' Cathi said.

I'd never seen a woman drinking, but I wondered if Cathi was. Her face was flushed and her eyes challenged first Effie and then me. Something was definitely wrong with her.

'Did you go home to Hushpuppykenya?' I asked.

'Hushpuckena,' she corrected. 'Yes, I saw my parents. They disapproved of me going to Pensacola without Phil, just like they disapproved of me going to graduate school. There doesn't seem to be much that I do that they approve of.' She waved a hand in the air.

'How about some coffee?' Effie asked. 'I was just about to brew a pot.'

'I'd really like a drink. Have any bourbon?'

'No,' Effie said, even though we did. 'I drank the last bit last night. Meant to go to the store, but it slipped my mind.' She got up to make a pot of coffee.

When I looked up, Mama Betts was standing in the doorway from the hall. She was taking in the scene with another dose of disapproval. I didn't think anybody had to explain anything to her.

'Mrs. Cummings is a friend of Walt's,' Effie said. 'Mrs. Cummings, this is my mother—'

'Mama Betts,' Cathi supplied, as she stood up. 'I've heard so much about you from Bekkah's father. About all of you. Is Arly here too?'

'He went to the baseball field,' Mama Betts supplied. 'He'll be back. How about some supper?' She didn't wait for an answer, either, but went to the refrigerator and began to put together some leftovers to warm up. Nobody had cooked because we had the hamburgers from Mobile, but there were lots of things in the refrigerator. In a couple of minutes Mama Betts had Indian corn, crowder peas and okra and some pork chops warming with sweet potato casserole.

'That smells wonderful,' Cathi said. She was supporting herself at the table on her elbows. 'I shouldn't have come here. Walt would be very upset with me if he knew. But I just had to see what it is he can't leave here.'

Her voice caught and for one awful moment I thought she was going to cry. That would be it. Effie might throw the hot coffee on her. I chanced a look at Effie and saw that careful mask still in place. There was no softening.

'Walt talks about you all the time,' Cathi continued. She was watching Effie pour three mugs full of strong black coffee. Mama Betts kept her back to the table. She was stirring her pots with a vengeance.

'He talks about you and Bekkah the most, but he has plenty to say about Mrs. McVay and Arly.'

It was strange to hear Mama Betts called by her formal name. I couldn't remember hearing anyone do it before.

'And does Walt tell you how much he loves his family?' Mama Betts asked.

'Yes, ma'am, that's exactly what he tells me. And he tells me that this road here, Kali Oka, has cast some spell over his wife and children and over him. He can't seem to leave it any more than he could leave his family. It doesn't matter that he could have a real future in Columbia.'

Mama Betts filled a plate with food, and Effie pushed a mug of coffee over to Cathi.

'And I'll bet you tried your best to convince him to stay in Missouri,' Mama Betts said as she placed the steaming plate in front of Cathi.

'I did, which didn't impress Walt worth a damn.' She laughed, but it had a broken sound. 'It seems to be my lot in life to fall for men who always care about something else more than they could ever possibly care about me.'

'Perhaps you should select men who aren't already obligated,' Mama Betts suggested as she carefully placed a cloth napkin and flatware in front of Cathi.

'Sound advice,' Cathi agreed. 'Sound advice. And I've given it some thought. You see, I think I fall for these men *because* they care about someone or something else. That was the thing about Walt. He loves his family.' She looked around the kitchen, and her eyes wouldn't completely focus on me. 'Each one of you. And I thought if someone could love me that way—'

'Better drink that coffee before it gets cold,' Effie said. 'Bekkah, get your friend some aspirin. Make it three. She's going to need them in the morning.'

The mannequin face was gone. Behind it was anger, fear, and maybe just a touch of compassion. I did as she told me, unwilling to ignite a temper I knew could scorch the hide off me at twenty paces.

When I got back to the kitchen, Cathi was sampling the sweet potatoes with admirable appetite. 'This is really good,' she was saying again and again. 'Really good. I've never had this before.'

Mama Betts took a seat at the table. 'Eat the food, Mrs. Cummings. You've had a bit to drink, and I don't hold with drinking and driving. You know an awful lot about us here on Kali Oka. Now there are some questions Effie and I would like to ask you.'

Effie waved me onto the porch. I followed her out into the darkness, wondering if I'd be the first to feel the heat of her anger.

'Who is this woman?' she asked.

'One of The Judge's students. She's from Mississippi originally.'

'Yes, I've gathered that much. What is she doing here in Jexville? Nobody comes to Kali Oka Road on the way to someplace else. Walt is still in Missouri; what's she doing here?'

'I don't know.'

'Is she someone you made friends with on your little vacation?' The anger was creeping back into her voice. The dreaded vacation, my week of betrayal, was coming back to life.

'Yes, Mama. I met her and she was nice to me. While Daddy was busy, she took me places.'

'Did you invite her here?'

'No.'

'Well, she's in no condition to drive any farther. She'll have to stay in your room, since she's your friend.'

'I'll make up the sofa to sleep on.'

'Bekkah, what went on between that woman and your father?'

I couldn't see her in the dark. Was she angry or worried? Judging from her voice, I couldn't tell. 'I think she fell in love with Daddy, but he didn't love her back. If he did, he'd stay in Missouri, wouldn't he?'

'Is that what he told you?'

'Not exactly. He asked me a question too.' The anger was like some flower opening up inside my chest. It pushed against my ribs and hurt. It crowded inside me, demanding to get out, to hurt her back.

'What question?'

'He wanted to know why you loved Kali Oka Road more than him, why you expected him to give up his life to live here.' I hit the outside screen door and ran. I heard it slam hard behind me, but I kept running. Picket appeared at my side as I ran harder and harder into the woods toward the spring. I hadn't asked Cathi Cummings to drop by Chickasaw County. I'd never even told her where I lived. She'd come here on her own. What was happening was between Effie and The Judge and Cathi. I had nothing to do with it. Nothing.

I ran harder along the familiar path, dodging limbs and branches by instinct and memory, but I couldn't outrun the ugliness. No matter what I told myself, I couldn't outrun my guilt.

I made it to the spring, each breath a slicing knife in my lungs. Picket was at my side, her breath coming in sharp pants. My fingers found the smooth bark of a wild magnolia that grew beside the little pool of water, and I slipped to the moist, cool earth to catch my breath.

I was ashamed of myself. Terribly ashamed. I'd done the unforgivable lashing out at Effie with a half-truth to cut her as she was cutting me. I wanted to cry, but my eyes were dry and burning. I reached into the pool to draw some water to my hot face. My fingers caught something in the water, a piece of material.

Involuntarily my fingers closed on it, and I pulled it toward me. It was heavy, something big. As I pulled I saw the familiar material of the white dress I'd buried only ten feet away. But I'd buried it deep, and put rocks and leaves on top of it. It couldn't be the same dress.

I saw the blood stains all down the front.

My scream echoed again and again on the stillness of the August night.

Chapter Twenty-four

Cathi Cummings left in the middle of the night. She came into the living room where I was sleeping and sat on the arm of the sofa.

'I'm sorry, Bekkah,' she said. 'I'm sorry and ashamed.'

I pretended to be asleep. I hated her for coming to my home, for bringing Missouri to Kali Oka Road. For hurting Effie. Daddy was coming home in two days, and now she'd ruined it. Effie would be coiled and ready to strike.

'If I could have had a daughter like you . . . ' She brushed her hand over my hair. 'There's something wrong inside, I can't . . . Damn!' She removed her hand. 'Whatever else happens, Bekkah, know that your father loves you more than anything in the world. Just remember that. No one can ever take that away from you.'

She stood up and I heard her car keys jiggle in her hand.

'Don't come back here,' I said.

'I won't. I won't come here again. I was wrong to come here at all, but I had to see. Now I'm going to try to get a job in Mobile. There's a paper there.'

'Go back to Missouri. Or go back to your husband.' Mobile was too close.

'I can't, Bekkah. I can't go forward and I can't go back.' She tried for a laugh, but it fell in brittle pieces around her.

'What about your husband?'

'What about him?' She went to the front door, pushed back the lacy curtain and looked out. In the darkness of the room she was a small silhouette. 'If there was ever anything worth going back to there, I ruined it when I drove south and came here.' She sighed. 'I know you hate me, but if you ever need anything, you can call on me.'

'I have my mama.' I was hateful, and I knew it.

'Sometimes you can't always tell your mama everything. I hurt you, Bekkah. And I hurt your father and your family. I'm not a fool. I know that. I'd undo it if I could. But I can't. So just remember. We're a lot alike, you and I. We see what we want, and we don't intend to hurt others.'

'I'm not like you, and I'm not stupid. I know you were nice to me to be with The Judge.'

'You're wrong there, Bekkah. I spent time with you because I liked you. We are alike. Neither of us are hypocrites. If I hadn't liked you, I'd have made sure I was busy when you were around. I only like you more because you're Walt's child.'

'Go away from here, Cathi. Leave us alone.'

'If you need me, call information in Mobile and get my number. Then call me collect. I won't let you down.'

She walked out the door and into the night. I heard her car crank. The lights swung through the open window across the living-room ceiling, brushing the portrait of Effie that Mama Betts had had painted when Effie was sixteen, her dark hair in curls about her shoulders and her lips tinted a ripe red.

I had only to wait until morning to see how terrible it was going to be.

Mama Betts woke me and got me ready for the barn with a sack lunch and a cold biscuit in hand. She also woke Arly and packed his lunch for work at the nursery.

She was making a fresh pot of coffee for Effie when I opened the kitchen door to leave. Her pale eyes locked with mine.

'Don't come back until late,' she said softly. 'Everything will be fine by then.'

I knew it wouldn't. 'Cathi's going to get a job in Mobile.'

Mama Betts nodded. 'She can get a job in hell for all I care. She won't be bothering this family.'

'Daddy could have stayed in Missouri. I mean, if that's what he wanted, he would have done it. Mama ought to know that.'

'I have a lot of respect for your father, Bekkah. You're preaching to the choir.'

'But Effie's . . . ' I gripped the door handle. 'She's going to blame Daddy for what happened. It wasn't his fault.'

'Not entirely.'

'It wasn't his fault at all.' I made myself slow down. 'He can't tell Cathi what to do or not do. You can plainly see that she does what she wants.'

'Yes, I can plainly see that.' Mama Betts had made up a tray with coffee and toast. 'Get on out of here before your mother starts looking for you. Since Walt isn't here to take the heat, you'll bear the brunt of it if you don't skedaddle.'

'Well, The Judge will be here tomorrow. Then everything will get back on track.' Just saying the words made me feel better. Walt and Effie might fight and raise hell, but it would be over and life on Kali Oka would go back to the way it had always been.

'Your father isn't coming straight home.'

I thought that I hadn't heard her right.

'Close your mouth, Bekkah. You look like one of those Fairleys from down Wilson Ferry Road.'

'Not coming home? Why not? He has to come home. I need him.'

Mama Betts sharpened her gaze. 'What's going on with you, Bekkah?'

'Daddy's supposed to be home Friday. He said so days ago. I've been waiting for him.' My voice drifted to an end. 'He promised.'

'I called him this morning and told him what had happened. He's going to New Orleans first. I'm sending Effie there to meet him.'

'She won't go. Not now.' Hell would freeze over before Effie met The Judge anywhere, unless it was a lynching tree or electric chair. She didn't believe in capital punishment, but she was mad enough at Walt to vote for his extermination. I hadn't forgotten the way she looked and talked the night before.

'She doesn't know he's going to be there. It's a trick.'

'She's going to murder you.'

Mama Betts shrugged. 'I'm too tough to cook and too old to care. I told Walt everything that happened. When I wake Effie, I'm going to tell her that Rita Sheffield called and wants to meet her for the weekend in New Orleans. Effie will go.'

'She'll go to spite Daddy.' Mama Betts' plan might work, but I needed The Judge home with me. I had to tell him about the Redeemers, and the babies, and the white dress and scrap of lace I'd hidden away in the old fort Alice and I had built in the woods two years ago.

'I called Rita out in California. She's agreed to it. She'll play along if Effie calls her.'

'I don't want to be there when Mama sees it's The Judge instead of Rita.'

'Let them have it out in front of strangers. It won't do for them to be here.' She looked sharply at me. 'There's been enough dissension in this house to last a good long while.'

'When will they come home?' I felt the beginning of a

slow headache. I never had one unless I had the flu, but this one was different. It was dull and slow, letting me know that it was going to get bigger, stronger and meaner as the day went on.

'I'm hoping they'll stay gone a while. Effie's ahead on her book. Walt doesn't have to be in Hattiesburg until late September.'

'That's a month or better.'

'I see they have taught you something at school.'

'They can't be gone a month.'

Mama Betts put her hands on her hips, the tray of coffee and toast momentarily forgotten.

'Bekkah, your parents need some time alone. You and Arly can start school without them. I'll be right here, just like always.'

'Couldn't Daddy come here first, before they leave?' If I didn't talk with him soon, it might be too late. The Redeemers might sell another baby. Or something might happen to Magdeline. Or Selena might come after me to retrieve her dress.

'It would be better if they left straight from New Orleans.'

'Left! For where?

'Maybe California. Your mother would love to see Rita. It's been seven years. Effie and Rita used to be best friends, like you and Alice. You were only five when Rita was home the last time, and you know Effie isn't one to travel.'

'What makes you think she'll go now?' Effie didn't travel. She hated leaving Kali Oka Road.

'She loves Walt a lot.'

'Grandma?'

Mama Betts looked closely at me then. I hardly ever called her that, only when I was very upset.

'What's eating at you, Bekkah? You've been odd for a day or two now.'

'Can I call Daddy before he leaves?'

She picked up the tray. 'You can call him in New Orleans tonight. He's already gone and you have to scat. Effie's coffee will be cold and I want everything perfect.'

She disappeared down the hall, coffee cup rattling in the saucer as she carried Effie's tray. The image brought back a long-ago memory of the time that Effie had been very sick. Dr. McMillan had come to the house every day to check on her, and she was too weak to get out of bed. The doctor had told Daddy out in the front yard that Effie should never try to have another child.

For weeks Mama Betts had prepared food for Effie and helped her eat it. Not since she'd recovered had I seen a tray of food going down the hallway. It wasn't a good sight.

Even though it was early morning, the day wrapped around me like a damp wool blanket. The grass was soaked with dew, and the air wasn't much drier. August, the month when south Mississippi returned to the tropics. Steam and heat. The possibility of hurricanes. In a few short days school would start. Alice was excited. Jamey Louise was torn between desire to show off her tan and new curves to the high school boys we'd see every day and the knowledge that she'd be separated from Greg. At Chickasaw Consolidated grades seven through twelve were housed in one building with three wings. Effie said it looked like a chicken hatchery. She said it was an architectural blight, and that if children learned anything it was a miracle.

I dreaded school, the changes, the boredom and the confinement. But then I dreaded the idea of spending every day on Kali Oka Road too. This summer I had lost every safe place I knew. As I walked along, kicking the large rocks that showed up in the loose red dirt of

Kali Oka, I felt the pull of the Redeemers and Cry Baby Creek. As much as I was afraid, I also wanted to go there. Since The Judge wasn't coming home right away, what was I going to do? What had happened to Magdeline? Maybe if I could just see her and know that she was okay, I wouldn't feel so guilty and worried. I had to get Greg alone and ask him a few questions.

The weathered sign at Nadine's driveway moaned even though not a leaf or blade of grass moved in a breeze. The air was perfectly still, yet the sign groaned again. The sound sent a shiver down my spine. I was being silly about that dress. But how had it gotten in the loft?

There was an unearthly stillness about the barn as I walked beneath the chinaberry trees toward the rusty gate. I was a little early for work, but normally Nadine and Greg were already around. There wasn't a sign that anyone was there. The barn door was cracked open, a violation of the rules that Nadine had imposed. We were either to open or shut the door, not halfway in between.

The wind whispered through the chinaberry leaves, a feather-light touch. I stopped at the gate, all senses alert. Picket clung to my leg, her ears forward and her mouth open, panting. There wasn't a sound except the mournful sigh of the sign on its rusty chain.

Truck and horse trailer were in place. Garbage spilled out the back door of the house and down the steps. I stood in the sunlight-dappled driveway, afraid to go forward. Something was wrong.

Something terrible. Something even worse than that bloody dress I'd found.

I considered for a moment going to get Alice. She could help me tell the story of what we'd seen. But Alice hated Nadine. And there was a good chance Nadine would tell Alice about what we'd seen in the preacherman's house.

I forced my fingers to the latch on the gate and then walked through.

I heard the tiny rocks scrunch under my feet and the call of a single crow. I saw the bird, big and glossy, sitting on the telephone wire to Nadine's house. Mama Betts said one crow was a sign of death. I looked for another, but the blue-white sky was empty.

My hand was on the barn door, and I listened. Inside, there was the sound of faint sobbing. My own breath caught in my throat, a painful knot.

The door moved beneath my hand, frightening me so that I jumped back. Jamey Louise stepped out of the darkness, pushing me roughly back.

'Don't go in there,' she said harshly. She put her hands on my shoulders and pushed me away.

'What is it?' I looked beyond her shoulder but could see nothing. There was only the sound of broken sobbing.

'Bekkah, stay out!'

I looked at her face and saw it was streaked with a dried brown substance. Her blue-and-white-checked sundress, her favorite, was soaked in sticky blood.

'What?' I was stricken by the sight of so much blood.

Jamey's face tightened, but she didn't cry. 'There's nothing you can do,' she said. 'Nadine told me to keep you out.'

'What is it? Is she hurt?' I felt the hammer of my earlier headache strike home. My knees quivered. 'Is someone dead in there?'

Jamey Louise grabbed my arm and walked me back to Nadine's house. There was a water hose at the corner, and she turned it on her face and then her body, washing the blood away in pink rivulets that ran down her legs and into her sneakers.

With the blood gone, her face was pale and her eyes sharp like a doll's glassy gaze. She washed her legs over and over again.

266

'What happened?' I thought about running home, just leaving without asking any questions. I could go to Alice's house and help her with Maebelle V. and the other children. We could ask her older sisters about the seventh grade. Alice loved to think about it, to plan what it was going to be like to be with the juniors and seniors in the halls.

'Cammie is dead.'

I looked at Jamey Louise. I'd never thought she could be so mean. I really looked at her. Fine golden hairs curled at her forehead in wisps, like baby hair. Her skin was clear tan, translucent now that the dried blood was washed away and the color had returned. In her clear brown eyes was . . . pity?

'Somebody snuck in the barn early this morning and hurt her,' Jamey Louise said. 'When Nadine got up, she found her and tried to save her. But she died. Just when you walked up.'

Jamey's hand grabbed my arm and her fingers bit into my skin. I wanted to slap her away, to slap her in the face as hard as I could, but I couldn't lift my hand. In fact, I was falling backward. Only Jamey Louise's tight grip on my arm kept me from slamming backward. As it was, I sat down on the ground, right in the puddle of water Jamey had made while washing away the blood. Her sundress was soaked and stained beyond repair.

'There's nothing to be done,' Jamey said, sitting down beside me.

I was breathing through my mouth, and I thought of the Fairleys on Wilson Ferry Road. But when I tried to close my mouth I couldn't breathe. Something was clawing at my throat, working up toward the base of my head.

'I've got to go get Daddy to bring the backhoe,' Jamey said. 'Want to walk with me?'

I looked at her. I heard what she said, but I didn't understand it. She got up and tugged me up with her.

'Walk with me,' she said. 'Daddy will give us a ride back.'

'Backhoe?'

Jamey looked past me. 'Yeah. Nadine couldn't get her out of the stall. We're going to have to drag her out to the field and bury her.'

I rejected that information too.

'The other horses are okay,' Jamey offered. She patted my arm. Nadine said it was strange that they didn't make a sound, or she would have heard it. Whoever did it just slipped in and . . . ' She stopped. 'Libby and Cora are home this morning. You know Libby has a job at the Kettle, waiting on tables. She made twelve dollars in tips last night. That's the most any waitress has ever made on a Thursday night.'

We were walking down the driveway. Picket had taken up with us, and she was sniffing the trunks of the chinaberry trees.

'Who did this?' I asked Jamey. 'Who?'

'Nadine doesn't know. She can't figure it out. Whoever did it was strong. Cammie was, uh, stabbed a lot. We couldn't find the knife.'

'Trapped in that stall, she didn't have a chance.' I said the words before I thought. 'Mama Betts said those horses shouldn't be penned up all the time. She said it wasn't natural.'

'If she'd been in the pasture, they could have shot her,' Jamey said. She laced her fingers around my wrist and pulled me along with her. I didn't resist. I didn't want to go to the barn, and I didn't want to go home. At least Jamey knew where she wanted to go.

We'd left Picket several trees behind, and I looked back for her. The barn door was still open only a little, and Jamey had left the gate to the pasture unlatched. It

268

had swung wide open, hanging slightly askew.

'The gate.' I stopped. 'I'd better close it.'

Jamey waited while I walked back. Picket was half buried in some undergrowth beneath the big chinaberry tree where Alice and I had once hidden our Coca-Colas. I called to her, but she only wagged her tail, refusing to give up her quest.

I didn't want to leave her at the barn. 'Picket!' I clapped my hands and the noise was too loud. Still, Picket burrowed away.

'Come on,' Jamey urged. 'Nadine needs me to get back.'

I went to grab Picket by the collar. Once I got her attention, she'd follow me. I reached deep into the undergrowth, remembering the Cokes and how Greg had found them and drank them. My fingers touched something sleek and polished. It was wood, but it wasn't a stick. Instead of grabbing Picket, I tugged at the wood. It was heavier than I imagined, and I couldn't lift it with one hand.

Picket had inched over to give me room and still dig at whatever had caught her fancy. I pushed the tangle of bushes and weeds back, and my breath caught. Picket had thrown a good bit of dirt on the crucified Jesus from the Redeemer church, but I had no doubt that was what I'd found. Except someone had painted the face black. It looked like spray paint of some kind. Whoever had done it hadn't taken a lot of pains to be neat either. The spray covered Jesus's face, part of the crown and some of his neck and chest.

'Bekkah, get that dog and come on if you're coming!' Jamey said.

I grabbed Picket's collar and pulled her out of the shrubs. 'We're coming.' Once I had her back in the driveway, she gave up and decided to mind me, just like I knew she would.

'What'd she have, a rabbit?' Jamey asked.

'Must have been.' I felt like my feet weren't completely touching the ground.

'Well, she can chase the chickens at our house. She hasn't been around this summer, and they've all gotten fat and lazy.'

Jamey was trying harder to be nice to me than she'd ever been. I walked along with nothing to say.

'Libby said she'd show us all how to use makeup before school started, if you'd like to learn. Just a little mascara and maybe some rouge and lipstick.'

'Yeah.'

'Even though we're seventh graders, it's going to be high school for all practical purposes. Libby started wearing makeup in the seventh grade, I mean to school. She wore it before that when she could get away with it.'

'Libby's always been beautiful.' I felt like someone else was talking. Someone else had taken over my body and was walking it down the road with Jamey Louise babbling about crazy things. And that person was babbling back.

'Jamey, are you certain it was Cammie?'

'It was her stall. Blood was everywhere, all over the walls and the horse.' She shrugged. 'The ones that are the same color look the same to me. There was so much blood . . . '

We were halfway to the Welfords. 'Who would do such a thing?' I remembered Mr. Tom and the horror of his death. Someone sick had done it. Someone so sick that they needed to be locked away from society, Mama Betts had said. She had said that if it was someone on Kali Oka Road, they'd do something evil again. She'd warned me that such sickness didn't go away, that it just boiled and simmered and fermented until it spewed out again in another mean and cruel act.

Mama Betts thought it was someone from the Redeemers who'd killed Mr. Tom. I'd even thought it was Greg until he'd said he didn't do it. Was he lying? I didn't know. I couldn't seem to think it through.

'Nadine said she was going to catch whoever had done this, and she was personally going to make them suffer,' Jamey said. 'I'd hate to be at Nadine's mercy. You know there's the old storage area under the end of the barn. They said old Rathson McInnis used to chain his slaves down there to punish them. That was so no one else could hear them scream when he tortured them.'

'Jamey!' I'd never heard any such thing. 'That's crazy.'

'No, it isn't. Mama said it was true.'

'Have you seen the room? Have you been in it?'

'No. Who has time to explore when Nadine's cracking the whip? Anyway, all I was saying was that if she could find out who'd done this, she could chain them down in the little room and torture them for days before she finally finished them off. I'll bet no one would ever find the body.'

Jamey Louise was only trying to take my mind off what had happened to Cammie, and for a moment it had worked. I wished there was a room beneath the barn, and I wished I could find whoever had hurt Cammie so much. I'd do to them what they had done to her.

Two tears slipped down my cheek. Jamey saw them and started walking faster. She gave up talking and settled on motion. By the time we turned down the drive to the Welfords' house, I was crying good, but without making a sound.

I sat on the steps, and Emily Welford brought me a glass of lemonade while they sent Libby in the truck to find Gus out in the field. He was turning the ground for some fall turnips.

Condensation dripped off my lemonade glass and hit my shoes at just about the same pace the tears dripped off my chin. Emily and Jamey and Cora stood over me, but no one said anything. They all thought us Riches weré silly about our animals. Horses died, cows went to butcher, and unlucky dogs and cats met death in numerous tragic ways. The Welfords had lost livestock to lightning, stray dogs, poachers, colic, birth, infection, and theft. The death of an animal was insignificant to them. But they were too kind to say anything to me about my unstoppable tears. They just stood over me and waited for Gus to drive up on the tractor.

He came in a cloud of dust and diesel, hot and sweat-streaked and weathered beyond his years. 'Sorry about that horse, Bekkah,' he said as he climbed the steps and took the glass of lemonade Emily held for him. He drank it all in one swallow, the ice clanking back into the bottom of the glass, hardly melted. Emily took it for a refill and they went inside.

The window was open, and I listened to Jamey tell what had happened. Nadine had gone out to feed and found Cammie down in her stall, hamstrung and with at least thirty knife wounds. She'd bled to death slowly, unable even to struggle to her feet.

Jamey described the stalls and the barn.

'Better get after it. In this heat she won't last long,' Gus said. He came back out the door, patting my head as he went down the steps.

'He's gonna go get the chains, so it'll take him a little while,' Jamey explained. 'You want to ride on the tractor with him? I'll walk.'

'No. You ride. I have Picket.' I wanted to be alone.

'Why don't you go home?' Emily suggested. She'd come out on the porch again, sliding out of the screen so silently I hadn't even heard her. 'Go home and see if

Effie won't take you to the river for a swim. It's the last week before school. You might not get another chance.'

'Maybe I will.' The tears were still dripping slowly off my face, but it wasn't like I was really crying.

'Bekkah, honey, she still has eight other horses. It isn't the end of the world,' Emily said. 'Maybe next summer, if you ride as good as Jamey says you do, maybe Effie and Walt will get you your very own horse.'

'Maybe.' There would be no replacement for Cammie. 'I'd better be going.'

Picket hadn't even bothered to hunt for the chickens. She came out from under the porch as soon as I stepped down. Together we walked down the drive.

I thought about going home. I thought about going to Alice's. My feet took me back to the chinaberry drive, back to the barn. There was still no sound, or sight, of Gus getting the tractor ready to drag Cammie out of her stall and to a grave. I wanted to see her for myself. To say goodbye. Then I would go home.

The barn was as still as when I'd left it. I walked past the tree with the vandalized crucifix beneath it. I remembered it was there, it just didn't have anything to do with what was happening to me. Not yet. Once I had dealt with Cammie, I would think about the crucifix and what it might mean.

The barn door was still cracked and I went to it, slipping inside into the dim coolness.

There was nothing except the shuffle and snort of the horses as they ate hay and shifted their weight in the stalls. Cammie's door was open, and I knew it would be horrible, but I walked there and looked in.

Jamey had not exaggerated. Blood was everywhere. It covered the walls and the hay and the bedding. And the dead horse that lay on its side, one eye open and glazed.

273

Color was impossible to tell because of the blood, but I knew the slope of the muzzle, the shape of the ear.

It wasn't Cammie.

I knew it instantly. The dead horse was Caesar, the big gelding that lived two stalls down. His entire head was soaked in blood, covering the blaze that stopped three inches above his nostrils. He was the same dark bay as Cammie, but he was slightly bigger, and a gelding. After the weeks of grooming Cammie daily, of going over her inch by inch, I knew her. My fingers knew the feel of her. The poor dead horse lying in the stall was not my Cammie.

I staggered backward into the center aisle. Caesar's stall was two doors down, and I ran to it, not daring to breathe. Cammie stood with her head in a far corner, munching her hay. When I whispered her name, she swung around to look at me, calling a soft greeting. Several straws stuck from her mouth, and she pulled them in as she walked over to me for a head rub.

'Cammie.' I whispered her name, unable to believe that she was alive, uninjured. I opened the door and slipped inside, running my hands down her sleek neck and chest, tangling my fingers in her mane and pressing my face against her so that my tears were soaked into her shining coat.

'I thought it was Cammie, too, at first.'

Greg's voice startled me. Not that he was there, but the quality of his tone. I turned to him. The barn light wasn't good, but his eyes were swollen, his face splotched and ugly. Blood covered his long-sleeved white shirt.

'Stay away from her.' I hissed the warning.

Greg backed up two steps as if I'd slapped him.

Shock passed over his face, and I moved forward to confront him. 'What was Caesar doing in her stall? Who changed the horses, Greg?'

His eyes narrowed as he realized my meaning. 'Go to hell, Rebekah Rich.' He turned to walk away, and I noticed that he moved stiffly, as if he'd injured himself.

Or as if some large animal had stepped on him in an effort at self-defense.

Chapter Twenty-five

From the leafy seclusion of the tallest chinaberry tree I watched Gus chug down the driveway and into the barn. They had to tear the front of the stall away to get Caesar out into the aisle, and then they dragged him to the back of the field. Gus used a box blade on the tractor to dig a grave for the big thoroughbred. It wasn't deep, but it seemed sufficient.

Nadine and Jamey watched. When it was over they followed the tractor back to the house. Gus drove on home; there was still work to be done in his fields. Without a word to Jamey, Nadine went into the house, slamming the back door behind her. Jamey Louise ambled down the driveway toward home, her shoulders rounded and her footsteps dragging. In a little while I heard the sounds of hammer and nails from the barn. Greg was rebuilding the stall. The rhythm was uneven, ominous.

Nadine's frustration carried clearly to the outside. She was slamming doors and throwing things. I wondered if she might call my house to explain that Cammie was fine. Knowing Nadine, she'd just wait for me to come by the barn on my own. Throughout the entire summer she'd never called my house once.

When I was certain Greg would be busy in the barn, I climbed down from the tree and went to inspect the crucified Jesus in the bushes. I crawled into the high grass and shrubs and made sure I was hidden from sight. I pulled at the heavy crucifix until I could see it clearly. Someone had taken spray paint and deliberately ruined it. I didn't know much about wood – The Judge had never been the kind of man who carved or hammered or sawed – but I thought there had to be a way to get the black paint off. The detail of the carving was beautiful, if terrible. I ran a finger down the smooth wood. If the black paint was removed, some of the fine detail, like the blood from the crown of thorns, would have to be redone and repainted. But surely someone at the Redeemers could do the work.

I realized then that the crucifix had not been thrown away. It had been stolen. The vandalism was part of a twofold act of meanness. Destroy and steal. I didn't have to ask how it had come to be on Nadine's property. Greg could have taken it alone. The crucifix was heavy, but lifting those big bales of hay all summer long had given Greg impressive muscles. I could barely drag the crucifix along the ground, but Greg could have done it. And there was also the possibility that he might have had a little help from the other Redeemer boys.

I covered the wood carefully, so that no one would be able to tell that I had been there. I needed my wagon, and Alice. But before I did that, I wanted to talk with Nadine. Checking to make sure that the sound of hammering continued in the barn, I hurried to the steps.

Flies buzzed the garbage, and I had an irrational urge to tell her how filthy and nasty it was to throw her trash out the back door like she did. I knocked three times before she came to open it.

'Bekkah, where did you go? We could have used some help getting Caesar out of that stall.'

'I went with Jamey, and then I needed time to think.' The smell of the garbage was making me dizzy. 'Can I come in? I need to tell you something. About Caesar.'

Nadine looked behind her, as if someone might object. I had the peculiar thought that maybe she didn't live alone. Then she stepped back. 'Okay. Come in.' She signaled me inside, then closed the back door, shutting out some of the garbage smell.

I followed her from the narrow entrance down a hall and into the kitchen.

I'd never been inside Nadine's before, not even to go to the bathroom. Either I held it or crouched down in one of the stalls, the way Nadine said all the professional riders did in big barns. The practice was unpleasant, but I didn't want to seem like a sissy so I did it. Looking around the filthy kitchen, I knew I didn't want to see the toilet.

Paper plates, fast-food wrappers and TV dinner boxes spilled out of paper bags and onto the floor. There were empty cans of soup and dirty pots. Stains were spattered down the front of the cabinets and even the refrigerator. There was a bare light bulb, and above that, on the ceiling, was what looked like spaghetti pasta and sauce. Had Nadine thrown a spoon or dish? I didn't feel that I could ask.

There was a table, but it was covered in dirty dishes and half-eaten sandwiches that served as a landing strip for flies.

'This place is a mess,' I said before I thought. I had a clear picture of Mama Betts' face in my mind. Her disapproval was extreme.

'I can either ride or clean, and I'd rather ride,' Nadine said, not in the least offended by my remark. 'When I was growing up, we had maids, and I guess I never got in the habit of cleaning up after myself.'

'Nobody on Kali Oka Road has a maid.'

'I know,' Nadine said, and she laughed. She led the way down a hall cluttered with dirty clothes and into the living room. The curtains were drawn, and beneath them were old yellowed shades. The combination effectively kept the light at a minimum, but I could see that the furniture was all antiques. Good solid pieces that Mama Betts would tend and dust with loving attention. These hadn't seen a dust cloth in years, and they'd been scarred and mistreated. Nadine threw herself on an old Queen Anne sofa and draped one leg over the battered back.

'What's on your mind?' she asked. She was concentrating on a stain on the ceiling where the roof had leaked. It was vaguely shaped like a heart.

'Nadine, it's Caesar . . . You didn't hear anything?' I leaned forward. 'Not even a sound?' Greg wouldn't disturb the horses. They trusted him.

'You think I wouldn't get up and check if I heard a horse making a racket?' She turned her attention from the stain and looked at me. There was a stillness behind her eyes.

The room smelled of dogs. By my count there should have been two left. 'What about your dogs? They didn't bark? Picket would have gone through the screen door if someone had been in our yard.'

'The dogs are dead. They got distemper.'

'They weren't vaccinated?' Nadine knew everything about horses. She should have known to get her dogs shots.

'I was waiting on some money.' The stillness in her eyes burned away, revealing heat. 'What are you, part of the Spanish Inquisition? Is somebody paying you to make me feel worse than I already do?'

'I'm sorry.' Nadine's mood was volatile. I could see that Caesar's death had shaken her tremendously. I had to be careful what I said. 'Dr. Hilbun only charges a couple of dollars for shots. Mama Betts or Effie would have loaned you the money.' They might dislike Nadine, but they'd have loaned her the money to get her dogs shots. I took a seat on one of the wingback chairs. The rich brocade of the fabric showed a design that had once been beautiful and elegant. Time and misuse had faded the beauty.

'I have a trust fund, from my parents' deaths, you know. I thought the money would come in on time.' Nadine shrugged. 'By the time I was certain that Mac had it, then the others caught it from him. They just died one right after the other. Greg buried a couple for me. I buried the rest.'

'Yeah, I saw him.'

'And what did he say?'

Nadine's question threw me. Did she suspect what I did? 'Greg didn't say much, just that the dogs died.'

'Good.' Nadine swung her leg off the back of the sofa and sat up, both feet flat on the ground. 'Any other questions about my animals? If not, maybe you should go back outside and do your chores. I have a headache and I think I want to take a nap.'

I sat on the edge of the chair. Anger grew inside me so fast that I wasn't certain what it was I felt. I wanted Nadine to do something, to hunt for who had hurt Caesar, not to take a stupid nap. What was wrong with her? 'None of this had to happen! Not the dogs and not Caesar! How could someone kill an animal like that and you not hear a thing? You brought Greg here! You allowed him in, and the animals trusted him!' The smell of the house, the dimness of the room – I felt as if my head was going to split.

'Are you daring to imply that this was my fault?' She was perfectly still, but the fire in her eyes burned brighter.

'Why was Caesar in Cammie's stall?' I wasn't going to run away from her. Not this time. How could she not have heard? 'Why was he moved?' I had to have some answers.

'You're very tenacious, Rebekah. I had thought you

might be, but then I wondered if I had misjudged you.'

She was staring at me with a curious expression. 'I don't care what you think about me. Caesar's dead.'

'I don't owe you an explanation,' she paused, 'but I'll give you one. I moved Caesar last night. His foot was giving him some trouble, and Cammie's stall is slightly bigger. I thought it would give him more room to move around.' She slowly sat forward. 'You think whoever killed Caesar meant to kill Cammie, don't you?'

I didn't say anything.

'Maybe Greg? Maybe to get even because he found out we'd gone to the church?'

I hadn't put my thoughts into real clear ideas. 'Jamey Louise thought it was Cammie who was dead. That's what she told me.'

'That Jamey, she's worked here all summer and doesn't know one horse from another.' Nadine sighed. 'They were both bays, but that's the only way they resembled each other. Just thank God it wasn't Cammie. In the dark they would resemble each other. Greg wouldn't have known that I'd changed stalls.'

As suddenly as it had come, my anger evaporated. I was about as wrung out as Effie during one of her tantrums. 'No one else was hurt at all?'

'No one. It was like some maniac got loose in the stall with poor old Caesar. He fought, but he didn't know how to strike out at a person. He'd always been treated with kindness. He never expected to be . . . killed.' Nadine looked away at the window shade. A branch from one of the overgrown camellia bushes brushed against the screen, creating moving shadows. 'Why would Greg do this?'

'I don't know. Who else would?'

'That's the question, isn't it? Who else?' Nadine stood. Her wild, slightly green hair hung past her shoulders. Well water and bleach had combined to give it that funny cast, and she needed more bleach. Even in the dimness of the room her roots were darker than the rest. 'Say it wasn't Greg. Who would do this?'

'Someone mean. Meaner than anybody I've ever known or read about.'

'Is that the way you see Greg?' she asked.

'Maybe.' I swallowed. I'd watched Greg with the horses. He petted them when he thought no one else was looking. 'He's strong enough.'

'Yes, strong enough.' Nadine was staring at the ceiling again. 'But why? Motive is the thing. Did Greg have a motive?'

It was the crucifix. That was the reason I'd suspected him. That tortured Jesus, his face blackened, hidden so carefully in the weeds and bushes. But did that mean Greg would kill a horse?

'No,' I finally answered her. 'Maybe it was a stranger on the road.' It could not really have been anyone I knew. Not Greg or anyone else.

'Maybe not a stranger,' Nadine whispered, 'maybe someone from my past.' She turned back to face me, and her eyes glowed in her pale face. 'My last husband was . . . not exactly normal. He was very charming. A handsome man with the kindest gray eyes. But when he didn't get his way.' She swallowed and I could tell her mouth had gone dry by the way her throat worked. 'He could become very abusive and mean.'

A car passed on Kali Oka Road. I could hear it, but I couldn't see because of the shades and curtains. Nadine got up and pulled back the shade, staring for a moment as the car disappeared.

I thought about calling the sheriff. Joe Wickham would probably tell Effie and Walt if I called him, but it would be better than doing nothing. I hadn't considered that someone from Nadine's past might have followed her to Kali Oka Road. That would explain a lot.

'Would you like something cold to drink?' Nadine asked.

I would, but the thought of that kitchen effectively quenched my thirst. I'd get some water from the hose before I left. I could wait until then. 'Thanks, but I'm not really thirsty.'

'My husband drank water with a twist of lemon in it.' She moved back to the sofa and reclined. For a moment she stared at the ceiling. 'I shouldn't tell you this. No one should have to know this kind of thing.'

'What?' My curiosity blossomed. Nadine had never talked about her past. The first day I'd met her, she'd told me her parents were dead and she'd been married three times. During the whole summer I'd never known her to have a date or even to go into town. Mrs. Huff, the post mistress, had told Emily that not a single letter had been delivered to Nadine since she'd lived there. Just bills. Not even magazines.

'Aren't you afraid to know?' She looked at me. 'Knowing things can change you. You experience them, secondhand.'

She was playing with me in the way she liked to do. Testing. 'I'm not afraid. Tell me.'

'I hardly knew Phillip when I married him. I met him at a dance at the country club.' She stared at me, watching how her words affected my features. 'My parents had just died, only weeks before. They'd been my whole world, them and the horses. I was lonely . . . ' She didn't finish.

'What happened after you got married?'

Her smile was amused. 'If I told you those things, your mother would surely skin me alive.'

'Where is he?'

'Phillip? I haven't heard from him since I moved here. You see, that's really why I came to Kali Oka Road. I wanted to get as far away from him as I could. The only thing I took were my horses and my dogs and cats. Everything else I left. After I filed for the divorce, Phillip was really upset. He said he was going to kill me.'

'Nadine, where is he now?' The hair on my arms stood on end. He could have followed her from the very beginning. He could have been watching all along.

'I don't know.' She shrugged on the sofa. 'I called home this morning after I found Caesar. I have an aunt there, and a few good friends left. Phillip hated the horses. He hated anything that I cared about. Whatever I loved, he wanted to destroy.'

'Was he there?'

She sighed. 'No. He left shortly after I did. No one knows where he went. My family's lawyer had him evicted from the house after the divorce was final. He hasn't been seen or heard from since then.' She stared at the ceiling again. 'He's a very, very smart man. That's what makes him so dangerous.'

Nadine sat up, rubbing the back of her neck. 'If he was the one who killed Caesar, he'll be back. The horse was a warning.'

'A warning?'

'He likes to make me anticipate. When we were married, when he would decide to hurt me, he'd only hurt me a little first. Then he'd wait.' Her gaze was focused behind me, her eyes sharp with anger. 'Part of his torture was telling me how I deserved to suffer. He'd quote from the Bible, just an appropriate verse or two, and he'd hurt me a little more. He said he wanted to give me a taste of what was coming later. It was the waiting that was the worst. That and having to thank him for saving me from my sins. Redeemed through suffering.'

'Nadine,' I spoke very calmly. She'd thought she'd make me afraid, but she hadn't. It was worse than Selena's ghost, worse than going into the barn by myself

285

late in the evening when I expected to find the wrathful ghost of old Sheriff Sidney Miller. 'We have to call the sheriff.'

'No!' She put both hands on her knees and leaned forward. 'That's exactly what he would want me to do. I've called the police before. They won't help a woman if it's her husband.'

'But you're divorced.'

'Around here that only makes it worse,' she said. 'Let the bastard come on. I know he's around now. And I know what he's up to. I don't want any lawmen in the way, because when I see him, I'm going to kill him.'

The room was stifling. Sweat trickled from the base of my hairline down my neck, slipping farther along my spine and down to the waistband of my shorts. The bends of my legs were sweating. After what Phillip had done to Caesar, he deserved to die. I didn't doubt it for a moment. But he could come back and kill the other horses, or Nadine. She was alone. She needed someone to help her.

'Do you still think Greg had anything to do with this?' Nadine asked.

In all of his days at the barn, I'd never seen Greg act as if he wanted to hurt one of the horses. It had been the crucifix and doubts about Mr. Tom that had made me suspect him all along. That and the fact that things on Kali Oka Road had changed since the Redeemers had moved there. 'Redeemed through suffering.' A horrible, terrible thought crossed my mind.

'Nadine! What if your husband is with the Redeemers?'

The smile she gave me was cunning. 'Oh, Bekkah, don't you think I've thought of that? That's why I hired Greg in the first place, to ask him about the men there. But he won't talk. That's why we went to the church that day. We weren't just being nosy. Phillip is smart. I

286

thought that perhaps he might be down there waiting for his chance to strike at me.'

'Could he do that? I mean, the Redeemers are pretty weird.' She was staring at me like I'd grown another head. 'I mean, could he fit in with them?'

'If anyone had the background to fit in with religious fanatics, it was darling Phillip. He knew the scriptures inside and out, and he knew exactly how to twist them to his own means. That's what preachers do, they get a herd of folks to follow them like cows.' Three short chuckles escaped her. 'Why, Phillip could be Rev. Marcus the preacherman himself.'

I took a short breath. 'You think your ex-husband is the preacherman?'

'That remains to be seen, Rebekah. That remains to be seen.'

Chapter Twenty-six

Jamey Louise returned to the barn about eleven o'clock, but she didn't stay longer than three minutes. The heat and the flies and the smell of the blood must have gotten to her. She looked pale and drawn as she passed beneath me in the driveway. After leaving Nadine, still reclining on her sofa, I'd climbed back in the chinaberry tree and waited.

When I was certain Nadine wasn't coming back out to the barn, I climbed down from the tree and went inside. Greg wasn't in any of the stalls, so I climbed the ladder to the loft, clearing my throat near the top as a warning of my approach.

He was sitting on a bale of hay, facing me, when I pulled myself up onto the straw-covered floor.

'If you don't mind, I'd prefer some privacy,' he said coldly.

His long-sleeved shirt, filthy with dried blood and sweat, was buttoned wrong, cuffs hanging loose. Barely visible behind the bale of hay was some kind of container.

'I'm sorry, Greg.'

'Sorry that it wasn't me, or sorry that you thought it was?'

I was afraid to step any farther into the loft, so I hung at the end of the opening. 'I'm glad it wasn't you, and I'm sorry I jumped to that conclusion. I . . . ' It was too hard to explain exactly how my mind had made that leap. Most of it was the crucifix, but some of it was the way Greg was looking at me now, like he could hurt me.

'Whenever anything goes wrong on Kali Oka Road, the Redeemers will always be blamed.' He turned his head away from me when he spoke.

I wanted to ask him outright about the preacherm in, but he wouldn't answer. He never talked about he Redeemers. I'd have to find a way to get him to talk. 'it's because y'all act like you've got something to hide. You clump up down there and run people off—'

'Just nosy children who snoop around and then run back down the road to lie about us! Those are the only people who've been run off.'

'Maybe you should have invited others to your church.'

'So they could laugh and make fun of us? Point at us and call us hillbillies and primitives? Yeah! You act like Kali Oka is the first place we've ever been. Why do you think we move so much?' The last was spoken quietly.

'You make yourselves different, and around here that means dangerous.'

'Even to you, Bekkah Rich?' He sat slumped on the bale of hay. 'Are we so dangerous to you that you'd go into our church and paint the crucifix black like you did?' he asked.

I wasn't even shocked that he thought I'd done such a thing. 'I didn't do that.'

He smiled. 'Then who? You're the only one around here who's shown any interest in what goes on at our church. You're the one who's been peeping in the church windows. I saw you staring at it that day, looking like it was some sort of evil thing.'

'I didn't do it.'

'Then who, Bekkah? Who would do such a thing while we were out of town? I know you were in the sanctuary.'

He smiled, but he looked as if he were too weary to sit up a minute longer. He seemed to drift forward and catch himself. 'I didn't tell anyone else, but I knew you were there.'

'How?'

'I saw Picket's tracks. She must have gotten her paws wet and then walked in the red dirt. There were perfect paw prints and then a little pile of dirt where she laid down beside one of the pews. You must have been in there a while before you decided to paint the crucifix.'

My heart felt funny, like pressure had been added to the beat. I felt it in my temples, along with a burning shame. 'I was in the church, but I didn't touch that crucifix. I swear it.'

'Then who did?' he asked.

'I don't know. It was fine when I left. I swear it on a stack of Bibles.'

Greg stood, and he really did falter. His hand shot out and grabbed the beam that supported the roof just in time to keep from falling on his face in the hay.

'Greg!' I started forward, but he warned me back with a look that was cold.

'Don't worry, Miss Rebekah. I didn't tell anyone that you were there. I would have gotten blamed for that anyway. Just know that your meddling has a price tag hooked to it.'

'What are you talking about?' A whisper of fear tickled my neck. 'What kind of price tag? I didn't hurt anything. I didn't want to go in the church, but I got frightened and there was no place else to go.'

'Digging up graves?' he said, and his voice was ugly again. 'Looking to see if the Redeemers had murdered someone? That's the gossip, isn't it, that we murder people who try to leave us. That we're a cult and that we worship Satan.'

'It was Magdeline. I was worried about her.'

'Sure,' he said. 'You're worried about her so you almost get her strapped.'

'How? What are you saying?'

'If Rev. Marcus even thought she was talking to you, he'd half kill her. The women aren't allowed to talk to anyone outside the church.'

'I never talked to her. I never tried to talk to her. There's no reason she should be in any trouble because of me.'

'When Rev. Marcus saw the paint job on that crucifix, he said he'd give the congregation three days to come up with a confession.'

'That's stupid. Everyone was gone to Hattiesburg. None of you could have done it.'

'Exactly.' Greg swayed a little on his feet but caught the beam again. 'He said someone in the church had to tell our business and our plans, or the intruder wouldn't have felt so free to sneak around and desecrate the crucifix. So he said we had three days to confess. And then . . . ' Greg stopped.

'Then what?' I demanded.

'Then he would start with the beatings.'

'Greg, my father's in New Orleans, but I can call him. He'll know what to do. He can stop this from happening.'

'It's too late.'

'Did he—'

'He beat Jim first, as an example. But Jim wouldn't say anything. When he couldn't beat it out of him, he said I was next. But then he changed his mind and said it was Georgie. The discipline is public. Georgie couldn't have taken it. He would have wet his pants. So I said I did it.' He took a step toward me. 'The only thing that made it bearable was that I knew how awful you'd feel when you saw that I'd taken the beating you should have had.'

What he was saying was like a riddle. 'I didn't do it, Greg. I didn't. And I don't know who did.'

He shifted his weight from foot to foot. It was like slow motion. I knew he was going to fall, and the edge of the loft was only three or four feet away from him. If he fell wrong, he could roll off the edge and down to the center aisle of the barn ten feet below. I lunged forward and grabbed his arm, pulling him back against several bundles of hay. He cried out as his back came in contact with the hay and rolled quickly to his stomach. I could see where his shirt had dried and stuck to his back. It wasn't Caesar's blood, not on his back.

'Those bastards,' I whispered, sitting down beside him. 'Don't move, Greg.' I didn't know what to do.

'There's some water by the hay,' he whispered.

I got the container he'd been trying to hide. He wanted me to soak his shirt so that he could pull it off without tearing the scabs away. It was obvious he'd slept in the shirt, but I didn't ask.

'Greg, come to the house. My grandmother will help you.' I was surprised to find that I was crying.

'No. If she sees my back, she'll call the sheriff.'

'Why is everybody here so afraid of the sheriff? Joe Wickham isn't Satan. He needs to be called. That son of a bitch should pay for this, and my daddy will see that he does.'

'Bekkah!' His hand shot through the hay and grabbed my ankle. 'No lawmen. Nobody! You hear! Not at the Redeemers.'

'What is it you have to hide?' I asked. I started to tell him that I knew about the babies, but I stopped.

'Ask yourself the same question.' He jerked the collar of his shirt, tearing it half free of his back. Fresh blood covered the material in a matter of seconds.

'I'll get Nadine. She'll know what to do.' I was panicked. He was hurting so much, and he was so mad.

'Run, Bekkah. That's what you always do, isn't it?'

'What should I do, Greg?' I was crying hard.

'Run home. Run to Nadine. Then when you stop running, think for a moment what it might be like not to have anywhere to run to.'

I stood clenching and unclenching my fingers in the rag that had been in the bucket.

'There's some epsom salt in Cammie's grooming kit.' I picked up the pail of bloody water. 'I'll get some hot water from Nadine's kitchen.'

Greg was still white from pain. It occurred to me that he might be in shock. His features were sharp-edged, testimony to his sheer determination not to cry.

'What will you tell Nadine?' he asked.

'That Cammie has a sore I want to soak.' How had Nadine failed to see his condition? 'Would it hurt if I told her? She's good at doctoring things.'

'I'd rather she didn't know. Jamey either.'

'Jamey doesn't know?' The barn was dim, even with all of the lights on. It had been a gruesome morning. But if Jamey didn't know today, she'd know soon. She was constantly touching him, running her hands along his arms and shoulders and back. Maybe I should call Jamey. She might be able to talk some sense into Greg.

'Go on home, Bekkah. I'm not going to die.'

I took the pail and climbed down the ladder. At the back door I called Nadine, but she didn't answer. When I slipped inside I didn't see her, but I could hear her foot thumping up and down on the floor in the living room. I could imagine her, sprawled on the Queen Anne with one leg bent and the heel rising and falling in a regular rhythm, as if she listened to music. I tried to hold my breath while I got the water, but I had to breathe. The smell, the events of the day, what I had left to do, it all made me queasy. Nothing felt real anymore. I had only to tend to Greg and then I could go home to Mama Betts.

Greg was sitting with his head in his hands on the bale of hay when I got into the loft with the hot water and the salt. I'd also brought along some of the yellow salve Nadine used on the horses when they were cut. It said for use in horses only, but I'd gotten it in small cuts on my hands when I was doctoring a horse. It hadn't killed me. Maybe it had helped hold off infection.

There was a big bottle of methylate at home, but I didn't think Greg would let me go get it. I was afraid it would kill him if I tried to use it on his back. Even with the shirt still on, it looked bad.

It took thirty minutes of soaking to get the shirt pulled free. I took it down the ladder and soaked it in another bucket of cold water. Not that I cared for the shirt, but it was so coated with skin and scab and blood that it had to be washed clean before he could think of wearing it again. If he didn't account for it, those bastards might beat him again.

The crisscrosses on his back lapped over and over each other.

'Coat hanger,' he said, knowing that I was wondering what he had been struck with.

'My father will kill him.' I didn't realize I spoke out loud.

'My parents gave their approval.'

'They belong in jail, then.'

Greg laughed. It was the saddest sound. 'They feel the same way about me. I confessed to destroying the crucifix, Bekkah. It's not like they just decided to beat me.'

'Even if you had done it, they shouldn't have done this.' Some of the wounds were cut deep into Greg's thin coating of muscle. I wondered about stitches, but there was hardly a place to stitch to.

The salt water I'd made had been very mild. Nadine had said salt water was a good healing agent, and it also helped relieve soreness. She hadn't said that it would sting and burn.

'There's some peroxide down in the tack room. Maybe we should use some of that before the salve.'

'I don't know.' Greg sounded weak. 'Will it burn?'

'Probably.'

'Maybe tomorrow. I don't think I can take it now.'

'Let me get one of Arly's T-shirts. It'll be cooler, and you'll sleep better.'

'No!'

'Greg.' I was standing behind him and I put my hands on his arms. 'I'm going home to get one. Arly won't ever know, and Mama Betts won't catch me.'

'Bekkah . . . '

'I'm going.' I took off down the ladder before he could protest. He was a lot sicker than he wanted me to know. Passing Cammie's stall, where Caesar had been killed, I didn't look. When I got to the barn door, I started running. Picket fell into step beside me. We ran and ran in the hot August day, churning up small clouds of Kali Oka behind us.

Two terrible things had happened in one day, and nobody wanted to call the sheriff. I might not call Joe Wickham, but I was going to call The Judge. As soon as it turned dark. Mama Betts would have his number and I'd call him in New Orleans. He had to come home and take care of this. Effie too. Bad things were happening. Until then, though, I couldn't let Mama Betts see me. She'd know something was bad wrong if she took one look at me.

I sneaked around to Arly's window, pried off the screen and slipped in. I had to stand on an old tub we used to haul leaves to the ditch to burn. It was barely high enough, but I managed to jump to the sill and wiggle up. It was a lot easier breaking out of the house than in, I decided.

I got two white T-shirts, then slipped down to the bathroom for some aspirin and whatever else I could find. There weren't any bandages nearly big enough for Greg's back. There was one roll of gauze, but it wouldn't cover much territory. In the back of the shelves where we kept our towels I found some old cotton diapers. I took four of those and some tape. They might make big bandages, and I could tape the corners of the diaper to his chest. He had to have something to keep the dirt out of his wounds.

When I heard Mama Betts go outside to hang some clothes, I sneaked into the kitchen and got a brown paper sack. I filled it with biscuits from the morning, bread, slices of fresh ham, a hunk of cheese, some apples, and a knife. I'd make Greg some sandwiches, without the deadly mayonnaise.

I made a dash to the study and grabbed a collection of stories by Poe and one of Effie's books. Since I wasn't willing to risk meeting Mama Betts in the yard, I waited until I heard the screen door slam as she came back in, and I went back out Arly's window. I couldn't get the screen to fit together right, so I did the best I could and took off. In Arly's perpetual state of horniness, he probably wouldn't even notice if a few mosquitoes got in and feasted on him.

I beat it back to the barn as fast as I could with all the things I was carrying. When I got to the loft, Greg was lying on his side. A few pieces of hay had gotten into the salve, so I picked them out and made him a diaper bandage by taping the corners of the diaper to his collarbones and the front of his stomach. It took the whole diaper to cover his wounds. Then I made him put on the T-shirt. In my haste to escape, I'd forgotten a blanket, but I made him take two of the aspirin.

'I need to rest for a while,' he said.

I went down to the tack room and got the cleanest horse blanket I could find and took it up to him.

'Greg, Nadine would drive you home,' I suggested.

Then I remembered those rooms at the church. The horse blanket was surely as clean as those urine-soaked mattresses. Maybe cleaner. And the barn was certainly cleaner than Nadine's house.

'I can get you to my house.' I pressed him because all of the hard edges had dropped away from his face. His eyes were soft, liquidy, yet dry. He smiled.

'No can do,' he said, then reached and touched my leg. 'Thanks. You didn't run away.'

I slapped together some bread and ham and cheese into a rough sandwich for him and left the rest of the food with him, along with some bottles of water I hauled up for him to drink in case he woke up thirsty.

I went down to the barn, cleaned out Cammie's stall, taking it down to the red clay floor, and then covered it – walls and floor – in as much lime as I could throw on it. Nadine had not come out of the house, so I got Cammie out of her stall and brushed her. I only meant to saddle her and ride around the yard. But once the saddle was on, I led her out of the gate, mounted her under the chinaberry tree and took off down Kali Oka Road. I hadn't gotten a chance to ask Greg about the preacherman. I couldn't wait for the right time. The Redeemers drew me down the road. I might not have any answer to my questions, but at least I'd look at them. With any luck, maybe I'd see Jim or Georgie or even Magdeline. If I did, I intended to talk to them.

Chapter Twenty-seven

Holding Cammie on the road took all of my strength and know-how. She spooked at mailboxes, gates, whenever the road shifted colors from brick red to coral. Rutted tire tracks made her balk and try to rear. She'd never been down the road in her entire life. It was as if I'd taken her to a different continent, a place of danger and the unknown. If I hadn't been so determined to bring her under control, I might have turned back to the barn.

When we stood at the bridge to Cry Baby Creek, Cammie was coated in sweat and foam on her neck. The dust we'd stirred in approaching the bridge in crab-like scuttles and lunges settled over us, giving Cammie's gleaming mahogany coat a sticky pink topping.

Across the bridge, three Redeemer women stared at us. Picket stood just in front and to the right of Cammie, her hackles raised.

'It's a public road,' I challenged them.

The women said nothing, but they didn't turn away. Some fifteen feet behind them a young girl darted behind a tree. She was about eight, and she peeked out at me, curiosity plainly overcoming her fear of me.

One of the women heard her and turned quickly. 'Get inside, Ruth!' she commanded, pointing toward the sanctuary. 'Get the others and get inside.'

The child looked past the woman at me. I waved to her. 'I won't hurt you,' I called out. 'Don't be afraid of me.' I'd seen men, women, teenagers and young children, but no babies.

'Ruth! Get inside or Rev. Marcus will tan your hide.'

The young girl fled, not even daring a look over her shoulder.

The youngest-looking of the Redeemer women spoke to the other two, then turned and ran back into the woods. She was going for some of the men, maybe even the preacherman. They acted as if they thought I intended to harm them, as if by standing in the road and looking at them I might do them some horrible damage.

The very thin grip I'd kept on my anger snapped. Digging my heels into Cammie's side, I urged her forward. She bolted onto the wooden bridge without having time to consider her action. Her momentum carried her forward another stride before she heard the hollow wood echoing beneath her. She panicked, rising high on her hind legs and pawing the air.

The two Redeemer women fell back, screaming. From high on the horse's back I could see their faces twitch as they threw up their arms to ward off the horse's hoofs.

Cammie had no intention of going any closer. She twisted in midair and started back to solid ground.

'I know what you do here!' I called at the women. 'I know.'

There was no stopping Cammie with the simple snaffle bit in her mouth. She tore out for home, stretching out long and frightened as she pounded the red clay road toward Nadine's.

By the time I got Cammie to stop, she was heaving and blowing. There was no going back to Nadine's in that condition. I walked past the creaking sign and kept going to my house. Cammie was too tired and exhausted to even put up a protest when I turned her down the drive to my house.

Mama Betts was taking in the clothes that had dried on

the line. It rained every afternoon, and she timed her wash so that it was ready to come in long before the sky clouded over with the heat-rain. She paused, clothespin held aloft, as she watched me come down the short drive.

'Looks like you've had a ride,' she said, folding a towel and dropping it into a basket at her feet.

'She's too hot. I'm afraid she'll get sick.'

'Take her to the back and put the water hose on her. Just her feet for a little while.'

I remembered Nadine telling me the same thing about an overheated horse, or one that had been ridden hard. Cool the feet and legs with water before you let it touch the chest or body. I was impressed that Mama Betts knew that fact.

'I know you think only Nadine knows a thing about horses, but you forget I was born before cars were invented. In fact, before there were water hoses. We'd have to take a horse like that down to the creek and let her wade around for a while.'

I left Mama Betts taking down the last of the towels. The hose was behind the house, and I turned it on and let the cool water wash over Cammie's front legs. I shifted the spray front to back, front to back, front to back, in a slow and endless pattern. There were rainbows in the spray of the water as it spread around the finger I held at the end of the hose. When I was a little girl, Effie had told me that rainbows were magic. She said if I could step inside one, I'd be granted a wish. If only that were true.

'Where's Nadine?' Mama Betts answered.

'Up at the barn.' I inched the water higher up Cammie's hocks.

'Does she know you've had this horse on the road?'

'No, ma'am.'

'Shall I call her to come down here?'

'No, ma'am. It's okay. I just wanted to cool Cammie

off.' I looked up at her. 'I wanted to come home for a few minutes.'

'She's a beautiful horse. When I was a teenager, I was courted by a man who had a beautiful bay mare. Truth told, I liked his horse better than I liked him.'

'What happened to him?'

'Oh, he found out where my sentiments were and it hurt his feelings. He found a girl who liked him.'

I smiled. Mama Betts could always make me feel better.

'I didn't bring Cammie here to show off. I just wanted to come home.'

'Effie's gone over to Pam's to get her hair styled. She's leaving for New Orleans as soon as she gets back.'

I'd never really doubted that Mama Betts could get her to go. 'I have to talk to Daddy.'

'You can call them both tonight, see if they're still alive.' She chuckled. ''Course, Effie might turn around and come straight home, you know. She might come back to get me.'

'She might.' I inched the water up to Cammie's chest. She lowered her head for some of the spray. I'd have to clean and oil the bridle, but it didn't matter. Cammie wanted to be hosed off.

'Bekkah, when you finish up at the barn, why don't you go over to Alice's for the afternoon? I don't want you around here when Effie comes back. Might just give her an excuse not to go. Or she might want to take you with her.'

I wanted to go to New Orleans. I wanted to escape from Kali Oka Road, from what had happened at the barn. From what might happen next. 'Okay, I'll go over to Alice's. Can she have supper with us?'

'Make it late, about seven. I know she'll bring that baby.' Mama Betts sighed. 'I thought once I raised Effie, I'd be done. Little did I know I'd be raising hers and the young'uns down the road.'

I smiled. 'You love Maebelle V.' Mama Betts always grumbled about Maebelle, but when the baby was in the house, no one else could hold her or change her or feed her.

'I do,' Mama Betts said suddenly. 'God help me, I do love that little redheaded child.'

I allowed the water to cascade over Cammie's chest. I spared the saddle as much as I could while giving her back end a good rinsing. With Mama Betts watching, with what might have been some approval, I mounted.

The cold water had revived some of Cammie's foolishness, and she sidestepped away from a terra cotta pot of geraniums.

'That horse is pretty, but she lacks good sense.'

'I don't think she's ever been away from a barn.'

Mama Betts snorted. 'It's a wonder she hasn't turned mean. Keeping animals penned up and running around in circles will make 'em crazy. Just like people. They have to be allowed to do what comes naturally.'

I'd heard this lecture before. Mama Betts thoroughly disapproved of everything she'd heard about Nadine's horse care, especially the confinement.

'I'll see you tonight. With Alice and Maebelle.' To prevent an answer, I nudged Cammie into a trot.

'Hey?' Mama Betts called out when I was halfway down the drive. 'Bekkah!'

I turned Cammie into a tight circle and stopped her. 'What?'

'You look mighty pretty on that mare. You're a natural.'

'Thanks, Grandma.' I turned back to Kali Oka and rode toward Nadine's.

The barn was as deserted as when I left. A pinch of guilt tweaked at me as I unsaddled Cammie and put her in her stall. I intended to take her down the road again as soon as possible. Mama Betts was right. Keeping animals penned up might not be the best thing for them. Cammie had enjoyed going down the road, and once she learned that it was part of what she was supposed to do, she'd like it more. I cleaned and oiled the saddle and bridle. It took well over an hour, and still there was no sign of Nadine, Jamey Louise or Greg. I thought he'd have to come down to go to the bathroom, at least. When I'd finished everything I was supposed to do, I went up to the loft. He was lying on his side, asleep.

His face had a flushed tinge that didn't look good. I woke him with a gently shake.

'Bekkah?' He acted like he didn't know me.

'How're you feeling?'

'Hot.' He pushed up on one arm, his face contorting. 'Would you hand me that water?'

I gave him one of the bottles, and he drank it down. I found the aspirins I'd hidden in the straw and gave him two more. He took them without any sign of stubbornness.

'I think if I sleep some more I'll feel better.'

His face was puffy from sleep, and when I touched his forehead, he felt slightly warm. 'Greg, won't you please let my grandmother look at your back?'

'If you'll get out of here and let me sleep, I'll be fine.' He pushed at my hand and eased back down on the horse blanket. 'Bekkah?'

'What?'

'Who killed Caesar?'

I didn't know what to say. 'We don't know.' I waited a minute, but his eyes were closed. 'Greg, where did Rev. Marcus come from? Do you know?'

'Up state. Near Memphis, I think.'

'From the Delta?'

'Gossip before he came was that he'd grown up in a rich family and gave it all up because the Lord told him to.' Greg opened his eyes and looked at me. 'Only the women believe that, because they want to. It makes him sound noble or something.'

'I wouldn't believe anything he said, a man who could hurt a young boy the way he hurt you.'

'You live in a fairy tale, Bekkah. I looked at your mother's book. She dedicated it to you, for your help.' He reached out his hand and touched my leg. 'You live some place I've never even dreamed about. If you're smart, you'll stay away from the church. Don't be asking questions, and don't be going down there. Where Rev. Marcus came from and where he goes ain't none of your concern.' He closed his eyes and in a few minutes he was breathing slow and shallow.

'It is my business if he killed Caesar,' I whispered.

Maebelle's fingers grabbed my left braid, and she pulled with all of her eight-month-old strength.

'She'll jerk you bald,' Alice warned. Her attention focused on my hair, she advanced across the Waltman front porch, avoiding the two places where the wood had gone soft with rot. 'How are you going to wear your hair this year? Pigtails are too little-girlish. Nobody wears buns anymore. What are you doing to do?'

It was an issue I hadn't given a terrible amount of thought, but it was far better than the things that kept edging up in my head. 'What do you think?'

'Cut it shoulder-length and see if it'll turn up on the ends.'

I shook my head, partly to get Maebelle's wandering attention and partly in denial. My hair would never flip up. There was too much of it, and it was too fine with a will of its own.

'I'm getting mine cut.' Alice sat down on the floor beside the straight-backed chair where I sat. We'd come out on the porch to escape the mayhem of the house. Agatha Waltman was five months along, and she was as mean as a hungry lioness. She had everyone in the house jumping from chair to chair. She wouldn't allow Alice to leave the yard, but she didn't want her inside with Maebelle V. Mrs. Waltman said the sight of Maebelle made her bottom hurt, and she was getting ready to go through it again. I'd started to ask her why she got pregnant again if it hurt so bad, but Alice had dragged me out the screen door, which had no spring and two enormous holes in it.

'Don't do anything stupid,' she'd hissed in my ear. 'You may not be one of her young'uns, but she'll take your head off and roll it home for you.'

I laughed. There had been a time when I was afraid of Agatha's harsh tongue and quick hand. Not today. But I didn't want to make it harder for Alice. If we aggravated her mother, Mrs. Waltman wouldn't let Alice come for supper. More than anything in the world, I didn't want to be alone. If I was alone, I'd think about what had happened.

'Hey! Bekkah!' Alice waved her hand in front of my face.

I looked up to see she was wearing a sundress, not a lot different from the one Jamey Louise had worn to the barn that morning, only Alice's was aqua. While I'd drifted off in my own private little nightmare world, Alice had gone inside and changed clothes. The dress made her eyes snap with color.

'You like it?'

I nodded.

'Connie Shoals gave it to me for baby-sitting her two young'uns last week. She didn't have any money, but she said I could have this dress because Marvin wouldn't let her wear it anyway. She had this big bruise on her arm. It wasn't really one big bruise, it was like four smaller ones that sort of oozed together, like he'd grabbed her around the arm and squeezed real hard.

And her cheekbone' – she pointed beneath her right eye – 'was bruised too. She said she hit herself with a cabinet door.'

'Did he hit her?' I didn't want to hear this.

Alice nodded. 'I'd say so.'

It was stupid to ask, but I did anyway. 'Did she call the sheriff?'

Alice laughed. 'If she called Mr. Wickham every time Marvin slapped her around, Joe Wickham would have to move in with them.'

'Is it so much to ask for people to behave?'

Alice tugged one shoulder strap on the dress, adjusting it over her new bra strap. Alice had gotten her bras two weeks before, and she said she was getting bigger every night. In the aqua sundress she looked like she had breasts. 'What's wrong with you, Bekkah?'

'I hate the idea of going to school.'

'This year it'll be different. We'll be around all the high school kids.'

'Yeah, and they'll make us feel like babies. Look at Arly. He's only gonna be in the ninth grade, and he acts like I'm a gnat.'

'That's 'cause you're his little sister.' Alice laughed. 'Some of those ninth-grade boys are going to think you're pretty, and that's going to get Arly's goat good and proper.'

I laughed with Alice, even though I had trouble believing what she said. I had difficulty thinking about school and boys. I wanted to tell Alice about Caesar and about Greg – and about Nadine's ex-husband. But I couldn't.

She took the baby from my arms. 'Let's go to the swing.'

We went out and Alice held the baby while I pushed them both high into the darkening leaves of the tree and the fading twilight. Twice I thought I was going to cry, but I blinked back the tears. Alice had her back to me, so she couldn't see. She just talked on about school and the two days of freedom we had left.

'Tonight, after supper, you can show me what clothes your mama got you for school.'

'Sure,' I agreed, not really thinking.

'Did you get sundresses or more shifts?'

I tried hard to remember. Effie and Mama Betts had brought some things for me in Mobile. I'd tried them on. 'Both.'

'Miss Effie is always trying to get nice things for you,' Alice said. 'You act like you don't care.' There was gentle disapproval in her voice. 'Once those boys start after you, you'll know every dress in your closet, and what shoes match.' The disapproval had gone and she was teasing me.

'I'd like that, Alice. More than you'll ever know.'

Darkness had nearly claimed the day, and I told Alice it was time to eat. She considered telling her mother we were leaving, then decided to go without bothering. In her mood, Agatha Waltman might simply change her mind and decide Alice couldn't go. Chances were that if we just left, she'd never miss us.

'I ought to get some diapers for Maebelle,' Alice said, eyeing the front door like it might hold a bogeyman.

'We've got some old ones at the house. Come on.'

'And a bottle?' She rolled her eyes.

'We've got some of those. It tickles Mama Betts to fix things for Maebelle. Let's go.'

Alice didn't require any more urging, and we slipped through the woods to my house. I watched the kitchen clock as we ate Mama Betts' field peas, okra, cornbread and pork chops. I didn't think I'd be able to eat until I started. Then I realized I'd gone all day without. Alice was hungry, too, which pleased Mama Betts.

'Good to see young'ns with a healthy appetite.'

Across the table, Arly grabbed the last piece of corn-bread on the plate and grinned, his mouth full of food.

'You need a trough,' I told him.

'I have to eat this way or you'll grab all the vittles.' He grinned again, almost letting the food drop from his open mouth.

'If I see that mouth open one more time, except to insert food, I'm going to tape your hands to your chair and feed you myself. Maebelle has better manners,' Mama Betts said, giving Arly a look over the top of her glasses.

It seemed like the first time all summer that I'd really looked at Arly. He'd grown at least four inches, and his skin was a smooth golden brown from working in the sun. Mrs. Arnette let the boys in the nursery work without shirts. Effie had teased Arly a bit about it during the summer, saying Mrs. Arnette liked to watch the young boys flex their muscles and sweat. Instead of getting irritated, Arly had agreed with a grin.

Since he was saving up to buy a car, Arly had been working from seven in the morning until six at night. He wouldn't tell anyone how much money he had, but he was spending some of it on Rosie Carpenter and the drive-in. They changed the feature every week, but Arly and Rosie would go sometimes on Friday, Saturday and Sunday night, when Effie let him use the car that often. I thought they'd lost their minds, but Alice said they never watched the movie the whole way through. Eavesdropping on her older brothers and sisters had given Alice a wealth of knowledge I didn't have.

When supper was over, Alice and I helped Mama Betts clear the table while Arly played with Maebelle. It was eight by the time we were done, and I asked Mama Betts if I could call The Judge in New Orleans.

'I expect they're out having dinner, but you can call,' she said. She gave me the phone number, and I went into the hall. What was I going to tell The Judge? I hadn't planned anything, and as I picked up the black receiver, the horror of the day threatened to overwhelm me. All I had to tell him was that I needed him. That he had to come home to me.

I dialed, and was shocked to hear a strange woman answer. 'Monteleon, may I help you?'

I asked for Walt Rich's room, and she put me through. The phone rang at least a dozen times before she came back on and said there was no answer. I didn't leave a message. If they got in late and found I'd called, it would frighten the daylights out of them. I'd try again later. I'd stay up all night if I had to.

We all watched *Dr. Kildaire*, and for a brief time I forgot Kali Oka and concentrated on the wonderful doctor. Alice and I both agreed he was dreamy, and Arly said he was going to barf. Mama Betts played with Maebelle V.

At nine I tried to call again. Still no answer. I placed the call again at ten. They weren't back.

Arly and I walked Alice and Maebelle V. home. We left her at the edge of the woods and watched her sneak in the back door, careful not to let it slam. If she wasn't caught going in, no one would ever recall where she'd gone or what she'd done. It seemed odd. Mama Betts and Effie knew just about every move Arly and I made.

'We need about ten brothers and sisters,' Arly said. 'Then we could get by with doing whatever we wanted.'

'We might get to do it, but we'd still have to pay for it.' I started home, and to my surprise, Arly didn't even try to scare me once.

Chapter Twenty-eight

I wore my hair down and my bra for the first day of school. I'd never been so miserable. The heat in the school was compounded by nervous seventh graders crammed together in one study hall for registration while, outside the double doors, high schoolers went about their business, going to lockers, talking, laughing, looking good no matter the heat.

There were hundreds of new faces. In Chickasaw County there were community schools for grades one through six. In the seventh, classes were consolidated. There were girls and boys from Two Forks, Shuntee, Brushy Creek, Pixley, Fairley's Hollow and Crossroads. Alice and I were swept up in the milling crowd as friends sought each other above the hubbub.

Alice wore her aqua sundress and her eyes were wide beneath her bangs. She was ready for school, as was Jamey Louise. I saw her standing on a chair in a yellow dress that showed off her tan. She waved at me.

Even though we were mighty seventh graders, it didn't keep the girls from squealing as they met friends they hadn't seen all summer. The hot season of isolation was over. School was in, and there would be ball games and dances and spend-the-night parties. The yellow school buses would bring us together and deliver us home every day.

The boys ganged up at the end of the study hall, and I

saw some I knew from the year before. Frank Taylor jerked my hair with a healthy tug.

'Where's the 'tails, Bekkah Rich?' he asked, grinning.

'Tomorrow,' I promised him, lifting my hair with my hand. Sweat was running down my back. Pigtails might be stupid, but they were cool. I was dying, and the bra was rubbing a raw spot in my rib cage.

'You look like you feel bad,' he said.

I hadn't slept for three nights. Each time I closed my eyes and drifted into blackness, I heard the screams of a horse that became the cries of Greg. 'I'm fine,' I lied. 'It's so hot in here.'

'I hear your folks are out in California.'

'Yeah, they're headed that way. Hollywood.' I'd been trying to find The Judge and Effie each night, but they'd left New Orleans and headed toward the West Coast. Effie had called once and Walt once. I'd missed both calls because I wasn't home. Mama Betts had assured them all was fine on Kali Oka. She didn't know the torments I was suffering. Since my parents weren't certain how far they'd make it each day in their travels west, they couldn't say where they'd be until they got to Rita's. By then it would be too late. Walt couldn't just turn around and rush back. I'd lost my chance with him.

'Bekkah?' Frank was staring at me. 'Maybe you want some water or something?'

I shook my head and forced a smile. 'Thanks, Frank. I've got a lot on my mind.'

'You're pretty close to your mother, aren't you?' He shifted from foot to foot, and he kept his back turned to the other boys.

'Yeah.' It was easier to agree than to try to explain. There were so many things to worry about. Greg had disappeared completely from the barn. Jamey Louise had stayed in a vile mood for two days. Then she just said she'd had it with Greg and the barn, and she quit. She hadn't given me a chance to consider telling her anything about the beating Greg had gotten. That was like a trust between me and Greg, and I hadn't told anyone. Not even Nadine. And if I was worried about Jamey being mad, Nadine was a slow fuse burning. She was furious that both Jamey and Greg had quit without giving notice.

The other shoe I expected to drop was the Redeemers. For the first day or two after my ride to Cry Baby Creek, I had expected some repercussions. None had come. My relief was tinged with a bit of disappointment, and I realized I'd hoped in some crazy way to draw the Redeemers out, to make them come onto Kali Oka Road away from church property. If they'd called the sheriff on me, then I could have told Joe Wickham everything I knew. But they did nothing.

And I went to school. My work schedule at the barn had shifted to afternoons with the first day of school. After the packed, airless classrooms all day, the barn was an improvement. I did all of my chores first and took my time, so I could ride Cammie in the late afternoon.

Nadine did not come outside. I hadn't seen much of her since Caesar's death. My schedule became one of work and solitude. I rode Cammie and then put her away. The barn looked good, but it was a lot more work since Jamey Louise had quit. And Greg.

Since they'd gone, the barn took on a different atmosphere. Strange noises filtered from the loft, noises that piqued my curiosity and my horrid imagination. I climbed the ladder to the loft twice and poked my head up to look around, hoping for some sign of Greg, that he'd at least been by. But the ligthing was poor and the loft spooky. I didn't linger long or look very hard. The hay was piled high, and the faint rustlings undoubtedly came from Nadine's growing collection of rats.

Before I left for home on the third day, I took a quick

survey around the barn. When Nadine came out to feed, I didn't want her to find anything out of place. Outside the open barn door, the sky was turning shades of gold and pink and lavender. It was after seven – a good thing Effie was out of town or she'd be mad at me for being so late.

My shoulders ached, a good tiredness mixed with the stiffness that was a result of lack of sleep. Everyone at school seemed so excited to be there. All of the girls smiled, and all of the boys watched them. It seemed that everyone had left the summer behind but me. I was still trapped in my nightmares.

'Good night, Cammie,' I went to her stall and patted her muzzle. It was velvet, slightly warmed. Cammie was the one good thing about the summer. The best. I buried my face against her warm neck.

She stilled suddenly, and without looking, I knew her ears had pricked forward. She was listening to something. I thought I'd heard it too. A noise indistinguishable in the shuffling and snuffling of horses, the creak of old wood, the sigh of rusty hinges. Something that didn't belong.

Cammie tensed beneath my touch, and I eased away from her, looking to see where she looked. In the fading light of the day, there was nothing unusual that I could see in the barn.

I thought of a weapon. The pitchforks were at the other end of the barn, near the tack room. At the thought of me standing guard with a pitchfork, I tried to smile, but it didn't work. Someone had very recently been in that barn and killed a horse. Someone evil had visited. And left. Perhaps he had returned.

The noise came to me again, a whisper of a moan. It floated all around me, coming from nowhere in particular. It was the sound of something dying, something in pain. Or someone trying very hard to frighten me out of the barn.

'Get out of here!' I hissed the words through a jaw that didn't want to unclench. 'Whoever you are, just get away from these horses.'

Nadine was in the house. Maybe if I screamed she would come out. But she hadn't heard Caesar's death cries.

The sound came again, a low, throbbing moan.

My fears ricocheted from the real to the unreal. Selena had left her dress in the loft. Maybe she'd come back for it. I looked down to the end of the barn. The doorway was empty, but night was falling. Mama Betts would be worried sick about me. And where was Picket? She'd never go home without me.

I argued with myself that I was letting my imagination run away with me. There was nothing to prevent me from dashing home and getting Arly or Mama Betts to come back with me to search the barn.

But I could not leave the horses defenseless. Whatever, or whoever, was in the barn, I'd have to confront them. Greg had been right about me before. But this time I wasn't going to run away.

I whistled softly for Picket as I unlatched the stall door. I'd be a better target in the open aisle, but I couldn't cower in the stall forever. I had to get to a pitchfork. It was better than nothing.

There was no sign of my dog, and a burst of hatred unlocked some of the fear. If anything had happened to Picket . . . I shifted from stall to stall down the length of the barn toward the tack room. If anyone was watching me, I couldn't see them.

The moan came again, clearer now. It vibrated against my body. I felt it, filled with so many black things.

I prayed. For protection, for courage. For my dog and the horses.

Then my hand found the pitchfork and I stepped into the center of the aisle.

The moan slithered around me, more distinct than before. More unearthly. Given a choice, I decided I'd rather face Selena than the man who'd killed Caesar. Ghosts were frightening, but I'd never heard of one killing anything.

'Selena,' I whispered.

The moan answered me.

It seemed to come from above me. Was she looking for her dress? She'd hidden it in the loft one time.

The moan came again, low and soft, almost a sigh. It sounded as if someone said my name!

'Jesus Christ, son of God, protect me. I swear I'll be a better person. I'll say my prayers every night.' I stopped. What prayer could save me from that whisper, that horrible claim on my very soul?

Hefting the pitchfork with one hand, I started up the ladder to the loft. Whatever was up there, it was happy I was coming. It had stopped making any noise at all.

The loft was very dark. The last glimmer of evening light came in through a few cracks and crevices, but for the most part I was sightless. I eased to my knees and began crawling, feeling in front of me with one hand so that I didn't slip off the edge of the loft floor. Against all of Nadine's rules, I dragged the pitchfork beside me. It wouldn't do much good against a ghost, but it might if I found the person who'd killed Caesar. Maybe the horse had clipped him and hurt him worse than anyone knew. Maybe he'd been hiding around the barn for days, growing weaker and weaker, until he finally crawled into the loft to die. That gave me great satisfaction. Maybe I'd just leave him up there until he croaked!

When my fingers brushed against the shoe, I almost screamed. The only thing that stopped me was the terrible moan that came from whoever I'd touched.

My fingers closed on the leg, and I shook it.

'Help,' the voice answered softly.

The truth started to dawn on me, and with it came a terrible rush of guilt.

'Greg?' I inched closer, feeling the leg. My hand drifted up past his waist to the white cotton shirt. It was crusted on his back with something that I knew was infection and blood.

'Holy shit!'

I raced backward, crawling on my hands and knees in the hay. My foot slipped on the first rung of the ladder, but I managed to hang on and beat it down to the ground. In a moment the barn was illuminated. I hurried back up the ladder and stopped as soon as I saw him. He was sicker than I'd ever seen anyone. He lay on his side, curled into a ball. His body shook as if demon-possessed, and low moans slipped from between his slack lips.

'Greg?' I inched forward and touched his leg.

He moaned, but he didn't wake up.

'Greg?' I shook his leg pretty hard. 'Wake up.'

His body shook, starting at his head and moving down to his feet. I backed away from him, wondering if he was going to die in front of me. There was a terrible smell, as if maybe part of him had already died.

I was too frightened to cry. I stumbled backward to the ladder, afraid to take my eyes off Greg, afraid the shallow rise of his chest would stop if I looked away for even a second. For a long time I clung to the ladder, my feet on the second rung. Then I started down. Picket was waiting for me at the bottom. I hit the ground running toward the house and Nadine.

Darkness had finally settled in, and I thought of Mama Betts. She'd be worried sick about me. Maybe she'd come to look for me. She'd know how to make Greg well. She always knew how to make sick people better.

'Nadine!' I pounded the back door and screamed. 'Nadine!'

When there was no answer, I banged the screen open

and shut as hard as I could. 'Nadine!'

If she didn't come to the door, I'd go in and call Mama Betts. I'd tell her to bring the doctor and an ambulance.

'Nadine!'

'What in the hell is wrong with you?'

Nadine appeared at the kitchen door, her hair around her head in shaggy disarray. She'd been asleep.

'It's Greg. He's in the barn and he's hurt bad.'

'That little bastard can't come here to lick his wounds after he left me without help.'

Her voice was fuzzy, like each word slammed over the next. The screen door pulled back easily in my hand, and I stepped over a fresh sack of garbage near the door and entered. 'He's hurt bad.'

Nadine blinked three times. 'Where is he?' She ran a hand through her hair. She was dressed in an old T-shirt, too big and with holes, and her underwear.

'In the loft.' I had to choke back the tears. 'I think he's been there since Caesar was killed.'

'Three days?' Nadine said it like she was asking a question, but she wasn't.

'They beat him at the church. They beat him bad. I tried to doctor him, but I guess it didn't work.' I grabbed Nadine's hand and pulled her with me to the steps. 'I put that horse salve on his back.'

'Shit!' Nadine gathered momentum and started after me. As we hurried down her steps, she took the lead. Running barefoot in her T-shirt and panties, she raced across the yard in the dark.

She was halfway up the ladder by the time I started. At the top she halted. 'Fuck.' The word was a simple statement. 'What the fuck happened to him?' she asked down to me.

'The preacherman beat him. Greg confessed that he'd painted Jesus's face black on the crucifix, but he didn't.

Someone else did, but they were going to beat Georgie and Greg confessed.'

'The stupid little fuck.' She went on up.

When I cleared the opening, she was crouched beside Greg, her hand on his head. 'He's burning up with fever. It's a wonder he isn't dead from infection. Get a flashlight from the house,' she ordered. 'In the bedroom, beside the bed.'

With Nadine's presence, a sense of calm touched me like a cooling hand. I ran as fast as I could, but I wasn't panicked. I turned on the light in the kitchen and followed the hall towards the front rooms. It wasn't a large house, and the door to the bathroom was open. Dirty towels covered the floor, and I went past. The next door was closed. When I opened it, I found what looked like a storage room. There was a terrible smell, so I closed it back. The next door gave access to Nadine's bedroom.

There was a switch for an overhead light, so I hit it. Nothing happened and I stumbled over shoes and things on the floor until I made it to the bed and found the bedside lamp. The flashlight was beside it.

'Bekkah! Hurry it up!'

I could hear her hollering at me through the open windows. She was worried, really worried.

As I reached for the flashlight, I knocked a bottle of pills off the table. The cap wasn't on good, and they spilled across the floor. I picked up as many as I could. They were tiny, like Mama Betts' blood-pressure medicine, sort of, except hers were a pale orange color. These were red. The label showed they were for Nadine Sellers for sleep. I tucked one in my pocket. Maybe it would help Greg.

I tried to think of anything else I might bring from the house for Greg. I stopped in the bathroom and looked for some clean towels, but I couldn't find them. I gave it up when Nadine hollered again.

319

By the time I got back to the loft, she had Greg on his stomach with his shirt pulled off. The diaper bandage I'd made was stuck to his back, crusted with dried blood and a yellowy substance.

'What else did you put on him except the salve?'

'I cleaned it with salt water.'

'How deep were the wounds?'

'Some were deep. Maybe a quarter of an inch. They beat him with a coat hanger. It was the places where they criss-crossed that were the worst.'

Nadine nodded. 'This bandage has to come off. We need to get him to the house.'

'Nadine, we have to call Dr. McMillan.'

'Let's get him down first.'

'The doctor could help us.' I didn't see how we were going to get Greg down from the loft. He weighed as much as Nadine, even as skinny as he was. He was tall and gangly, but working all summer and eating Jamey's lunch, and part of my lunch, had begun to fill him out.

'We're going to tie him in the horse blanket and lower him out the loft with the winch, like we get the hay up.'

'We could kill him.'

'If he doesn't get some help, he's going to die, Bekkah.' Nadine went to the ladder and started down. 'I'll get some rope.'

Greg tried to turn on his side, but he was too weak. We had to get him out of the barn. Nadine knew what she was doing.

She came back with the rope and tied Greg in the horse blanket. Nadine put another rope through the winch that was used to hoist hay into the loft through the top door in front. Then we dragged Greg over to the opening.

It took both of us holding the rope with everything we had to lower him, but we did it, slowly and carefully. When he was almost to the ground, Nadine sent me down the ladder to grab him so he wouldn't hit too hard.

Together we hauled him to the house.

'It's almost like moving a dead body,' Nadine said.

I didn't answer. I was afraid we'd killed him with such rough treatment.

We left the horse blanket at the steps and got Greg out. He was moaning a lot more, and he felt even hotter to my touch.

'Run the tub full of lukewarm water,' she ordered me. 'We'll soak the bandage off him and cool his fever at the same time. Just lukewarm.'

I rinsed out the tub as good as I could and put in the plug. It seemed to take forever for the water to fill it. When it was done, I checked once again with my elbow to make sure it wasn't hot. That was the way Alice tested Maebelle's bottles. It felt just slightly warm, so I went back out to help with Greg.

Nadine had stripped him. In the light that spilled out the back door, his butt and legs were moon white against the darkness of his arms. It was like someone had cut him in half, two separate pieces of different boys. I looked away, embarrassed.

'Help me get him up.'

Nadine was lifting him by one arm, but he was struggling.

'Bekkah!' She spoke sharply.

'He's naked.'

'Well, aren't you the one with sharp eyes?' Nadine's voice cracked. 'Get over here and help.'

I'd seen Arly naked at the creek when we used to go skinny-dipping. But that had been a few years back. And Arly was my brother.

'Bekkah, either help me or go home.'

I went to Greg's other side and bent so that I could wrap his arm around my neck. My face was almost as hot as Greg's back, but I lifted him. I assumed we were going to drag him into the house and put him into the tub.

'We should call the doctor.'

'And pay for it with what? You think the Redeemers are going to reimburse me for a doctor's visit?'

I hadn't thought about money at all. 'Dr. McMillan will do it for free. I mean, he wouldn't make you pay.'

'Let's get that bandage off and worry about a doctor after I take a look at him.'

We started up the steps, Greg dragging between us. 'He isn't going to die, is he?' I was panting with exertion.

'Not if I can help it. Now shut up and help.'

Once he was in the tub, Nadine sat on the side and made sure he didn't drown. Water had splashed up on her T-shirt, and it was molded to her body. The night was sticky hot and she didn't seem to mind.

I'd taken a stand at the doorway, my face averted. Greg would be humiliated to know that I had seen him exposed. Nadine treated him like one of her animals. She took no notice of his sex.

'You'd better get on down the road,' she finally said. 'The Redeemers are going to be looking for this one, and your folks will be after you. Before I know it the law will be down here arresting me for kidnapping.'

'The Redeemers don't care about Greg. He's been gone for days and they haven't even bothered to ask around.'

'He's too old to sell,' Nadine said. She bent forward to work at the tape I'd put on his chest to hold the diaper in place.

'Nadine?'

She stopped picking at the tape and looked at me. Her hair, wild and uncombed, fell across one eye.

'Did that horse salve make him sick?' I had to know.

'I doubt it. He needed some real medicine, but I suspect he would have gotten sick no matter what you did.'

A heavy rock shifted off my heart. 'I'll telephone Mama Betts and tell her I'm coming home. Do you need help getting him out of the tub? Arly could come over to help.'

Nadine shook her head. 'I can manage, but the phone is dead. You'll have to go home.'

'Dead?'

Nadine had gone back to picking off the tape. Greg was stirring slightly in the water, acting as if his eyes wanted to open.

'I forgot to pay the bill so they shut the phone off. I never used it anyway.'

'I'd better go, but I can come back and help.'

Nadine shook her head. 'I can manage. You know, that horse salve didn't hurt him, but it could have been the salt water that sent him into shock. Salt is very abrasive, Bekkah.'

I swallowed. 'I wanted to get help, but he wouldn't let me. I thought the salt water would help. I made it just a little warm and real mild.'

'He's a tough kid. He won't die from it.'

'Nadine . . . ' I swallowed again. 'Did I almost kill him?'

'You had a little help, what with the Redeemers, but Greg's tough. He'll pull through this. I'll take care of him until he's better.'

'I'll pay for the doctor. I've been saving up to buy some boots and clothes for the horse show, but I have enough for the doctor.' If Greg was sick because of me, I wanted to make it right.

'There's nothing a doctor can do that I can't,' Nadine said. 'Once I get the bandage off and the wounds cleaned out, I've got some antibiotics in the refrigerator. A few penicillin shots will kick this infection in the butt. He'll be fine.'

'Shots?'

She pulled the tape on his right shoulder free. 'Yeah, I can give them to people as well as animals. Greg's going to be fine, and I don't think he'd want to call the doctor. It might start too many questions about his family down at the end of the road.' Nadine looked directly at me. The yellow bathroom light glittered in her eyes. 'And we don't want lawmen going down there. Not yet. Not until we have a chance to find out for ourselves, do we, Bekkah?'

Chapter Twenty-nine

Mama Betts was waiting for me on the screened porch, almost hidden in the darkness. I sensed more than saw her. I anticipated that she would be there. The screen door slammed behind me in the darkness, and she didn't say anything as I stood in the doorway. I couldn't tell if she was too mad to talk or waiting for me to start.

'Mrs. Andrews' telephone has been disconnected,' she said.

'She didn't pay the bill. She ran out of money, and she said she never used it.' I'd never known anyone who didn't pay their bills. Mama Betts would be scandalized. I wanted that, but I didn't know why.

'Bekkah, it's nine o'clock. And a school night.'

'Greg got hurt at the barn. I had to help Nadine, and I would have called, but the phone was out.'

'Is he hurt badly?'

'I don't know.' My voice broke.

'Do you need to call the doctor?'

I shook my head but realized she couldn't see that in the dark. 'Nadine says she'll watch him tonight. She has medicine.'

'Is Nadine a doctor?'

There was a blade of sharpness in Mama Betts voice. She cut swiftly, accurately.

'No, ma'am, but she knows some about doctoring.'

'What happened to him?'

This was the hard question. But I was tired of lying. Sick of trying to think up what to say so that I told just enough and not too much.

'The preacherman down at the Redeemers beat him with a coat hanger.'

Mama Betts stood up. 'He beat him, with a coat hanger?'

'I tried to doctor him—'

'Bekkah Rich, you know enough to call a doctor to someone who's injured.'

'I know enough, Mama Betts, but Greg didn't want a doctor. Those people are strange. They don't want him associating with others, outside the Redeemers. He wouldn't have a doctor, and he wouldn't come down here for you to help him.'

'He'd of had a doctor – and the sheriff – if I'd had anything to do with it!'

'And he might have suffered more because of it.'

Mama Betts stopped talking. In the darkness she brushed past me, opening the kitchen door and flipping on the light. I followed her inside and watched as she brought a plate of food from the oven and put it on the table for me. I wasn't hungry, but it would be easier all around if I ate.

'How sick is the boy?' She took the chair across from me.

'His back got infected.' I was suddenly afraid to tell her that he'd been in the loft for days. Not afraid that I would be blamed, but afraid that she might think he was going to die. I'd see it on her face, and I couldn't stand it.

'Does he have a fever?'

'Yes, ma'am.' I ate a bite of pea salad. The peas were crisp and fresh. 'Pretty high too. He was moaning and . . . well, I couldn't wake him.'

Mama Betts folded her arms on top of the table. 'When was Greg . . . beaten?'

'A couple of days ago.'

'And you found him where?'

'In the loft.'

The look I didn't want to see passed over her face. She looked at the tabletop. 'Bekkah, has that child been up in the loft since then without anyone to care for him? Without food or water?'

'I took him some food and water.' I swallowed the salad. It no longer had any taste. 'That was the first day, though.' I held my fork and watched her not look at me.

'Nadine has penicillin? She has a way of giving it to him?'

'Yes, ma'am.' I wanted Mama Betts to go, to look at Greg. She'd know if a doctor had to be called. I wasn't certain Nadine was a good judge of how sick Greg was. If it cost more money than I had, Mama Betts would take care of it. Even if he had to go to the hospital.

'She can give an injection?' Mama Betts was following her own thoughts.

'Who?'

'Nadine. She can give Greg something to fight the infection?'

'She said she was going to give him some shots.'

'Bekkah, do you really think that if I called the doctor to go down there, Greg might suffer from it?'

I didn't answer right away. She was putting me in a spot to make a terrible decision. One I'd already made once when I tried to help Greg. One I'd botched too. 'Greg led me to believe that he'd be in more trouble if the doctor was called. He was hurting bad, and he'd rather suffer than have the doctor.'

Mama Betts didn't say anything. She stood up suddenly. 'Eat your supper and then go take a bath. There's school tomorrow.'

'Did Effie and Walt call?' The idea of them almost made me cry. Effie would tuck me against her side and hold me while Walt did what ought to be done. My need for them was a vice grip in my gut.

'They called about eight. They wanted to talk with you, but I said you and Alice were out enjoying the last of the summer evenings.'

Mama Betts had lied to cover my tail.

'I didn't want them to worry the way I was worrying.'

'Thanks, Mama Betts. They don't need to worry.' I sighed.

'Clean that plate, Bekkah. You look wrung out and peaked.'

She started out of the kitchen and down the hall. I stopped her with a call. 'Mama Betts?'

'Yes?' She came back to the doorway.

I fiddled with the scalloped potatoes on my plate. 'Is Greg going to be all right?'

'I'm assuming Nadine Andrews has sense enough to get a doctor if she needs one.' She went down the hall, and then I heard the sound of water running in the tub. I finished as much of my supper as I could and took the plate to the sink. I was almost too tired to bathe, but I went to the bathroom, shucked off my clothes and sank into the deep, warm water.

The face of the crucified Jesus came to me. The black paint had eradicated his features. The eyes and lips and the blood were all black, giving him a sort of flat appearance. He didn't seem to suffer as much.

Who had done such a thing? If not Greg, then who? The Redeemers weren't looking for any more answers, not since Greg had confessed. But they might be looking for the crucifix. Had Greg stolen it, or had he been sent out of the Blood of the Redeemer's church with the crucifix?

And Caesar? That was beyond imagining. It was something from a nightmare, or a *Twilight Zone* episode where some foreign creature had landed on earth and didn't know the rules. Whoever had done that couldn't be from Kali Oka Road. Not even from the end of it.

I thought back to the ride I'd taken with Cammie, the terror of the Redeemer women, as if I might force the horse to stomp on them. They were more afraid of me than I'd ever been of them, and it wasn't just the horse either. Dressed in their gray shifts, they reminded me of rabbits caught in the open by a big dog. Too far from the hole to run and hide, they stood frozen in place until their heartbeat pulsed against their ribs.

But the men were another story. I remembered the one who had chased me the first time. And Georgie's father – big and tall and strong and doing nothing to help his daughter. There was the dwarf too. And above all, the preacherman. Rev. Marcus, who touched Magdeline and probably made her pregnant. Rev. Marcus, who might be from Nadine's past. Funny that she hadn't gone down there and looked at him. Maybe she would now. One good look would tell her if he was her ex-husband. In the stillness of the August night, that seemed improbable. It was hard to remember who had come first, Nadine or the Redeemers. They were interwoven in the summer with Alice and Maebelle V., the heat, and the appearance of Selena at Cry Baby Creek.

My wet hair floated out beside my head like lilies in the quiet pools where Cry Baby Creek widened near the Pascagoula River. A whippoorwill started up outside the open bathroom window, a lonely cry that brought me back to Greg. Whip Poor Will! Whip Poor Will! Mama Betts had told us when we were little that the hoot of the owl and the cry of the whippoorwill foretold death. That couldn't be true, though, because I heard the call of the bird almost every night. Besides, Greg wasn't going to die. Nadine would take care of him. He was sick, but not that sick. He was too young. Just a boy. Whatever infection had set in, he'd be able to fight it off.

I forced my body to lie still in the water. It was an old claw-foot tub, deep and spacious. I braced my feet against the end and held myself steady. The house was too silent around me. Effie was gone, her absence a vacuum in the quietness of the old house. The Judge was gone a lot and I was used to that, but tonight it seemed that they'd never come back. Maybe Daddy had finally gotten Effie away from Kali Oka Road and she'd never want to come back, not even to get me and Arly.

If she knew what had happened, she wouldn't think Kali Oka was so safe. Maybe she wouldn't want to stay here at all. Or maybe she and Daddy would go down to see the Redeemers. They'd find out what was going on down there and just who the preacherman was. If something was happening to babies, The Judge would figure it out.

In all of the times I'd been to the church, I hadn't seen a baby. There were children, to be sure, but they were all older. It might only mean that there was a nursery in the church, a place where young babies were kept during the day and during church services. I tried to remember if there had been any babies in the congregation the time I'd seen the singing dwarf and the testimonials.

I couldn't recall a single infant.

But Magdeline's face was clear, in every detail. Her fear, her courage. Her determination to come forward and tell her story.

It had cost her dearly.

Had she been angry enough to blacken the face of Jesus? Would she let Greg take the blame? I couldn't begin to answer those questions.

I'd never given much thought to the other Redeemers I knew from my eavesdropping. Jim had been beaten too. And Georgie was part of it. I couldn't remember the other boys names, but I had an image of them. Did they know how bad Greg was hurt?

The questions tore at me as the bath water cooled.

'Bekkah?'

Mama Betts' knock on the door made me bolt up straight in the tub.

'Get out of there and get in bed. It's going on ten o'clock. The bus will be here at seven in the morning.'

'Okay.' I pulled the plug by wrapping the chain around my toe. Even though the water had cooled considerably, I still felt a chill when I got out and started to dry. A premonition of winter tickled my mind. Things would be better when the earth cooled. When summer was over and the oppressive heat was not smothering down on everyone.

I dried my hair as good as I could with a towel and hurried barefoot to my room. The cool sheets settled over me, and I snapped the light out. Homework would have to wait.

When the hand grabbed my ankle, I sat up straight in bed and opened my mouth to scream. A strong hand covered my mouth and forced me back to the bed.

'Bekkah, you idiot, it's me, Arly.'

He shook me for good measure, sending the breath from my lungs in rapid bursts.

I managed to punch his hands off me. 'What do you want?' I wanted to kick him as hard as I could in the shin.

'You stay away from Frank Taylor, you hear?'

Arly had lost his mind. Lusting for Rosie Carpenter had finally driven him over the edge.

'What are you talking about?'

'I saw him playing with your hair at school. He's been watching you, hanging around the hall where you have classes. Stay away from him. He's trouble.'

'Arly, if you ever did have a brain, it must have leaked out your ear.'

'I mean it, Bekkah. Frank Taylor is trouble. He's already got one girlfriend.'

331

'Well, he can have a dozen for all I care. Now get out of my room.' Frank Taylor had been the very last thing on my mind, even below what I was going to wear to school the next day.

'He's going to ask you to the ball game.'

'Arly, I'm going to count to ten. If you aren't gone, I'm going to call Mama Betts. She'll make you go.'

'He's only doing it to make me mad.'

'One, two, three . . .'

'He just wants to get back at me because he liked Rosie before she started going with me.'

'– four, five, six, seven . . .'

'He's telling people Rosie went all the way. He'd say the same thing about you, you know.'

'Ten.' I took a lungful of air in a real dramatic way.

'Okay.' Arly opened the door. The hallway had a small night-light burning, and I could see his silhouette. He ran his hand through his hair. 'I'm trying to warn you so you don't look like an idiot and a . . . slut.'

The word was like a slap. 'You stupid boys! All you think about is diddling some girl. None of you do it, but you think about it with everything that happens. And you make everything dirty because of how you think.' The more I talked, the angrier I got. 'You aren't warning me, you're having some kind of stupid battle with Frank. It's about you, not me. But just so you'll know, I'll do whatever I damn well please. I'll kiss who I want to, and if I want to go all the way, it doesn't have a thing to do with you. Get out!'

Arly was frozen in the doorway. 'You're crazy.' He was whispering. He backed up one step. 'You're just a stupid kid. Can't you see that I'm trying to stop you from ruining yourself? Frank's a hound dog.'

'Fuck you, Arly.' I threw my pillow at him, wishing it was a rock. 'Get out!' I screamed.

Mama Betts' door burst open.

'What's going on here?' She padded down the hall. I could hear her bare feet. 'What's going on? Arly, what is it?'

'Bekkah's crazy. She's saying she's going to . . . do things with boys.'

Mama Betts hit the overhead light switch, flooding my room with light.

'Bekkah?' she asked.

'Get him out of here. Everything is crazy. There are people who kill animals and beat people with coat hangers, and he's worried about Frank Taylor pulling my hair!' My voice rose to hysteria. 'Get out!' I threw my other pillow at Arly.

'Go to your room, Arly,' Mama Betts said.

'You didn't hear what she said, Mama Betts. She said she was going to . . . she used a word that—'

'To your room, Arly. Now!'

She waited in the doorway until he went stomping down the hall and slammed the door to his room.

'Rebekah, where did you learn to talk like that?'

The question was softly put, but there was iron in it. And disappointment.

'Leave me alone,' I whispered.

'Okay. But in the morning, before school, I want you to go for a walk with me.' She didn't wait for an answer. She shut off the light and closed the door. I was left in the darkness with a burning fury and images that made me twich in the clean sheets.

The bus bumped along Kali Oka Road. Arly had gone to the back near Jamey Louise, where he was drilling holes in my head with his stare. There were several other kids already laughing and talking, but I'd taken a seat by myself near the front where I had a clear view of Kali Oka stretching red and dusty. I saw Alice standing at the side of the road with about seven other Waltmans waiting for the bus. Alice had on a pink shift, and her hair was curled under around her jaw. She was smiling, eager for school. On a day-to-day basis her life was far more difficult than mine, yet I was the one who constantly stayed in trouble.

During our walk Mama Betts had said she was shocked and disappointed in me. No matter what was happening, I had no reason to speak the way I'd done to Arly. She also said that when I got home from school, she wanted me to walk to Nadine's and check on Greg. But I was to come straight home. I couldn't work there and I couldn't ride. Not for the rest of the week. Come the weekend, she would decide then if I could go back, depending on my attitude.

Since I didn't say anything back, she said I wasn't making it any easier on myself by acting like a bloated toad.

Alice hurried toward me, her smile slipping off her face as she looked at me.

'Jesus, you look like you're going to prison.' She slipped down beside me on the green vinyl seat.

I tried hard to smile, but tears threatened instead. I cleared my throat and looked down at my books. In a moment she swung around and looked back at Arly. Even she could feel him staring at me. 'What's going on?'

The kids in the back of the bus were laughing, and one of them hit Alice in the back of the head with a rolled-up sheet of paper. Alice ignored them. 'What is it, Bekkah?'

'It's a lot of things.' I looked at her. 'Alice, the preacher beat Greg with a coat hanger. He's real sick.'

'How sick?'

'I think he ought to go to the hospital.'

The bus churned forward, stopping every quarter mile or so to let children on. Alice and I huddled together whispering, oblivious to everything except the feelings of horror and guilt.

'We should have told someone—'

'Told 'em what?' Jamey Louise nudged down on the seat beside Alice. It was a tight squeeze, but we could all fit. We made room for her, but we didn't answer.

'What's going on with you and Arly?' Jamey asked. 'You usually ignore each other. He's back there acting like he wants to kill you.'

'He does.' I almost wanted to laugh at the stupidity. 'He thinks Frank Taylor is going to ask me to go to the football game, and it's worrying Arly that Frank might try to make time with me.'

'Because of Rosie,' Jamey said. She followed Arly's thinking perfectly.

'He's such a jerk.'

Jamey laughed. 'Frank or Arly?'

'Both of them.' I smiled for the first time in a long time. 'Jamey?' I hesitated, then plunged on, 'Greg's sick. He's been sick.'

The smile froze on her face and then melted away. 'What kind of sick?'

'He got hurt. At the church.'

'Is he bad?' She grabbed the seat in front of her so she could lean out and look at me.

I shared a look with Alice. 'He's pretty bad. He's at Nadine's house. That's why he didn't see you at the barn. I don't think he wanted you to know.'

Jamey Louise rearranged her books. 'I'm sorry to hear that,' she said. When she looked up, her eyes were a clear, dark brown. 'I hope he gets better. I guess maybe he doesn't fit in my life much, but I wouldn't want him to be hurt. I mean, Greg's a nice guy. But, well, the summer's over. School has started again.'

I didn't say anything. I couldn't. Alice looked out the window. 'Are you going to the game Friday?' she finally asked.

Jamey nodded. 'It's going to be great. We're going to

stomp the Bulldogs this year. Mark Soloman said we have the best offensive line we've ever had. The Panthers are going to smear Dykesville. Are y'all going?'

'Probably,' Alice answered. She nudged me with her elbow, trying to get me to participate. 'I'll have Maebelle V., though, so it won't be the most fun I've ever had.'

'Is your mama going to let you date?' Jamey asked. 'I mean, this year.'

'Even if she said yes, which she wouldn't, I'd still have to take the baby.' Alice laughed. 'Can you imagine anyone taking me on a date with a ten-month-old?'

'What about you, Bekkah?' Jamey pressed. 'If Frank asks you, will you go with him?'

'I can't date.' It was almost as if they spoke another language, one that I understood but didn't appreciate.

'Effie Rich would have a duck if she thought her baby girl was going to a game with a boy,' Alice said. 'Can you imagine that?' She nudged me in the ribs again, trying hard to get some response.

'Then why's Arly so worked up about Frank Taylor?' Jamey asked.

'Because all of the blood's gone to his pecker,' I answered. 'His brain's gone to sleep.'

Jamey and Alice laughed so hard they held the back of the seat. The only problem was I hadn't meant to be funny.

Chapter Thirty

Kali Oka was so hot it burned all the way through the soles of my new penny loafers. Thick lavender clouds hung on the eastern horizon, inching over the sky with the promise of rain, a brief shower that would only thicken the humidity and bring no relief from the heat. School had been endless hours of hell. The classrooms were hot and the teachers irritable. Frank Taylor had indeed asked me to meet him at the ball game. I'd agreed, just to show Arly that I'd do what I damn well pleased. He could stew in his own juices.

I hadn't bothered to change out of my school dress, and Kali Oka seeped over the sides of the loafers. Hot, dry quicksand that left my footprints wide and wallowed behind me. I'd wear a blister if I wasn't careful, but I was almost to Nadine's.

If Greg had gotten worse, Nadine would have gone to Mama Betts for help. I had to believe that. Still, my feet dragged as I ambled toward the line of chinaberry trees, dark green in the blistered sky.

I made it to the driveway and stopped to check on the crucified Jesus. He was still hidden in the weeds and shrubs, still blackened and still heavy. Open and upturned toward what should have been heaven, his blackened eyes seemed to expect no help. I took care to hide him well and went to the back door and knocked.

Nadine looked rough. She was still wearing her holey

T-shirt, but she'd added a pair of riding pants with holes and white cotton socks like the boys wore with their jeans.

'How's Greg?' I asked when she didn't invite me inside.

'He's sleeping.'

I smiled. 'Then he's better.'

She nodded, her golden eyes sparking for a moment. 'Just a little, but I think with some rest and that penicillin, he'll be back on his feet in no time.'

'Nadine, what if the Redeemers come looking for him?' I'd thought about that all day at school. 'Will you give him to them?'

Nadine laughed. 'You want him for yourself, Bekkah? Did you like something you saw?'

'No.' I could feel the heat rushing to my face. She'd made me remember him naked. It made me angry. 'I don't want him. But I don't think they should have him.'

'Well, I want him,' Nadine said. She was smiling again, tormenting me the way she loved to. 'Maybe I'll keep him forever. Make him my fourth husband.'

If she was being funny, she wasn't laughing. I didn't know what to say. Greg was just a kid.

'Of course, he's more suitable for you, isn't he, Bekkah?'

I ignored her jibe. 'Jamey wouldn't come see him. She wanted me to come over and learn some new dance steps.' The smell of the garbage was sweet, cloying. I knew if I looked close, there would be live things in it so I looked at my shoes, the pennies winking in the brown leather. 'Greg was Jamey's boyfriend, but since they aren't a couple anymore, you can have him.' I tried to sound grown up, like she did.

'Well, thank you.' She smiled at last. 'Greg will be delighted to know that he's been handed from woman to woman.'

'I can't work this week, or ride.'

'Punishment?'

'Yeah.'

'For staying here so late?'

'Naw. I said something to Arly that got me in trouble.' I grinned.

'Must have been fuck,' Nadine said, laughing. 'Women shouldn't say that word, Bekkah. Men do and say what they want, and women are punished for the same thing. That's fucking justice for you.' She grinned at my expression. 'Well, work out your prison sentence and hurry back. Cammie will be eager to get out for a workout.'

'You'll ride her for me, won't you?' The idea that she might be trapped in a stall bothered me. She'd be helpless if someone came around to hurt her. I realized I couldn't stay away, no matter what Mama Betts said. Not after Caesar.

'I'll do what I can, Bekkah. Cammie is sort of your responsibility. I've got all the others . . . and Greg.'

'What about your ex-husband? Have you found him?'

'I haven't heard a word.'

'Maybe we can go down to the Redeemers. If he's there, you'll see him.'

'Then again, maybe they'll come up here for Greg,' she answered. 'Listen, I'd better go see how our boy is doing. I'll tell him you came to check on him.'

'Nadine, if he needs a doctor, Mama Betts would pay for it.'

'I'll keep that in mind, Bekkah. If he keeps getting better, there won't be a need for that.'

She stepped back, disappearing into the darkness of the small room. I turned and jumped down the steps, eager to get away from the smell. Where was Greg staying? On the sofa? There wasn't much other place in the house. I'd only seen Nadine's bed and the sofa. It would be a lot better than what we'd seen in the

Redeemers' church. Still, if I'd had a choice, I would've had Greg down at the house with Mama Betts. I walked home, feeling strange that I hadn't seen him.

The rest of the afternoon I worked in the flower beds with Mama Betts. We didn't talk much, but it wasn't because there was trouble between us. I had a lot to think about, and she wanted me to think. We cleared out the dying begonias, each trying to remember exactly how the spider lilies would come up in another week or two. They were the old-fashioned red ones, blossoming overnight into lines of vivid powder puffs. Mama Betts loved flowering bulbs, and the yard was filled with lilies in the summer and fall and daffodils and paperwhites in the spring. She called some of the big yellow daffodils Prince Alberts. She'd had a son named Albert who died when he was seven months old. There was a picture of her holding him on her lap, a fat, happy baby. No one ever said why he died, but Effie was born several years later, the only other child Mama Betts had.

Mama Betts wore her big old garden hat, a flop-brimmed straw antique that she'd had ever since I could remember. She was on her knees, digging in the dark soil. The skin on her arms hung loose and jiggled as she worked. I realized suddenly that she was old.

'How old are you, Mama Betts?' I asked.

'Old enough to know that's a rude question.'

I laughed. 'Really? We always have a cake for your birthday, but never any candles.'

'We'd burn the house down, child.' She was putting the weeds in a small pile.

'Really?' I pressed.

'I've tended this garden for sixty-seven years, and I was six when I first started.'

I did the math in my head. 'You're seventy-three!'

'I was born in 1890.'

I sat back on my heels and looked at her. She kept working, ignoring the way I stared.

'You're finding that hard to believe, are you?' She laughed. 'Just think, when you're my age, you'll probably be living on Mars, where the sky is pink and folks rent wings to get around.'

'When I'm seventy-three, I'll still be living right here on Kali Oka Road, just like you.'

Mama Betts' hands fumbled in the dirt. 'Keep your options open, Bekkah, there's a lot of world out there.'

'What are you saying?'

'This is a different world for women than the one I grew up in. You have different choices. You can travel, go to school.'

'And I can stay here and ride horses.'

She didn't miss a dig with her trowel. 'And that, too, if that's what you truly want. Plenty of your girlfriends will make that choice – to marry young and stay right where they are.'

'You did that. And Effie.'

'No, Effie did not. She waited to marry. She was considered an old maid.' Mama Betts laughed. 'She was twenty-four.'

'She was old.'

Mama Betts put her trowel down and used her hands to balance she laughed so hard. It was funny at first, but then I felt left out. 'Well, Nadine's not much older and she's been married three times.'

Mama Betts' laughter sputtered, then died. 'Three times?'

I knew I'd messed up. 'Well, she says a lot of things to try to, well, upset or shock me.'

'Did she say if these husbands divorced her or if they're dead? Maybe she's just had a run of bad luck.'

I hoped Mama Betts was kidding, but I didn't think so. 'Her parents are dead. They died in a car wreck.'

'Along with her three husbands. Must have been a car-load.'

Mama Betts was being sarcastic, which meant she was irritated. It was best to drop the subject. 'I'm going to get some iced tea. Want some?'

'Sure.' Mama Betts picked up her gloves and trowel. 'I think I've had enough.' She took the hand I offered as she got to her feet. 'I'm going to take a rest on the porch.'

'I'll bring the tea out there.'

'By the way, Bekkah, you never said if that Taylor boy asked you about the ball game.'

I held the screen door open for her. 'He did, and I told him I'd sit with him at the game.' Mama Betts stopped but didn't turn around. I let the screen door bang. 'I don't care about him at all, but I'm not going to let Arly bully me.'

'We'll ask Effie tonight if she thinks you're old enough to meet boys at games.'

I sighed. 'Mama Betts, even if she says no, there's no place where I can sit that boys aren't allowed. I can't stop them from sitting on the bleachers, you know.'

'You have a point, Bekkah. How about that tea?'

Arly came home and went straight to the bathroom to clean up. By the time he got to the table, hair wet and plastered to his head where he'd combed it back, Mama Betts had supper on the table. He was popping to ask me about Frank Taylor, but he knew better. When he finished gobbling, he stood up. 'Buster Schultz, the preacher's son at the Crossroads Church, is coming to pick me up. We're going to study together.'

Before I could even make a rude noise, Mama Betts said, 'I think not. You're going to wash these dishes and do your homework in your room.'

Arly's chin dropped. 'Why is that?'

'You had no business in Bekkah's room last night, and you have no right interfering in her choice of friends.

Her activities are restricted and so are yours.'

'But—'

'No buts, Arly. Think next time before you sneak into someone else's room and try to bully them into doing what you want. Now you'd better call your friend and save him a trip out here. But get off the phone fast. Walt and Effie are due to call in fifteen minutes.'

My grin of victory sent Arly slamming down the hall. It was almost worth it to be punished to see him taken down a notch or two. He'd gotten unbearable since school started. He thought he was too old to ride the bus and wanted to drive Effie's car, but Mama Betts had put her foot down. The old gater-looking Edsel remained parked behind the house. Arly had permission to use it on Saturday nights for his dates to the local drive-in. There wasn't any other place to go in Jexville, but most of the teenagers went to the show and then drove into town for a burger or to sit in parking lots and gather up.

'Finish up,' Mama Betts nudged me gently. 'It would be best if you were out of the kitchen when Arly comes back to do the dishes. I don't want anything starting between the two of you.'

I turned my attention back to the butter beans and ham and listened for the sound of the telephone. Arly made his call and then retreated to his room. I cleared the table and went to my room until the shrill ring brought me running.

'Hello.' I had so many things to tell The Judge. I wanted to get first in line.

'Bekkah, honey.' Effie's voice was curly with happiness. 'We're having such a wonderful time. We're at Rita's, and it's wonderful to see her. Walt's been at one of the studios all day talking with a writer. It's so exciting. They may want him to consult on a film. Rita set it all up for him. I think she did it so the two of us girls could have some time alone together. What would you think

343

about maybe spending Christmas vacation in Hollywood?'

'It would be fun.' I was free-falling, spinning end over end in atmosphere too light to stop my weight. 'Mama?' I wasn't certain who I was talking to.

'What, honey?'

'You're having fun in Hollywood?' Effie never had fun anywhere except Kali Oka Road. We'd taken vacations, and she hated hotels and diners and bathrooms where strangers went.

'It's an exciting town. Rita has done well here, Bekkah. She's opened a lot of doors for us, and California is really beautiful. It's dry and cool at night. You must be suffocating in the heat and humidity.'

'Is The Judge there?'

'He wanted to say hi to you, but he's in a meeting. There's some film about a journalist who's accused of murder. They asked Walt first about working with the writers to make sure they got the details of the newspaper business correct, but he had some good ideas for the story, so he's helping them with that. Bekkah, they're going to pay him a lot of money. More than he makes in a year as a teacher.'

'Sounds great.' My parents had fallen over the edge of the world. No matter how hard I tried, I couldn't imagine Effie in Hollywood. Not smiling, at least.

'Walt and I are so happy. This was the best trick I've ever had played on me. And Bekkah,' she paused, 'I don't want you to worry about that Cathi Cummings woman. Walt explained things.' Her voice tightened, and I could hear it even though she tried not to let on. 'I'm sorry I was so hard on you, Bekkah. That wasn't fair. I know it wasn't your fault.'

'That's okay.' I tried to sound cheerful. 'Effie, when Walt gets in, would you ask him to call me?'

'Is something wrong? Do we need to come home?' All

enthusiasm was drained from her voice.

'No, of course not.' I laughed. 'I have a question I need The Judge to answer for me. It's for school.'

'Okay, I'll tell him, but it might be a couple of days.'

'It'll keep,' I said, feeling as if my heart would break. 'When are y'all coming home?'

'Bekkah, if there's trouble, we'll start back now. It would take us two or three days.'

'There's no trouble, Mama. I just miss y'all.'

'We miss you, too, honey. Would you put Mama on the phone?'

I signaled Mama Betts, who was standing down the hall, watching me closely. She took the receiver and answered what I knew would be Effie's first question.

'Yes, Ef, things are fine around here. Nothing out of the ordinary. Arly and Bekkah are at each other's throats, but what's new about that? No, nothing is wrong. School is fine. Both of the kids are falling into the routine. No. No.'

I turned back into my room and softly closed the door. A couple of days and The Judge would call me. Maybe sooner. Then I could tell him about Greg and the beatings and about Caesar. He'd come home and it would mess up his movie deal.

I opened my science book, but the words had no meaning. I knew them all, but none of them were linked in any way that made sense. What was I going to do? The hot night closed in on Kali Oka, and the same old whippoorwill started his nightly call.

Chapter Thirty-one

'Is Greg feeling well enough for me to see him?' I toed the top step at Nadine's with my sneaker. It was almost five. I'd helped Mama Betts at the grocery store, and she'd driven me down to Nadine's to let me out. I could still hear her turning the car around in the drive, her curious eyes taking in every detail she could see. I hoped the garbage wasn't visible.

'He's taken a turn for the worse,' Nadine said. She was standing in shadow, and I couldn't see her eyes to know if she was teasing me or not.

'Really?'

She pushed the door open. 'Come see for yourself.'

I was afraid, but I followed Nadine through the kitchen and down the hallway. She went to her bedroom instead of the living room. Nadine pushed open the door to reveal Greg propped up in bed on pillows, Effie's book in his hands as he read.

'Bekkah.' He sounded surprised and embarrassed. He wore no shirt, and the sheet covered his lower body, which I tried not to look at but thought might be naked too.

He put the book down.

'Nadine said you'd relapsed,' I said, casting her an accusing look. She was smiling like a shark.

'Nadine's a great doctor,' Greg said. 'I'm feeling much better. The fever's gone, and my back's starting to heal.'

'That's good.' I twisted my hands.

'Have a seat and talk with Greg,' Nadine suggested, indicating the foot of the bed. 'He's tired of my company.'

'That's not true.' He looked at her, a split second of a look that said he was not tired of her, that he was grateful, and something else. He shifted his gaze to me. 'I'd never have thought Nadine would be so . . . kind.'

She went to the door. 'Bekkah, would you like a Coke? I was about to get one for Greg. He needs to eat and drink.'

'Sure,' I said.

'I have to give Greg a shot in an hour, so the Coke is a bribe for him to behave,' Nadine said as she walked out.

She left the door open, and I took a seat on the very edge of the bed. 'Nadine really gives you shots?' I made a face. 'Dr. McMillan gives them to us. It's awful.'

'Yeah.' Greg's face was slightly flushed. 'It's pretty awful, but I'm feeling so much better, I can't complain.' He picked up the book. 'Your mama writes real good. I thought I'd be too old to read this, but I like the story. Does it end happy?'

'Effie told me never to tell the ending of a story first. You have to read it to get there.'

Greg put the book down beside him, his finger still tucked in his place. 'How's school?'

We felt like strangers, talking about things that didn't matter to the other. 'I hate it. It's hot and the teachers are fat cows.'

'How's Jamey Louise?'

'She's fine, Greg.' I swallowed. 'Her studies keep her busy.'

'And the boys, I'll bet.'

I didn't say anything for a few rough seconds. 'I'm glad you're better.' I stood up. There wasn't anything else to say, and I wished Nadine would come back with the

Cokes. I hated Jamey. I should have lied to Greg and said she asked about him.

'It doesn't matter,' he finally said.

'Did you take the crucified Jesus and put him by the chinaberry tree?'

'Yeah, I took it. I figured if I was going to get beaten to death for painting it, which I didn't do, then I might as well take it.'

'What are you going to do with him?' I couldn't imagine. What could be done with the thing?

Greg looked toward the window, but it was all covered up and there was nothing to see except the yellowish shade and curtains. 'I've been thinking, but I haven't come to any decision.'

'You'd better take it back.'

He shook his head. 'No, it won't go back to them. It's ruined for them anyway. Even if someone could clean the paint off, nobody there would be able to look at it without thinking about how it had gotten painted black. And about who did it. If I'm going to have to go back there, it can't.'

'Go back?' I never thought Greg would consider such a thing. 'After what they did to you?'

Anger moved across his face. Like summer lightning, it pulsed and disappeared. 'You don't understand, Bekkah.' He spoke so softly I had to move back beside the bed to hear him. 'Where else can I go? I don't have any schooling. I don't have any other relatives. I've been with the Redeemers since I was a little boy. I don't know anything but them.'

He twisted his head on the pillow so our eyes didn't meet. I wanted to tell him something, that there was a place for him, somewhere he belonged. I'd just never been much good at lying because it sounded pretty.

'What about aunts? Other relatives?'

He shrugged one shoulder, then winced at the pain.

349

'When I was about three the Redeemers got me. My real parents are dead. John and Rachel Singer sort of adopted me. At least they took me in. My real parents died somehow. I was little and I don't remember. I think my name was Calendar.' He paused. 'I can remember being made to say my name again and again so I would know it if I ever got lost. I was really little.'

'Calendar, like a year's time?'

Greg nodded. 'Sounds like I made it up, I know. I quit telling people because no one believed me.'

'It's not that I don't believe you, it's just . . . an odd name.'

Now I understood how Greg's family would let the preacherman beat him so. He didn't belong with them, didn't want to belong.

'Forget it,' he said. 'Maybe I did make it all up. Or dreamed it.'

'Greg, you can't go back there.'

'I have to, until I'm sixteen, anyway. When I'm old enough to get a work permit, I can learn to drive. I can get a job somewhere maybe.'

'You can drive at fifteen here, and Nadine would let you stay here.'

'I can't clean lofts for the rest of my life, Bekkah. I've never even been to school. I'm gonna have to go to a city, some place where there's jobs for people like me.'

'Plenty of folks here don't have educations.'

'Yeah, but they own land. They farm. They have something they can work toward. I couldn't buy myself a cup of coffee.' Bitterness had entered his voice.

'We'll figure something out.' There had to be another alternative. If Greg went back to the Redeemers, they might hurt him worse.

There was the sound of a car on the road. It slowed outside the house and I heard it turn in the drive. 'Who could that be?' Nadine's bedroom window didn't front on the house, but I could look out it and see part of the road. It was too late to see the car, but the dust cloud hung steady in the air.

'It's them,' Greg said. 'The old Chevy. I know the sound of the motor.'

'Them who?' But he didn't have to answer. My skin rippled. The Redeemers. They'd come for him at last. After nearly a week they'd finally decided they missed him.

'John and Rachel. Rev. Marcus loaned them the car to come get me and the crucifix.' He didn't budge in the pillows.

There was loud knocking at the front of the house. I'd forgotten that Nadine even had a front door. Her light footsteps went toward it. She passed the bedroom door and didn't even look in. The front door creaked open, and Nadine didn't offer a greeting.

'We've come for the boy,' a man's voice said.

In the bed, Greg was completely passive. He stared at the ceiling as if he'd gone into a trance.

'What boy?' Nadine asked, an edge of cunning in her voice.

I slipped to the door and peeped out. I couldn't see clearly, so I stepped forward. Nadine stood, arms akimbo, blocking the doorway. By her stance I could see she knew who she was dealing with.

'We've come for Greg.' The man spoke again. 'We're his legal guardians, and we demand that you return him.'

'Well, that's too bad,' Nadine said. 'You can just put yourself in your car and drive straight back to that hellhole you call a church. Greg's not going anywhere. In case you're dimwitted or something, the beating you people gave him almost killed him. Get off my property or I'll have the sheriff down there checking into what goes on.'

351

'Greg is our son.' For the first time I heard a woman speak. Her voice sounded heavy with grief. I inched forward down the hall. I had to look at them, to see the kind of people who would allow their son, adopted or not, to be beaten in such a way.

I saw the dark brown of her dress first. Then her hair, rolled on top of her head. Her face was lined and weathered, and she was thin, like Greg. The man beside her was tall and thin too. He looked tired and angry.

'The boy needs to come home,' the man said. 'The longer he stays away, the harder it's going to be on him. He did something wrong and he got punished. It's over now, unless he wants to drag it out and make it worse for himself.'

Nadine snorted. 'Greg is extremely sick. He's not going anywhere. Not for a long time. His back is terribly infected. He needs medicine and care, something you people don't know a thing about.'

'I can take care of him,' the woman said. 'If he'll come home, I'll make sure he heals properly. I would have seen to him, but he ran off.'

'He's not going back there.' I surprised myself by saying the words. Everyone turned to look at me.

'Who else is in this house?' the man asked, and there was an growing anger in his voice.

'None of your fucking business.' Nadine's lazy voice was as much an insult as her language. 'Now get off my property.'

'We want the boy.' The man was furious. His eyes had narrowed to slits, and he tried to see behind me and Nadine into the house. 'Greg, get out here now before you make trouble for your . . . friends.'

'Greg's too sick to get up, you jackass,' Nadine snapped. 'Get off my property or you're going to have more trouble than you can manage.'

'We want the boy.'

352

'People in hell want ice water.' Nadine's arms dropped to her side. 'Bekkah, go in the bedroom and get the shotgun and bring it here. These people may need some convincing that it's time for them to leave.'

'John.' The woman grabbed his arm. 'Let's go. We can't afford no trouble like this.'

'Greg shouldn't be here.' The man glared at Nadine. 'Our son shouldn't be here with hussies and—'

The woman tugged his sleeve. 'John, please.'

'If you want Greg so bad, why don't you send the preacherman down here to get him?' I challenged. I wanted Nadine to see Rev. Marcus, to see if he was her ex-husband come to hurt her.

'We'll get our boy. You'll see,' the man said, but he was backing down the steps with the woman tugging his arm. 'Greg'll soon tire of your . . . filthy flesh.' He smiled, and it was mean and hard. 'He'll come home. You'll see. He's got no place else to go and he knows it.'

'Come on my property again and you'll see what price trespassers pay around here.'

'That's something you'd better keep in mind yourself.' The man spoke to me. 'We know you've been poking around our property, Miss Rebekah Rich. There's laws that protect us too.'

I stood frozen at Nadine's side.

'Get out of here.' Nadine slammed the front door closed.

I walked back to Greg's room. His face was turned away from me, toward the wall. 'Go home, Bekkah,' he said, and he sounded like he was a hundred years old.

'They can't make you go back, Greg. They can't. We won't let them.'

'Just go home,' he answered. 'Please, just leave me alone.'

At school the next day I hemmed Jamey Louise in a

corner of the library where we could talk for a few minutes without getting demerits. I asked her to visit Greg. I told her he was hurt bad and feeling low. She said she might on Saturday, if her mama didn't take her to get her hair styled. She wanted it cut short around her face and long in back, she said, demonstrating the style with her fingers as best she could. I knew she wasn't going to see Greg.

It was Friday, the night of the first game of the season. Alice and I were riding to the game with Arly, a fact that was like sticking needles under his fingernails. He also had to bring us home, which meant he couldn't go off parking with Rosie during the middle of the game. I was cutting into his petting time something fierce, and he didn't bother to hide his resentment.

The game excited me about as much as the idea of going to the dentist. I was going, though. I'd be a social outcast if I missed the first home football game. Even though my mind was down Kali Oka Road at Nadine's house.

My punishment was still in force, so I didn't go to the barn Friday afternoon. I helped Mama Betts as much as I could with the laundry and her garden, even volunteering to wash the supper dishes. I wanted to ride Cammie on Saturday, and I was hoping my attitude had improved in Mama Betts' eyes. She was looking on me with a little more favor.

By seven, Arly and I were in the car, headed to pick up Alice and Maebelle V.

'How much trouble can you get in with a baby?' Arly asked, delighted we were stuck with Maebelle V.

'I'll try hard to find out and tell you tomorrow,' I said, flipping my hair over my shoulder. 'Frank loves my hair down.'

That steamed him to the point he wouldn't talk. We picked up Alice and Maebelle V., and Arly didn't say another word all the way into Jexville.

The football stadium is at the elementary school, which is strange because it should have been at the high school, but Jexville Elementary School had once been grades one through twelve for all the townspeople.

When it was decided that the Negroes were eventually going to go to school with us, the school board decided that all of the grades seven through twelve would go to the same school. That way all of the older black kids would be bussed into town, where they would be easier to watch. There weren't that many negroes in all of Chickasaw County, and they were resisting desegregation as much as the whites, but 'plans had been made for all contingencies.' What the school board meant was that they'd have the system they wanted already in place.

Only the elementary schools were kept in the communities, a point of serious concern to Effie and delight to Arly. Back last fall Effie had gone to a school board meeting and warned that bussing all of the teenagers to town would destroy the community school system. It had been a carbuncle on her butt for months. She couldn't sit down to eat without getting all worked up over it. And she tried to stop it. Boy, did she try.

Effie had a reputation among the folks in Jexville 'cause she actually attended public meetings. Old Sherman Smith, the superintendent, and Effie were bitter enemies from way back. They'd tangled over books, curriculum, personnel, budget, facilities, nutritional values, and bus routes.

During the meeting on consolidation, he said Effie was half a bubble off. He said it was common knowledge in the county that she had a hormone imbalance, or otherwise she'd be content to stay home and raise her children like a normal woman. He said it was a commonly known fact that she was such a bitch her own husband took jobs out of town to get away from her.

Effie had responded that any southern county that would elect a man named Sherman deserved to be left in ashes. Somehow she'd heard the story how his father, a forty-acre farmer from the Pixley Community, had taken one look at Sherman when he was born and declared him the ugliest baby God had ever created. His daddy named him Sherman after the hated and feared Union general, a name he said that went with his son's face.

At any rate, her comment broke up the school board meeting, but it didn't change what happened. The schools were consolidated, and the new high school was built immediately. But when they built the new high school they didn't have enough money to build a new football field too. So the ball games were held back over at the elementary school.

A grove of pine trees surrounded the field, and Arly found a good spot and parked where nobody could accidentally bump into the car. He'd washed it up and waxed it before he found out that Rosie was in trouble with her parents, so she couldn't ride to the ball game with him. She was meeting him in the bleachers. I wondered if I could manage to get Frank to sit with me somewhere near Arly. It would serve him right.

Once we were out of the car, Arly took his leave. Alice and I and Maebelle wandered over to the concession stands, where the smell of buttered popcorn made my mouth water even though I'd just had supper. I had fifty cents, so I bought two Cokes and a popcorn to share with Alice.

We walked on to the bleachers to eat and scout around for Frank. Alice was interested in a ninth grader named Mack Sumrall. He shaved his head close except for three little tufts of blond right at his forehead. I thought he looked like a Hereford bull with his thick neck, square head and forehead curl, but Alice thought he was pure temptation. He was also ninth-grade quarterback. Next year he'd be a star with the high school team. Frank didn't play ball because he had an afternoon job at a nursery. I was glad he didn't play, because he had a real neck and all his teeth. Since I'd accepted his invitation to sit with him at the game, I'd given him a little thought. In a way, with his dark eyes and tan, he was handsome. He talked more than the other boys too. And he didn't have time to hunt. I liked him for those things.

We were munching down the popcorn when Alice poked me. Jamey Louise was out on the football field, hanging on the arm of Dewey Merritt, the Panthers' tight end. He was a junior who everybody said had a professional career ahead of him – if he could keep his pecker in his pants – that was what everybody said, even Dewey himself. Jamey Louise looked up at him, and he bent down and brushed her lips in front of everybody.

Alice sucked in her breath. 'He's a junior,' she said softly.

'Jamey's a lot more advanced than he'll ever be, no matter how old he is.' I felt sick when I thought about Greg. Like it was my business.

'Hi, girls. I didn't realize I was going to have three dates.' Frank took the seat beside me and lifted Maebelle V. from Alice's hands. I was impressed. Arly wouldn't touch Maebelle V. if she was drowning. He held Maebelle high in the air, and she gave him a drooly grin. When he jiggled her, she squealed with delight.

'She's easy,' he said, handing her back. 'How about you, Bekkah?'

Before I knew what he was doing, he slid his hands under my arms and pulled me into his lap.

'Frank Taylor, put me down or I'm going to—'

He jounced his knees up and down. 'I heard you liked to ride those horses.'

He was laughing, and so was Alice, and even Maebelle V. My face was red, but I laughed too. It was fun to be at the game, to watch all of the people talk and laugh and eat. Under the bright lights of the stadium, with the band tuning up thirty yards away, I felt thirteen and grown, and very much a part of what was happening. When Mack strolled over and took a seat beside Alice, it was perfect. The four of us and the baby rooted for the Panthers. Jexville won 21–18, and Frank lifted Maebelle in his arms and danced out onto the football field with her.

Arly, who'd settled far enough away that I hadn't seen him, finally stood up and gave us all a black look. It was time to go home, and no dillydallying.

'Looks like Arly isn't having the time of his life,' Frank commented smoothly. 'Why don't I take you and Alice home?'

The idea sounded a lot more appealing than riding with Arly. I'd teased him pretty hard, and he wasn't going to be easy to soften up.

'I'll ask,' I said. 'You do have a driver's license?' It was a Mama Betts' question, and it popped out of my mouth before I could help myself.

'Of course, Officer, would you like to see it?'

Alice laughed and I turned red. Suddenly the idea of riding home with Frank Taylor made me a little uncomfortable. After we let Alice and the baby off, I'd be alone with him. The idea made my heart hammer. Jamey Louise would know exactly how to behave.

And if I never did it, I'd never learn.

'Arly!' I yelled across the crowd to him. He was already heading for the car with his arm around Rosie, hoping, no doubt, to get a few moments of privacy before we descended on him. 'Frank's taking me home.'

He didn't move much. He just stopped and looked. His gaze went to Frank, then me, then Alice and the baby.

'I don't think so,' he grinned.

'That's 'cause you don't think. You take Rosie and we'll

go with Frank. At least he talks to us and acts human.'
Arly wasn't the boss of me.

'Mama Betts said for me to bring you home.'

I could tell he didn't really want to, but he was acting
on what he felt was his duty. 'Look, you can have some
time alone with Rosie, and we'll go on home. Once I'm
there safe, Mama Betts won't care. Alice and Maebelle V.
will look out for me.' I dared a glance at her and saw the
amusement on her face.

'You'd better go straight home. I'll be right behind
you.' Arly pulled Rosie a little closer to him. Her smile
widened. 'Taylor, you drive careful,' Arly ordered.

'You're gonna get old before your time, Arly,' Frank
said easily. 'It's only nine miles. I think I can make it.'

'Straight home,' Arly warned again as he started to
walk away. He even looked back over his shoulder. 'I'll
be ten minutes behind you.'

'That's probably true,' I said to Alice and Frank.
'Rosie's on detention and can't stay out. Arly will have to
come straight home.'

Frank had parked his pickup on the edge of the field,
where it didn't take long to get out onto the highway and
head toward Kali Oka. The center line of the highway
whizzed through the windshield, and Alice cooed to a
very sleepy Maebelle V. while her hair blew from the
open window. I was sitting close enough to Frank that
our hips brushed. Alice was pressing against my other
side, but it wasn't the same.

'Sure is a good baby,' Frank said. 'She didn't cry at all.'

'Naw,' Alice said. 'Maebelle V. does everything
Bekkah and I do. She doesn't have time to cry.'

We rode along, listening to the radio and talking about
whether the Beatles were better than American singers.
Bands were Alice's second passion, after makeup, and
she knew everything about everyone. She kept me and
Frank laughing until we pulled up at her house.

'Go straight home,' she teased me as she thanked Frank for the ride and slammed the door.

'She's a great girl,' Frank said.

'The best best friend ever.' I held my hands in my lap, not knowing what to say or do. Everything had been fine until Alice left, and now I felt altogether too close to Frank.

'What's down at the end of this road?' Frank asked, sort of casually putting his arm along the top of the seat.

'Cry Baby Creek.' I didn't want to say the Redeemers. For one night I wanted to push all of that to the back of my mind, to forget.

'Ever heard the baby crying?'

I swallowed. 'Not only the baby but the mother too. It was terrible.' I looked up at him, and in the glow of the truck's old dash his face was different. His lips were slightly parted.

Frank eased the car a little down the road from Alice's house and cut the engine beneath the branches of an old water oak. 'Tell me all about it,' he said. 'I love a good spooky story.'

'Here?'

'Well, I didn't want to park in your yard. I don't think your grandma would think a lot of that.'

He was right. Mama Betts wouldn't let me sit out in a car and talk to a boy. But right on the main road someone was liable to come along and think we were having car trouble. It could make a big scene if that someone was Arly.

Frank cranked the engine. 'I have a solution,' he said softly. 'We'll ride down to the end of the road, and you can tell me on the banks of the creek.'

'Frank!'

'You aren't afraid, are you?'

'No, but Arly will be home.'

'We won't be gone longer than fifteen minutes. Just

long enough for the story and to listen for the baby. I've always heard about the legend, but I've never heard the baby really cry.'

I wanted to go, for a couple of different reasons, but I was already in trouble with Mama Betts. I'd never been down to the Redeemers at night. Not when they were there. What did they do on a Friday night? Frank wouldn't be afraid to look with me. But he wasn't going down to the creek to spy on Redeemers. Or to listen to the ghost of a dead baby. I wasn't sure I wanted to go parking.

Frank eased the truck in the road, and before I could protest, we were already past my house.

Chapter Thirty-two

The moon was a thin crescent in the sky, and looking at the stars made a tide of guilt suck at my heart. The Judge and I liked to walk at nights, and he was teaching me the constellations. Now here I was in a pickup truck with a boy, riding close in the warm September night. It made me squirm, and Frank took that as a signal he could drop his arm around my shoulders.

We passed Nadine's, and I wanted to tell him about Caesar and Greg, but it was all so gruesome. That kind of talk had no place on a night like this. It would take a mental midget not to realize that other girls didn't talk about stabbings and beatings when they were riding in the moonlight with a boy for the first time.

As the familiar trees and fields and houses slipped by, I tried to think what Jamey Louise would do. Well, she wouldn't talk at all. She'd squeeze her arms together and show her breasts. And she'd rub on the boy. Maybe trace her fingers along his arm. Look up at him and invite a kiss. All of the things I'd never be able to do without feeling like a fool. Besides, I didn't know if I liked Frank Taylor well enough to invite a kiss from him.

'Chain Gang' and 'Love Potion' played on the radio, and I couldn't think of anything to say. Not a single thing that I thought Frank Taylor might be interested in hearing. The things I did every day didn't have anything to do with him, and shoveling horse manure wasn't exactly a topic likely to win his heart. The things my family talked about would only make me seem weird to him. So we parked in silence at the last turn in the road, the very same spot where Nadine and I had parked, and I sat beside him, holding my own hand in my lap. Elvis sang 'Love Me Tender,' and I couldn't decide what I wanted.

'I never knew you to be so quiet, Bekkah,' he said softly.

'I'm listening for the baby.' Even as I said it, a tingle of fear traced deliciously along my spine. I listened over the radio for the sound of a baby, or at least some noise coming from the Redeemers. They weren't far, just around the corner.

'Maybe we should walk on down to the creek to get a better listen.'

'I don't know.' I was suddenly afraid. If they caught us snooping, they might hurt us. They'd hurt Greg.

'Then you want to stay here?' Frank asked. His arm tightened, his fingers brushing my right upper arm.

A cat caught in a car motor couldn't have been more glad to get out. I scooted across the seat, opened the door, and had my feet on the ground before he could get out from behind the steering wheel.

'You make it awfully hard to be a gentleman. I would've opened your door for you.' He talked easily as he came around the truck.

He was teasing me, but it still made me feel hot and awkward. 'Arly isn't much on showing me how boys are supposed to act,' I told him. 'He's more likely to slam the door on my hand.'

Frank laughed and slipped his hand around mine as we walked down the road toward the creek.

Crickets chirred in the still night, but there was no other sound. When we'd gone a little farther, I could hear the gurgle of the creek. Before the Redeemers, it had been a friendly sound. Now I wasn't so sure. My feet scuffed in the dirt.

'It's still warm enough for a swim,' Frank suggested.

It was, but the idea boggled my mind. I looked at him, in his jeans and shirt.

'We could wear our underwear.'

'Mama Betts would murder me,' I said. 'Besides, we don't have time.' As soon as the words were out, I knew he'd laugh at me. As if I'd consider the idea of swimming in my underwear with him if we had time.

He did laugh, and he squeezed my hand.

Would the Redeemers hear us? 'Shush! If you want to hear the baby, you're going to have to quit talking.' I pointed at the bridge in the pale moonlight. The old wood was silvered, and the vines that grew along it were black in the night. The sound of the creek, heavy with the August and September rains, was softer than I'd ever heard it. It was a sigh and a whisper tinged with regret. Before the Redeemers, Cry Baby Creek had never sounded sad. They were over there, and they might be watching us.

'Maybe we should go home,' I said.

'We haven't even listened for the baby,' Frank protested.

I drew him toward the woods on the right side of the bridge. If we were going to listen for the baby, I wanted to be secluded.

'There's a log over here,' I whispered. 'We can sit on it, but only for a few minutes. Then I have to go home.' He didn't resist as I led the way. The old log I was thinking of had fallen in a curtain of scuppernong vines. The wild grapevine had grown up over some small dogwoods and laced around some pines until it created a natural arbor, but there was also a pretty good view of the creek.

When we were seated, I told him about hearing the baby and seeing Selena. I left out about trespassing and

365

the graves and going into the church to spend most of the night. I just told him the high points, and how Selena had seemed to be in such pain, and that maybe she hadn't killed her own baby, but that maybe it had been the preacherman.

Telling the story made my skin crawl, and I started hearing a few things in the woods around us. Frank eased a little closer and put his arm around me. I had to admit to myself that it was a comforting feeling. It inspired me to add a few more details.

'Listen!' Frank tightened his hold on me. 'There's someone in the woods, over by the creek.'

My heart started, but I knew Frank was pulling my leg. 'Don't try to scare me,' I warned him. 'Selena's ghost will get us both.'

His hands tightened painfully on my wrists. I started to protest, but something in his face made me remain silent. His eyes were riveted on something just behind my head.

'What?' I whispered.

'There's someone watching us,' he said, his hands pulling me in closer to him as he eased backward along the log.

I started to twist and look, but his hands held me facing him. 'No,' he whispered, 'just come on with me. Easy.'

If he was trying to romance me, he was doing a terrible job. My heart was hammering and my brain was light. I had to concentrate on doing what he said, and I had to look around and see what he saw.

Frank stood up, his eyes never wavering from behind me. As I stood, I turned and looked too. There was a flash of movement that left small limbs and leaves vibrating. And nothing else. Frank's arms tightened around me.

'I don't see anything.' My heart started to calm, and I was more aware of how tightly Frank was holding me. It made for a different rush of feelings.

'Over by that cedar, see?' He pointed and I sighted down his arm. The bank was empty, but it had been the place I'd seen something.

'You're just trying to spook me,' I accused him. I didn't want to believe there was anything there. The thought of Selena wailing in her bloodied dress came back to me. 'Let's get out of here.'

'You're the one telling the ghost stories,' he reminded me. 'I thought you were enjoying telling about Selena.'

'I did see her. Alice and I both did. It was . . . I'd expected to feel some other way than I did. It frightened me, but it made me so sad too.'

'Feeling sorry for a ghost? Now, that's a new one, Bekkah Rich.' I heard the tenderness in his voice, and I knew it was now or never. If I looked up at him, he'd kiss me, which after all was what we'd come down here to do. Up until that moment I hadn't realized what I'd really wanted to do. I lifted my chin and met his eyes.

For one second his look was hot on me. His gaze flicked up and behind me. His face changed expressions, shifting to amazement and then fear. Swiveling, I turned to look, but there was only the movement of the dogwood branches, where something rather large had been. And it had been very close to us.

'Holy shit.' He grabbed my hand. 'Let's get out of here.'

'What?'

His grip tightened. 'Run, Bekkah.' He maneuvered me in front of him and pushed.

'What was it, Frank?' He was really scaring me. Something had been there, but what?

'Go, Bekkah. Run!' The urgency of his voice pushed through my questions. I ran. Small limbs struck me across the face, almost blinding me. Behind me, Frank ran hard too.

'Get in the truck and lock the door.'

I thought at first that he was playing with me the way that boys do, but his voice frightened me. He was afraid, really afraid, not just spooked by some ghost story. He put me in the truck, locked the door himself and then went around to the driver's side, got in, locked the door and cranked the engine.

In a spurt of sand and gravel we turned around and headed home.

'What did you see?' I demanded. 'What?' I was panting, and I could feel a place beneath my eye where a limber branch had cut a welt.

His gaze caught mine in the rearview mirror. We were both white and shaken.

'It's worse if you don't tell me,' I demanded. 'What I imagine is only worse. You don't know what's been going on here on this road. What did you see?'

'A woman.'

'In a white dress, with long dark hair? Was it Selena again?'

'No. She wasn't wearing a white dress.' He spoke slowly, as if he didn't want to tell me any more.

'Did she have long brown hair, about my age? Maybe it was Magdeline.'

'No, Bekkah.'

'Dammit, Frank, this is like pulling teeth. Tell me what you saw.' He didn't understand about the Redeemers. It might have been one of them wanting to escape. They might have wanted us to help, and we'd run off like scalded dogs.

'She was naked. And she had a knife.' His gaze flicked to the mirror and watched my face. 'She was staring at your back, and when she saw that I'd seen her, she disappeared.'

I looked hard at Frank Taylor to see if I could tell that he was lying. 'You're just trying to get even with me for my scary story.' I couldn't decide whether to be mad or pleased.

He put his hand on mine and squeezed it. 'I'm not lying, Bekkah. You saw the limbs move. I couldn't make that up. She was there, and then she was gone. Like a wild animal.'

He was scaring me again. 'That's crazy, Frank. There aren't any wild people living on Kali Oka Road.'

'What's across the creek?' he asked.

'Just those Redeemer people.' As soon as I said it, I wondered. They were strange, but they didn't run around naked in the woods with knives. I doubted they even took their clothes off to take a bath, especially the women.

'That's the bunch of folks moved here during the summer, some type of religious nuts?'

'That's them. They stay down there. Nobody knows what they do.'

'What do you know about them?' he asked.

More than I was ever going to tell him. 'Not much.' I shrugged. The worst of the fear was wearing off as we traveled down Kali Oka toward home. It had to have been one of the Redeemers spying on us. Frank had just imagined the naked woman. He'd seen someone, and he'd made the rest up. He was trying to scare me, and he'd done a pretty good job of it. Up until now.

'Folks in town say they've been run off other places. They've been so quiet down at the end of your road, everybody's forgotten about 'em. Maybe I should ask around, see what people know.'

He pulled the truck into the yard, and I was relieved to see that Arly hadn't gotten home yet.

'Bekkah?' His hand caught my upper arm and he held me. 'Promise me you won't go back down to the creek.'

All of my thoughts of a few moments before disappeared. He was afraid. Even safe in my own yard, Frank was a bit unsettled by what had happened down at the creek.

'Maybe we should go in and talk to your granny.'

'No!' I was surprised at my own tone. 'I mean, there's no need to. I'm not allowed to go down to the Redeemers. It would just upset Mama Betts for no good reason.'

'But she had a knife . . .'

'Frank, we're home. You can quit trying to scare me now.' I looked at him. 'You got me good back there, but it's okay now. I'm home and I won't be going down there.'

He didn't let me go. 'I wish I was making it up, but I'm not. I saw that woman. She looked half wild. As good as I could tell, she was naked, and I saw that knife.'

The front porch light came on, and Mama Betts was silhouetted in the door. 'Bekkah? Is that you?'

'Thanks for the ride, Frank.' I felt awkward and suddenly guilty. I didn't understand either emotion, I only knew I had to get out of that truck. 'Don't bother being a gentleman.' I slid across the seat away from him, opened the door and stepped to the ground. 'Thanks again,' I said through the open window. I turned to the house. 'It's me, Mama Betts. A friend gave me a ride home so Arly could smooch a little with Rosie.'

Mama Betts held the door wide. 'You children are as wild as March hares. You leave in one bunch and come home in a different state. Was that you going down the road toward Cry Baby Creek in that pickup truck?' Frank turned back into the road as she was talking. In a moment his taillights were gone.

Mama Betts had been sitting on the porch swing, watching and listening for us to come home. I hadn't considered that possibility.

We went into the kitchen, and I opened the refrigerator door. I was suddenly starved. 'Yeah, I wanted to show

Frank Taylor Cry Baby Creek. He'd heard the legend but had never seen the creek.'

'That's no place for a girl and a boy.'

I chanced a look over the refrigerator door at her face. Thunderclouds. I had to think fast. 'We saw someone in the woods. Or at least Frank saw her.'

Mama Betts hesitated. She knew she was being bird-dogged off the trail. 'Who did he see? If you're making this up, Bekkah, you're going to be in real trouble.'

I grabbed an apple and some cheese and went to the table with a knife. 'I didn't see anyone. Frank saw her. He said she had a knife.' I edited out the naked portion.

Mama Betts snorted. 'Yeah, and then he tried to hold you close.'

'Something like that.' I grinned at her. 'But I didn't fall for it. I knew he was trying to scare me. And if you heard us drive down the road, you know we didn't stay long enough to get into any trouble. I showed him the creek and told him the story. Then we came home.'

She sat down at the table with me. 'Listen, Bekkah, you're growing up, sometimes a lot faster than Effie or Walt or me want to see. When you go off with Arly to something, you have to come home with him. Okay?'

'Alice and Maebelle V. were with us.'

'You leave with Arly, you come home with him. That's the rule until Effie and Walt get home.'

It wasn't unreasonable, and not as harsh as I had expected. 'Okay,' I agreed.

We heard Arly pulling into the yard, and Mama Betts went to the door.

'Don't fuss at Arly,' I requested with a measure of pleading in my voice. 'This really wasn't his fault. He didn't want me to ride with Frank, and I sort of engineered it to get under Arly's skin more than anything else.'

Mama Betts didn't turn around. 'I didn't think you had

any real interest in going off down a lonesome dirt road with a boy. At least not yet.'

'Arly hates Frank. It's personal between them, and I was sort of getting his goat.'

She turned around, and to my surprise she was smiling. 'This time I won't say anything to Arly, but I'm going to tell him the same thing I told you. Leave with him, come home with him. No exceptions.'

'Okay.' I put the apple core in the garbage and got the dish cloth to wipe off the table. 'Thanks, Mama Betts.' I hurried off to bed before Arly could get in the door.

Saturday morning Mama Betts relented and let me go ride Cammie and work at the barn. I didn't know who'd been helping Nadine since Greg was laid up and I was under punishment. I knew Jamey Louise had quit for good. There would be a lot of work to do, and I wanted to ride more than anything. The night before, I dreamed I'd ridden Cammie in the woods. We'd floated beneath the canopy of trees, the wind whispering in my ear and the hot sand spurting out behind us.

I went to the house first, but no one came to the door. I thought about going in, just to make sure Greg was okay, but something held me back. If he was in there and didn't hear me calling, then he was asleep. In that case I didn't need to be in the house. But where was Nadine? The truck was parked behind the house. Wherever she'd gone, she'd gone on foot.

I escaped the back steps and the flies as quickly as I could and went to the barn. The door was shut completely, and I opened it wide. Before I could see anything, I heard the horses. They were restless, shifting in their stalls. Someone was kicking a wall over and over again. I knew they hadn't been out. For nearly a week they'd been penned up without any way to walk or move. Expecting the worst, I went and looked in the first stall.

To my surprise, the bedding was clean. There was fresh water, as if Nadine had just been through with the hose. Mounds of hay were neatly stacked in the left rear corner. Bacchus shifted in his stall and struck out with his front hoof. His ears went back to his head.

He was furious. I held out my hand as a peace offering, and he snapped at me, his teeth clicking together. He'd never had a great disposition, but now he was mean.

I heard Cammie's soft whicker, so I walked on down to her. She danced up and down in the stall, eager for my pets but unable to stand still. I was furious with Nadine. She had no right to confine the horses if she wasn't going to ride them. Even Mama Betts knew that much.

The far end door of the barn was closed, and with a sudden decision I went down to open it. The sudden shaft of daylight penetrating the barn made the horses shift and jostle even more.

I thought I heard something in the hayloft, a scurrying of some kind, a noise like a giggle, but the horses were so restless I couldn't be certain.

'Nadine?' If she was up there she'd surely let me know. 'Nadine?' There was no answer.

I knew then what I was going to do. There might be hell to pay, but I didn't care. I slid the bolt on Cammie's stall open and flung the door wide. She charged forward, cornering the stall and sprinting down the aisle like Satan was riding her tail. One by one I let them all out. The barn was churning with dirt and the sound of hooves pounding outside.

I might have to spend the entire day trying to catch them, but it would be worth it. I walked to the door and looked out. They were bucking and leaping, snorting and running. I'd never seen anything more beautiful in my life, and I was a little frightened that they would run into a fence or slip and fall and break a hip with their antics. But they were magnificent. The September sun beat down on their gleaming coats, and beneath their hides, muscles rippled.

In fifteen minutes the show was over. They bent their heads and began to explore the sorry mixture of weeds that had taken over the pasture. There wouldn't be much of nutritional value, but they would enjoy the pleasure of grazing. From Mama Betts' frequent comments I knew how important it was for grazing animals to graze. 'All creatures to their natures,' Mama Betts had told me a million times. 'When we domesticate an animal, we take on the responsibility of caring for it and providing for it, but we aren't allowed to change its nature completely. That wasn't what God intended.'

Picket was running around the pasture, frolicking with any horse who would join her. I'd never seen her go after the horses, but it was with such playfulness that I knew she intended no harm. I whistled her up and went back into the barn. I'd clean tack as penance for letting the horses out. It wouldn't make Nadine any less mad when she saw what I'd done, but it might make it easier for her to forgive me later on. She hated cleaning tack, yet she demanded that it be kept spotless. As I got out the rags and saddle soap, I couldn't help but compare the barn with her house. Why would she live in such squalor and demand that the barn be so immaculate? Maybe it all did have to do with having a maid in the house. It occurred to me that if a person was doomed to act like they were raised, I'd spend the rest of my life cleaning and ironing and working. It wasn't exactly the future I wanted to see for myself.

I cleaned the two close-contact saddles and was working on the saddle I used to jump when I thought of the crucifix. My fingers ached from working under the leather. I was determined to do the best cleaning job Nadine had ever seen. Looking for the crucifix would give me a break. I got up from the cement block and walked through the barn. The old wood shifted, making the loft creak. It was an eerie sound that brought the memory of Greg nearly dead, Selena's bloody dress and the ghost of Sidney Miller back to me in a rush. Without the horses snuffling companionably in their stalls, the barn was an altogether different place.

The sun was bright outside the door, and I stepped into it, forcing my mind away from the frightening flights of fancy. I'd tried not to think about Frank Taylor. What had he seen, if anything? Maybe he just didn't want to kiss me and had taken me down to the creek to get back at Arly more than anything else. It wasn't an idea that made me feel exactly special, but I poked around at it anyway. It was distinctly possible. I'd agreed to sit with Frank to get at Arly; why wouldn't Frank do the same thing using me? It stung a little, but it was worth considering.

I crawled up in the weeds and shrubs that had grown thick around the chinaberry trees in a considerably lower state of mind than when I'd walked out of the barn. I searched the shrubs and weeds, once casually, and a second time with greater care. The crucifix was gone. I broadened my search, going from tree to tree. I searched the whole line and found nothing. It was gone.

Greg was in no condition to move it. As far as I knew, we were the only two people who knew where it was. Except for Nadine. He'd probably told her. Nadine was extremely strong for a woman, but I didn't know if she could move the crucifix far. It was so awkward. Maybe she could have dragged it. I checked the driveway. There was no sign that something heavy had been pulled along in the dirt.

I walked around the house to the window that would have been Nadine's bedroom. I tapped on the pane, hoping that if Greg was awake he'd call out to me. I tapped again. The window was shut tight, and it was still hot. The weatherman had promised a kiss of autumn during the next week, but it hadn't arrived yet. Not by a long shot. If Greg was in that room he was either dead or extremely sick.

'Greg?' I tapped the window. What if the Redeemers had come down here in the dead of night and killed Greg and Nadine? What if they were lying in there, in the heat, in a pool of blood? What if they'd found the crucifix, or tortured Greg until he told them where it was, and then took it off to hide the evidence? I crept back around the house, dodging from bush to bush, until I was in the line of chinaberry trees. I climbed into the top of the highest one. It wasn't a great place to be caught, but it gave me the vantage of a lookout. I scouted down the road as far as I could see. Nothing. The horses were grazing happily in the pasture, and Picket lounged in the door of the barn. There was no sign of any of Nadine's cats. They'd simply vanished, one by one. She'd told me they were half wild, a mixture of strays she'd taken in. They were probably in the woods, hunting.

Except for the silence of the house, everything seemed normal. Except for Greg and Nadine's absence, everything seemed perfectly fine. The Spooners' new car was coming down the road, and I thought about running out and flagging them down for help. They'd walk in Nadine's house with me and look for – I wouldn't imagine the bodies. It would make a lot of trouble for Nadine if Greg was okay and he was caught in her bed with all of that trash in the house. There wasn't anything wrong with what was going on. Not a thing. But I knew enough about the way people thought to know it would look bad. If I brought any strangers into this, it would change things forever.

Slowly I climbed down from the tree. I had to go in there. To look. To see if everything was okay or if my wild imagination had taken over. Surely it was all okay.

Greg was . . . I couldn't begin to figure it out. The best thing was to look and then think up a plan.

The door was unlocked. I slipped into the kitchen, ignoring the disarray. I tiptoed down the narrow hallway. Nadine's door was closed. It took every bit of courage I had to knock softly, so softly.

'Greg?'

Outside the house the old sign creaked on the rusty chains. It was the sound that I clearly remembered. It had started my friendship with Nadine. It had given me the wonderful summer of horses and jumping. And Caesar. And Greg.

I turned the knob and opened the door. The room was an oven, hot and stifling. The windows were closed tight and shades and curtains drawn. There was no light in the room, but the one from the hall filtered in. There was a withered form in the bed, a misshapen twist of legs and arms and torso covered by a sheet.

'Greg?' I couldn't stand it. I knew by the stillness that he was dead.

I was afraid to leave the doorway, afraid to turn and run, afraid to breathe or think. I had to be sure, though. There was no blood. He looked as if he'd been broken in many places. But there was no blood.

I stepped to the edge of the bed. My fingers closed on the sheet and I drew it back. There was a wad of pillows and a blanket twisted and knotted. The bed was empty.

More than anything in the world I wanted to hear The Judge's voice. I tried to imagine what he would say to me. He'd be calm, and he'd tell me, *Bekkah, you let that imagination get the upper hand again. A good reporter observes before jumping to conclusions. Imagination is a magical thing, but there's always a price involved. Think, girl. Think. You're okay. It's Saturday morning, almost noon. Mama Betts packed you a good lunch, and it's waiting out in the barn. You've got to finish that saddle and get those horses back in their stalls. Now come on, don't panic. No sense in behaving like a fool.*

His voice calmed me, made me draw a breath. I felt the bed with my palms, just to be sure. I no longer believed my eyes. When I backed out of the room, I remembered to close the door. I walked through the rest of the house.

It was empty. No bodies, alive or dead.

I was standing in the kitchen, looking at but not seeing the cans and boxes and packages stacked on the table. There was a tablecloth beneath the mess, but I couldn't be certain if it was a floral pattern or not. There was too much stuff. Nadine didn't seem like the kind of person who would have a tablecloth. I was bemused by that idea, thinking of going over and looking at it closer.

I knew I should get out of the house. It didn't make sense to stand around, staring at nothing important. I only needed a few seconds to breathe, to think and try to get over the scare I'd given myself.

Through the open back door I heard the sound of the old sign singing on its chains. I hated that sound. I knew what it was and it still made my heart thump painfully. *It's just the wind, Bekkah.* The Judge was talking to me again. Just the wind, I assured him back.

The hair on my scalp prickled just before I felt strong fingers grasp the nape of my neck.

Chapter Thirty-three

'Find something interesting?'

I heard Nadine's question above the loud scream I let loose. Her strong fingers clamped around the back of my neck, and she shook me hard.

'Hey! Bekkah!' She shook me again. 'Bekkah! It's me!'

By the time I made myself look at her, there was amusement glittering in the depths of her dark eyes.

'If you're not careful, you're going to have to clean your pants,' she said, taking her hand off my neck.

My fingers automatically went there, rubbing where she'd dug into me.

'I only meant to startle you,' she said, raising her eyebrows. 'I didn't intend to give you a coronary. The way you were jumping around, I thought I was going to break your neck.'

I still couldn't talk. The words were choked in my throat, blocked by another scream that wanted out but wasn't needed. I swallowed hard. 'You scared the shit out of me.' It was part accusation.

'So I noticed.' She grinned. 'Jamey Louise always insisted you were real spooky. She had some really mean schemes worked out to get you.'

Her attitude angered me. 'I thought Greg was dead.'

Her eyes flickered. 'Oh, really?'

'I thought the Redeemers had come in here and killed him and you both.'

'So you took the opportunity to turn all the horses out, even though I expressly told you they weren't to go out.'

All amusement was gone from her face. Beneath the cold glitter of her eyes I saw anger. She'd had the fun of scaring me, now she was ready to attack.

'They were kicking their stalls. Bacchus tried to bite me. It won't hurt them to be out.'

Nadine took a step toward me, and the look on her face made me back up a step.

'You're an authority on horses now?'

'They're out there grazing, just like they should be. What harm has it done?'

'Maybe none, this time.' Her eyes narrowed. 'The trouble is that you disobeyed me. Deliberately. Now I don't think I can trust you with the horses anymore.'

'I stayed right here to watch them. I was going to put them back up before I left. I would never have left them alone.'

'And if one got in the fence, could you cut it out? Where are the wire cutters, Bekkah? Would you have had the nerve to come in here and get the gun and put an injured animal out of its misery?'

'The wire cutters are in the tool box in the tack room.'

'Can you use them?'

'Yes.' I'd cut wire before when Arly and Alice and I had built our secret fort in the woods.

'And the gun? Could you put it against the horse's temple and pull the trigger?'

I thought of Caesar. My gaze wavered and I looked down at the floor.

'I thought not.' Nadine's voice was nasty. 'Before you're so willing to risk an animal, you might think about the responsibility you're taking on.'

'Nadine, I just let them out in the pasture. They should be allowed to graze. Mama Betts said—' I stopped.

Nadine was looking at me with a glow in her eyes. They were amber, not brown.

'So now your grandmother is a trainer. She knows all about show horses and how to care for them. Maybe she'd like to come down here and teach me the proper way to manage my barn.'

'That isn't what I meant.'

'Since your grandmother is so smart, why don't you go home and let her teach you to ride?'

'Nadine, I—'

'Get off my property. Get that cur dog of yours and get off my land. Those horses will be worthless to show. Their coats will be bleached and ruined, and all because of you!'

'Nadine, if you'll let me—'

'Now, Bekkah. Go now before I get even madder.'

'What about Greg?'

'You lost your right to ask questions when you violated my trust. You're a spoiled brat. Get out of my sight.'

Words raged around in my head, but I couldn't force them out my mouth. I wanted to tell her that she was mean and cruel and liked to frighten people. That she had more than a little of the bully in her. I wanted to tell her that she was a pig living in filth and wallowing in nastiness. But I said nothing as I marched to the end of the driveway and called Picket to come home with me. I didn't turn around and look back into the pasture. I couldn't bear the thought of seeing Cammie, and I knew Nadine would never relent and allow me to tell her goodbye.

About halfway home I stopped fighting and let the tears go. I'd known Nadine would be mad about the horses. I knew it and I'd done it anyway. Because they needed to get out. I could see that. I hadn't meant to defy Nadine, I'd only tried to help the horses.

I didn't want to go home and I didn't want to go to

Alice's. I turned down our drive and headed for my old swing. I'd been there about fifteen minutes when Mama Betts came out of the house with a load of laundry. She'd already washed and hung up one load.

'Bekkah?'

She sounded like she didn't believe I was there. I tried to wipe the evidence of tears off my face, but I knew my eyes were swollen and my breathing ragged.

'Ma'am?'

She put the laundry basket down on the ground. 'Come into the house. We need to have a talk.'

I was too numbed to even think about what I'd done wrong now. I followed her into the kitchen and took my seat.

'Something happen at the barn?' she asked, but there wasn't a lot of sympathy in her voice. Something was really wrong.

'I turned the horses out in the pasture, and Nadine told me not to ever come back.'

Mama Betts studied my face. Her fingers drummed on the table. 'I was going through some dirty clothes in your room. When I shook out the pockets of your shorts, this fell out.' She reached into her apron pocket and put the tiny red pill on the table. 'What is it?'

'I don't know.'

'How did it get in your pocket?'

She was acting like it was arsenic or something. 'I got it at Nadine's. I knocked her pill bottle over, and when I picked them up I put one in my pocket, for Greg.'

'Greg takes these pills?'

I shook my head. 'I thought it might help him, but I forgot to tell Nadine that I had it. I knew it was medicine and I thought it might help.'

Mama Betts' hands trembled. 'Bekkah, this is a prescription drug. It's very potent and very dangerous. To make someone sleep. It isn't to be played with. I called

Mr. Hartz down at the drugstore, and he told me what it was. Taken wrong, this medicine could kill a healthy person.'

I nodded. 'But no one took any.'

'You shouldn't have had this in your pocket. Mrs. Andrews should keep her medicines out of the way.'

'It wasn't her fault. I went to get the flashlight and knocked the pills over. I was scared for Greg. I took one thinking it might fight infection, and then I forgot I had it.'

Mama Betts nodded. 'It's just as well she's put you off her property.' Her face softened. 'But I'm sorry for those horses. If she doesn't let them be horses, she's going to pay a terrible price.'

I thought of Cammie, and I felt the tears freshen again. Nadine would leave her in a stall all the time. There'd be no one to ride her, and it was all my fault for disobeying.

'Maybe when Walt and Effie get back we'll talk to them about buying that horse for you, Bekkah. She's a lovely animal and you handle her well.'

'When are they coming home?' I'd begun to believe they'd never come back.

'Soon, I hope. I'm too old to worry over you children the way I do. It was easier when you were babies, crawling and destroying everything in sight.' She reached across the table and held my hand. 'I love you, Bekkah. And Arly too. That's hard work for an old woman.'

'Mama Betts?'

'What is it?'

'Will Cammie die if she isn't let out of the stall?'

She shook her head. 'No, not just up and die. But it works on a horse's nerves. They get twitchy and foul-tempered. Then they pick at their feed and start vices like weaving and cribbing. They don't digest their food, and like people, they get sick.'

383

'Colic.' I'd heard Nadine tell terrible stories about horses with twisted guts. They died in agony.

'It happens. It's beyond me why that young woman would want to pen animals up like that. It'd be easier on her to let them in the pasture. Less stalls to clean, less work, better for the horse.'

'It's their coats. She doesn't want them bleached out.'

'Well, Bekkah Rich, use your brain. Why doesn't she let them out at night?'

She went outside to hang her clothes, and I was left alone in the kitchen with a lot to think about.

I'd come to no clear conclusions when September rolled into October. The days passed, and though I went to the edge of Nadine's property more than once, I hadn't caught a glimpse of the horses. They were in the barn, latched into the ten-by-ten stalls.

My grades fell, spiraling from the top of my class to Ds and a few Cs. Mama Betts' repeated admonitions did no good. Frank Taylor's attentions, and my talks with Alice, were the only things I had to look forward to.

The brief spell of Indian summer the weatherman had promised finally touched Kali Oka Road. The air was golden, crisp. It didn't last but two days, but it gave us all the promise of fall and some relief from the humidity and heat. Every afternoon I worked with Mama Betts and tried not to think of Cammie or wonder about what had happened to Greg.

The telephone conversations between Mama Betts and Walt and Effie grew more intense. The president was sending troops to some Asian country where Mama Betts said we should not go. Ollie Stanford's trial was starting in Meridian, and there had been death threats on his life from a local chapter of the Ku Klux Klan. The North had erupted in race troubles, and the mood of the country was growing ugly. I sat on the hardwood floor in the drag of the attic fan and listened to Mama Betts' side of the conversation and knew exactly what Walt and Effie were saying back.

They would start home in two weeks, when Daddy's contract was up. He'd been paid a tremendous amount of money. Effie, the woman who never left Kali Oka Road, wanted to go to Europe.

. With my hair spread out behind me on the waxed oak floor, I couldn't believe how things had changed. The attic fan hummed and pulled, but nothing else was the same.

Arly was getting ready to ride the pep squad bus to Poplarville with Rosie. Frank had asked me to ride with him, but I couldn't endure another Friday night game. No matter how hard I tried, I couldn't understand how football could be important to anyone with good sense. I hated it when the players crashed into and on top of each other. I hated it when they piled on top of Dewey Merritt and Jamey Louise got nearly hysterical, running out on the edge of the field with tears streaming down her face, only to be dragged back to the sidelines by the sympathetic cheerleaders. It wasn't just a game, it was a blood sport, though Jamey didn't have sense enough to know it. Soon enough someone was going to get hurt, and hurt bad. It seemed a stupid waste.

I told Frank I'd rather go skating on Saturday, or maybe even go fishing. That seemed to make him feel better about the game, but Alice warned me that I'd messed up bad. She said the bus ride was the place where a lot of important things got done in a boy-girl relationship. The trip to Poplarville was one of the longest and therefore the best. The chaperons got tired on the trip home, and while the big old bus lumbered through the night, kisses were given and taken. It was romantic as all get out. Alice was so excited her hair never stopped bouncing because Mack Sumrall had asked her to go with him.

As it turned out, the night was not all romance and stars for her. Agatha Waltman handed Alice a crushing defeat before the bus motor was even cranked. Alice was going to have to take Maebelle V. with her.

Mama Betts was outraged when she learned that Alice was going to drag that baby over a hundred miles there and a hundred miles back on an old school bus with a football game thrown in. When I offered to keep Maebelle V. since I was staying at home anyway, Alice and Mama Betts both thought it was a good idea.

I was waiting on Alice to deliver Maebelle while Mama Betts talked on the phone to Effie in one of those conversations where their voices were quiet but strong. Mama Betts was telling about a visit that Huey Jones, the grand wizard of the local KKK, had paid on Ollie Stanford's wife. Mrs. Stanford lived in one of those shotgun shanties in the Oak Grove area, which was on the edge of Jexville. Mrs. Stanford worked as a cook and maid for Camille Dossett, one of the founding widows of Jexville.

Mama Betts was telling how Mrs. Stanford had met old Huey on her front porch. She'd asked him to get off her property, but Huey had laughed, saying he'd come to check on a gas leak. Huey worked part-time for the Magnolia Gas Company, reading meters, when he wasn't too busy drinking to work. He told Mrs. Stanford it would sure be a shame if her little shanty had a gas leak and blew up one night when she and the young'uns were asleep inside.

Mrs. Stanford started crying, and all of her children, standing at the ragtag screen door, started crying too. Huey started laughing until the shiny black Cadillac of Camille Dossett pulled up in front of the house.

Mrs. Dossett is older than dirt, and her eyes are hardly

above the dash of that big old car, but she still drives it all over town. Folks just get out of her way if they're smart 'cause that car is solid, and she'd bump over someone and not even feel it.

Anyway, Mama Betts was telling how Mrs. Dossett got her umbrella out of the car, even though it was a hot and sunny day, and she shook her umbrella at Huey Jones and put him on the run.

Huey said he'd be back, and Mrs. Dossett told him that if he was planning on modeling any bed linens, he might better wear them up to her house before he tormented her maid and cook any further.

I didn't get to hear what Huey said back because the screen door banged and I went to get the baby. Arly was going to give Alice a ride to school, where the pep bus loaded up behind the band bus. It was a Jexville convoy.

'I'll make sure Frank behaves himself,' Alice promised me as she handed the baby over. 'That Krissy Elkins has been eyeballing him hard. She might make a play tonight on the bus.'

'I shouldn't have to go to every game just to stake my claim.' I was irritable, and it wasn't Alice's fault. She was just being a friend.

'I'm only telling you because you need to know.'

Arly walked into the kitchen. He nodded to Alice and called over his shoulder to Mama Betts that he was gone. I watched them walk out with a mixture of feelings. Part of me wanted to go, just to be in on some of the fun. Another part of me was worried. I had to see Cammie, and I had to figure out how to do it. Greg was also niggling at the back of my mind. Greg and Caesar and Magdeline. And the preacherman. There was too much unfinished business down Kali Oka.

Mama Betts and I watched an episode of *Route 66* and then I begged her into letting me watch a rerun of Boris Karloff's *Thriller*. It was my favorite show, but I couldn't watch it with Arly because he always scared me afterward. This Friday night seemed like a gift from heaven. All through *Route 66* I laid on the sofa with my head in Mama Betts' lap and thought of impossible schemes to get Cammie out of that barn. Nothing I dreamed up was good enough.

Maebelle V. was curled in against me like a spoon, sound asleep. Her little top lip looked like a kewpie doll's, a delicate edge of a curl.

When the show was over, Mama Betts made me hot chocolate, scooped up the sleeping baby and left me alone to watch my scary program. She didn't like *Thriller* and she warned me that if I frightened myself, I'd have to sleep in my own room anyway.

The cocoa smelled delicious as I snuggled back into the pillows and watched these two young boys not much older than Arly have a flat tire on a deserted road. They were going to have to spend the night in this big old abandoned mansion where pigeons flew up and fluttered right under their noses, almost making me spill my cocoa.

Just by the way they were walking and looking around, and the music, I knew something terrible was going to happen any minute. My heart was racing with excitement, and I forgot about Frank and Greg and Nadine, and even for a little while, Cammie. I forgot that my parents were over a thousand miles away at a time when I needed them more than I ever had. The plight of the boys Biff and Timmy was uppermost in my mind. The pigeons took on a hellish cast, leading the boys up into attics and turrets and rooftops where something dark and evil lurked – and waited.

Sure enough, they discovered an entire room full of decapitated bodies. A family. Except one of the places where a body should have been was empty. And then there was the sounds of footsteps and an ax striking the walls. The pigeons fluttered horribly, fleeing the roof of the old mansion in a whirlwind of wings and guttural noises. I knew whoever was coming up the stairs didn't have a head. It was just a body, no head, and an ax.

Mama Betts would have asked me how he could see to kill Biff and Timmy if he didn't have any eyes, but those logical questions were irrelevant to me. I was in the thrall of 'Pigeons from Hell.'

'I can't believe you enjoy this kind of thing.'

I screamed and whirled around on the sofa to find Mama Betts standing behind me, her long nightgown flowing around her and her Bible in her hand.

'I was trying to read, and that music. It's enough to scare Satan from the pits of hell.'

Mama Betts was a relief. With her standing there it wasn't so bad to watch the mud-crusted feet with the head of the ax dangling by them ascend the steps to the tower where Biff and Timmy would certainly meet their doom.

'Rebekah Rich, I can't believe you enjoy this kind of thing.' But she stood there with her finger tucked in the pages of her gilt-edged Bible, waiting to see what happened.

Two steps from the top, and the television went back to Biff and Timmy trying to make something to escape out the third-floor window with. If they jumped, they'd be broken to bits by the fall. They were tying curtains and sheets together while constantly watching the door of the turret room where they were. They could hear the steps, and the head of the ax thumping on the floor with each step.

They tied the last knot, threw the rope of sheets and curtains over the side, and Timmy went out the window. He was younger and smaller. Biff urged him to hurry.

The ax-feet were coming along the hallway now, making a beeline for Biff's room.

Biff and I both knew the knots wouldn't hold his weight and Timmy's at the same time, so he had to wait until Timmy was on the ground. He looked up, and his face registered stark terror at what he saw. Then the ax blade bit deep into the wood by his hand.

Mama Betts walked over to the television and switched it off. 'That's enough of that.'

'But—'

'But nothing. No wonder you can't sleep at night and toss and talk.'

'Me?' I knew I wasn't sleeping well, but I didn't know I'd been talking. 'What do I say?' I was afraid to ask.

'You talk about knives and blood and white dresses and—' She stopped. She sat on the arm of the sofa and stroked the bangs back from my face. 'Effie and Walt will be home before you know it. You and Arly have been great. I know it hasn't been easy.'

I swallowed. 'It hasn't been so bad.'

Mama Betts chuckled. 'Every time you've gone down that hallway, you've looked at the telephone with such desperate longing. Either you're waiting for that boy to call, or you keep thinking Effie and Walt will dial us up.'

'There was something I wanted to tell The Judge.'

'I thought as much. Now, I've got that baby sound asleep in my bed. When Alice comes in with Arly, she'll come to your room. Just tell her to stay, and she can take Maebelle V. home early in the morning. Agatha won't know how many young'uns are asleep under her roof. I doubt she knows how many she's had.'

'Thanks, Mama Betts.' I knelt on the sofa and kissed her soft cheek. It was dry, like it had been dusted with a thin coat of powder, and I remembered that she didn't sweat anymore. She said old bodies didn't make sweat or hair coloring anymore. That's why she always smelled good and her hair was whiter than the sand beaches at Gulf Shores, Alabama.

'Sleep tight, Bekkah.'

I went on to bed. *Thriller* was over, and even if it wasn't Mama Betts wouldn't let me turn the television back on. My body wanted to sleep, but my mind wasn't ready to give up. I lay on the clean sheets, smelling the sunshine where they'd dried on the clothesline and thinking about Greg. Had he gone back to the Redeemers? What had he done with the crucifix? Had they hurt him more? I closed my eyes against the memory of his back, but I only found Caesar's mangled body behind my closed eyelids.

Two weeks. If I could hang on for two weeks, Daddy would be home and I could tell him everything. I had no way of knowing if anyone had been back in Nadine's barn and injured another of the horses. She might be hurt herself, and those animals trapped in stalls with no way to get water. I tossed on the bed. For more than two weeks I'd pushed all of my nightmares to the back of my mind. But tonight, aided by the gentle flutter of the pigeons' wings, the ugly images attacked.

No matter what position I got in or what I tried to think about, the worst of my imagination took hold and served me up a terrible picture. When I was certain that Mama Betts had drifted off to sleep, I got up and slipped out the front door into the still night. I went to the swing. My slipperless feet dug into the oval bare patch of ground just beneath the swing, and I moved softly into the night air. The chains creaked gently, such a different sound from the chains on the old sign at Nadine's. This was comforting, a cre-e-ek of lulling motion. I swung slowly back and forth and waited for Alice and Arly to come pulling into the yard. Once Alice crawled in bed with me, she'd want to talk about the ball game, and mostly the bus ride home. Mack would have kissed her, and we'd have to decide how much tongue was allowed for nice girls. I wouldn't have to face the darkness alone.

391

I gave my body to the motion of the swing and tried to imagine Alice and Mack on the bus, along with Arly and Rosie, and Jamey Louise and Dewey. It was a vision of tangled limbs and eventual disaster.

A noise in the blueberry bushes made me look up. Someone was standing there, just between the two biggest bushes. It looked to be a grown boy. Close to Arly's age and size. His hands were at his sides, empty. And he simply stood, staring at me.

I put one foot on the ground and dragged the swing to a stop. I was terrified. The folds of my billowing nightgown settling about my legs was like the touch of a hand from the grave. The boy and I stared at each other. When the blueberry branches shifted in a errant breeze, he disappeared. I was acutely aware that I was in my nightgown, barefoot. My hair was down my back, unbraided and unbrushed.

The yard was completely dark, except for the silvery light of stars and the half moon. It was impossible to see clearly. When I looked at the place where I'd seen the boy, it was empty.

I'd imagined him. The breath whooshed out of me on a long, trembly sigh. I'd frightened myself nearly to death. Along with everything else that was happening, I was getting visits from Biff or Timmy off a Boris Karloff show. It was time to go inside.

'Bekkah?' The voice was male, sad.

I jerked around to find the owner, but I didn't see anyone. The yard kept the secret of whoever had spoken.

I eased to my feet. I'd make a dash for the door and pray that no cold and clammy hands clutched my nightgown.

'I'm sorry, Bekkah. I didn't mean to scare you.'

Then I saw him again. He was such a distance away, and the branches of the blueberry bushes blocked my view. I couldn't see him clearly, but I recognized his voice.

'Greg?' I waited.

'Nadine said you were never coming back to the barn.'

I wanted him to come closer so we could talk, but I was afraid if I asked him to he'd leave. 'She's mad. Maybe she'll get over it.' I tried to sound hopeful, even though I didn't think Nadine ever forgot or forgave.

'Nadine is . . . ' His voice drifted to a stop.

'Come over here,' I said. 'Come and sit with me. I can get us a snack from the kitchen. Mama Betts made a fresh coconut cake.'

He walked toward me, bigger than I remembered. He'd been so sick, I'd forgotten that he had grown so muscular over the summer.

'You shouldn't be out in your gown,' he said.

The gauzy cotton folds had settled around my legs, outlining my body. I felt my face heat up, and I was glad it was dark. I could tell him that I'd seen him in less than a gown. At that thought I grew hotter still.

'I've been wanting to thank you, Bekkah. You've been a good friend. My only real friend.'

'It wasn't anything.' It embarrassed me; what I'd done was minimal. 'Let me go get a couple of pieces of cake. It's wonderful.'

His hand closed over mine on the swing chain. 'Don't go. I wanted to talk to you about Nadine.' He put his hand on the big tree trunk and leaned against it. 'She's . . . She said some things today about you—'

'She was pretty mad.'

'That's an understatement.' He blew a sigh out. 'She said you'd never come back. That the horses would rot before you saw them again.'

'But they're okay, aren't they?' I dug my toe into the dirt.

'Yeah, they're okay. But don't forget them, Bekkah.

Maybe this will all blow over and you can come back. Nadine just gets mad and she acts like she's . . . never going to get over it.'

'Watch Cammie for me, Greg.'

'I will, while I can. It's that . . . Bekkah, I can't stay there much longer. I—'

I heard the sound of a car and recognized it long before the headlights cut down the drive and captured me in the high beam like a terrified rabbit. The place where Greg had stood was empty.

Chapter Thirty-four

Alice decided to stay for breakfast instead of rushing on home Saturday morning. Maebelle V. perched on Mama Betts' hip while she cooked us French toast and bacon. The morning had a crisp snap to it that the warm night hadn't prepared any of us for. Winter was making me a promise.

Across the table, Arly watched me like a hawk, and Alice kept shooting me sympathetic looks. Krissy Elkins had made her play for Frank. Alice assured me that he'd behaved like an honorable gentleman, but that hadn't kept Krissy from sitting beside him on the bus ride home, and, well, Alice hadn't been able to watch them the entire time on the way back. Seems that Mack's face kept blocking her view.

She thought I was upset and quiet because of that. Frank would be mortally wounded to know that the late-night visit of Greg the Redeemer had pushed his sitting by Krissy Elkins to the nether reaches of my poor brain. It wasn't that it didn't hurt my feelings, I was just too torn up by Greg's visit and what it might mean to take time to feel anything about Frank and Krissy. Sometime during the late night of Alice's excited whispers, I'd decided to go to the barn. I'd ask Nadine about a price for Cammie. Maybe if she thought I was going to buy her, she'd let me ride her again even if she hated me.

'Bekkah?' Mama Betts dangled the Log Cabin syrup in

front of my face. 'Are you going to eat that French toast or stare it into another dimension?'

Mama Betts didn't like *Thriller*, but she liked *The Twilight Zone*. The Judge teased her about having a crush on Rod Serling.

I took the syrup and puddled my plate to the edges. The bacon was afloat in maple. Alice and I ate three pieces each, a real Saturday treat. We didn't have French toast or pancakes unless the weather was cold, and then not often. I ate with a big show of appetite, just to let Arly know that Frank Taylor didn't bother me a bit.

Mama Betts was bathing Maebelle V., so Alice and I took the first load of clothes to the line to hang them. I enjoyed putting them out in the sun. The day was crystal, the humidity much lower than usual. The clothes would dry fast and stiff, the way I liked them when I ironed them.

'Bekkah, you okay?'

'Sure.'

'You didn't like Frank that much, did you?'

'Not enough to cry over him.' I grinned to take the sting out of my words. How could I explain that the things happening in my head were so different from kisses and crushes that I couldn't take time out to let a boy break my heart?

'Jamey Louise said you wouldn't be upset. She said you cared more for that bay horse than you ever would for a boy.'

I let it ride. Jamey Louise had a sharp eye and a sharper tongue. But she wasn't as wrong as she could have been. 'Jamey hurt Greg pretty bad, you know.' I shook out the last towel and pinned it to the line. It was red and blue and yellow-striped, beautiful in the clear October sun. I couldn't get Greg off my mind.

Alice nodded. 'Jamey acts like there never was a Greg. I asked her one time if she ever saw him, and she pretended like she didn't know who I was talking about. She was ashamed that she'd spent all summer smooching with him.'

'Because he's a Redeemer. 'Cause he's different.'

Alice started to say something, but we heard a vehicle on the road. It didn't sound like one of the regulars, and we paused to watch. Nadine's old green truck churned by, going twice as fast as was safe or necessary. A cloud of dust boiled out behind her.

I handed Alice the empty basket. 'Listen, I may not have another chance to see Cammie in a long time.' I watched the road as I spoke, afraid that it might be one of Nadine's little jokes, that she'd turn around and drive right back home because she'd know what I was thinking of doing.

'You aren't going there? She told you not to come back.' Alice was worried.

'If she doesn't catch me, she'll never know.'

'And if she does?'

'What can she do? The worst would be tell Mama Betts. She'll fuss at me and ground me. I don't have a boyfriend anymore, so what's the big deal?' I put it together in my head, unwilling to look beneath the surface of what I was about to do. I had to see Cammie. I had to. Maybe then I could sleep without dreaming about her. And if Greg was back at Nadine's, I wanted to see him too. He'd been trying to tell me something. Something important. There had been something very different about Greg, but I couldn't put my finger on what.

'Bekkah, this is wrong.' Alice thrust the clothes basket back at me.

I refused to take it. 'I'll be back, Alice. Cover for me if you can. If you can't, don't worry about it.' I turned and ran, glad to see that Picket had fallen in beside me.

The barn door was opened a crack. It gave me pause, but I didn't tarry long with indecision. Nadine had gone.

There was no telling when she would be back or where she might have gone to. I slipped inside.

An unfamiliar odor came from the center of the barn. A dark suspicion blossomed in my brain. Greg had said something about checking on Cammie. The first stalls were clean, hay stacked neat, good water. I smelled Cammie's before I looked. When I did look, my heart pounded with fury. Her floor was squishy with muck. I got her halter and slipped it over her head. In the semidarkness of the barn, she rolled her eyes and nipped at me. I spoke softly but firmly and put her in the cross ties. I hadn't intended to take the time to groom her, but her coat was crusted and rough where she'd lain down in the stall and manure had dried on her. I started crying as I cleaned her up. Every time my hand touched her hide, she flinched and danced away from me. I found the saddle in my hands without even thinking about getting it. Once she was tacked up, though, I knew I was taking her down the road. I'd never bring her back. Never. I didn't care what happened to me, I wasn't leaving Cammie behind.

She shied almost out from under me as I tried to mount, but I managed to struggle into the saddle by clinging to her mane, and then was nearly upset again as I tried to urge her through the narrow gate I'd left open. Once we were through, we started down the drive at a trot. She twisted and spun under me, but I managed to keep my legs on her and push her into something of a forward motion.

At Kali Oka, I loosened the reins and let her go.

'Run, Cammie, run!' I whispered. 'Run free.' Nadine had once told me that a horse's only defense was flight. We were fleeing, both of us. Only this time I wasn't running away.

We went down toward the Redeemers because the road was less traveled, and I wasn't certain how much control I'd have over Cammie for the first half hour or so. She was too nervous to listen to any of my aids. She simply had to move for a while, and I did my best to sit on her back without interfering. I would have put her in the pasture, but I wasn't certain I could catch her again before Nadine returned, and I was determined to take her with me.

If Nadine wanted to punish me, she could find a way that didn't involve Cammie. I had to get Cammie away from Nadine. When we pulled up to a halt at the bridge at Cry Baby Creek, I wasn't prepared to find Magdeline standing just on the other bank. There wasn't another Redeemer in sight.

We stared at each other. Between my legs Cammie blew and trembled. I knew better than to try to force the issue of the bridge, so I turned her toward the bank of the creek. With very little reluctance she stepped into the water. I let her have a small drink, then urged her to the other side. When we climbed over the lip of the bank, Magdeline was still there, watching us.

'I can help you,' I said. I was as breathy and trembly as Cammie.

Magdeline only stared at us. I thought for a moment that they might have cut out her tongue.

'Magdeline, I can help.'

'Where's Greg?' she answered. There was no expression on her face.

'He's okay.' I tried to reassure her. She looked wild.

'He hasn't been here for weeks. Rachel said you and that woman with the horses had him. She said you'd turned him to the ways of sin.'

She didn't smile, not even a hint. This wasn't the same girl who'd pointed the finger of fornication at Rev. Marcus. Magdeline had changed in ways that I couldn't begin to define. Her . . . personality was missing.

'Do you have him down there?' she asked as if she

hadn't heard what I said. 'Tell him he has to come back here.' Desperation finally cracked the shell of her cold mask. 'Tell him. Please!'

'Greg was badly injured, but he's fine now. Magdeline, I can help you. Me and my family.'

'Where did he go?' A tear slipped down her face.

'Come with me, Magdeline. Come to my house. My grandmother will help you.'

'Greg promised me that he wouldn't leave me. He swore it.' She turned to look back at the church. 'I can't pretend much longer.' She spoke more to herself than to me.

'Are his . . . parents still looking for him?' I didn't really know where he was staying.

Something changed in her face. 'Maybe they wouldn't tell me.' She looked up at me, as if she might be able to see the truth sitting on the end of my nose. 'Maybe they would keep it a secret. To scare the rest of us. To say that Greg had gone off, fallen away. They said he would be punished in a terrible way.' She spoke faster as her eyes searched my face. 'I'll hunt for him here.'

'He must be around. I saw him last night. I know he's at Nadine's part of the time.'

'I've seen him, too, but I can't talk to him,' she whispered. She sidled toward me, completely unafraid of the horse. 'I see him at night sometimes. Always at a distance. He's with a girl. I thought it was you. She has on a white dress. They stand by the creek together.'

I could barely talk. 'Are you sure? I mean, are you sure it's Greg?'

She shook her head, and her beautiful hair shimmered down her back. 'They're faraway. At a distance. And—' – two tears leaked from the corners of her eyes – 'they touch each other. Like lovers.'

'Magdeline, come with me now.' She wasn't right somehow. The things she was saying were mixed up. If she was describing what I thought she was describing, it would be Greg and Selena. But Selena was a ghost. None of it made sense, but I knew it was important to get her to come with me. Mama Betts would find someone to help straighten it all out.

'If you see Greg,' she put her hand on Cammie's shoulder, 'tell him that I'm pregnant. He promised not to leave me. Will you tell him?' Tears dripped off her chin, but she didn't seem to notice.

'Yes, I'll tell him.' My voice was little more than a whisper. 'I'll tell him. I'll even look for him just to tell him.'

Her hand drifted to my knee. 'Greg said you lived in a beautiful world. He said it was a dream.'

'Magdeline, let me help you. Greg must have told you that I wanted to help. Get up here with me, and we'll ride to my house. My grandmother is smart. She'll know what to do.' I was begging her. If Greg was at the Redeemers, he wouldn't let her suffer so. If Greg wasn't there, Magdeline had no one to protect her. And her baby.

I reached my hand down to her as I shook my foot free of the stirrup. 'Put your foot in the stirrup, and I'll pull you up.' Cammie stood steady as a rock.

Her fingers closed on mine. They were cold and soft, without any real strength, and I had the craziest sensation that she was already dead.

'Hey!'

We both turned to look at the tall, gaunt figure of John Singer striding toward us. Cammie danced backward and Magdeline shook her hand free of mine.

'You're on Redeemer land now,' he called as he rushed toward us. 'This time you're going to pay.'

'Where's Greg?' I asked him, doing my best to hold Cammie still. 'Come on, Magdeline,' I whispered. She stood about four feet from me, frozen.

'You've made your last bit of trouble.' John Singer reached for the reins, and I let Cammie step away from his hand.

'I want to talk to Rev. Marcus,' I told him.

John Singer smiled. 'Get down off that horse, and we'll take you to him.'

'I'll wait here. Tell him I have a message for him.'

Magdeline was looking at me like I'd gone mad. Singer's eyes shifted from me to her, calculating. 'I'll get the reverend,' he finally agreed. 'Just you wait here.' Very quickly his hand darted out and grabbed Magdeline by the arm. While she was off balance, he dragged her toward him. She made no effort to resist, not even when he shook her arm fiercely. 'You can't seem to learn, girl,' he said as he pushed her roughly ahead of him. 'What did you tell her?'

'Hey! Leave her here.' I nudged Cammie forward a step or two.

Singer looked over his shoulder at me, then turned Magdeline to face me. 'Tell her you want to stay here.' He paused, then shook her. 'Tell her.'

'I have responsibilities in the church,' she said, looking beyond me at the far bank of the creek. 'I can't talk anymore. I'm neglecting my duties.' She turned away voluntarily, preceding Singer down the path toward the church.

The look he gave me was filled with satisfaction. He turned and stalked after her, circling his fingers around her arm.

I remembered something. 'Maggie!' I called her name loudly. Even in Singer's tight grip she turned back to look at me. 'I won't leave you here. I swear it.'

Singer thrust her forward, and they disappeared behind a clump of pines and elderberry bushes.

I didn't have long to wait before Rev. Marcus came through the clearing. The sun crested in the wave of his Brylcreemed hair. His clothes were crisp, expensive, and they hung on his body to show the leanness of his waist and hips. In contrast to the other Redeemers, his shoes gleamed with polish. To my surprise, he was alone.

'You have a message for me?' he asked.

His blue eyes looked up at me with nothing more than mild curiosity. He was a damn fine actor.

'Nadine Andrews wants to see you.'

'The woman with the horses?' There was no recognition in his voice or face, only a mild and contemptuous interest.

'Yeah, that's her.'

'Tell her to come down here. I'll be glad to talk with her. I have an interest in a young boy she's . . . sheltering.' His lip curled on the word.

'You nearly killed Greg. If it hadn't been for Nadine, he might have died.'

'The Bible states clearly that to spare the rod will ruin the child. His back will heal. It's his soul that I'm concerned about. Mrs. Andrews,' he almost sneered the words, 'may have condemned the boy to hell. I suspect the three of you will spend eternity roasting in the flames.' His gaze fell on my leg. 'I can redeem you, though. You're young. You aren't hardened in the ways of sin. I could work with you—'

'What kind of punishment do you get for selling babies?' My legs tightened involuntarily on Cammie's sides. She backed up, her body tensing beneath me.

His eyes narrowed. 'You tell Greg to get his butt back here. Whatever he's been telling you, he's going to pay for. And you, you'll pay for interfering here. You've snooped and pried since the day we moved here. God's going to punish you with a mighty blow. He is a just God and a righteous God. He protects his flock.'

I tickled Cammie's sides, and she lunged forward. The

preacherman broke off his tirade and fell back. 'It won't be God but the sheriff who comes after you,' I promised him.

'We have broken no laws here. The First Amendment guarantees our right to religious freedom. We have learned that there is nothing in this world but blood and redemption.' He spread his hands out, palms up and looked toward the heavens. Peace and compassion spread across his features. 'Upon the cross the Lord Jesus gave his life, his very flesh and blood, for us. That sacrifice bathes us all in his blood and allows us the choice of eternal redemption. I offer you that choice, Rebekah.' He brought his gaze down to rest on me. 'Yes, I know your given name, and a good one it is. Rebekah, a woman of the Bible. You could be a lovely servant of God. You're a warrior, Rebekah. Fierce, courageous. I like that, a bit of spirit in a young woman. I would welcome you into our flock. I have need of someone like you. A special place beside me. Exalted, esteemed. I had hoped that Magdeline might earn that place, but she is too weak.' He lifted an eyebrow. 'But you are strong, Rebekah. Everyone would recognize your special destiny, and they would worship you. You have a choice today, damnation or redemption. What will it be?'

It was exactly the way Nadine had told the story of Selena. Exactly. That knowledge gave me courage, and I wasn't afraid, not for myself. He could never catch me on Cammie. 'If anything happens to Maggie, you'll go to prison for the rest of your life.'

'That isn't the right choice.' He shook his head sadly. 'You will suffer as all sinners suffer. What is it you love? What things do you cherish the most? Those are the things God will take away from you. One by one. And the agony for you will be knowing that you brought it on yourself. Everything you love will suffer because of you.'

'It's you who's going to suffer. When my father gets home—'

He smiled. 'I have suffered, and I am redeemed. My suffering is past.'

'Let Maggie come with me.'

'She has no desire to leave with you. She is loved here, cared for. We'll make sure that she is protected.'

'And her baby? What will happen to her child?' I hurled my knowledge at him. 'What will happen to the child you fathered with Magdeline?'

Surprise touched his features, but he erased it in a moment. 'A child,' he murmured the words. 'I'll provide a decent and loving home. That is what we do here. We find homes for children.'

'You sell them.'

He looked at me, an appraising glance. The warmth and compassion that had softened his face as he looked toward heaven was gone. He was thinking of something mean and terrible. It flickered behind his eyes. 'God is preparing a special punishment for you. Very special. He will smite you to the ground and crush your bones beneath his heel.'

I turned Cammie, ready to run. At the thicket of pines I saw a motion. Two Redeemer men were struggling with something in the underbrush. When I heard the yelp of fear and pain, I knew they had Picket.

Chapter Thirty-five

Cammie bolted forward and then shied right. I lost my stirrup and felt myself sliding down her neck. My fingers clutched mane, and I managed to stay on top of the spinning horse. When I looked at the preacherman, he was grinning. 'I told you God was going to take away the things you loved.'

'Let my dog go.'

'We have a right to dispose of any animals that trespass on our land. The dog is vicious. She has to be destroyed.' He looked from me to the two Redeemers, and Picket yelped again. They were holding her down, one with his foot on her neck while the other tied her legs together.

'Stop it!' I tried to make Cammie go to Picket, but the thrashing and commotion frightened her. She shied and tried to bolt.

'Picket!' I screamed her name. 'Picket!'

I dug my heels into Cammie's side and she shot forward, covering the ground between me and the two Redeemers in three strides. I didn't know what I was going to do, but when I saw the Redeemer lift the large knife in the air, I hauled back on the reins.

Cammie skidded to a halt, trembling.

I couldn't stop looking at the knife. It was at least nine inches long, a steel blade that glittered in the sun. I thought of Caesar. Stabbed over thirty times. The

Redeemer who held the knife grasped Picket's tied mouth and lifted her head, exposing her throat.

'Let her go,' I whispered.

'Get off our property.' Rev. Marcus had walked up closer to the horse. 'If you ever come here again, we'll be the ones who call the sheriff. The damage you've done is irreparable. Greg is gone. Magdeline will be punished. We'll do whatever it takes to cleanse her.'

'What about Picket?'

'We don't allow pets. Poor Magdeline found a stray cat this summer. It had to be destroyed. It was very upsetting for her. I told her it didn't have a soul, but she insisted on burying it. Quite a little drama. Now get off our property.'

'Let me have my dog.' I couldn't leave Picket. I remembered the day Magdeline and Georgie had buried the cat. They were both crying. And the preacherman would kill Picket too. In cold blood. Just to be mean. 'Let her go and we'll leave. Forever.'

He nodded to the two men. As they picked Picket up by her legs, swinging upside down, he laughed. 'Go home, Rebekah. Maybe your dog will come later. Maybe not.'

He walked away from me, following the men who had my dog, back toward the church.

'Wait a minute,' I called after him. 'Wait!'

He kept walking, a casual, not hurried walk that told me he'd never turn around.

I turned Cammie toward the creek and we crossed. On Kali Oka, I held her to a trot. She'd spent most of her nervous energy, and she settled down to a pace that covered the ground. I went straight back to Nadine's. No matter what had happened between us. No matter how much she hated me, she had to help Picket. Nadine would go in there blasting. The Redeemers had killed Caesar. I was certain of it. I'd seen the knife, a hunting blade capable of such terrible wounds.

Nadine's truck was parked in the driveway. I rode Cammie into the barn and put her in an unused stall at the end. I left the saddle on her but pulled off the bridle so she wouldn't accidentally step on the reins. I'd give her water when I found Nadine.

I ran to the house, not bothering to knock. Whatever was in my way, I jumped over it.

'Nadine!' I called her name as loud as I could. 'Nadine! Help me.'

I went through the house twice before I accepted that she wasn't there.

The barn.

I hurried outside, running hard. The barn door was wide open, as I'd left it. I ran into the shadowy depths and blinked while my eyes adjusted. The barn was silent except for the noises of the horses. There was no sign of Nadine.

I checked the tack room and the feed room.

'Nadine?' I called her name.

Up above me in the loft, there was the sound of scurrying, small noises that sounded as if someone was trying not to laugh.

'Nadine?' I went to the ladder and called. 'Are you up there?'

Silence.

Had I ever climbed into the loft and found anything I wanted to see? I put one hand on a rung and slowly pulled myself up. My head cleared the loft floor, and for a moment I was dazzled by the shafts of light coming in from the hay door, which Nadine never allowed open unless a load was being delivered. Then I saw her.

She was a silhouette, her hair tumbling down about her shoulders, her naked breasts revealed by the intense backlight. She was sitting on something, moving slowly forward and back, her profile clear and tilted up, reverent. She put her arms behind her neck, lifting her hair and letting it fall through her fingers. Sweat glistened on her face and breasts and torso. She was dancing, slow and sexy, to some music I couldn't hear.

It took me a moment longer to notice the pale naked legs of the man she was astride.

'Hush!' she whispered, giggling. 'She won't come up here. She's terrified of the loft. Just be quiet and she'll go away.'

'Nadine—'

His protest was cut short as she leaned over him and let her hair drape in his face. She pushed back suddenly, and he groaned.

'Forget her,' Nadine whispered. 'Say it, Greg.' She increased the tempo of her movements. 'Say it!'

'I love you,' Greg whispered. His hands reached up and tangled in her hair. He lifted it off her back and let it fall through his fingers, and the sun turned it into spun gold.

The only thing I could think about was Charlie and Earnest, and how I'd watched them feed from Nadine's mouth. I was unable to look away even when I didn't want to see.

Nadine bent over Greg, pushing a breast into his mouth. The golden sun furrowed her spine, splitting her down the center in soft white hills.

My feet felt below me until they touched the next rung. My body descended, but my gaze clung to them until I dropped below the loft floor. When I touched the ground I found Cammie's bridle. The sweat had dried on her, crusting her hair into little tufts. She took the bit eagerly, and I led her into the yard before I mounted. When I was clear of the gate and walking down the drive, I looked back. Nadine's body whipped back and forth in the sun, much faster than before, her hair a wild dandelion riding the action of her hips.

I turned Cammie toward home and let her run.

Arly was waxing the car under the big cedar tree. He looked up at the sound of hoofbeats, and at another time I would have been delighted to see the reluctant admiration in his eyes. I stopped by the car and leaped to the ground. 'Get the keys. Those church people have Picket, and they're going to kill her.'

Arly stopped his rubbing motion on the hood of the car. He looked at me like I'd grown another head.

'They've got Picket?' He couldn't grasp what I'd said.

'Arly, they caught her and tied her up. They said they'd kill her. We've got to go down there right now and get her back.'

'Mama Betts!' He dropped the cloth on the car and turned to the house. 'Grandma! You'd better get out here.'

Mama Betts stopped at the screen door and then walked into the yard.

'Bekkah says those church people have Picket. She says they're going to kill her.'

'They are!' I grabbed Mama Betts' arm. 'They tied her up and she was screaming. I couldn't stop them. They had a knife. And I know they killed Caesar, Nadine's horse. He was stabbed more than thirty times.'

A blankness passed across Mama Betts' eyes, just a second of complete stillness before she spoke. 'I knew when Mr. Tom was killed that something evil had come on this road.' She dried her hands on her apron and started walking to the house. 'Get the keys, Arly, I want you to drive us to the sheriff's office. We could call him, but he'll delay. If we go there, I can force him to action faster.'

'There's not time!' I ran after her, dragging Cammie behind me. 'They're going to kill Picket. Joe Wickham won't do anything. Not about a dog. He'll just think up excuses.'

Mama Betts didn't stop. 'We can't go down there and get her, Bekkah. We'll get Joe Wickham. He has legal authority to go on their property. We might have to get a warrant, but we'll get the legal power, and we'll go get the dog.'

'They'll kill her!' I grabbed the bow of her apron. 'We have to go down there now.'

'What are you doing with that horse?' She didn't turn around.

'I took her. And I'm not taking her back.'

'Arly! Get the wax off and let's go. I'm getting my purse. Bekkah, unsaddle that horse and put her in Picket's old pen. She'll have to stay there until we can do something else.' She paused. 'Better yet, ride her down to the Welfords'. Put her in his barn and be sure she has some water. She's hollowed out. Now go! And walk her there, don't trot her! We'll drive by to get you.'

By the time Grandma got Joe Wickham motivated, with all his warrants and finding his deputies and all, Picket would be dead. I had to think of something better to do.

'Cammie's pretty hot,' I felt her chest. 'You'd better not wait for me.'

Mama Betts walked up and put her hand on the horse's shoulder, then her chest. 'You need to walk her. Use the hose and walk her in between. Arly, let's go.' She didn't move as Arly opened her car door for her. 'Bekkah, you stay right here in this yard with that horse. Don't you get any idea in your head. You stay away from those church people until we get back.'

'What if they kill Picket?'

'If they'll kill a dog, they might hurt you. Stay away from down there. You swear?'

'Mama Betts, I . . . ' My lying ability wasn't up to her direct stare. 'I'll take care of Cammie, I swear that. I don't have anybody to go down there with me, and I'm afraid to go alone.'

Mama Betts nodded. 'Take care of that horse. I don't know how long this will take. Joe can be difficult, but you stay in this yard.'

She got in the car and slammed the door as Arly was driving away. Even though he wouldn't admit it, he loved Picket as much as I did.

I hosed Cammie's legs with cold water and walked her to Jamey Louise's. I had to think of something to do. Something faster than Joe Wickham, and more powerful.

Jamey didn't say anything about how I'd gotten Cammie when I asked if she'd walk the horse for another fifteen minutes and let her stay in their barn for an hour or so. She got a water bucket and said she'd take care of her.

'How's Greg?' she finally asked. She held Cammie's reins and the water bucket.

'Jamey, too much has happened. The Redeemers have Picket.' To her credit she knew better than to say Picket was just a dog. She didn't understand why I was so terribly upset, but she let it pass. I thanked her for looking after Cammie and ran back home. I'd thought of something to do. It was an act of sheer desperation, but I had to do it.

The house was quieter than I'd ever heard it when I went to the hall and picked up the telephone receiver. The operator was very helpful in getting the number for the newspaper in Mobile. I knew Cathi was there because I'd seen her name above some stories. Mama Betts had been snorting about it.

The operator put the call through for me, and I hung on to the black telephone like it was my lifeline.

'Hello.'

I recognized Cathi's sleepy accent hidden by a gloss of living in other places.

'Cathi, it's Bekkah.' I drew a breath. 'There's nobody else I could call or I wouldn't be calling you. Some people down the road from me have my dog and they're going to kill her. They've been doing some terrible things. Will you help me?' I got it all out in one lungful.

'What is it that I can do?'

I couldn't tell if she was being mean or just asking a sincere question. 'Go with me down there. Make them give me Picket back. You can do it. You aren't afraid of them.'

'How can I do that, Bekkah?'

She sounded tired, like maybe she'd been up for several days, the way Effie sounded when she got to the end of a book and couldn't stop writing to sleep.

'They've been selling babies down there. They beat the children there with coat hangers, and they nearly killed one boy.'

'You know this for a fact.' All languor was gone from her voice. She was alert.

'I saw his back. I saw the records where it showed how much they got for the babies. Nadine wrote it all down.'

'Wait a minute. Who's Nadine?'

'The horse woman, remember?'

'Right. And she's got it written down. And the boy that was beaten. Where is he?'

'He's sort of staying with Nadine.'

'Why hasn't Walt done something about this?'

This was the question I knew she'd ask. 'The Judge and Effie have gone to Hollywood. They've been out there for a while, and I didn't want to tell him on the phone. There wasn't anything he could do from that distance anyway.'

'Hollywood?' Shock echoed in her voice. 'What in the hell is Walt doing in Hollywood?'

'Cathi, if you don't come on, they're going to kill Picket. Please! You can get here from Mobile a lot faster than Mama Betts can get the sheriff.' I wiped the tears from my face.

'I'll be there in thirty minutes, Bekkah. I can't make any promises about the dog, but I'll try.'

Thirty minutes. Mobile wasn't that much father from Kali Oka Road than Jexville. Thirty minutes. Did Picket have that long to live?

I tried not to think about what they might be doing to her. My imagination had been called gruesome, but I didn't need much imagination when I thought about Caesar. I paced the hall, then the kitchen, and finally the yard. By the time thirty minutes was up, I was at the end of the driveway walking up and down the road.

I'd decided that I wasn't going to tell anyone about Nadine and Greg. If there was any way possible to get that memory out of my mind, I was going to do it. I felt like I'd lifted up a rotten board and exposed wriggling grubs and white creatures never intended to feel the sun on their slick skins.

Nadine and Greg were breaking some kind of law. It had to do with age, and I'd heard Effie and The Judge talking about it one time before. Old men weren't supposed to do it with younger girls under the age of sixteen. Old men who did went to jail. I wasn't certain if the same law applied to older women and young boys, but I thought that it must.

The entire thing brought up some feelings in me that I didn't understand and didn't want to think about. There had been a terrible kind of beauty in Nadine's body glistening in the sun. The idea of what she was doing to Greg made me walk faster.

I thought about them in the barn, because as uneasy as it made me feel, it was better than thinking about Picket.

I heard the car coming down Kali Oka, and I knew it was Cathi before I recognized the shiny red Pontiac. She stopped and I ran around to the passenger side and got in.

'It's at the end of the road,' I managed.

She gunned the motor and red dust blasted out behind us. She was going too fast over the rutted road, but I didn't try to stop her, and to my relief, she didn't ask any questions.

When we got to the creek, she pulled right up to the bridge and stopped.

'Stay in the car,' she said.

'No.' I got out even as I spoke.

'Bekkah, let me talk to these people. Maybe they'll give me the dog. If you go up there, they'll lose face in front of you. You're a kid and that won't be easy for them.'

I slumped against the car. 'What if they've hurt her?'

'Don't borrow trouble before you have to,' she said. 'Get in the car and lock the doors. I left the keys in the ignition. If anything happens, drive home. Don't wait for me. If I'm not back in half an hour, go on back to your house. I can walk if I have to.'

She was talking like she thought they might hurt her.

'Remember that my editor knows where I am. Tell your grandmother that.'

She wasn't making a lot of sense, but I nodded.

'We are a lot alike, Bekkah.' She turned away and started over the bridge. I got in the car as she'd told me and locked the doors.

When she was about fifty yards on their property, one of the men came up to her. She took something out of her purse and showed him, and he went away. In a few minutes he returned with Rev. Marcus.

I couldn't hear what they were saying, but the preacherman was waving his hands and striding around like he was delivering the sermon on the mount. Cathi wiped her face, and I wondered if he'd spit on her. She took a notebook out of her purse and started writing.

The preacherman made a snatch for the notebook, and she twisted it out of his grip. I could tell she was shouting at him. For a minute I thought she was going to slap him full across the face, but she got a grip on herself and didn't.

I couldn't stand it anymore, so I slipped out of the car and inched toward the creek where I could hear.

'If you don't get that dog, I'll have the district attorney's office in here investigating before the sun goes down,' Cathi said. She was mad and her voice was raised. 'My father and the attorney general happen to be very close friends.'

'There's no dog here,' Rev. Marcus replied. His voice was strained, but it was under control.

'You've got two minutes. I have enough on you to keep a team of prosecutors busy for the next five years.'

'We haven't seen any dogs around here. We don't allow pets. It's a church policy. We're a God-fearing religious organization, and there's nothing you can do to us. Nothing. Now you'd better get off Redeemer property before I have to press charges against you.'

'The dog or more trouble than you can manage. You have a minute and a half.'

'We haven't seen any dogs. The young woman you're talking about is a liar and a troublemaker. She's made up this entire story to torment us.'

I ran across the bridge and stopped at Cathi's side. 'You liar. You took Picket with her legs tied.' I saw one of the men who'd helped catch her. 'He did it.' I pointed at him. 'Ask him about selling the babies. Ask him about the horse he killed.'

Cathi shifted to my side, close enough so that I could smell the perfume she wore. 'Go to the car, Bekkah,' she said slowly. 'The reverend is going to get Picket and bring her to me right now, aren't you, Reverend?

Bekkah can identify the men who took her dog. You may be willing to spend several months in jail while the charges are being investigated, but are they?'

The man I'd pointed at stepped forward. Rev. Marcus tried to ignore him, but he moved closer still. 'It ain't worth all of this,' he said slowly. 'You said this time would be different. You said we'd be able to settle down and live. You said—'

'We've done nothing wrong.' Rev. Marcus spoke to the man, but he looked at Cathi. 'That girl was trespassing. You both are. If anybody has a right to call the law, it's us.'

'Call them.' Cathi put her hand on my shoulder. 'Call them while we stand here, if you dare.'

'Oh, I dare,' he said, his face twisting with hatred.

'I know you come from the Delta,' Cathi said. 'I know about your past. I know about your ex-wife and how you hurt her. She's wanting to talk to you—'

Rev. Marcus pointed at the man who'd tied Picket. 'Get the goddamn dog now!' He leaned forward. 'You don't know anything about me, and you'd better shut up.' He stood right in Cathi's face. 'This had better end here, or I'll slap a lawsuit on that newspaper of yours like it's never seen before.'

'You're right, this had better end here. Nothing had better happen to this girl or her dog, or anything else she loves. She told me about the threats you made. Bullying a child may excite you, Mr. Marcus, but I find it sick and disgusting. It had better stop.'

Picket raced through the trees toward me. She was a red and gold blur, and I stepped away from Cathi and called her to me. She almost knocked me over as she tumbled against me. I grabbed her collar and held tight as I kissed her and felt all over her body.

'Get out of here,' the preacherman snarled.

Cathi grabbed my shoulder and pushed me toward the

creek. 'I don't know anything about you or your background, but before night falls, I will. Anybody who's capable of picking on a young girl and a helpless animal is capable of anything. If you have a past, Rev. Marcus, it won't be secret for much longer.'

'You're going to burn in hell, bitch,' Rev. Marcus spat. 'All of you. I can see you toasting in the flames. And I'm laughing.'

'Get that dog and get in the car,' Cathi said under her breath. Her fingers were about to break my shoulder as she pushed me toward the bridge. 'Stay in front of me.'

Picket and I were almost at the bridge when I saw Magdeline. She was off to my left, hiding in the woods. If she hadn't moved, I never would have seen her. I stopped on the bridge and Cathi slammed into my back. She was backing up, watching the preacherman and the other Redeemer men. There weren't any women anywhere in sight.

'Move!' she snapped at me.

'It's Magdeline,' I whispered. I motioned to her to come with us. In that instant she disappeared into the woods. I walked on to the car, afraid if I delayed any longer the Redeemers would see her and try to catch her. At least I knew she was still up and walking.

Chapter Thirty-six

Cathi wouldn't come into the house. I fixed her a glass of iced tea with lemon, and she drank it sitting in the swing. She knew Effie wouldn't want her in her house, and there wasn't any point making a big issue out of it. When she finished her tea, she got out her notebook and started asking me questions.

Selling babies was what she asked about first, then the beatings Greg had gotten, then Caesar and finally Nadine and how she might be Rev. Marcus's ex-wife. She wanted me to take her down to Nadine's, but I still had to figure out a way to keep Cammie, and I wanted to wait for Mama Betts to come back with Joe Wickham.

I was going to be in big trouble, but as I lay in the grass with Picket, I didn't care. Her legs were real sore, and she whined whenever I touched them and rubbed them, but she wasn't bleeding. Her muzzle was cut where they'd put a wire or something around it to keep her mouth shut, but I found some roast beef in the refrigerator and she ate that in two gulps.

'Bekkah?'

'What?' I got up on an elbow so I could look at Cathi. She looked worried.

'Will you give me Walt's number in California? I want to call him. He should know about this. Some of the things you've told me are . . . extremely serious.'

My fingers curled in Picket's ruff. 'I can't. It would hurt Effie too much if you called out there. That would be bad enough, but if she found out I'd given you the number, she wouldn't give me a chance to explain.' Cathi tried not to show her disappointment, but it was there. 'What I will do is call The Judge myself, and I'll tell him how you helped me.'

'You should tell him everything you've told me. I can't believe this has been going on here and nobody but a thirteen-year-old girl knows.'

'Nadine knows.'

'Yes, and that's another matter. We need to go down there.'

I explained to her about stealing the horse, an issue that didn't seem as serious to her as it seemed to me. Maybe it was because she hadn't seen what I'd seen in the loft.

'Maybe we should take the horse back,' Cathi suggested.

I shook my head. 'She's not going back. Nadine isn't taking care of her right.'

'You said Nadine knew everything about horses. If I remember, she was the best thing since sliced bread.'

'She's punishing me with Cammie. She got mad at me about something, so she threw me off her place.'

'All summer long I've thought of Kali Oka Road as this long stretch of red dust where the most exciting thing that happens is when two cars have to figure out how to pass each other. You've been thrown off two places in a matter of weeks. You've got wild religious cults who sell babies and beat children to a bloody pulp, horse theft, animal abuse and murder. If you had a little deviant sex going on here, it would be a complete Faulkner novel.'

She was staring at me, but I didn't dare meet her eyes. 'Is there something else, Bekkah?'

'I can't take Cammie back. Mama Betts will figure out a way to work it out.'

Part of it was pure, raw hope. Mama Betts might tell me I had to take Cammie back too. I heard the car – I wouldn't have long to wait.

Mama Betts saw Cathi – and Picket. When she got out of the car she called the dog over to her and inspected her carefully. 'No permanent damage, but they weren't exactly careful how they treated her.' She looked at me and then at Cathi.

'I called her and she came. She went down there and made them let Picket go,' I said as I stood up and went to Cathi's side. Arly came around the car and gave Picket some pets and hugs. All the time he was casting these undercover looks at Cathi.

'The sheriff said if you and the dog were on Redeemer property, we had no right to demand the dog back.' Mama Betts stood very still. 'I want to thank you, Mrs. Cummings, for saving Picket. That dog's a special part of this family, especially to Bekkah.'

'Mrs. McVay, there're some things happening on this road you ought to know about.' She looked at me, and I knew she was going to tell everything. 'I think it would be a good idea if you told all of this to the sheriff. I know I'm going to be doing some investigating for the newspaper. If what Bekkah tells me is true, there are some dangerous people living down at the end of this road.'

They went through the whole thing, and I had to answer questions with Arly listening to every word. After the first five minutes Mama Betts suggested we all go sit on the screened porch, and Cathi consented to that. I was telling the part about Nadine and I sneaking into the church when Arly exploded.

'Good Jesus Christ,' he said, 'you'da been better off with Frank Taylor than running up and down the road.

423

Only you could get in so much trouble on Kali Oka.'

'Hush your mouth, Arlington Rich,' Mama Betts warned him. 'In fact, take that big mouth of yours out to the yard and finish waxing that car. You drive it so much the wind's wearing the paint off.'

When I'd finally told everything again, I looked at Mama Betts. 'What about Cammie?'

'Mrs. Andrews hasn't missed the horse yet?' Mama Betts looked down toward Nadine's like she expected to see her materialize in the driveway, shotgun and rope in hand, ready to lynch me for horse theft.

'She knows I have her,' I said before I realized my mistake.

'You saw her?'

'Well, she'll see that my saddle is gone.' I was doing the very thing I'd vowed never to do again, sculpting the truth to protect different people.

'Go on down there with Mrs. Cummings. Tell Mrs. Andrews that you have Cammie and that you'd like to buy her. I'll call the Welfords and make sure you can keep her in their barn for a while, until we can get something built here.'

'Will Effie let me keep her?' I couldn't believe it.

'When she hears what you've been up to, I suspect she'll want to keep you in the backyard for the rest of your life.'

I grinned. 'It's been a hellacious summer, but if I get Cammie, it's going to be worth it. And that mean preacherman said everything I loved would be taken from me.'

'He's a sick man,' Cathi said softly. 'Extremely sick to use cruelty to an animal to frighten a child.'

'And to use the name of the Lord as his own personal punishment.' Mama Betts brushed her apron even though it was spotless. 'You two go on and get this done. If Mrs. Andrews is going to make trouble, I'd just as soon get it all over at once. Bekkah, if she won't sell, you have to take that horse back.'

Cathi rode me down to Nadine's in her car. She kept looking over at me, but I didn't say anything. The closer we got, the more nervous I got. As soon as we turned in the drive, I saw Nadine's truck, but my gaze went up to the loft. I dreaded what I might see.

The hay door was pulled shut.

'Bekkah?'

'Nadine can be pretty nasty.'

She patted my hand. 'So can I.'

She noticed the garbage as soon as we were out of the car. 'Good Lord, nasty is right. What nightmares are hiding around here?'

'Nadine used to be rich. She's not used to taking care of things around the house. She keeps the barn spotless, though.' I remembered Cammie's stall. 'Well, unless she's mad.'

'Your grandmother's hair would stand on end.'

I hurried up the steps and knocked, hoping Nadine would come outside. I didn't want Cathi to go inside for a couple of reasons. The inside was as filthy as the outside, and I had no idea where Greg was.

'Come on in, Bekkah, and bring your friend.' Nadine's voice came from deep inside the house.

'Oh, shit,' I mumbled under my breath. There wasn't time to hesitate. Cathi pulled the screen open and walked in ahead of me.

'The health department would have this place bull-dozed,' she whispered.

'I hardly ever come in here,' I answered.

Nadine was in her favourite pose on the old Queen Anne. One foot tapped the floor lightly while the other was hooked over the back of the sofa.

'Where's my horse?' she asked, not bothering to sit up.

'At Jamey's.'

'I suggest you bring her on home.'

'Nadine, Mama Betts said I could buy her if you'll sell her to me.'

Nadine eased up into a sitting position. Her face was in shadows.

'Could we turn on some lights?' Cathi asked.

I made the introductions and explained to Nadine that Cathi was a friend of my family's from Missouri who was living in Mobile now. 'Those Redeemer people had Picket, and Cathi came over and made them give her back. She's going to—'

'Bekkah gives me too much credit. I'm not a child, and they couldn't frighten me with their threats. Do you know anything about those people?'

'Not the first thing, and I want to know less.' Nadine reached over and snapped on a lamp beside the sofa. The glow cast one of her eyes in shadow, and the other was an amber dart aimed at me.

'But you said the preacherman—'

'So you want to buy Cammie?'

I was pulled up short. Nadine obviously didn't want to talk about how the preacherman might be her ex-husband. At least not in front of a stranger.

'Bekkah would love to have the horse. She's very attached to her, as I'm sure you know,' Cathi said smoothly.

'I've always wanted her, from the first day. Effie said back in August that maybe I could. If we have enough money.'

'How much do you think she's worth?' Nadine was watching me, but pretending to be disinterested.

I looked at Cathi for help.

'She's a nice mare,' Cathi said, even though she'd never seen her, 'but the Riches aren't wealthy people. They'll pay a fair price.'

'I've never bought a horse.' I was telling Nadine the

obvious. 'What would you sell her for?'

'A thousand dollars.' Nadine grinned.

'Oh . . . ' It was so much money. More than we'd ever be able to pay.

'Bekkah's parents are coming home soon. Since the incident with the dog and the Redeemers, her grandmother wants to keep Bekkah right at home all the time. Would you consider letting her keep the horse in her yard for a few days, until her parents get home? Then they'll either be able to buy the horse or Bekkah will bring her back.'

'What if something happens in the meantime?' Nadine asked. She didn't act like she really believed anything would happen. It was some sort of duel between the two of them.

Cathi reached down into her purse and brought out a checkbook. She started writing a check. 'It's Nadine Andrews, right?'

'Right,' Nadine said.

'A-n-d-r-e-w-s,' Cathi spelled as she wrote, like maybe she wasn't certain how to write Andrews.

'Exactly,' Nadine said.

'Here's a check for two hundred dollars. Consider it a damage deposit. If the Riches buy the horse, it can go toward the purchase price. If they don't, you can tear up the check. If the horse is injured, apply it toward the vet bill.'

Nadine took the check. 'She's your responsibility now, Bekkah.'

'Bekkah tells me you're from up around the Delta,' Cathi said, sitting back in her chair like she intended to visit for a spell.

Everything had happened so fast. There was a current going on between the two women. They were sizing each other up. I knew Cathi didn't like Nadine. But Nadine had been so much more reasonable than I'd ever expected. I felt like I was swimming way over my head, and I kept trying to touch bottom but could never find it.

'Cleveland.' Nadine's voice was bored. 'Ever heard of it?'

'Oh, yes,' Cathi said. 'I grew up around those parts. I spent many a happy evening at the Twilight Café. Best swing band in the state.'

'The Twilight was fun.' Nadine's gaze never wavered from Cathi. 'I spent most of my time in Memphis. I'd do whatever I could to get away from Cleveland. Nothing but cotton and dust.'

'And the prison.'

'And the prison,' Nadine agreed. She smiled. 'It's funny to come from a place where everybody knows it by a prison.'

'Well, the entire state has a reputation, doesn't it?'

'So now you're living over in Mobile, Alabama? Do you find it any different?'

'Not as many strange characters to write about in Alabama.'

Nadine actually laughed out loud. 'I like that.' She picked up the check off the coffee table and read it. 'Cathi Cummings. I don't know the name.'

'I was a Newman. I married a Cummings.'

Nadine nodded. 'I know that family.' Her gaze intensified. 'The Newmans were a big family. Lots of different branches.'

Cathi stood up. 'Bekkah's grandmother is probably worried to death. We'd better get on home. It was nice to meet you, and I'm sure the Riches will be in touch with you in the next three or four days. Bekkah's told me how much you've taught her, so you can rest assured that she'll take good care of that horse.'

Nadine stood up too. 'We'll work out something on the saddle if you want. I don't really need it anymore.'

'Thanks.' I couldn't believe Nadine.

'Maybe you'd want to get Cammie's blanket and grooming kit from the barn.'

I looked at Nadine then. I saw it in her eyes. She was deviling me. She knew I'd seen her and Greg in the barn, and she was dangling it right in front of Cathi.

'Bekkah?' Cathi said. 'Why don't you get the kit and stuff? Since I have the car you can take it home now.'

I couldn't look away from Nadine. She was dying with laughter, but it only showed in her eyes. 'Okay.' I broke the look and hurried out the back door.

The barn was shut tight. Just as a double check, I looked in every horse's stall. They had water and hay and the shavings were clean. Even Cammie's empty stall had been thoroughly cleaned. I wondered if Greg or Nadine had done it.

The thought of Greg made me look up at the loft. I didn't want to see him. Not ever again. He and Nadine could do whatever they wanted to do. I had Cammie and Picket, and Cathi was going to look into the Redeemers. I was finished with it all.

I gathered up Cammie's stuff as fast as I could and ran out of the barn. Cathi was waiting at the car. There was no sign of Nadine, and we drove out of there.

'She's a very interesting woman,' Cathi said. 'She knows better than to live the way she does. Either she doesn't care, or she's making a point.'

'What kind of point?'

'That's what's so interesting. By the way, I asked her about the Redeemer boy, Greg. She said he hadn't been around since the beating. Do you think he actually went back there?'

'No, he isn't there. When I was down there today, Magdeline, the girl I told you about, she was asking for him. All the Redeemers think Greg is at Nadine's.'

We pulled into my driveway. 'Get your things and jump out. I've got to get back to the office before I'm canned.'

'Thanks, Cathi. I'll call Daddy tonight.'

'If you could leave my name out of it, I wouldn't mind. I didn't ask for his telephone number to call for myself, Bekkah. I wanted him to know what's going on. He needs to come back here. He and your mother both.'

'I'll tell him. And you can bet that Mama Betts will too.'

Cathi reached over and gave me an awkward hug. 'Friends?'

'Sure.' I hugged her back. 'Thanks, Cathi.' I got out and got my stuff. Cathi backed up and drove away.

When I went into the kitchen, Mama Betts had some fresh greens cooked and cornbread. 'I was going to fry some chicken, but I got sidetracked by a trip to the sheriff's office instead.'

'Greens are fine.' I wasn't hungry, but I wasn't going to chance trouble over supper after everything I'd been into.

'Gus said they'd keep the horse, but you need to go over and help fix up a water bucket and feed trough. She'll have to get by tonight on hay. Gus didn't have any sweet feed.'

I didn't want to say it, but I knew I had to. 'Nadine wants a thousand dollars for her.'

'Isn't that a bit pricey? She's a pretty mare, but she's not—' She stopped in mid-sentence. 'We'll see.'

'Cathi gave her a check for two hundred as a down payment.'

'If we get the horse, Walt will send her a check for that amount.'

'Mama Betts, we can't spend money like that on a horse.' It almost killed me to say it, but it would hang there, unspoken, if I didn't.

She sighed. 'Bekkah, your father is making a lot of money in California. I think maybe he can get that horse for you.' She sighed again. 'The horse is the easy part. It's the rest of it that's worrying me to death. I wonder what's

430

become of the Redeemer boy, Greg. I'm worried sick about him. And that Madgeline child too. What will become of them? And I'm concerned about what you've seen and learned, and what you've gotten into.'

'Are you going to call the sheriff?'

'I'm going to talk to Walt first. Then we'll see. That Joe Wickham,' she sighed for the third time, and she wasn't given to sighing. 'He's a decent man, but he doesn't want to take on any church groups. He didn't say it, but I know he's thinking if he takes after the Redeemers, then some of the other churches are going to get worried.'

'That doesn't make any sense. Why should the other churches care?'

'They get touchy about rights. See, if Joe Wickham starts to look into one church, then he just might decide to look into another one. There're a lot of little churches scattered all through this county, and they aren't much more sophisticated than the Redeemers. They all think non-members are out to persecute them.'

'Joe wouldn't do that.'

'Well, come election time, if the churches go against Joe, he's out of office, and he knows it. And we both know the ministers carry a lot of sway on who votes for who in Chickasaw County.'

It was too much for me. 'Mama Betts, if an older woman . . . ' How was the way to say it?

'Well, go on.' She stopped cleaning the top of the stove and waited. 'If an older woman what?'

'Gets involved with a younger boy, is it against the law?'

'How young?'

'Oh, I don't know. Fifteen or sixteen.'

Mama Betts looked over her glasses. 'There's no law protecting young boys in Mississippi, but public opinion would go a certain distance to putting an end to such a thing. Now, is there a reason you're asking this question?'

She suspected. The way she held her hands so still told me she was putting two and two together, and it was adding up to trouble.

'Do you think your friend Greg is being abused by some of those Redeemer women?' she asked. The idea troubled her a lot. 'Did he ever insinuate such a thing?'

'Not really.'

'Bekkah, physical abuse is one thing. Sexual is another breed of cat. Those people can be in very serious trouble.'

'He never said such a thing at all. I was just wondering. Because of the selling babies and all. And I was thinking about Magdeline and if she's really pregnant, and if she is, who it belongs to.'

'You've been doing some grown-up thinking for a thirteen-year-old girl.'

'I'm not a baby anymore, Mama Betts.'

'No, child, you're not. And that breaks my heart. This summer you've grown up, and what you've seen is the ugly side of what people can be. That's the worst of growing up.'

'Greg said I lived in a fairy tale.'

Mama Betts picked up my empty plate. 'And his life has been a living hell. I'm hoping we can change that for him.' She put the plate in the sink and turned to me. 'If Greg wanted to come here to live, how would you feel about that?'

The question took me so completely by surprise that I must have shown my shock and disapproval. After what had gone on with Nadine, I never wanted to see Greg again. I didn't think I could face him. But where would he go?

'Not a good idea, huh?'

'I don't know. I mean, well, it's just out of the blue.' I

had to be careful because I didn't know what I felt. 'What would Arly say?'

'I'd say I'm not sharing my room.' Arly walked into the kitchen. 'Can I go down to Rosie's house to work on my algebra? She said she'd help me, and she makes the best grades in the class.'

'For two hours. Then home.'

'Bekkah's the one you'd better keep home. I haven't been in half the trouble she's been in. Not in my entire life.'

I thought about rubbing a piece of cornbread into his just washed hair, but I knew Mama Betts would tear my butt off its hinges.

'Arly, I suspect your folks will be coming home soon. That algebra grade better be up from a C, or you and Bekkah both will spend the rest of the year in your rooms.'

When the car had cranked and left, Mama Betts wiped off the table for the second time. 'I wanted Arly gone,' She said. 'It's time to call your father, and I think it might be easier for you if Arly wasn't hanging around.'

Chapter Thirty-seven

Mama Betts spoke with Effie for a moment, then gave the telephone to me. She got a book from The Judge's study and went into her room, closing the door.

'Bekkah, what's going on?' Effie asked. The line fuzzed, and I felt again how far away they were. I didn't want to tell them. Not now. They'd feel helpless, and Effie would feel guilty, like if she'd never left, none of this would have happened. But it had all been going on before she left, and when she realized that, she was going to be mad.

'It might be better if I told Daddy,' I said. 'I've got some questions . . . he could . . . ' The Judge wouldn't go all to pieces, but it was difficult to say that to Effie, because then she'd think the worst.

There was a pause. 'I'll get Walt.' She put the telephone down, and I could hear a buzz of conversation in the background. I hadn't seen Rita Sheffield in years, but I recognized her little laugh. She was petite, almost doll-like, and no matter how old she got, she'd always sound young.

'Bekkah, honey, what's wrong?' The Judge's voice was warm, concerned but overlaid with a hint of humor. It was like saying that nothing really serious could be wrong, maybe just something that needed a drop of oil here or a screw tightened there.

'There's been some trouble on Kali Oka Road, Daddy. Some serious trouble.'

'Can you give me the specifics?' The humor was gone.

Even as the tears started, I smiled. No matter how bad the trouble, The Judge would always ask for specifics. The Detail Man, as Mama Betts called him.

I started at the beginning, about the day the Redeemers moved on the road and how they'd run me and Picket away. I went on to Greg and working at the barn, and how he'd gotten beaten once because I stole his shirt and how he'd been beaten again, with a coat hanger, because of the crucifix that had been painted black and had now disappeared. When I told him about Caesar, the horror of it was so clear that I had to stop talking for a little while. The Judge talked to me then. What he said didn't matter, but he spoke softly and told me that he loved me. I didn't do a good job of telling it, but at last it was all told. All except for Greg and Nadine. I didn't see how that figured in with anything else, so I left it out.

'Bekkah, I want your solemn promise that you won't go anywhere near those church people.' He was calm, but there was a steely edge to his voice. 'Effie's going to catch a flight home tomorrow. We'll make the arrangements and call you back to tell you what time she'll arrive. I've got a bit more work to do. I think I can finish up in a few days. Then I'll sell the car and come on home by plane too. I don't want to spend the time driving.'

'Daddy, I had to call Cathi Cummings.'

'I see.' He thought for a minute. 'If you called her, I'm sure there was good reason.'

He was asking me what that good reason was, so I told him about the Redeemers snatching Picket and how the preacherman said I'd lose everything I loved and that I would suffer endlessly. 'Cathi came over from the newspaper and made them give Picket up,' I finished. 'She's going to investigate them.'

'She's a good reporter.' There was no trace of what he was feeling in his voice.

'What is it, Walt?'

I could hear Effie in the background, and I felt sorry for The Judge. He was going to have to figure out a way to tell her all of this and get her on a plane by herself.

'Let me talk to Effie,' I requested.

'Bekkah, I want your word that you'll stay at home. You've got the horse at Jamey's. Stay with Arly and your grandmother.'

'Okay.'

'Here's your mother.'

There was a rush of breath. 'Bekkah, are you okay? Walt looks like he's going into shock. What is it? Is it Arly? Is your grandmother ill? Has something happened? I knew I shouldn't have left home. I knew that if I didn't watch out for you, something terrible would happen.'

'Mama.'

The dead calm of my voice frightened her into silence.

'I'm perfectly fine. Mama Betts and Arly are both just fine. Even Picket's okay now, but it's been tough around here. I told Daddy everything, and he's going to tell you.'

'Bekkah, what is it?'

'Daddy will tell you all of it. It's pretty long, and I made some bad decisions. I know that, but nothing terrible has happened. Not yet.'

'We're coming home, sweetheart. We can leave tonight, just as soon as Walt—'

'I know Daddy has to finish his work, and it doesn't matter right this minute. I just want you to know one thing.' I paused.

'What?'

'Everything here is perfectly fine. That's all you have to remember. We need your help, yours and Daddy's, to get everything straight, but so far . . . ' Caesar was pretty awful. There was no fixing that, no going back and changing what he'd suffered. And Greg. And maybe Magdeline, if she was really pregnant. 'I can't wait for y'all to come home,' I finished.

'Walt just said he was booking a flight.' Effie was flustered. I knew she'd feel responsible. The flight to Mobile would be horrible for her. Kali Oka was her haven, her charm. For all of her life she'd believed that as long as she stayed on Kali Oka, she'd be able to protect her world. Her children. The people and things she loved. And somehow she'd been lured away. She'd gone to California, and she'd broken her magic charm. She'd even begun to dream of visiting other places, tempted by new sights and sounds. All along she'd expected to be punished.

'Mama, all of this started to happen before you left. I should have told you, but it didn't seem so bad. It all started back in June, with the Redeemers and when the horses came. None of it has to do with you at all. It would have happened if you'd been here or not.'

'I'll be home as soon as we can make the connections.'

She was already in the air, flying as hard toward me as she possibly could. California and all she'd experienced and liked were dust. I could hear it in her voice.

'Bekkah, you and Arly stay with your grandmother. You hear?'

'Yes, ma'am.'

'Put Mama Betts on the phone.'

I put the receiver down and knocked on Mama Betts' door. She'd been waiting because she came with her slippers on.

'I've ruined everything for her,' I said softly. 'She blames herself, just like I knew she would.'

'Effie has to learn not to take on everything. Control is an illusion, Bekkah. You remember that. And know that you can't make everything right, not even for someone you love more than life itself.'

'Effie, darling,' she picked up the phone, 'we're all fine here. Yes I think it would be best if you came on home now, but don't get so worked up . . . '

I went into my room and closed the door. Now the summer was over. Really over. I could taste the end of it at the back of my throat.

Chapter Thirty-eight

Arly took off from school Monday and drove Mama Betts to Mobile to meet Effie's flight. I went to school. After a long debate Mama Betts decided that would be the best way to handle it. Arly wasn't directly involved in what-all had happened, so he was the driver. That would free Mama Betts to thrash it out with Effie before I got in it. I knew Mama Betts was right, but it was wasted hours for me in that schoolhouse. I was little better than a mouth breather. No matter how I tried, I couldn't think of anything except Effie coming home.

At the end of fourth period, when Krissy Elkins made some snide remark to me at my locker, I was so busy imagining and breathing that I didn't even hear it. Alice did, though, and a set-to occurred which the assistant principal had to break up. It was a virtual hair-pulling, and Krissy got dragged down the hall by Mrs. Ethel Shepard and Mrs. Lila Simpson, the two heavyweight home ec teachers. She was in deep shit.

Alice had bit her own lip when Krissy shoved her palm in Alice's nose. Alice had to go to the teachers' lounge to lie down. I went to sit with her while the teachers went on back to teach.

'What did Krissy say?' I asked Alice as soon as the principal and teachers left us alone. The morning had been a disaster. Alice's nose was still dripping blood, and I couldn't even call Mama Betts to come get us. The Waltmans had a pickup, but Mr. Waltman was gone in it most of the time. He showed up at home when he ran out of money for liquor or gas, or both. To my knowledge, Agatha Waltman couldn't drive at all.

'She said you'd done it down by Cry Baby Creek with Frank Taylor.' Alice's voice was slightly choked and muffled because of her nose, but I heard her clear enough.

'That I'd done it?' I heard her; I just didn't believe it. 'Where would she get an idea like that?'

Alice lifted the cloth off her nose and gave me a look that as much as said my brain was drawing blowflies. 'Frank told her, you nitwit. Who else would know you went down to Cry Baby Creek?'

I was cut to the bone. Frank hadn't even kissed me. Hadn't even tried. Now he was telling Krissy Elkins, that kinky-headed gossip monger, that I'd done it. In the dirt. At the end of my own road. On a first date.

'Take it easy, Alice,' I said. 'I'll go get us a Coke.' The truth of the matter was that I'd been wanting to hit someone or something all day long. If Krissy Elkins was still in the home ec room, I was going to shove her head in the flour canister.

'Don't do it, Bekkah.'

Alice had the cloth back over her nose and her eyes closed.

'I'm just going to get a Coke.'

'Let Arly handle this,' she said slowly. 'He tried to warn you. He tried to warn both of us. He said Frank Taylor had a reputation.'

'One he doesn't deserve. All he does is *say* he did something. He probably hasn't screwed anybody. He's just bragging and lying.' I remembered the moment just when I thought he was going to kiss me. I'd wanted him to. And he'd . . . 'He's a coward. He was too scared to even try to kiss me, and he said he saw a naked woman in the woods with a knife.'

'That's a good one.' Alice's laugh was muffled by her nose.

'What a yellow belly.' My anger was blowing over, and I was considering the implications of what it meant for a boy to make up a tremendous lie to avoid kissing me.

'Seems like with his reputation as a hot dog he would've jumped on a naked woman and done it with her. Surely picking on a thirteen-year-old hadn't worn him out.'

'If Mama hears about this, she'll be furious.' As nice as it would be to let Arly handle the situation, I didn't know if I could afford the price. If he didn't tell Effie, he'd hold it over my head for years to come. If he got mad and told her that I'd been down to Cry Baby Creek with a boy, there was no telling what she'd do to me. Mama Betts was a lot easier to get around than Effie.

'Forget about it, Bekkah. I'll talk to Frank.' Alice sat up. 'I hope he gets sores on the end of his—'

We both laughed as the social studies teacher, Margie Fay Pierce, came in to check on us. Alice's nose had quit bleeding, so we were allowed to go back to class. It was only another fifteen minutes before Alice cornered Frank in the hallway.

'I hear you've been talking about Bekkah,' she said, sort of casually, but her voice was still funny because of her nose.

'You've heard wrong,' Frank said. He looked over at me. 'I thought you were going to call me about fishing Saturday. I waited around until three o'clock.'

'I had some trouble at home.'

He looked at me harder, then back at Alice. 'What's going on?'

'Krissy Elkins said you've been telling it around school that you screwed Bekkah down at Cry Baby Creek.'

Frank's gaze held Alice's, then shifted to mine. 'That's a damn lie.'

'We both know it's a lie. The question is why you told that little hussy Krissy.'

Frank sighed. 'I didn't tell Krissy any such thing. I told her Bekkah was telling me the legend of Cry Baby Creek.' He looked from me to Alice and back.

'That's not what she's saying,' I said slowly.

'Then I'll make sure she stops,' Frank said. He shifted his books to his other arm and walked over to me. 'I'll call you after school. We need to talk.'

'If I'm busy, just call Krissy,' I said as I walked by him.

'If you'd gone to the game like I asked, Krissy Elkins wouldn't have had a chance to start anything.'

'Tell Alice about the naked woman with the knife,' I suggested. My own hurt feelings gave the statement a nice hard edge.

Frank slammed his locker shut. 'I'll tell you what, Bekkah. You call me when you want to talk. Until then I'll stay out of your way.' He stalked down the hallway just as the bell for next class rang.

'Bekkah, you don't think those Redeemers are running around the woods without their clothes, do you?' Alice was watching Frank disappear, and she was worried.

'I don't know what to think, Alice.' I didn't have any of my books or anything for the next class, and I didn't care. I wanted to go home.

'Are you gonna tell Arly?'

'Not in this lifetime.' I motioned her toward the ladies' room. It was a foul and disgusting place, and we normally avoided it, even if it meant holding it all day until we got home.

'I can't stay here,' I told Alice. 'I've got to get home.'

'It'll look worse if you leave.'

'It isn't about Frank or Krissy,' I said. 'Effie's coming home today. She's flying into Mobile.'

Alice was suitably impressed. 'Where's your daddy?'

'He's coming later.'

'Is Effie sick?'

I hadn't really told Alice anything. 'It's about me. I told The Judge about the Redeemers. About Greg and Magdeline and all the rest. He's sending Effie home while he finishes working on some movie.'

Alice sputtered. 'Your daddy's working on a movie and you never said anything? Do you think he met Richard Chamberlain? Or Tab Hunter? I'd even settle for Jerry Lewis's autograph.'

Alice's questions stopped me dead in my tracks. I'd never given it a thought. The Judge worked on things all the time. He was always meeting people and talking and writing and lecturing. It had never occured to me that he might meet someone I'd seen on television or at the movies. And I'd fixed it so that he had to leave all of that and come home.

'You okay?' Alice asked.

'I have to go home.' I was going to be sick right there.

'Let's get out of here.' Alice grabbed my arm and dragged me into the hall. She had the right idea. If someone was sick, that bathroom would only make it a million times worse.

'Go on to class,' I told her. 'You're going to get in real trouble if you follow me.'

She shrugged. 'I'm already in trouble for fighting with Krissy.'

'Rebekah Rich, please report to the principal's office.'

The voice cut across on the intercom system, going into every classroom and echoing out in the hall. Alice shot me a look.

I shrugged. 'Who knows?' We walked together down to the end of the first hall, where Charlie Upwell reigned as the man with the big paddle. He wasn't all that swift with proper grammar, but he was one of the best football coaches in the South, and he could run a tight ship. He kept the rules enforced, and he gave me a glare as I walked in, Alice slightly behind me.

'I didn't realize you had a Siamese twin,' he said, looking at Alice.

'I was sick,' I answered.

'You've got a visitor.' He nodded toward the private office where he took the boys to paddle them. 'You,' he nodded to Alice, 'get back to your classroom.'

Alice fled, and I opened the door to find Cathi Cummings sitting in a straight-backed chair.

'I've been doing some serious checking around,' she said, motioning me to close the door. 'I've found some very interesting things about the Blood of the Redeemers.'

'What?' I was glad to see Cathi. With everything else going on, I felt that she was on my side.

'Tell me about your friend Nadine first. I'm having a hard time finding out anything about her. I made some calls to Cleveland, and I couldn't locate any Andrews or anyone who knew anything about a woman whose parents died in a car crash and who'd been married three times.'

'Why are you checking on Nadine?'

Cathi picked up her notebook. 'First of all, a good reporter checks on everything. Your daddy must have told you that. Second, if she was married to this Redeemer minister, then she's going to have the goods I want. She didn't seem too willing to talk to me, but if she knows what I need to know, I might be able to make it worth her while.'

'You mean, bribe her?'

'She didn't turn down the money I offered for Cammie. If she had money once, it's gone now.'

'She had her phone disconnected.'

Cathi nodded. 'Try hard to remember anything she

said,' she urged me. 'Anything at all could be very important.'

I sat down in another hard chair and thought. 'She said her husband was mean to her. She said she met him at a dance at the country club after her parents died in a car wreck.' I shrugged. 'She said she took only the horses and dogs and cats and left everything else just to get away from him.'

'So she left him in her family home.' Cathi got up and paced. 'He must have been some son of a bitch. And she came down here, and now her money's running out. I wonder why she can't get her hands on more.'

'She said her trust was supposed to pay her, but that it hadn't. That's why she's short on money.'

'I'm going to the Delta for a few days.' She eyed me. 'Want to come?'

I shook my head. 'Effie flew home today.'

Cathi nodded. 'And Walt?'

'He's finishing up some work. He'll be home in a few days.'

'I wish he were here now. He'd know how to go about this better than I do. I have to say that the newspaper is less than enthusiastic about my wild goose chase. When I tell them I'm going up to the Delta, they're going to hit the ceiling. If I had any vacation time built up, I'd use it.'

'Wouldn't it be easier to get Nadine to just look at Rev. Marcus? I mean if he is her ex-husband, wouldn't she know him?'

Cathi reached for the telephone, then thought better of it. 'That's true. But think about this. If he is her ex-husband, do you think it's merely coincidence that she showed up on the same dirt road in a state full of dirt roads?'

'She followed him?' It had never occurred to me. 'But they've been here all summer. Why didn't she go down there and see him? I mean if she knew, then she should have expected he might hurt one of the horses.'

'Exactly.'

'And Greg. She hired him just to get at the preacher-man?'

'Very possibly. This could be something strictly between the two of them. Something unfinished. She may have something on him that could ruin him, and if she does, she's not going to give her weapon to me. She may be just waiting for her chance to get even with him. If there's a connection, I'll find it in Cleveland.'

'Cathi, could you look up a missing boy?' I wasn't certain I wanted to help Greg or not, but I could at least ask.

'You mean Greg?'

Cathi was one step ahead of me. 'He said he thought his name was really Calendar, or something like that. He was about three, maybe four, when the Redeemers got him.'

'Got him?'

'He was orphaned. No one else wanted him.'

Cathi picked up her purse. 'I'm going to drive straight on to the Delta. When you get home, I want you to call the newspaper and tell them I was called away. An emergency.'

'They're going to fire you,' I warned her.

'That might not be the worst thing,' she said. 'I'm not sure I want to stay in Mobile. It's a small town . . . ' She faded away. What she meant was that she'd given up the idea of staying close to The Judge.

'If I had to live in a city, I'd go to New Orleans. There's an amusement park and a place to ride horses along the banks of the river.'

She pulled me against her for a hug. 'It has everything, huh?'

'Almost.'

She opened the door. 'Can I do anything for you before I go?'

'Take me home,' I whispered. 'I can't stay here any longer.'

She made the arrangements with the principal, and in a matter of minutes we were driving through the bright October day.

The pecan leaves had started to fall, and I knew that in only a few weeks the beautiful green orchard would look like skeletal fans opened to the sky. I loved fall and winter. No one else liked the cold but me, and I couldn't wait until I could ride Cammie down the road through the frost. No matter how much trouble I was in, I still had Picket and Cammie. And no matter how much Effie and The Judge fussed at me, they'd get to the bottom of things for Greg and Magdeline. It was nice to know that Cathi was already getting the ball rolling.

She pulled into the yard and I got out. 'Be careful,' I said, meaning the long drive. In some stretches the road was poorly maintained, and the area was isolated. The Judge had taken us through the Delta only the summer before on one of his educational vacations. It had seemed liked a slow drive through hell.

'*You* be careful,' she said. 'and stay away from the Redeemers. And Nadine.'

'I'm restricted to the yard,' I told her, 'except to see Cammie.'

'Good.' She waved and pulled out. I went in the house to forage around in the refrigerator and to wait for Effie to come home.

Arly was more than glad to drive Mama Betts into town. She wanted to pick out some material to make new curtains for the kitchen, and she said Arly could go to his last class while she shopped. He was so excited about having the car at school that he didn't even think that he was being hustled out of the way so Effie and I could have some privacy. I knew exactly what Mama Betts was up to, especially when she didn't raise a stink about me being home.

Whatever she'd said to Effie had calmed the fires. Mama met me with a hug that nearly broke every bone in my body. She was crying a little and looked real guilty. It was interesting to see that Mama Betts could do to her exactly what Effie did to me. Hand-me-down guilt.

When we were alone in the house, Effie asked if I wanted to sit on the porch and talk. I sat beside her and waited for her to start asking the questions.

'Your father and I have come to an agreement,' she said. 'I'm so sorry we were so far away when all of this happened and you needed us. But it has given us time to make some decisions, about us and you children.'

I was going to be grounded for the next twenty years. I looked down at my hands.

'We're going to stay on Kali Oka for the rest of this school year, and next summer we're going to travel. We may go back out to Hollywood, all of us as a family, or we may go to Europe and spend the summer in Spain.'

I couldn't believe this. 'Mama Betts too?'

'She wants to stay here. And I don't blame her. She wants us to be a family. Me and you and Arly and Walt. Just for a few months we'll be all together, just us.' She swallowed, and I knew that what she was saying might not be her idea completely.

'And Picket?'

'Picket will stay with your grandmother, where she'll be happy.' She took my hand. 'Bekkah, I've never wanted to leave this road, for several reasons. None of them are good enough by themselves, but all put together, they became too important. It's going to be hard for me, and I'm going to need your help.'

I was completely confused. 'Why? Why do we have to go anywhere?'

'Your father is the kind of man who has to learn new

450

things.' She looked at me and smiled. 'You should have seen him in Los Angeles. He was absorbing everything he could. He didn't like the movie people, but he learned how they worked. Then he started mentioning a few ideas to Rita. Wonderful ideas.' She kissed my forehead. 'Anyway, watching him like that, I knew that I'd been very selfish. My thoughts come from inside me, from my dreams and from the way I see the light in the trees around that little spring in the woods. All I have to do is sit here, right in this old swing, and let my imagination go. Mama Betts used to tell me all sorts of things, little fancies and stories. They're all here, right on this road, waiting for me to pluck them up and use them. I told you, Kali Oka is magic for me.' She sighed. 'But there are other kinds of magic. And we, you and I, have to learn to look at them too.'

'Why?' I was being stubborn, but the idea of leaving Picket and Cammie and Mama Betts, even for a summer that was still a lifetime away, didn't sit well with me.

'You sound like me,' she said, 'and that's the best answer I have for you. You're too young to let this road become your life. And I'm too old. That's what I wanted to tell you.'

'Are things okay? With you and Daddy?'

She looked down at her hand for a moment. 'Yes. They're better than they've been in a while. We love each other very much, you know. I think maybe I took that for granted a little. Families should experience things together.'

None of it made sense to me. 'What about the Redeemers?'

The softness left her face. 'That remains to be seen. I'm debating whether I should go down there alone or with the sheriff.'

'Joe Wickham won't go. Mama Betts called him.'

'I'm certainly not afraid to go down there and have it

451

out with that bully myself. The idea that he'd beat a child and steal Picket . . . ' Her face was white with anger. 'Did they really shave that woman's head?'

'They cut her hair off with scissors, but it was real short.'

'Because she dyed her hair. What a sin.'

'At least they didn't beat her,' I pointed out.

'It's easy to punish women and children, isn't it, Bekkah?' Effie rose from the porch swing. 'I think I am going down there. It's time they met a woman they couldn't bully or intimidate.'

'No!' I grabbed her hand. 'No!'

'Bekkah!' Effie turned to me with a look of surprise. 'You're terrified of them.' She spoke softly, more as an observation to herself than a comment to me.

'Mama, you don't know how mean they are.'

'Why don't we go take a look at that horse you want us to buy for you? Emily said she was a beauty.'

It wasn't a subtle change of topic, but I was willing to let it work. 'Can we?' I hadn't dared hope Effie would really think about buying her.

'Right this minute. We'll leave Mama Betts a note telling her where we've gone.'

'Effie, why aren't you going to punish me for going down to the Redeemers and all?'

She had started into the house to write her note. 'I didn't say we weren't going to punish you. That hasn't been decided, Bekkah. When Walt gets here and we sort through all of this, then we'll decide. This isn't something that can be done with a snap of the fingers.' She looked at me and lifted her eyebrows. 'After all, you've had the entire summer to get yourself into this mess.'

It seemed like it had been a million years since I'd smiled, but I did then. 'I missed you and The Judge so much. Every day I wanted to call and beg you to come home.'

'Why didn't you?' Effie was plainly curious. 'I've wondered and wondered that. I thought maybe you didn't have enough trust in us.'

I shook my head. 'No, it wasn't that. I kept thinking I could get out of it. That nothing else would happen until you came home on your own. Every time I talked to you, something wonderful had happened out there. It all sounded so good, and I thought it would be wrong to tell you this because I knew you'd both come running home.'

Effie walked back to me and kissed me softly on the forehead. 'You've just given the perfect example of why families need to stay together. Think about that when you think about what fun we're going to have next summer. Think about how important it is to your father.'

Chapter Thirty-nine

I gave Cammie a serious talk about how important it was for her to behave before I brought her out of the Welfords' dark barn and into the sunlight. Dazzles sparked in the deep mahogany sheen of her coat, and she greeted Effie with a soft whinny. She'd been out every day in the Welfords' pecan orchard, and her coat was magnificent, better than it had ever been before. The rolling eyes and nervous dancing were almost gone. I wanted to ride over to Nadine's and show her, but I was also hesitant. I didn't have the money to buy her yet, and I didn't want to run into Greg. I'd never be able to face him without thinking of the loft, of the sunlight, and Nadine's web of golden hair.

'Ride her,' Effie commanded, and I did. Cammie was as good as gold. She walked, trotted, and cantered with the steadiness of an old and reliable mount. She was perfection. When I stopped beside Effie, Cammie rubbed her head against my mother's palm. At last even Effie couldn't resist the temptation to climb aboard. Effie was trembling so hard I had to give her a leg up to get her in the saddle, but she got on and walked one time around the pecan orchard. I knew what it cost her to pretend not to be afraid. I could see the slight trace of blood where she bit her lip. But I acted like I didn't. Effie slid to the ground, gave Cammie a hug, and said Walt would send the money to Nadine as soon as he got home. A check would also be sent to Cathi Cummings.

'I owe Mrs. Cummings a thank-you,' Effie said, a curious smile on her face. 'For more than one thing.' She laughed and left me to ride while she walked home.

As I watched my slender mama walk toward home, I felt my life settle back around me. There would be differences. Either Kali Oka had shrunk or my horizons had stretched. It didn't matter. I'd already begun to plan how I was going to get Effie and The Judge to include Alice in our vacation plans. Agatha Waltman could find some other slave to tend to her young'uns. If we went to Spain, we'd be only a hop, skip and jump from Paris, and I wanted Alice to see it – before she up and married Mack Sumrall and started producing bullet-headed brats of her own.

All that night through supper, with Alice and Maebelle V. present to welcome Effie home, we laughed and giggled, and I schemed. Alice shot me some suspicious looks. To have been so upset at school, I was certainly in the catbird seat. I just enjoyed my grin and the way Alice would look when she saw that rainy Paris street where the woman in the red suit and hat walked her dog.

When the phone rang it was Frank Taylor, inviting me and Alice on a picnic Saturday with Mack Sumrall. I held my breath while I asked Effie. I wanted to talk with Frank, but it would be so much better if Alice was along. Mack didn't matter one way or another, but he made Alice happy so I was willing to put up with him.

'You're too young to date,' Effie said, slicing the magnificent sweet potato pies Mama Betts had made.

'It's not a date. Not a real date. It's a picnic, down at Bernard's Lake. There'll be a bunch of other people there too.'

'Okay.' Effie didn't look up, but I caught the hint of a grin at her mouth.

It was all going to be fine. The Judge had made

arrangements to fly home Saturday. He'd sold his car and Effie was going to meet him at the airport in Mobile. Together they were going to pick out a new one for him before they came home.

The week passed in a haze of golden sun, school, Cammie, and giggles between me and Alice. It wasn't summer, not like any summers of the past and certainly not like the one I'd just survived, but it was almost as good. Sometimes I thought about the other horses down at Nadine's, and I worried about them. Her cats had all disappeared, and the dogs were dead, so she had nothing to tend to except the horses, and Greg. Even the thought of them together made me physically cringe. I didn't care that they were screwing, it was just that Greg wasn't but two years older than me and Nadine was a woman. She'd been married three times. It didn't seem right, no matter how I tried to think of it. It was also the only thing I hadn't confessed about. In some tangled way I had become a part of what they did, and it made me anxious.

Friday afternoon I went to ride Cammie early. I'd promised Gus I'd help him clean the barn. When I got there Jamey Louise was waiting for me. She'd even started working.

She was raking old hay into a pile outside the barn door for Gus to move, and I was shifting the good bales up front. Gus was getting ready for the winter hay to come in, and he had to make a place ready for it. It was the work that Greg had done, over and over again, at Nadine's. Maybe we were both thinking about him, but it was Jamey who spoke.

'Have you seen him lately?' she asked.

I knew who. For a second I wanted to tell her what I'd seen. She'd feel as angry as I did about it. But good sense held me back. Jamey's reaction would make me feel good, but then she'd never be able to keep her mouth shut. It would be all over school and Arly would hear it. Then I'd be in more trouble.

'His back is getting better.'

'Is he back down with the Redeemers?'

'I don't know.' I spoke sharply because the truth was, I didn't know. And it bothered me. Greg didn't have many choices of where to be. The Redeemers or Nadine's. One would hurt him physically, and the other? The preacherman had said Nadine would steal his soul.

'Bekkah?'

'Yeah?' I didn't break the rhythm of my work.

'Would you go down to Nadine's with me to look for Greg?' She put her pitchfork down. 'Please. I ought to tell him some things. I should have done it a long time ago.'

'I don't think Greg's studying on a talk with you,' I said.

Jamey Louise was the one person who didn't need to go down there and catch them at something.

'The way I ended it wasn't right.'

'That's over and done, Jamey. Might as well let it go.'

'I'd like to. It's just that lately I've got to thinking how I'd feel if someone treated me that way.'

'Developing a conscience?' I teased her gently. I knew how bad it was to hurt somebody, intentional or not. 'It's best just to let it alone. I mean it. Greg's gone on. He was hurt for a while, but he put it behind him. It might be worse to go down there now and dredge it all up.'

Jamey went back to work. She didn't say anything else, but I could tell she was still thinking about talking to Greg. I could go down to Nadine's and leave him a message to come to Jamey's. I was going to have to go down there Saturday and give Nadine the check for Cammie. Once she took that check in her hands, Cammie would be mine. Forever.

I finished with the barn and rode, and Picket and I headed for home. Effie had cooked some collard greens,

458

cornbread and barbecued ribs. I was starving.

We'd all sat down to eat when the telephone rang. Arly nearly broke his neck getting to it. He and Rosie had been arguing, and she'd threatened not to go to the Friday night game with him. Once again I'd decided to stay home. Alice was going to bring Maebelle V. over to keep me company. Even though it was a home game, Alice wanted to yell and jump and cheer and run up and down the bleachers and drive Mack Sumrall wild with desire. All of that was hard to do with a baby slobbering on her shoulder.

Effie coming home from California was the reason I gave Frank for not going to the game, and it was partly true. I wanted to be home alone with Effie and Mama Betts one last night before The Judge returned. The week had been too wonderful. Effie had restored the magic of Kali Oka, and knowing that it would change when Daddy came home only made it more bittersweet. I wanted to see The Judge more than anything else in the world, but his coming home would shift the balance in the house. This was the last night for me, Effie and Mama Betts. In the past week we'd gone back to the way it was when I was almost a baby. We were going to make popcorn and watch *Thriller* all together with Maebelle V.

'It's for you, Bekkah.'

I came out of my daydream long enough to get up from the table and go to the phone. Arly was giving me some kind of serious look. 'It sounds like Mrs. Pierce, the social studies teacher from school. Bekkah hasn't been keeping up with her grades,' he informed Effie. 'It must be serious for her to call here on a Friday night.'

I gave him a look that should have penetrated his heart like a spear. I put the receiver to my ear.

'Hello.'

'Bekkah, it's Cathi Cummings.'

My gaze slid to Effie. She was pretending to eat, but

she was watching me closely.

'We're eating supper. My mother is home from California.'

'I know, and I'm sorry. This is important. I've got a line on those Redeemers. Listen closely. They were up in the Delta, just like Nadine said, but it was four years ago. They'd taken over an old campground on Lake Beulah, just near the town of Beulah. They weren't there six months before all hell broke loose. Some woman claimed they'd taken her baby against her will. She said her parents had snatched the infant and given it to the Redeemers to raise, and she wanted it back. As it turned out, the baby wasn't with the Redeemers, so she claimed that they'd sold it, like black-market babies.'

Cathi was talking so fast I had trouble following her. Effie was watching me, and twice she'd started to get up and come into the hall, but Mama Betts had stopped her.

'Are you listening, Bekkah? This is very important.'

'Go ahead.'

'Things got ugly. The Redeemers were attacked by several people in the Beulah community. The woman, a Dianne Salter, got the local people stirred up. She was from Beulah, or at least she was living there when all of this took place. She's sort of a fuzzy character because when she left, no one knows where she went or exactly where she came from. Once the Redeemers left town, she didn't stay long. She'd lived in a trailer court, had just had the baby with no evidence of a father. A strange case, from what I can tell. Trailer trash but not exactly. She had long brown hair, a very bold young woman. I've got to find out where she went, Bekkah. Folks around here say she never got her baby back, but there was never a report filed with the local sheriff. She started all of this trouble and then did nothing. None of this makes sense, and after four years people don't remember the fine details. It seems like I'm running around in circles, just catching a whiff of the real story but not able to grab it.'

'I can see that.' Effie was listening to everything I said. I shifted my weight from my right foot to my left. If I turned my back to Effie, she'd wonder. I wanted to call her to the phone, to tell her it was Cathi Cummings, and that she was trying to help out with the Redeemers, but Effie was so happy. She was doing everything right, and Daddy was coming home tomorrow. I couldn't throw Cathi into the middle of them, especially not when she didn't mean anything to The Judge. I knew that.

'Bekkah, is something wrong?' Effie got up and came toward me.

'No, ma'am.' I smiled at her and pointed at the phone. 'It is Mrs. Pierce. She wants to know something about a paper I wrote, and she wants some help with the Fall Festival booth.'

Effie looked meaningfully at the table, meaning I should say I'd call her back after supper. I put my hand over the receiver. 'She's going to Mobile in a few minutes, and it's something she wants me to get tomorrow, from the woods.'

'Okay,' Effie said. She went and sat down and started eating again. Arly cranked up a conversation about how he needed to buy his own car. That got Effie and Mama Betts involved, and they forgot about me.

'I'm sorry,' Cathi said, 'but this won't wait. I wouldn't put you in a spot like that for anything, Bekkah, but I have to know. What was Nadine's maiden name? I can't find a damn thing on a Nadine Andrews, not anywhere in the entire county. No one in Cleveland's ever heard of her. She must be using one of her married names.'

'Why do you need that?'

'Nadine's the last link I have to the preacherman. No one in Cleveland knew anything about the Redeemers, or at least they won't own up to it. These little churches protect each other against outsiders. Beulah's only about twenty miles from Cleveland. If Nadine was married to the man who became their preacher, then I can trace him through her marriage records, if I can find anything.'

'I don't know her name. Try the horse people around there. She had a big stable, and she's shown in Madison Square Gardens.'

'I've already tried that. Nobody around here remembers her. There are several big estates with stables, but they mostly fox hunt.'

I didn't know what to say. Who would ever forget Nadine once they'd met her? I remembered the pill bottle, the one with the little red tablets in it. The prescription had been typed out to Nadine Sellers. I told Cathi about that and spelled the last name.

'I'll check that,' Cathi said. 'In the meantime, would you go down there and simply ask her?'

'Sure.' I remembered what Cathi had said. 'I didn't think you wanted to do that, to be so direct.'

'It isn't a good idea, but I'm up the creek without a paddle here. I can't go any further unless I have something to check. So far I've managed to dig up a bunch of gossip, some juicy rumors, and not a single supporting fact. There's not even a record of the Redeemers renting the old campsite. They apparently just moved in and took over, without anyone's knowledge or permission. I wouldn't be surprised if they didn't do the same thing at Kali Oka. I can check those records when I come back through.'

'Well, I can take care of the other for you, Mrs. Pierce. Would tomorrow about five be okay?'

'I'll call back then,' Cathi said quickly. 'Bekkah, stay away from those church people. If they really are stealing babies, they're capable of anything at all. If they think you might expose them, they'll try to hurt you.'

'I understand. I'm going on a picnic tomorrow.'

'Talk to you at five.'

Cathi hung up, and I said a few more school things and put the receiver back. My appetite was gone.

'Are you in trouble at school?' Effie asked carefully.

'No, contrary to what Arly thinks, I'm doing fine. My teachers all think I'm wonderful.' I made rabbit teeth at Arly. I had to do something to shift the attention from the phone call, but I didn't have to worry. The screen door banged, and Alice came in with a gleefully squealing Maebelle V.

'I swear, I think she'd rather stay here than at home,' Alice said, fixing on Mama Betts' persimmon pudding with a hopeful eye.

'Help yourself,' Mama Betts said as she reached out her arms for the baby.

'I'd rather be here too,' Alice said. She got a bowl from the cabinet and spooned up a portion of pudding.

'Quit gabbing and eat,' Arly said fiercely. He'd slumped back into a bad mood.

'Arly's being stood up by Rosie,' I explained with a bit of delight to Alice. 'He's going to be a bear, so watch him.'

'Sorry,' Alice said to Arly. 'Y'all will patch things up.'

'What's the quarrel about?' Effie asked.

'Nothing.' Arly lowered his gaze to his pudding and started shoveling it into his mouth.

'Rosie's getting even with Arly because he gave old hyena-face Beth Burgess a ride in the car Wednesday after school.' I grinned at Arly, proud of my secret knowledge. He'd made me ride the bus, pretending that he was going over to Buster Schultz's house to study for an hour.

'Loyalty is a serious part of a relationship,' Effie said.

'Loyalty!' Arly pushed his bowl back and stood. Alice recognized the signs of imminent departure and went after her pudding. 'I gave Beth a ride home. It was on the way to Buster's. Buster and Raymond Rollins were with me.'

'Yeah, but she had to sit in the front seat.' I couldn't resist.

Alice kicked me under the table.

'Are you going to the game stag?' Alice asked. She was meeting Mack there but riding with Arly, as usual.

'Yeah!' Arly got his jacket from behind the chair. The nights were getting cold. That was the only thing that tempted me to even think about going. I loved being outside at night when my breath frosted in front of me.

'You can sit with us,' Alice said. 'Mack won't mind.'

'Nothing like being a third wheel, Arly,' I said, and then regretted it when I saw the hurt look on his face. 'You could take Alice and then come back home. We're going to make popcorn and watch the TV. It'll be fun.' I didn't want him to stay home, but he looked so down-trodden.

Arly slipped his arms in the jacket. 'Rosie'll show up at the game. Maybe I can explain it to her.' There wasn't much hope in his eyes.

I was sorry to see him in such a state. I'd gotten so used to teasing him and being teased by him that I hadn't realized his feelings were so delicate.

'Have a good time,' Effie and Mama Betts called after them in unison as they banged out the door.

Mama Betts wiggled Maebelle in the air. 'Get this baby's bottle, Bekkah, and let's get the television warmed up. I think I'll wait until this one goes to sleep to wash the dishes.'

'You watch, I'll wash,' Effie said.

'No, I'll wash.' I got up and cleared the table so there would be no further argument. The sooner everything was done, the sooner we could all pile up on the sofa and get the bejesus scared out of us during *Thriller*. Even

Mama Betts had agreed to watch it all the way through. It was Friday night on Kali Oka Road.

I was humming and packing the picnic lunch Mama Betts had put together for us when Alice finally woke up. She'd been so happy when she'd come home the night before. She and Mack had had a seriously good time, she said. Frank Taylor, a solitary man and one who had avoided Krissy Elkins like the plague, had sat with them for a while, as had Arly. Alice was certain that both me and Arly would overcome the difficulties of love.

Mama Betts was out in the garden, and I had Maebelle V. on the floor beside me. She was rolling wooden thread spools around and having a time of it.

Alice picked up the baby and held her on her lap, kissing her ears and face and neck until Maebelle shrieked with delight. She was a baby that loved lovin'.

She was also going to spoil our picnic if she had to go along.

'Any chance we can escape without that baby?' I asked.

'I asked Sukey if she'd keep her, but she wouldn't,' Alice said. 'I don't know what else to do.'

'Couldn't your mother keep her just one Saturday? I mean, we never get to do anything like a picnic, and . . . ' It wasn't Alice's fault, but it just wasn't fair. Everything we did, we had to drag Maebelle along with us. It wasn't that we didn't like her, but there were some things a one-year-old just didn't fit in doing.

'I'll ask,' Alice said, bundling up the baby's things. 'She's going to say no, but I'll ask. I'll take her on over, and if Mama won't keep her I'll have to get some clean diapers and bottles and things. I'll be back shortly.'

'Okay. We've got chicken salad, bacon and cheese, roast beef and horseradish, potato salad, dill pickles, cheese curls, some chocolate chip cookies, and tea.'

Alice's eyes were wide with delight. 'I'll be right back,' she said, lifting Maebelle and all of the baby stuff. She went out the door while I put the napkins and the red-checked tablecloth on top of the basket. I was looking forward to this picnic more than I wanted to admit.

Frank and Mack were supposed to pick us up at eleven, and we'd be back by two. Effie said that was plenty of time to eat and talk and walk around the old lake. It was too cold to swim.

I had everything ready when Alice returned thirty minutes later. Her arms were conspicuously empty.

'Maebelle?' I was afraid to ask. Alice had probably put her down at the door in an attempt to trick me.

'Mama got so aggravated at me she said one of the others could watch Maebelle V. and for me to get out of her sight.'

'She was mad?'

'Let's just say she was in a bad mood, but that doesn't change much. Every day she's a little bigger and a little meaner. You'd think she'd figure out how to keep from getting pregnant. I mean, your mother doesn't.'

The idea of Effie pregnant was terrifying. It could happen too. She was younger than Alice's mother. It could actually happen. I pushed that aside and focused back in on Alice's problem. 'Do you think you'll have to pay when we get back?'

Alice shrugged. 'It'll be worth it, whatever the price. Betty and Rhonda never have to keep any of the younger kids. They go to choir practice and Y-teens all the time. They never have to take a baby with them. I'm surprised I don't have to take Maebelle V. to school with me. If it wasn't against the rules, I'm sure Mama would make me, whether I learned anything or not. In fact, she told me she didn't care what kind of grades I made. She just thinks I'm going to meet some boy and get married, and the sooner the better. She'll probably send Maebelle V. on my honeymoon!'

I laughed out loud even though I sympathized with Alice. Maebelle V. was almost as much a part of my life as hers. The frying pan clock in the kitchen showed 10:55. Alice and I picked up the lunch and went out on the porch to wait.

The day was wonderful. It was warm enough for shorts, but we'd decided to wear our brand-new Lady Lee Rider stretch jeans that Effie had brought us from California. Mine were sky blue, and Alice's were sort of an army green. They made us look very sophisticated, Alice said. Even Arly said he liked them and wanted Mama to write Rita and have a pair sent for Rosie for a Christmas present. They'd patched things up at the game, and Arly had promised never to let another girl, except me and Alice, ride in the car with him.

At exactly eleven, Frank turned into the yard. He tooted the horn, then thought better and jumped out of the truck and came up to the house with Mack at his heels.

Effie appeared like magic at the door.

'You kids have a good time,' she said. She smiled at Frank, but she was checking him out. His short-sleeved plaid shirt was ironed. His jeans were neat. He had on clean socks, and his shoes were shined. He passed. Then she cast a look at Mack Sumrall. She didn't get past his shaved head with the three little curls on his forehead.

'Mack had lice and had to get his head shaved,' I said innocently.

Effie's gaze quickly left his head, but she didn't miss the look he threw at me.

'Bekkah!' she reprimanded, realizing she'd been sucked into my joke.

I laughed. 'It makes more sense than just having it cut

that way.' Since Mack had been running around with Alice, I'd gotten to be friendly with him. I teased him about his haircut all the time.

'It's cooler,' Mack explained. 'Maybe now that winter is coming on, I'll let it grow a bit.' He grinned at Alice.

'Be back by two,' Effie said, kissing me on the head. 'Take care of my little girl, Frank,' she added, and there was extra emphasis on 'my little girl.'

We piled into the pickup and headed to the lake. Frank switched the radio on and we sang along for a number or two. It was a tight squeeze, all four of us in the truck, but it gave us the excuse we needed to sit close.

'Where's Maebelle?' Frank asked, suddenly realizing the baby wasn't with us.

'We escaped,' Alice said, grinning from ear to ear.

'Too bad,' Mack said, 'I thought we might use her for alligator bait.'

We all laughed and didn't stop until we got to the lake.

The blue October sky shimmered in the mirror of the lake, disturbed on occasion by a rock or a fish jumping. The upside-down trees would ripple into fragments and then reshape themselves on the still surface. We rode all around the lake and checked out the other picnickers. Some of the other kids we knew, but not well. At last we settled on a water oak that threw a giant shade that was perfect for our picnic. Frank helped me spread the tablecloth.

Frank and Mack were awed by the lunch Mama Betts had packed and kept trying to steal parts of it. We weren't really hungry, so we walked around the lake. Frank took the opportunity to lead me away from Alice and Mack, and we found a secluded log to sit on. I was greatly reminded of the night we'd gone down to Cry Baby Creek.

'You're thinking about that night,' Frank said. 'I didn't tell Krissy any of that, not about us doing anything. She made that up. But I guarantee she won't be repeating it. Not ever again.'

'After I thought about it, I didn't believe you'd said it. I'm sorry I made out like I didn't believe you about the naked woman.' At the time, I remembered that he'd fairly frightened the wits out of me. He'd been scared too.

Frank frowned. 'We should have gone after her. It makes me feel like a . . . coward.'

'What would we have done with her if we'd caught her?' I asked, almost laughing at the picture of the two of us wrestling down a naked woman.

'Good point,' he said, laughing out loud. 'It doesn't matter now, as long as you understand.'

When he leaned down to kiss me, I was prepared. Our teeth sort of chipped together. It wasn't painful, but it made me want to giggle. He steadied my head with his hands, and we finally made lip contact. It wasn't like what I'd expected. It was more pleasant, and once we got aimed at each other right, I found I had a definite talent for it.

'How many boys have you kissed?' Frank asked when we stopped for a while to breathe.

'You're the first,' I admitted, and he gave me a strange smile.

'We'd better go find Alice and Mack,' I said. The kissing was fine until we stopped, but then I realized I had a lot to think about. I was only thirteen. I knew plenty of girls my age were doing a lot more than kissing, but they were all looking to get married too. In some strange kind of way, the idea of spending the summer in Spain or Hollywood had taken hold of me. It was going to be hard enough to leave Kali Oka Road, and I didn't need to get addicted to kissing Frank Taylor to make it even worse.

'You're not like the other girls, Bekkah,' Frank said,

standing up and pulling me alongside him. 'Sometimes I think you jumped out of one of your mama's books.'

'You read one?' I couldn't believe it.

'Just one. The one about the girl from the woods who watched all the other children but didn't join in.'

'Starla Fern.' That was the character's name.

'Right. You remind me of her, in a way. You're here but not completely.'

I had the craziest notion to cry. What he said was a compliment, but it made me sad, and I could tell it made him sad too.

'Let's go find those two and have some lunch. We can't take a scrap back or it'll hurt Mama Betts' feelings. She's expecting you boys to eat hearty.'

Frank followed me back to the trail, and we stumbled around until we found Alice and Mack. Our clumsiness in the woods gave them plenty of time to sit up proper, and they were holding hands when we got there.

The rest of the time we stayed by the lake all together. We ate until we were so full we had to stretch out in the gentle sun, four stuffed sardines lying side by side.

When it was time to go, we laughed as we picked up our litter. There was still a hint of sadness between Frank and me. I wondered if I could be more like Alice, more real. She felt everything immediately, just as it happened. With me, it seemed that I had to think about it all too much. Thinking about it made me quiet on the ride home.

Frank and Mack had a glass of iced tea with Mama Betts and thanked her for the lunch. Frank leaned over and pulled Alice's hair. 'Next time don't forget the prettiest girl of the lot. I missed Maebelle.' He and Mack got into the truck and drove away.

'Those are nice boys,' Mama Betts commented to no one in particular. 'Mrs. Mapleson, the potter, called. She said she'd give you five dollars if you'd go down to Chalk

Gully and excavate some of that blue clay for her. She wants to throw some bowls tomorrow morning.'

Alice pulled at her bangs. 'I'd better go get that baby. Mama'll be fit to be tied. Maybe if she isn't too mad, she'll let me meet you at the clay pit,' she said.

'Maebelle loves the clay,' I agreed. I was feeling a little guilty for not having taken the baby.

'As much as I kick about taking care of her, I missed her,' Alice said.

'Who wouldn't miss that child?' Mama Betts threw in. She patted Alice's arm. 'Don't be thinking about young'uns, Alice Waltman. You'll have plenty of time to have your own. And you'll be a fine mama when you do.'

I got my bicycle out of the garage. I hadn't ridden the bike in a long time, it seemed. It was hard to look at it and not remember Greg and how he'd taken it apart piece by piece.

'Hope to see you in a few minutes,' Alice said as she picked up her purse and headed home.

The clay pit wasn't far behind our house, but it was really closer to the Waltmans. It was on our land, but both Riches and Waltmans had played in it since I could remember. Arly had once dug up the clay for Mrs. Mapleson, but he was too grown now, so the lucrative job had fallen to me. I shared it with Alice whenever I could.

For five dollars Mrs. Mapleson would want a big hunk of clay. I could probably get about twenty pounds in my bicycle basket. The stuff was dense and heavy. There had been a place near the back of the gully where Alice and I found a rich vein of pure turquoise clay. There was red and yellow clay, too, but it was the blue that was prized by the potters. It had something to do with the texture, Mama Betts said, since they more often than not glazed it with whatever color they wanted anyway.

I didn't have a long time to dig up the clay since Cathi was supposed to call at five and I still had to ride down to Nadine's. I was hoping to get the clay, get home and distract Mama Betts long enough for me to make a blistering trip down to the barn.

Even though the day was mild, Chalk Gully was hot. The afternoon sun reflected off the packed clay surface, but there were niches and smaller gullies where it was cool. The summer had passed, and Alice and I had not made a trip to pick wild plums or berries. In years past, we'd never have let such a thing happen.

I parked my bike under a wild willow. Picket was panting and on the alert for rabbits. Covered in blackberry brambles and kudzu, it was a perfect place for the bunnies. The kudzu had flowered with the purple blossoms that were so sweetly scented the air around them tasted like grape Kool-aid.

There was an old pond where water had collected from rain. It was filled with frogs and fish. It was a mystery to me and Alice how fish had come to live in an old clay pond, but Arly said the birds stocked it by dropping fish eggs into it. I didn't believe him for a minute, but it made as much sense as thinking the fish had sprung from the mud.

The edges of the pond were cracked and dried, and it was slowly evaporating. Unless we got some rain soon, it would be a mud waller and the fish would all die from lack of oxygen. The Judge had explained how that happened in stagnant water.

The vein of clay I was looking for was at the far end of the gully, up in a little niche where the top was covered with wild plum trees. It made a nice shade, and a good place for the last of the season's snakes to rest. I checked it out good before I scootched in there and started digging.

It was work tough on my hands, but there was also a

simple satisfaction. With two dollars and fifty cents, if Alice came to help, or the whole five, I would have almost enough money to buy the boots and coat I wanted. Without Nadine's trailer I wouldn't be going to many horse shows. I knew Effie and The Judge wouldn't go for hauling me and a horse all around the country. Maybe Nadine and I would patch things up and become friends again. Once Cammie was mine, maybe we could ride together.

It didn't matter whether I got to show or not, I wanted the boots and the coat. And I had to buy the saddle and bridle from Nadine too. If my folks bought the horse, it didn't seem right to ask them to buy anything else. A thousand dollars. That was a lot of money.

The clay was a dark teal, beautiful in the sunlight when I'd trenched enough of the red clay and dirt away from it. The vein was about ten inches wide. It seemed to run up about eight feet from the floor of the gully. I'd have a basket full in no time. I dug for a while, and then stopped to listen for Alice. She should have been there by now. She'd have Maebelle, but it didn't matter. The baby loved the clay. But the fact that Alice hadn't arrived yet had me worried. Had Mrs. Waltman been so angry that she'd slapped Alice again? It was a distressing thought.

Up above me Picket rustled in the briars. A high-pitched squeal cut through the air, followed by rapid yips. She was hot on the trail of some cottontail. I grinned and worked my trowel a little deeper into the wall. I was torn between wanting Alice to hurry up and wanting to get all the money for myself.

After another ten minutes I stopped again. If Alice didn't come on, I'd have the whole thing done. She'd never take half the money if she didn't do half the work, and I knew she needed cash as much as I did. She'd been eyeing a pair of loafers at one of the stores

473

in Jexville. She wanted those shoes bad.

Listening hard for the sound of Alice's squeaky bike or Maebelle's laugh, I dug a little more.

The high-pitched scream that wafted over the gully made me freeze with the trowel lifted. I was ready to plunge the sharp point deep into the clay, but I stopped. I'd never heard a rabbit scream like that. I didn't know what to do. I scrambled out of the niche and started climbing the wall of clay up to the briars.

The scream came again, floating on the golden air. It was a human, a grown woman. It came from toward Kali Oka, from the Waltmans' house.

The wail rose for the third time, a cry of loss and fury and . . . I knew then why Alice hadn't come to the gully. It was Maebelle V. It was an instant, instinctive knowledge that came as sure and thick as the grape smell of the kudzu.

Something terrible had happened to Maebelle V.

The clay was forgotten as I got my bicycle. It was rough riding from the gully, but I didn't have time to worry about tree limbs that clawed at my face or briars that snatched at my new stretch jeans.

The smell of the sweet kudzu mingled with the taste of fear, and my throat spasmed. Maebelle VanCamp. We should have taken her with us. It wouldn't have hurt to take her to the lake for a picnic, even the boys had said so. We didn't take her because of me.

Mama Betts was standing at the screen door, waiting for me.

'Someone's stolen the youngest Waltman,' she said, unable to even say Maebelle's name.

'Maebelle?' I saw her as she'd been only that morning, sitting on the floor drooling on the wooden thread spools. Her red curls had been tousled about her head, and her smile lopsided and wet. She was a skinny baby, hardly big enough to support her full name.

Mama Betts talked, something about Effie and Alice, but I didn't hear her. I was thinking about Maebelle. She had to be around the Waltman house somewhere. They'd just misplaced her. No one would steal a baby.

'It was ten years ago almost to the day that Evie Baxter was stolen. Everybody on Kali Oka remembers, but nobody wants to. They've forgotten that poor baby's name.'

I looked at Mama Betts.

'I knew when those church folks moved on Kali Oka it was going to be trouble,' she said. 'I knew it.'

The Waltman household was in a panic when I dropped the bicycle in the yard. The younger children were out poking in bushes and crawling under the house. They were all calling Maebelle's name.

Alice stood in the center of the yard, unmoving. She looked as if she'd been slapped hard. In fact, the print of a hand was still on her left cheek.

'She has to be around here somewhere,' I said.

Another ear-piercing scream came from the house. I had the impulse to run in and slap Agatha Waltman as hard as I could, right across the mouth. Now was a fine time for her to decide that she was really worried about her baby. It had been four hours since anyone had seen Maebelle V., not since just after Alice and I left for the lake.

'Where did you see her last?' I asked Alice. It wouldn't do any good to ask the others.

'I gave her to Betty and told her that I was going back to your house. They were sitting on the front porch.'

'Betty!' I called the Waltman a year younger than Alice. She was a dark-haired girl with clear blue eyes. She hardly ever spoke, but she was a favorite of the teachers at school.

'Where did you see Maebelle last?'

'I had her down by the mailbox. I went to get the mail, and we were playing in the sand. Maebelle had found a rock.' She looked nervously around the yard. 'Then Sukey came down to talk to me. Somebody was picking her up to take her to the church to practice for that wedding.'

'And Maebelle?' Alice questioned.

'I talked with Sukey for a while, and then I went home.'

'And Maebelle?' I asked.

'I don't know,' Betty said slowly. 'She . . . '

'Did you leave her at the mailbox?'

'I thought Sukey had changed her mind and taken her to the church.'

Alice started down the driveway at a trot. Betty and I fell in beside her, and I whistled to Picket to come along.

'How far could she get?' I asked. Maebelle V. could crawl, but she had to be around somewhere close by.

Alice started down the ditches with a silent Betty working the other side of the road. I walked with Alice.

'She's around here,' I reassured her. 'She couldn't have gotten far, and if anyone had seen her on the road, they would have stopped and taken her home.'

That was one good thing about Kali Oka. Everybody knew everybody else. There was no doubt that the redheaded baby girl with the curls and gurgling laugh was Agatha Waltman's. Or if they didn't place the child as Agatha's, they knew she belonged to me and Alice. Someone would have brought her home.

'She's probably asleep under some bush,' I told Alice. But the frown didn't disappear, and after we'd searched the ditches for half a mile in either direction, the tears started.

'I need to go home,' I told her softly. The Waltmans didn't have a phone, and it was time to call the sheriff.

476

Maebelle V. wasn't going to turn up tucked under a shrub asleep.

'Don't go,' Alice whispered. She looked at me, tears leaking from her eyes and down her face. 'She's gone, Bekkah. She's really gone, and I know in my heart she's not coming back. I feel it.'

Chapter Forty

Kali Oka Road rumbled like a thundercloud. Cars and trucks churned through the heavy sand, never slowing. When they hit the patches of hard red clay, they slung gravel far behind them. They were strange cars and trucks, driven by solitary men with tractor caps and fatigues. The national guard had been called out to hunt for Maebelle V.

In the distance there was the baying of the bloodhounds. Six of the state prison's best dogs had been flown into Jexville to hunt for the baby. Maebelle V. had been missing for twenty-four hours. There wasn't a trace of her.

The bloodhounds picked up her scent at the Waltman mailbox, but then they circled and cried, running on top of each other in confusion. Mama Betts said it was as if the angels had picked Maebelle up and disappeared with her into thin air.

The Judge had driven his new Volvo into town to talk with the district attorney. The honorable Rex T. Ransom had driven over from Pascagoula to personally oversee the search. Effie was disgusted by Ransom's sudden appearance and the ugly mood that was showing up along the road. Folks on Kali Oka who'd never mentioned the Redeemers had started asking questions about them. Effie said that rumors were simmering up and down the road, and that the delicious odor of terrible tragedy had wafted over to Pascagoula and drawn the district attorney by the nose.

'He smells publicity,' she said. 'He couldn't care less about the baby. He just wants to be around when the headlines are made. When Ollie Stanford's trial starts in Meridian Thursday, you can bet Ransom will manage to be there when otherwise he'd send his assistant. Goddamn vulture.'

Still, Daddy had gone down to tell him everything I'd seen. The Judge didn't see much use for Rex Ransom, either, but he was the elected authority, Daddy said. He'd reached out to touch Effie's shoulder and then mine, and said that we'd do anything we could to get Maebelle back.

Arly was in his room studying for a history test. He was mad because Effie wouldn't let him tie up the telephone to talk with Rosie, and she wouldn't let him leave the house.

Mama Betts and I sat on the swing on the porch and listened to the local radio station. There was a special broadcast with updates on the search for Maebelle V.

Once Daddy was gone to town, Effie paced back and forth, from the kitchen to the screened door and back into the kitchen.

'Why don't you go see if Alice wants to come over here for a while?' Mama Betts said.

'She won't. She's standing at that mailbox like she's suddenly going to see Maebelle sitting on the ground playing with a rock.' I was talking to Mama Betts, but I was a long, long way from Kali Oka Road. I couldn't bear the thought of Alice, the look on her face. She'd accepted that Maebelle was dead, and that no amount of hunting would bring her home safely.

I couldn't stand that thought. I simply abandoned my body, left it sitting on the porch. I was floating on Cammie's back. I could feel her muscles bunch and stretch beneath my legs as we galloped down a sandy lane. The pine needles were crisp. The air was clean, and I was free. I didn't feel anything but the ride. If I stopped or paused or even looked behind me, something terrible would happen. So I concentrated on the sound of her hooves, a rapid four-beat cadence as we ran. Me and Cammie, just ahead of the storm.

'How could they lose a baby, and who has her now?' Effie asked, stopping in the doorway. She brought me back to the porch with a bone-rattling reality. She didn't want to talk about the Redeemers, but I could see it in her eyes. She thought they had Maebelle V. That's why The Judge had rushed into Jexville. He wanted Rex Ransom to do something immediately, to sign search warrants and get a posse of men down there before the baby could be harmed. I'd heard them talking about it, whispering in the still of the night.

That was the sound I'd missed for the past month of the summer, the sound of angry secrets passing between my parents. The trip to California had banished the hiss of their hot words. They still whispered, but there was no longer the volcanic element of anger. No, this was worse. Now their voices were hushed with fear, with the dread possibility of what had become of a small baby.

A baby who would be safe today if I hadn't wanted a picnic without her.

'Bekkah.' Mama Betts touched my leg. 'Honey, I know this is hard on you. Especially hard on Alice. But it wasn't wrong of you and Alice to want a small piece of time for yourselves. Maebelle V. has a mama and a host of brothers and sisters, all who could watch her as good as you and Alice. This isn't your fault.'

'I know.' She was trying, but it didn't help. It was my fault. Mine more than Alice's. Alice would have taken her if I hadn't said not to.

481

'Why don't you go and check on that horse of yours?' Mama Betts suggested.

'Cammie.' I said her name but didn't move.

'Maybe just brush her a bit. It might make both of you feel better.'

I got up and walked off the porch. Why not go see Cammie? What else could I do? Before I realized what I was doing, I'd walked all the way to the Welfords.

Jamey Louise came out of the house with a glass of lemonade when she saw me coming down her driveway. 'I'm sorry,' she said. 'I'll bet that baby was almost like your sister.'

'Yeah.' I looked straight at Jamey, noticing her new red sweater and skirt, but I wasn't there any longer. I was riding through the woods again. The pine scent was wonderful. There wasn't a trace of kudzu in the air. I was riding in a place where kudzu would never grow.

'Mama said that if there's anything she can do . . . She's making up a casserole to take to the Waltmans.'

'That's nice. They'll appreciate that.'

'How many brothers and sisters does Alice have?'

'Ten, counting Maebelle,' I answered. I drained the glass and gave it back to her. There was the tartness of lemon at the back of my throat, but other than that I hadn't tasted a thing.

'Going to ride Cammie?' Jamey asked.

'Just around in the pecan orchard.'

'Bekkah, you want me to go with you?'

I smiled. 'No, I think I'd rather be by myself.' I got the saddle and bridle from the barn, along with a pad. I'd catch her in the orchard and saddle her there.

'You sure you're okay?'

'I just need some time to think.' I kept walking toward the orchard. I didn't look back because I didn't want to encourage Jamey to follow me.

Cammie came to me as soon as she saw me. It didn't

take two minutes to tack up, and then we were at the side gate to Kali Oka Road. I didn't think much about what I was doing. I hadn't intended to leave the orchard. I just rode to Cry Baby Creek.

The six old battered buses were in front of the church. Redeemer women were carrying bundles of things while the men were putting mattresses and bigger items in the first buses. They were leaving. It was exactly what I'd expected.

They had Maebelle, and they were going to make a run for it.

I saw Magdeline. She was standing at the back of the third bus. She'd stepped out of the way of an older woman who was carrying what looked like sheets. Her gaze roved over the church grounds, moving silently. She was saying goodbye, and she wasn't upset about it. She was just marking the places in her mind where things had happened.

She stopped when she saw me, sitting on Cammie, just across the creek. She stared at me, her face not showing how she felt one way or another. Her skin looked too clear, almost like I could see through it. I was hoping she'd make a dash to the creek to talk to me. At least I could ask her about the baby if she got close enough. Instead she turned her back to me and walked in among a cluster of women. They looked up, and then went back to their work. They didn't hurry, and they didn't stop.

'Where's the baby?' I cried.

My voice carried strongly on the creek. Picket stood poised just in front of me, her ruff standing on end.

No one even looked at me.

'Where's the baby? Give her back and nothing bad will happen.'

They didn't even look.

'My daddy's talking to the district attorney. He's going to put y'all in jail.'

One of the men started toward the bridge, but the preacherman grabbed his arm and roughly shoved him back toward the bus. They were loading pots and pans, big vat-like kettles.

'Magdeline?' I called out to her. 'Come on over here and I'll see that you're safe. Don't leave with them.'

From behind the bus Magdeline stepped forward. The Redeemer women froze in a cluster. The men stopped working. Even the preacherman halted in mid-command to some workers. Magdeline walked toward him. He put his hand on her shoulder, and she kissed his cheek and then went to get into the bus.

'Y'all better not try to leave Kali Oka Road.' I threw that at them as a last resort. Then I spun Cammie and we headed for the house. Instead of standing around yelling at the Redeemers, I needed to let someone know they were trying to run out. I hadn't seen Maebelle V., but they had to have her. If they hadn't sold her already.

The Judge was back from Jexville, and Cathi Cummings had arrived when I rode into the yard. I'd completely forgotten about her phone call. Mama Betts must have talked to her and told her about Maebelle V. Effie, Cathi and The Judge were all on the screened porch sipping iced tea and talking seriously. It was the same kind of voice Effie and The Judge had used when they were talking last night.

'Ransom won't do a thing until he's forced to act,' The Judge was saying.

'The Redeemers are packing up to leave,' I cried as I leaped to the ground, barely catching Cammie's reins.

'Now?' Daddy stood up, concern furrowing his forehead. 'Right this minute?'

'They aren't planning on staying the night. They're putting all the bedding and everything in the buses. They look like ants, all lined up and working.'

Daddy didn't wait to answer. He went to the telephone

and dialed the sheriff's office. Joe Wickham was already on Kali Oka with the volunteer search and rescue. They were a bunch of drunks, Daddy said, and when he came back from the phone, he was even more worried.

'It's liable to get out of hand,' he said. 'They're going to radio Joe and get him and the volunteers to go down there and stop the Redeemers from leaving until that baby is found.'

'Someone's going to get hurt.' Effie stood also.

'Is there anything I can do?' Cathi asked.

'I just wish you'd been able to find something concrete on those Redeemers. They look guilty as hell,' Daddy said. He paced the porch. 'I just have a hard time convicting a person on appearances.'

'Who else could have her?' I asked. 'Nadine said they sold babies. If she isn't there, they've already sold her to someone.' I could hear my voice rising.

'What about Nadine? Did you find out about her ex-husband?' The Judge stopped pacing long enough for me to answer.

I could tell that the three of them had shared everything. And Effie wasn't too upset. At least if she was, she was more upset by Maebelle V.'s disappearance than Cathi's appearance.

'I forgot,' I said. 'I'll go now.'

'I think you should stay home,' Effie said. 'Once those men get on the road . . . If they're drinking, they might hit you and that horse.'

'I need to see if Greg is there. He might know where they're planning on going.'

'That's a good idea,' Cathi said. She stood up. 'I'll go ask him. You can wait here.'

'He won't talk to anyone but me.' It was partly because I wanted to ask him, but mostly because he'd never talk to Cathi. The only way I was going to get anything out of him, if he was at the barn, was to threaten him with what

I'd seen. And I didn't want any witnesses to that. If I was going to make him talk, I had to be alone with him.

'Go on,' Daddy waved down the road. 'Be careful, Bekkah. Cut through the woods and stay off the road.'

'Mama?' I turned to her. 'Will you go check on Alice for me?'

'Mama Betts has made some pies. I was planning on taking them down to the Waltmans. I'll see her then.'

'Bring her back here if she'll come,' I requested.

'I'll try.'

'I'll go with you, if you don't mind,' Cathi said.

A look passed between her and Effie. It was one I didn't understand at all.

'There's four pies. I could use the help,' Effie answered her.

I didn't wait to watch what happened between them. I couldn't understand how all of a sudden they were talking all civilized and working together. Effie had even talked to Cathi about covering Ollie Stanford's trial and how having a real reporter there might help him get a fair shake. It didn't make sense, and I didn't have time to gnaw on it. Cammie and I trotted through the woods to Nadine's.

Even though the afternoon was breezeless, the old sign moaned on its rusty chains. Cammie hadn't been nervous since I'd taken her away, but she crab-stepped down the driveway toward the barn. The crowded limbs of the chinaberry trees must have made her feel confined.

From halfway down the drive I could see the barn door was pulled shut.

The stench of the garbage was worse, even though the days had cooled considerably. The gruesome pile against the steps didn't seem much bigger, just ranker. Nadine's truck and trailer were parked in the barnyard, but there wasn't a sign of life. I missed the darting shadows of the cats. It was strange how they'd all run away. Even wild cats usually stayed in a barn if they were fed.

'Nadine!' I called as loud as I could. I didn't want to get off Cammie, and I didn't want to go into the barn. If she and Greg were up to anything, I wanted to warn them that I was on the property.

'Nadine!'

Silence answered me back.

'Easy, girl.' Cammie was shifting and sidling under me. Her ears perked forward and her nostrils flared as the door of the barn opened a crack. No one came out, and no one said anything.

All of the flesh on my arms and back rearranged itself. I got off Cammie and against all of the rules tied her to the fence. I didn't want her inside the barnyard, and I didn't have a halter. I had to use the bridle and hope she wouldn't pull and break the leather.

The gate creaked under my hand, and I left it hanging on one hinge. I wanted all the paths cleared for my getaway.

'Nadine?' I walked across the yard.

There wasn't the sound of anything. Nothing. I stopped at the barn door. The interior was black, and at last I heard the snuffling of the horses. I let go of a sigh.

'Greg?'

His name echoed around the big old barn, not stopping anywhere.

'Greg? Are you in here?'

'Get out of here.'

It was Greg's voice, but it scared the hell out of me. He sounded like a disembodied spirit. I hadn't really expected to hear him. In my mind, he was down at those buses helping the Redeemers pack.

'Greg, somebody's stolen Maebelle V.'

'Bekkah, get out of here now. This isn't any place for you. Just get on your horse and get on home.'

I couldn't see him in the barn. The light was bad, and

487

he was deliberately hiding from me.

'Greg, the Redeemers have taken Maebelle V. If someone doesn't do something, there's going to be trouble.
Half the men in town are in the national guard, and
they're all out in the woods hunting for that baby. When
they find those church people have her, all hell's going to
break loose.'

'The Redeemers don't have no baby.'

He spoke with such conviction, as if he knew where
Maebelle was.

'Then where is she?'

He hesitated. 'I don't know for certain, but I know
the Redeemers don't have her. They don't steal babies.
They didn't steal me or anyone else. Folks give them
babies sometimes, babies from unwed mothers and
from families where children aren't wanted. We take
them in and give them to people in the church who
want a child.'

'Nadine found evidence. She found records of babies
being sold by Rev. Marcus.'

Greg mumbled a curse word under his breath. 'Nadine
found what she wanted to find, Bekkah. Can't you see
that?'

I wasn't following him, and I was annoyed that I
couldn't see him. He was up in the loft, I thought. 'What
are you getting at?' I stepped farther into the barn, my
eyes trying to penetrate the darkness.

'Take you, for instance. Nadine saw you as someone to
buy a horse. Right from the beginning she meant to sell
Cammie to you, a horse, by the way, that she got from a
man up near Jackson. Cleaned out his stables for him,
after she'd—'

'What are you saying?'

'That Cammie isn't any fancy show horse. She's just a
horse. Nadine told me she met this man, rode his horses
for a while.' Greg laughed and it was bitter. 'Rode him, I

488

suspect, and managed to get his horses from him.'

'Where is she?'

'I don't know. I came back here to wait for her. As soon as I figure out what to do with these horses, I'm going to leave myself. I just didn't want to go off without making some kind of arrangements.'

I was still struggling with the news about the horses and what it might mean. I didn't believe Greg. Not right off. There was no telling why Nadine had concocted such a story, but just because she'd told him didn't make it true. Nadine had a habit of lying, especially if she thought it was going to shock someone.

'I don't care about the horses or where they came from. Greg, we've got to find that baby. Maebelle V.'s been gone more than twenty-four hours now.'

'Nadine quit feeding the horses at the first of the week. That's why I'm still here. She said she'd had enough of them. Charlie and Earnest are dead. I found them Tuesday. Poisoned. Just like she'd done the dogs. And more than likely the cats too.'

'Greg, get down here and talk to me. I don't know why you're saying all of this. I saw you and Nadine. I saw you in the loft. I know what you're doing together.' The words rushed out in clumps. 'If you don't help me find that baby, I'm going to tell everyone.'

'Go ahead. I don't give a damn anymore.'

His body was a blur as he swung down from the ladder at the end of the barn and landed on his feet in the center of the aisle.

'I'd rather go to jail than go back with the Redeemers or stay here with her. John Singer, that crazy old bastard, was righter than he ever knew when he said she'd steal my soul and send me to hell. I've been living here all this week, watching her, wondering what she was gonna do next. Knowing I couldn't stop her.' He came down the aisle toward me, walking slow, catlike. 'She's hinted that she was the one who killed Caesar. That his foot was bad and wasn't getting better fast enough. She was tired of taking care of him. She said he was a summer horse, good for only a season.'

Greg was panting. His breath was a harsh rasp. He kept coming toward me, and I had never been so afraid of anyone in my life. A shaft of sunlight from one of the stall windows caught his face, and his eyes glittered like narrow slits of some hard stone.

'You ran out on me, Bekkah. You left me here by myself with her. My back was a mess.' In the shaft of light he turned slowly. He wasn't wearing a shirt and the scabs that still crisscrossed his back were black and ugly. The tissue around it was red welts, white at the edges.

'Nadine saved my life,' he continued, turning back around to face me. 'I owe her something for that, don't I? She said she wanted a baby. She said I could give it to her. A little Redeemer baby to make up for everything she'd lost.'

Even though he was standing still, he was panting hard, like he'd run a long way.

'Greg, nobody will hurt you. Just tell us where the baby is and we'll get her. Then we'll find a place for you to be safe. Mama Betts wanted to ask you to stay at our house. Arly even said he'd share his room.'

Tears ran down my chin and neck, tickling my chest as they slipped away to soak into my bra. Where in the hell was Nadine? She couldn't be far, her truck was in the yard.

'You have no idea what it's been like here,' he said. 'No idea,' he whispered.

'Jamey Louise wanted to come down here and talk with you, but I told her it wasn't a good idea. Maybe I was wrong. She said she had some things to tell you—'

'Jamey doesn't exist.' He waved his hand in the air.

'This whole summer was a lie, Bekkah. All of it. It's like spider's silk. You don't see the web. You just walk into it, and it has you.'

'My folks are waiting for me to come back. I wanted to ask Nadine something, but it can wait. You want to come back with me?' I had to get out of the barn.

'On that horse?' He laughed. 'All this summer I've been here, and nobody thought to teach me to ride.'

'We can walk her home, Greg. We don't have to ride.' I inched toward the door. Greg came forward, stepping out of the light so I couldn't see him clearly anymore.

'Are you crying?' he asked suddenly.

'I'm worried about that baby. Maebelle V. is like my own sister. I keep thinking she may be hungry or scared. She'll be crying for Alice to take care of her.'

'Are you trying to leave?'

'Greg, my parents are waiting for me.' He frightened me. I wanted to beg him to let me go, but I knew that would be the wrong thing. I wasn't his prisoner unless I admitted that I was. 'I have to go now. You can come with me if you want to, but I have to go.'

I sidestepped to the door. My hand was on it when he lunged at me, knocking me down and to the side. My head slammed against the edge of the door, and Greg pulled it back with a half-strangled cry.

Sunlight poured into the barn. Greg ran to the other end and threw open that door, flooding the barn with light. I sat up, dazed but not really hurt. A whirlwind of frantic activity, Greg ran to the first stall and slammed open the latch and door.

'Run!' he cried. 'Run! Don't stay here or you'll die!'

Bacchus bolted out of his stall, followed by all the rest of the horses. They thundered out of the barn, sending dirt flying. I noticed that their coats were matted and covered in filth.

'I can go now,' he said. 'But we have to come back and

491

do something with them later. We can't leave them here. They're innocent.'

He walked toward me, his thin body shaking. I managed to crawl to my feet. The blow to my head hadn't hurt me, but the fear had made my knees rubbery. I looked back at him, but my eyes traveled beyond, into the interior of the old barn.

At first I didn't believe it. I had to be imagining it. Greg saw the expression on my face, and he looked behind him quickly, as if he expected some demon to rush out of one of the stalls.

'Holy Christ,' he muttered. He almost dropped to his knees, but he stopped himself.

'Greg.' I whispered his name because I didn't know what else to say.

Hanging above Cammie's old stall was the crucifix with the blackened Jesus. The sunlight from the open doors caught it full, giving Jesus a purely satanic look as his blacked eyes turned to heaven, devoid of all expression.

There was something else dangling from the right side of the cross, material of some sort. I walked forward to look at it, and before I got much closer I knew what it was.

'Oh, no,' I whispered. 'No.'

Greg stood in the doorway while I ran to the crucifix. I had to get the ladder from the end of the barn, but I finally got it and climbed to the top.

I knew the bib. It was one that had been handed down through several different Waltmans. It was Maebelle V.'s bib.

Chapter Forty-one

They found her in the creek, about two miles from the church. The full skirt of the old christening gown had hung in the roots of a willow tree. The coroner said she was dead before she was put in the water, and that was a blessing, Mama Betts said.

They didn't want me to hear, but I eavesdropped after they'd given me a sleeping pill and some warm milk. They thought I was asleep in the clean, safe sheets of my bed, but I wasn't. I was sitting on the floor, listening at the crack under the door.

They said Maebelle's neck had been broken. That death had been fast. They spoke as if it were a television show they were talking about, and I knew it was because they didn't believe it had really happened. Not on Kali Oka Road.

Maybe Greg and I were the only people who believed it was real, because we should have seen it coming. We had all summer long to look at it. Somehow we'd managed to avoid seeing.

Effie told me they'd caught Nadine. When Joe Wickham and the posse had gone down to stop the Redeemers, they'd been just in time to see Nadine run out of the woods. It had taken four grown men to subdue her, and they'd been none too gentle. Nadine was wearing a blood-soaked dress and carrying a large hunting knife. The dress was old and white, and the blood wasn't fresh.

I figured it was the same one she'd been wearing when she pretended to be the ghost of Selena to scare me and Alice. At the edge of the woods they found a cheap wig with long dark hair. I wondered if that was when she'd decided to steal Maebelle V., when I told her the legend of Cry Baby Creek.

Nadine had been following me for a long, long time. All summer, in fact. She knew about the spring by the house, the secret fort where Alice and I played, about everything. I had no doubt that she'd seen me petting Mr. Tom and decided to kill him. She'd touched my entire life. It would never be clean again.

Cathi had taken me aside and told me that she'd finally found evidence of Nadine in the Delta, but it wasn't Nadine. It was Dianne Salter. Nadine-Dianne. The exact same letters. A very clever woman, Cathi said.

The Beulah police were looking for a dead baby in the woods behind the trailer court where she'd lived. According to hospital records, she'd delivered a healthy baby girl on October 22, 1959. After the first week or two, no one had seen the baby, and Dianne Salter had accused the Redeemers of stealing her child. Dianne Salter had leveled some damning accusations wrapped in a web of lies. And Nadine Andrews had brought those lies to Kali Oka Road.

There had been no parents killed in an automobile wreck. There were no marriages. There was no grand home in Cleveland with maids and antique furniture. There was no Nadine.

The woman I'd talked to every day for most of the summer did not exist.

Cathi stroked Picket's fur and told me that I was to put everything behind me and try not to think about it. She said that time would make the hurting fade.

Mama Betts ran my bath water and put out clean pajamas for me along with a cup of cocoa. She kissed the top of my head, and I felt her tears soak into my hair. Neither of us spoke. Maebelle was too much with us to talk. She had indeed loved that little redheaded child, and she grieved for her in bitter silence.

When I was clean, Effie gave me the medicine and put me to bed. In the still October night while crickets chorused outside the window and the whippoorwill sang, Effie held me for a long, long time and let me cry until the tears slacked of their own accord. Then The Judge came in. When I tried to talk, he shushed me and said that it would keep for a while, that the worst was over and that the best thing I could do was sleep and forget. He found an old storybook that I'd loved as a child and read to me until I closed my eyes and made my breathing slow and steady.

Listening at the crack in the door, I knew I would never forget what had happened. Never. No one on Kali Oka Road would ever forget. And it wasn't over. The voices out on the porch continued.

'I sunk a line into a small cluster of Salters from near Hushpuckena who've heard of a Salter woman who'd gotten herself pregnant by a rich man. She was a stable hand at his barn, but she disappeared from Hushpuckena. Gossip is that he ran her out of town,' Cathi was saying.

'No one will admit to being a close relative, and no one wants to come down here and help her out. It's sort of sad, sort of tragic,' Cathi continued. 'They're still looking for the baby up at Beulah.'

I imagined the men of Beulah with their spades digging around for the little dead baby. Where had Nadine buried this one? How many more were there that we didn't know about?

'Some of these questions will never be answered,' Mama Betts said. 'I pray that innocent child didn't suffer.'

'How long are they going to hold Dianne Salter in the county jail?' Effie asked. 'Until Rex Ransom can stage a theatrical hearing? Or until maybe he can stir up a riot and stand on the courthouse steps and quell it like the hero he wants to be?'

'Easy, Effie,' The Judge said, and I heard his chair scrape out as he got up and went to Mama. I knew he was putting his hands on her shoulders and giving them a light massage. That's what he always did when she started getting too angry.

So Nadine was still at the county jail. She'd be taken to Parchman soon. There were psychiatrists up there, and they'd have a go at her.

'How's Greg? Will they keep him in the hospital?' Cathi asked.

'He was in shock and badly malnourished.' Effie laughed, but there was no humor in it. 'He's more worried about those horses. Gus and Walt rounded them up, and Gus's feeding them. Greg made them promise. He's a lot like Bekkah in that regard.'

'Speaking of Bekkah, what about that horse of hers?' Cathi asked.

'Cammie's part of the family,' Mama Betts said. 'With everything else that child lost this summer, you can't think of taking away her horse.'

'Of course not,' The Judge said, exasperated a tiny bit.

Tears were leaking out of my eyes again. I hadn't been able to really stop since Greg and I had run back to the house with Maebelle's bib in my hand.

'The Redeemers managed to get out of town before anyone hurt them, didn't they?' Mama Betts asked.

'Some rocks were thrown, but no one was injured. Rev. Marcus said they would go somewhere else, try again. I urged him to become a part of the community wherever he went.' Daddy sighed. 'He wasn't impressed with my counsel. He said he'd be in touch, to see when Greg would be ready to rejoin them, as if he had no other place to go.'

'He doesn't,' Effie said.

'We'll talk about it tomorrow, after the funeral,' Daddy said.

They were going to ask him to live with us. I didn't have any feelings about it one way or another. In fact, I didn't think I'd ever feel about anything again.

'What about Bekkah?' Effie asked.

For a moment no one answered, and then Mama Betts' voice was as soft and worn as her skin. I couldn't make out what she was saying, and I fell asleep with my face pressed against the crack of the door, soothed by the whisper of their voices.

Everyone on Kali Oka Road was going to the funeral. Even Mr. Waltman had turned up, his face pulled and sagging toward a big nose that I didn't remember. No matter how closely I looked at him, I couldn't see a shred of Alice. Or Maebelle. I'd gone over to Alice's before the funeral to get her to ride with us. Mr. Waltman was sitting on the front porch in his good suit with his shoes off. He was clipping his toenails. I'd never seen any nails so thick and horny-looking. They flew from the snippers like deadly weapons.

Alice didn't argue when I told her to come with me, and Mrs. Waltman didn't try to stop her. Agatha Waltman was struggling to get her belly into a dress that someone had sent over for her to wear. No one had to tell me or Alice that since Maebelle V. was dead, Mrs. Waltman didn't care what Alice did.

The service was an ordeal. I sat on the family pew with Alice, and Effie and Mama Betts were just behind us. The Judge was a pallbearer, and Cathi Cummings had gone back to Mobile. Her series of stories on the Redeemers and Dianne Salter had created a stir in the world of newspapers.

Little tidbits of additional facts were floating down to Mobile from all over the state of Mississippi. Cathi had interviewed grammar school friends of Dianne who said even as a little girl she'd collected dolls and ribbons. One was never enough, and once she had as many as she wanted, she destroyed them all.

Her folks were found in Memphis, saying they hadn't talked to her in years. Not since she'd gotten pregnant and run away. They wanted no part of her now and refused to come down and visit her in jail even if the newspaper paid the cost of their travels. They said thanks but no thanks.

As far as the Redeemers went, they were being investigated by the feds. There were several different groups, all loosely connected. And there were homes in Texas and Hattiesburg where unwed girls had their babies. Cathi's newspaper stories had revealed a large network. No formal charges had been made yet, though. As far as anyone knew, Magdeline was still with them. When the buses had been stopped by Joe Wickham, everyone on them had been given a chance to leave, but no one had. Joe had no reason to hold them, so he'd let them go. They'd disappeared down the blacktop in one final blast of Kali Oka dust that soon settled and left nothing behind at all.

Mostly, to get through the funeral, I thought about Cammie and the ride through the clean pine woods. That way I sort of hovered above all the singing and crying and Alice sitting like a stone beside me, unable to react in any way.

I was relieved to see Mack Sumrall at the graveside. He took Alice by the arm, and I had a moment to back off by myself.

It was another golden October day. A Tuesday. Most of

the school was at the funeral. There was a Waltman in almost every grade. Mack said that classes had been dismissed for two hours so that everyone who wanted could attend.

Maebelle V. was being put to rest beside another brother, a stillborn infant who'd never even been given a name. Baby Waltman, November 3, 1957, was the only inscription on the little tombstone. Maebelle would have one that showed eleven months of life. Just her name and the dates.

I went to stand beside a line of cedars along the fence of the small cemetery. So many people had come, spilling out from around the red mouth of the grave like a flock of crows. I backed into the spicy shade of the cedars and watched.

'Are you okay?'

I didn't turn around. It was Frank Taylor behind me. I was glad he'd come to the funeral.

'I'm fine.' It was the biggest lie I'd ever told. But what else was there to say? 'I want to die' Or maybe, 'This is my fault'?

'And Alice?'

'I don't know. It's hard to tell right now.'

'Is there anything I can do?' He touched my shoulder, and I thought I would cry. Then I thought of something that only Frank would do for me.

'Take me to the jail.'

'Why?' He stepped closer behind me. I could smell his aftershave even though I hadn't turned around to face him.

'I want to see Nadine.'

'Dianne,' he corrected with some anger. 'Her name is Dianne Salter.'

'I want to see her.'

He put both hands on my shoulders and tried to turn me, but I made myself rigid.

'Maybe that isn't such a good idea.'

'I need to see her,' I said.

'If your parents say it's okay.' He wasn't going to argue, but he wasn't going to do it either.

'You know they won't let me. There's something I have to ask her, Frank. I have to know. No one else will take me. If you don't, they'll take her away and I'll never find out.'

'Even if you ask her, you won't find out the truth. She's a liar, Bekkah. Can't you see that! After everything she's done, don't you see that she won't tell you the truth about anything?'

'She will about this.' I tore my eyes away from the sight of the black dresses and the black suits. It was a slightly different version of the Redeemers. That made me shudder.

'Bekkah?'

I looked up at him, and I made sure I wasn't about to cry. 'I want to talk to her for ten minutes. No more. I know how to get into the jail without being seen. You can wait for me in the truck. All you have to do is drive me there.'

He shrugged. 'Okay.'

We eased back into the cedars, followed their line to the end of the fence and made our way to his truck. We were only a few minutes from Jexville, and we made the trip without talking. I was thinking about Nadine.

I made Frank stay in the truck just in case I got caught. There was no point in dragging him into it. The sheriff's office was empty, as I'd expected. Everyone was at the funeral. The key to the jail was hanging on the nail beside the back door, and I had it in a few seconds. The jail yard was freshly raked, and I was across it in no time. I opened the door to the jail and stepped inside.

Nadine was the only prisoner. She was on the bottom

floor in the last cell on the right. There were no provisions for women in the Chickasaw County jail, so it was a good thing she was the only prisoner.

She was sitting on her cot, waiting for me. The light from the barred windows cut across her face, leaving only her eyes revealed. They were a golden brown, alert.

'I wondered when you'd come,' she said.

'The horses are okay. Gus's going to take care of them until we can find owners.'

She waved her hand. 'I'm done with them. They shit too much.'

I put my fingers on the bars and felt the cool steel. Nadine was wearing an old T-shirt with a hole in the right shoulder and a pair of riding pants, knee-high socks and sneakers. Her hair was tangled and uncombed. There was a smudge of dirt on her right cheek and a cut on her forehead. Her wrists were badly bruised from the handcuffs. They said she'd struggled when they'd taken her down.

'Why, Nadine?' I tightened my grip on the bar.

'Why what?' She gave me that cagey smile, like she knew something really interesting that I didn't know.

'Would you rather I call you Dianne? Dianne Salter.' I meant it to be mean, but she only grinned wider.

'Call me what you like.'

'Why did you come to Kali Oka Road?'

'The Redeemers took my baby. I've been following them ever since, on and off now for four years. They had to be punished. You understand that, Bekkah, bad people have to be punished.'

'That's a lie and you know it. Damn you! They're going to dig up that little dead baby in Beulah. They'll find her just where you buried her. You murdered your own baby and buried her in that trailer court.'

Nadine looked out the window. 'Maybe. I guess only time will tell.'

If the bars hadn't been between us, I would have killed her myself. 'Don't you want to know about Greg?' I wanted to bait her, to tell her that he was going to have a wonderful life while she rotted in prison. I wanted her to know that all of us would be happy one day, that we'd get over what she'd done. But I didn't believe it enough to say it. There was no getting over Maebelle.

'I don't care what happens to Greg. It's insignificant to me. But if you do see him, tell him we were successful.'

'Successful?' Surely not in killing Maebelle. Was she implying that she and Greg had planned it?

'I'm pregnant.' She smiled. 'They won't execute a pregnant woman, and I doubt the state of Mississippi will kill a mother. At least not for a while.'

'They'll never let you keep a baby. Not in prison.' I backed away from the cell.

'I could ask that your family adopt it.' Nadine grinned her fox grin. She was tormenting me. I didn't know whether to believe she was pregnant or not.

'I hope there is a hell, and I hope you burn there forever.' I meant that. Every word of it. It had been stupid of me to come to the jail. Whatever I'd expected to find out, Frank was right. She was never going to tell me anything worth knowing.

'You want to know why I killed her, don't you?'

Her question startled me. I'd backed clear across the aisle so that my back was touching the other cell bars. 'Why did you?' That was exactly what I'd come to ask. Nadine always knew the questions.

'She wouldn't stop crying.'

'Maebelle never cried. Not really.'

'I guess maybe she was hungry.' Nadine shrugged. 'I thought I really wanted her until I had her. Then she was too much trouble. She wouldn't shut up.'

Nadine looked at me and laughed at the horror that was on my face.

'It wasn't Maebelle I really wanted, although from the first minute I saw her I was planning how to get her. It was you, Bekkah. You and Greg and Jamey Louise. Even cautious little Alice, who tried so desperately to avoid me. And I had you all. For the best part of a summer, you were all mine.' She lifted her chin so that the sunlight struck fully across her face. 'And I still have you, Bekkah. Oh, yes, I've collected the best of each of you.'

I turned and ran as hard as I could. I threw the key to the jail door on the ground. I didn't care if they ever got Nadine out of there. I didn't care if she starved.

Frank cranked the motor as soon as I'd slammed the door.

'Where to?' he asked. He cut a look at me but didn't comment further.

'Home,' I whispered. 'Kali Oka Road.'

When Frank failed to move the truck, I looked up. The Judge was standing at the truck window. I should have known that he would see me leave the graveside. He was standing on the curb, waiting for me.

'I guess I'd better ride home with Daddy,' I said. I reached across the seat and touched Frank's arm. 'Thanks.' Before he had a chance to be a gentleman, I opened the door and got out.

'Effie's worried about you,' The Judge said as he nodded toward the new black Volvo that was parked on the south side of the courthouse square. 'We'd better be getting home. Alice is going to spend a few days with us.'

I got in the front seat before I asked him. 'Does she hate me?'

'Alice?' He shook his head. 'No, Bekkah, she doesn't. She doesn't even hate herself. Nobody could have loved that child more than Alice did.'

He let that simmer as we spun along the highway. Neither of us talked, and I could hear the tires whirring as The Judge drove fast. I thought of Nadine in her cell, her shirt torn and her face dirty. And still she was triumphant. Maebelle V. was dead because she'd gotten hungry – and Nadine was alive and pregnant.

'She said she'd taken the best of us.' I spoke without intending to. 'She said she'd gotten us all, me and Jamey and Greg, and even Alice.' The words scalded me. 'I hate her.'

The Judge drove for a while. When I looked at him, his mouth was sad and I noticed the crook in his nose. Sometime, long before I was born, he'd broken it in a fight in New York City.

'Rebekah, that woman did take something from you. There's no denying that. She took your innocence, your trust. She took that from all of you.' He reached across to me and offered his hand. When I put mine in it, he smiled as he continued to watch the road. 'Now's the real test of your mettle. Now we see if you accept the mistakes of the past and go on without losing too much of yourself. Remember, from here on out, she can only take what you allow her to have.'

The turn off onto Kali Oka was coming up. He slowed the car, eased onto the red dirt and then pulled over to the right. When the car was stopped, he pointed down the road. 'This is your past, Bekkah, and a large part of your future. Nadine is gone, but your mother and grandmother and brother and me and Alice, we're all right here for you. It won't ever be the same, but it won't always hurt this much.'

'What about Greg?'

The Judge put the car in first and let off the clutch. 'I spoke with the juvenile authorities. Cathi is trying to follow up on his last name, Calendar. Rev. Marcus said they picked him up in Tupelo, so that's a place to start.'

'What if he doesn't have any relatives?' Greg had left the hospital without being discharged and without telling anyone where he was going. The Judge had found him, though.

'Effie and I decided to ask him to live with us, but he said no.'

'No?' I knew how much Greg wanted my family. He'd said it more than once.

'He says he won't live with us, but I do believe he's going to spend the rest of the school year with us.'

I felt a clash of emotions. 'Greg's going to school with us?'

The Judge shook his head. 'No, he's too far behind. But Effie is going to tutor him during the day for the rest of the year, and then next summer while we're in Europe, Greg will stay with Mama Betts and help her. After all, someone is going to have to tend to that horse of yours.'

'Greg said he would do that?'

'I think that was the deciding factor. He thinks as much of that horse as you do. In a year's time he'll be sixteen. He can get his license. With Effie's help he should be able to pass his GED. Then it's up to Greg. He's mighty young to be out on his own, but in most ways I suppose he's always been on his own.'

'Arly's going to share his room?' They must have bribed him with his own car.

'There are still a lot of details to settle.'

The Detail Man. He was home with us, and he would see to the fine print, make sure that nothing was over-looked.

The outline of the big cedar tree that shaded our side yard came into view. Arly and I had climbed that tree a million times. From the top of it I'd once been able to see everything in the world that was important to me. My home, Alice's house. Our secret fort. The spring. It was all still there. I just had to look for it.

'Go fast, Daddy,' I whispered. 'Make the tires sing. I have to get home.'

A selection of quality fiction from Headline